Series Volumes of Haun Classi

The Phantom of the Opera by Gaston Leroux (2020)

The Beetle by Richard Marsh (2020)

Vathek by William Beckford (2020)

The House on the Borderland by William Hope Hodgson (2020)

Of One Blood: or, The Hidden Self by Pauline Hopkins (2021)

The Parasite and Other Tales of Terror by
Arthur Conan Doyle (2021)

The King in Yellow by Robert W. Chambers (2021)

Ghost Stories of an Antiquary by M. R. James (2021)

Gothic Classics: The Castle of Otranto by Horace Walpole and
The Old English Baron by Clara Reeve (an omnibus) (2022)

*The Mummy! A Tale of the Twenty-Second
Century* by Jane Webb (2022)

Fantasmagoriana translated into English by
Sarah Elizabeth Utterson (2022)

The Picture of Dorian Gray by Oscar Wilde (2022)

…and more forthcoming

GOTHIC CLASSICS

THE CASTLE OF OTRANTO
BY HORACE WALPOLE

=== AND ===

THE OLD ENGLISH BARON
BY CLARA REEVE

(an omnibus of two books)

The Horror Writers Association
Haunted Library of Horror Classics
Presents:

GOTHIC CLASSICS

THE CASTLE OF OTRANTO
BY HORACE WALPOLE

=== AND ===

THE OLD ENGLISH BARON
BY CLARA REEVE

(an omnibus of two books)

Series Editors: Eric J. Guignard
and Leslie S. Klinger
With an introduction by Robert McCammon

Poisoned Pen
PRESS

Introduction © 2022 Robert McCammon
Additional supplemental material © 2022 by Eric J. Guignard and Leslie S. Klinger
Cover and internal design © 2022 by Sourcebooks
Cover design and illustration by Jeffrey Nguyen

Sourcebooks, Poisoned Pen Press, and the colophon are registered trademarks of Sourcebooks.

Published by Poisoned Pen Press, an imprint of Sourcebooks
P.O. Box 4410, Naperville, Illinois 60567-4410
(630) 961-3900
sourcebooks.com

This text of *The Castle of Otranto* is from the 1766 third edition, published by William Bathoe, London, UK.

This text of *The Old English Baron* is from the 1778 first edition, published by Edward and Charles Dilly, London, UK.

Library of Congress Cataloging-in-Publication Data

Names: Walpole, Horace. Castle of Otranto. | Reeve, Clara. Old English baron.
Title: Gothic classics : The castle of Otranto and The old English baron /
   by Horace Walpole and by Clara Reeve.
Description: Naperville, Illinois : Poisoned Pen Press, [2022] | Series:
   Haunted library of horror classics | Includes bibliographical
   references.
Identifiers: LCCN 2021023599 (print) | LCCN 2021023600 (ebook) | (trade paperback) |
   (epub)
Subjects: LCSH: Horror tales, English.
Classification: LCC PR1309.H6 G68 2022 (print) | LCC PR1309.H6 (ebook) |
   DDC 823/.0872908--dc23
LC record available at https://lccn.loc.gov/2021023599
LC ebook record available at https://lccn.loc.gov/2021023600

Printed and bound in the United States of America.
KP 10 9 8 7 6 5 4 3 2 1

This edition of Gothic Classics: The Castle of Otranto and The Old English Baron *is presented by the* Horror Writers Association, *a nonprofit organization of writers and publishing professionals around the world, dedicated to promoting dark literature and the interests of those who write it. For more information on HWA, visit: www.horror.org.*

CONTENTS

Introduction to the Novel by Robert McCammon   *xi*

THE CASTLE OF OTRANTO   1
Preface to the First Edition.   3
Sonnet to the Right Honourable Lady Mary Coke.   7
Preface to the Second Edition.   8
Chapter I.   14
Chapter II.   38
Chapter III.   60
Chapter IV.   81
Chapter V.   101

THE OLD ENGLISH BARON   119
Preface.   121
The Old English Baron: A Gothic Story.   125

About the Author, Horace Walpole   282
About the Author, Clara Reeve   284
Suggested Discussion Questions for Classroom Use   285
Suggested Further Reading of Fiction   290
About the Series Editors   295

INTRODUCTION TO THE NOVEL: MY EVENING WITH WALPOLE

I AM here in this candlelit library with the man of the moment, and let me add that this library is truly huge, with a cathedral ceiling, leather bound books from wall to wall, polite flames whispering in a large white stone fireplace, overstuffed chairs, sofas and love seats, Oriental rugs of many hues upon the timbered floors…yet there is a heavy silence here, and a sense that shadows hang in the corners of this chamber like intricate spiderwebs.

Yes, it is indeed true. One may call the architecture of this grand castle Gothic. It is named Strawberry Hill, and its builder and owner is sitting very comfortably—sprawled, actually—on a dark green sofa before me, his dark eyes glinting with candlelight, the sides of his equally dark hair standing out like the wings of an owl, and his narrow face chalky white as is the fashion of the time (though I do hear his pallor is so pale it alarms those who meet him). He is dressed in a simple gray suit, a ruffled shirt, cream-colored stockings, and small black shoes on rather small feet. The gentleman has graciously agreed to this interview, and so without further hesitation let us offer our first question to Horace Walpole, author, politician, essayist, and some might say true visionary.

Robert McCammon: I would like first to touch on your most famous work, *The Castle of Otranto*. Do you consider it a horror novel?

Horace Walpole: *Pardon me? I don't understand that question.*

RM: Well, you would hardly know it now, but *The Castle of Otranto* is destined to become very much more than you envisioned. It's going to be a Gothic touchstone. Edgar Allan Poe will—

HW: *Who?*

RM: Never mind that. I'm just saying that the Gothic influence of *The Castle of Otranto* is going to be seen in thousands of books and movies. If I was to try to list even a fraction of the titles, it would take up far more pages than I've been given for this interview.

HW: *I was going to offer you a glass of sherry, but obviously you have over indulged before reaching my home. Or have you recently escaped from Bedlam?*

RM: Yes, you can point to the movie *Bedlam*, too, starring Boris Karloff.

HW: *I should wish to point you to Bedlam. What is a so-called movie and what is this ghastly Boris Karloff?*

RM: Um…we should proceed a pace. Will you tell me a bit about yourself?

HW: *I was born on the 24th of September in the year 1717. This being the year 1766, my present age is forty-nine. I am the youngest son of Robert Walpole, who was the first prime minister of this great England. I was educated at Eton and at Cambridge. The Castle of Otranto was first published in 1764. I have my own publishing concern here, called Strawberry Hill Press. What else is there to know?*

RM: A lot, I think. I understand you have two pets, a spaniel and a squirrel?

HW: Had *two pets. My dear spaniel was attacked and killed by a wolf when I was travelling in the Italian alps. The squirrel escaped its cage and is somewhere in the castle, Lord knows where.*

RM: Oh. Well…about the castle. Gothic architecture, certainly. How did it come about?

HW: *Now you're speaking of something I find interesting. Oh yes, my Strawberry Hill! I bought the property when there was a single cottage on it, and I was determined to build a home of which I might be proud. Over the years it was built stone-by-stone, turret by turret, tower by tower and battlement by…you know the rest. In fact I doubt it shall be finished until 1776 or so, at which point I shall allow tourists in to admire my efforts.*

RM: Do you have a word to describe this castle?

HW: *I do, and one of my own devising. Gloomth. A combination, you see, of 'gloom' and 'warmth', which I find extremely comforting.*

RM: It's surely a big place.

HW: *It is my refuge. Also there are the gardens. Do you know I am considered a master gardener? My theory of gardening has been taken up all over the land.*

RM: What is that theory?

HW: *That Nature abhors a straight line, therefore you will find no straight lines in my garden. I don't care much for straight lines myself. I rather like complications…intrigue…the careful arrangement of shadows in a chamber. To my tastes, a delight.*

RM: Ah! Now you're talking like a writer of what many consider 'the' first Gothic tale. What are your work habits?

HW: *Some have accused me of lunacy, but I prefer to work in the late hours. I begin writing at ten at night and work until two in the morning. Would you consider that lunatic?*

RM: Um…those are *my* working hours.

HW: *Then perhaps only one of us is the lunatic, sir. I do fortify myself with many cups of coffee.*

RM: So do I, but I thought people of your time drank mostly tea.

HW: *Zounds, no! There's a coffee shop on almost every corner in London! I expect you wouldn't understand such a wild frenzy for the brew, in your era.*

RM: Well…let's go on. About *The Castle of Otranto*. What caused you to write the book?

HW: *I expect that as a writer—I suppose you're really a writer, though I have no evidence of your wit and intellect, so I shall let that pass—you are asked a particular question, that being: do you get your ideas from your dreams? In my case it was true. I had a dream in which I thought myself in an ancient castle, a very natural dream for a head like mine filled with Gothic story, and that on the uppermost banister of a great staircase I saw a gigantic hand in armor. That evening I sat down to write. And there it was. But I might add, when the book was first published I played a grand joke on the reading public. I did not present it as fiction, but as a genuine account of something that had really happened, and that I had simply discovered the manuscript. Wasn't that delightful?*

RM: I don't know, but I can't wrap my imagination around the image of a giant helmet with black feathers falling out of the sky as it appears in your book.

HW: Your *failure of imagination, sir. Not mine.*

RM: Just a minute. You said 'a very natural dream for a head like mine filled with Gothic story'. I thought you invented the Gothic story!

HW: *Is that what they say about me in your era? I am flattered, of course, and perhaps they mean it in the sense that I refined it, but I was very much influenced by those who came before me, as all writers are. The plays of Shakespeare…the ghost stories of medieval Europe… the folktales of the lands I happened to travel through…all those went into…if I may be a bit grotesque…the brainpan. And when I came across a tale that ignited my interest, I defined the moment as another word I devised, that word being 'serendipity'.*

RM: You came up with that word?

HW: *Indeed.*

RM: I understand you've been quite a writer of letters.

HW: *I have written thousands and hope to write thousands more. I prize communication as one of the greatest gifts to mankind.*

RM: Let me turn now to the manuscript I wanted you to read.

HW: *Oh, yes. The Old English Baron by Clara Reeve. I understand it won't be published until 1778?*

RM: Correct. What did you think of it?

HW: *Hm. A difficult question to answer. I can see that it is highly influenced by The Castle of Otranto, yet it takes a turn from the Gothic into the world of what I term the ordinary, so it leaves me somewhat faint. Tell me…in your era, do you have material that purports to be about one thing but at a crucial moment turns out to be about something else, much to the dismay of the reader who expected that certain something to be about what they at first thought it was about, but turned out not to be about?*

RM: Yes.

HW: *There you have it, then.*

RM: But you do agree it has a modicum of historical interest?

HW: *About that.*

RM: Well, I should be getting back to my era. Thank you very much for your time, and for giving us *The Castle of Otranto*. I have the feeling that 'Gothic' is a state of mind, and that it involves the convolution of imagination that dares to challenge the social standards of the day, and uses its power to transport the reader or viewer into a dream world…or, in some instances, a world of nightmare in which one might roam but afterward return safely to the land of reality. But hopefully with a heightened imagination and sense of self.

HW: *You're a long-winded cuss, aren't you?*

RM: Do you have any final word for our readers?

HW: *I shall offer what I once offered in a letter: 'To act with common sense, according to the moment, is the best wisdom I know; and the best philosophy, to do one's duties, take the world as it comes, submit respectfully to one's lot, bless the goodness that has given us so much happiness with it, and despise affectation'. In other words: find your happiness, and embrace it.*

RM: Thank you, and good evening.

HW: *I should like the last word as advice to your era. That being: Read.*

Robert McCammon
March 30, 2021
Birmingham, Alabama

Along with Joe and Karen Lansdale and Dean Koontz, Robert McCammon is one of the founders of the Horror Writers Association.

The Castle of Otranto

by Horace Walpole

PREFACE TO THE FIRST EDITION.

THE following work was found in the library of an ancient Catholic family in the north of England. It was printed at Naples, in the black letter,* in the year 1529. How much sooner it was written does not appear. The principal incidents are such as were believed in the darkest ages of Christianity; but the language and conduct have nothing that savours of barbarism. The style is the purest Italian. If the story was written near the time when it is supposed to have happened, it must have been between 1095, the era of the first Crusade, and 1243, the date of the last, or not long afterwards. There is no other circumstance in the work that can lead us to guess at the period in which the scene is laid: the names of the actors are evidently fictitious, and probably disguised on purpose: yet the Spanish names of the domestics seem to indicate that this work was not composed until the establishment of the Arragonian Kings in Naples† had made Spanish appellations familiar in that country. The beauty of the diction, and the zeal of the author (moderated, however, by singular judgment) concur to make me think that the date of the composition was little antecedent to that of the impression.

---

* This was a heavy, ornate printing style, also referred to as Gothic.

† The Aragonese kings of Sicily and Naples ruled from the 13th to the early 16th century.

Letters were then in their most flourishing state in Italy, and contributed to dispel the empire of superstition, at that time so forcibly attacked by the reformers. It is not unlikely that an artful priest might endeavour to turn their own arms on the innovators, and might avail himself of his abilities as an author to confirm the populace in their ancient errors and superstitions. If this was his view, he has certainly acted with signal address. Such a work as the following would enslave a hundred vulgar minds beyond half the books of controversy that have been written from the days of Luther to the present hour.

This solution of the author's motives is, however, offered as a mere conjecture. Whatever his views were, or whatever effects the execution of them might have, his work can only be laid before the public at present as a matter of entertainment. Even as such, some apology for it is necessary. Miracles, visions, necromancy, dreams, and other preternatural events, are exploded now even from romances. That was not the case when our author wrote; much less when the story itself is supposed to have happened. Belief in every kind of prodigy* was so established in those dark ages, that an author would not be faithful to the *manners* of the times, who should omit all mention of them. He is not bound to believe them himself, but he must represent his actors as believing them.

If this *air of the miraculous* is excused, the reader will find nothing else unworthy of his perusal. Allow the possibility of the facts, and all the actors comport themselves as persons would do in their situation. There is no bombast, no similes, flowers, digressions, or unnecessary descriptions. Everything tends directly to the catastrophe. Never is the reader's attention relaxed. The rules of the drama are almost observed throughout the conduct of the piece. The characters are well drawn, and still better maintained. Terror, the author's principal engine, prevents the story from ever languishing; and it is so often contrasted by pity, that the mind is kept up in a constant vicissitude of interesting passions.

---

* An extraordinary thing or occurrence regarded as an omen, a usage recorded as early as 1450.

Some persons may perhaps think the characters of the domestics too little serious for the general cast of the story; but besides their opposition to the principal personages, the art of the author is very observable in his conduct of the subalterns. They discover many passages essential to the story, which could not be well brought to light but by their *naïveté* and simplicity. In particular, the womanish terror and foibles of Bianca, in the last chapter, conduce essentially towards advancing the catastrophe.

It is natural for a translator to be prejudiced in favour of his adopted work. More impartial readers may not be so much struck with the beauties of this piece as I was. Yet I am not blind to my author's defects. I could wish he had grounded his plan on a more useful moral than this: that "the sins of fathers are visited on their children to the third and fourth generation." I doubt whether, in his time, any more than at present, ambition curbed its appetite of dominion from the dread of so remote a punishment. And yet this moral is weakened by that less direct insinuation, that even such anathema may be diverted by devotion to St. Nicholas.* Here the interest of the Monk plainly gets the better of the judgment of the author. However, with all its faults, I have no doubt but the English reader will be pleased with a sight of this performance. The piety that reigns throughout, the lessons of virtue that are inculcated, and the rigid purity of the sentiments, exempt this work from the censure to which romances are but too liable. Should it meet with the success I hope for, I may be encouraged to reprint the original Italian, though it will tend to depreciate my own labour. Our language falls far short of the charms of the Italian, both for variety and harmony. The latter is peculiarly excellent for simple narrative. It is difficult in English to relate without falling too low or rising too high; a fault obviously occasioned by the little care taken to speak pure language in common conversation. Every Italian or Frenchman of any rank piques himself on speaking his

---

* Saint Nicholas (approximately 270–340 C.E.) is the patron saint of many communities in Europe, and many miracles were attributed to his intercession. His habit of secret gift-giving eventually transmuted the saint in popular culture into Santa Claus.

own tongue correctly and with choice. I cannot flatter myself with having done justice to my author in this respect: his style is as elegant as his conduct of the passions is masterly. It is a pity that he did not apply his talents to what they were evidently proper for—the theatre.

I will detain the reader no longer, but to make one short remark. Though the machinery is invention, and the names of the actors imaginary, I cannot but believe that the groundwork of the story is founded on truth. The scene is undoubtedly laid in some real castle. The author seems frequently, without design, to describe particular parts. "The chamber," says he, "on the right hand;" "the door on the left hand;" "the distance from the chapel to Conrad's apartment": these and other passages are strong presumptions that the author had some certain building in his eye. Curious persons, who have leisure to employ in such researches, may possibly discover in the Italian writers the foundation on which our author has built. If a catastrophe, at all resembling that which he describes, is believed to have given rise to this work, it will contribute to interest the reader, and will make the *Castle of Otranto* a still more moving story.

SONNET
TO THE RIGHT HONOURABLE
LADY MARY COKE.*

THE gentle maid, whose hapless tale
These melancholy pages speak;
Say, gracious lady, shall she fail
To draw the tear adown thy cheek?

No; never was thy pitying breast
Insensible to human woes;
Tender, tho' firm, it melts distrest
For weaknesses it never knows.

Oh! guard the marvels I relate
Of fell ambition scourg'd by fate,
From reason's peevish blame.
Blest with thy smile, my dauntless sail
I dare expand to Fancy's gale,
For sure thy smiles are Fame.

—H. W.

---

* An English noblewoman (1727–1811), a one-time friend of Walpole, here mocked with
pseudo-gallantry.

PREFACE TO THE SECOND EDITION.

THE favourable manner in which this little piece has been received by the public, calls upon the author to explain the grounds on which he composed it. But, before he opens those motives, it is fit that he should ask pardon of his readers for having offered his work to them under the borrowed personage of a translator. As diffidence of his own abilities and the novelty of the attempt, were the sole inducements to assume the disguise, he flatters himself he shall appear excusable. He resigned the performance to the impartial judgement of the public; determined to let it perish in obscurity, if disproved; nor meaning to avow such a trifle, unless better judges should pronounce that he might own it without a blush.

It was an attempt to blend the two kinds of Romance, the ancient and the modern. In the former, all was imagination and improbability; in the latter, nature is always intended to be, and sometimes has been, copied with success. Invention has not been wanting; but the great resources of fancy have been dammed up, by a strict adherence to common life. But if, in the latter species, Nature has cramped imagination, she did but take her revenge, having been totally excluded from old Romances. The actions, sentiments, and conversations, of the heroes and heroines of ancient days, were as unnatural as the machines employed to put them in motion.

The author of the following pages thought it possible to reconcile the two kinds. Desirous of leaving the powers of fancy at liberty to expatiate through the boundless realms of invention, and thence of creating more interesting situations, he wished to conduct the mortal agents in his drama according to the rules of probability; in short, to make them think, speak, and act, as it might be supposed mere men and women would do in extraordinary positions. He had observed, that, in all inspired writings, the personages under the dispensation of miracles, and witness to the most stupendous phenomena, never lose sight of their human character: whereas, in the productions of romantic story, an improbable event never fails to be attended by an absurd dialogue. The actors seem to lose their senses, the moment the laws of nature have lost their tone. As the public have applauded the attempt, the author must not say he was entirely unequal to the task he had undertaken: yet, if the new route he has struck out shall have paved a road for men of brighter talents, he shall own, with pleasure and modesty, that he was sensible the plan was capable of receiving greater embellishments than his imagination, or conduct of the passions, could bestow on it.

With regard to the deportment of the domestics,* on which I have touched in the former preface, I will beg leave to add a few words.—The simplicity of their behaviour, almost tending to excite smiles, which, at first, seems not consonant to the serious cast of the work, appeared to me not only improper, but was marked designedly in that manner. My rule was nature. However grave, important, or even melancholy, the sensations of the princes and heroes may be, they do not stamp the same affections on their domestics: at least the latter do not, or should not be made to, express their passions in the same dignified tone. In my humble opinion, the contrast between the sublime of the

---

* A term that still is in use, meaning servants or attendants.

one and the *naiveté* of the other, sets the pathetic of the former in a stronger light. The very impatience which a reader feels, while delayed, by the coarse pleasantries of vulgar actors, from arriving at the knowledge of the important catastrophe he expects, perhaps heightens, certainly proves that he has been artfully interested in, the depending event. But I had higher authority than my own opinion for this conduct. The great master of nature, Shakespeare, was the model I copied. Let me ask, if his tragedies of *Hamlet* and *Julius Caesar* would not lose a considerable share of their spirit and wonderful beauties, if the humour of the gravediggers, the fooleries of Polonius, and the clumsy jests of the Roman citizens, were omitted, or vested in heroics? Is not the eloquence of Antony, the nobler and affectedly-unaffected oration of Brutus, artificially exalted by the rude bursts of nature from the mouths of their auditors? These touches remind one of the Grecian sculptor, who, to convey the idea of a Colossus, within the dimensions of a seal, inserted a little boy measuring his thumb.

"No," says Voltaire, in his edition of *Corneille*, "this mixture of buffoonery and solemnity is intolerable."—Voltaire is a genius*—but not of Shakespeare's magnitude. Without recurring to disputable authority, I appeal from Voltaire to himself. I shall not avail myself of his former encomiums on our mighty poet; though the French critic has twice translated the same speech in *Hamlet*, some years ago in admiration, latterly in derision; and I

---

* [Author's note:] The following remark is foreign to the present question, yet excusable in an Englishman, who is willing to think that the severe criticisms of so masterly a writer as Voltaire on our immortal countryman, may have been the effusions of wit and precipitation, rather than the result of judgment and attention. May not the critic's skill, in the force and powers of our language, have been as incorrect and incompetent as his knowledge of our history? Of the latter, his own pen has dropped glaring evidence. In his preface to Thomas Corneille's *Earl of Essex*, Monsieur de Voltaire allows that the truth of history has been grossly perverted in that piece. In excuse he pleads, that when Corneille wrote, the noblesse of France were much unread in English story; but now, says the commentator, that they study it, such misrepresentations would not be suffered— yet forgetting that the period of ignorance is lapsed, and that it is not very necessary to instruct the knowing, he undertakes, from the overflowing of his own reading, to give the nobility of his own country a detail of Queen Elizabeth's favourites—of whom, says he, Robert Dudley was the first, and the Earl of Leicester the second. Could one have believed that it would be necessary to inform Monsieur de Voltaire himself, that Robert Dudley and the Earl of Leicester were the same person?

am sorry to find that his judgment grows weaker when it ought to be farther matured. But I shall make use of his own words, delivered on the general topic of the theatre, when he was neither thinking to recommend or decry Shakespeare's practice; consequently, at a moment when Voltaire was impartial. In the preface to his *Enfant Prodigue*, that exquisite piece, of which I declare my admiration, and which, should I live twenty years longer, I trust I shall never attempt to ridicule, he has these words, speaking of comedy (but equally applicable to tragedy, if tragedy is, as surely it ought to be, a picture of human life; nor can I conceive why occasional pleasantry ought more to be banished from the tragic scene than pathetic seriousness from the comic), *"On y voit un mélange de sérieux et de plaisanterie, de comique et de touchant; souvent même une seule aventure produit tous ces contrastes. Rien n'est si commun qu'une maison dans laquelle un père gronde, une fille occupée de sa passion pleure; le fils se moque des deux, et quelques parents prennent différemment part à la scène &c. Nous n'inférons pas de là que toute comédie doive avoir des scènes de bouffonnerie et des scènes attendrissantes: il y a beaucoup de très bonnes pièces où il ne règne que de la gaieté; d'autres toutes sérieuses; d'autres mélangèes: d'autres où l'attendrissement va jusques aux larmes: il ne faut donner l'exclusion à aucun genre; et si on me demandoit, quel genre est le meilleur, je répondrois, celui qui est le mieux traité."**

Surely if a Comedy may be *toute sérieuse*, Tragedy may now and then, soberly, be indulged in a smile. Who shall proscribe it? Shall the critic, who, in self-defence, declares, that *no kind* ought to be excluded from comedy, give laws to Shakespeare?

I am aware that the preface from whence I have quoted these passages does not stand in Monsieur de Voltaire's name, but in

---

* [Editors' note:] "One sees there a mixture of the grave and the light, of the comic and the tragic; often even a single adventure exhibits all these contrasts. Nothing is more common than a house in which the father scolds, a girl occupied by her passions weeps, the son ridicules both, some relations take a differing part in the scene, etc. We do not infer from this that every comedy ought to have scenes of buffoonery and of gravity. Now there is gaiety, now seriousness, now a mixture. Then there are others in which tenderness moves one to tears. We must not exclude any type, and if I were asked which is the best I would answer, 'the one which is best made.'" From Voltaire's *L'Enfant prodigue* (*The Prodigal Son*), a 1736 play.

that of his editor; yet who doubts that the editor and the author were the same person? Or where is the editor, who has so happily possessed himself of his author's style, and brilliant ease of argument? These passages were indubitably the genuine sentiments of that great writer. In his epistle to Maffei, prefixed to his Mérope, he delivers almost the same opinion, though, I doubt, with a little irony. I will repeat his words, and then give my reason for quoting them. After translating a passage in Maffei's Mérope, Monsieur de Voltaire adds, *"Tous ces traits sont naïfs; tout y est convenable à ceux que vous introduisez sur la scène, et aux moeurs que vous leur donnez. Ces familiarités naturelles eussent été, à ce que je crois, bien reçues dans Athènes; mais Paris et notre parterre veulent une autre espèce de simplicité."* * I doubt, I say, whether there is not a grain of sneer in this and other passages of that epistle; yet the force of truth is not damaged by being tinged with ridicule. Maffei was to represent a Grecian story: surely the Athenians were as competent judges of Grecian manners, and of the propriety of introducing them, as the *Parterre of Paris.* "On the contrary," says Voltaire (and I cannot but admire his reasoning), "there were but ten thousand citizens at Athens and Paris has near eight hundred thousand inhabitants, among whom one may reckon thirty thousand judges of dramatic works."—indeed!—but allowing so numerous a tribunal, I believe this is the only instance in which it was ever pretended that thirty thousand persons, living near two thousand years after the era in question, were, upon the mere face of the poll, declared better judges than the Grecians themselves, of what ought to be the manners of a tragedy written on a Grecian story.

I will not enter into a discussion of the *espèce de simplicité,* which the *Parterre of Paris* demands, nor of the shackles with which *the thirty thousand judges* have cramped their poetry, the chief merit of which, as I gather from repeated passages in the *New Commentary on Corneille,* consists in vaulting in spite of

---

* [Editors' note:] "All of these characteristics are naive. Everything is convenient to those who introduce the scene and to the customs that you give them. These natural familiarities would, I think, have been well received in Athens, but Paris and our nation prefer another type of subtlety."

those fetters; a merit which, if true, would reduce poetry from the lofty effort of imagination, to a puerile and most contemptible labour—*difficiles nugæ* with a witness! I cannot, however, help mentioning a couplet, which, to my English ears, always sounded as the flattest and most trifling instance of circumstantial propriety, but which Voltaire, who has dealt so severely with nine parts in ten of Corneille's works, has singled out to defend in Racine;

> *De son appartement cette porte est prochaine,*
> *Et cette autre conduit dans celui de la Reine.*

In English,

> *To Caeser's closet through this door you come,*
> *And t'other leads to the Queen's drawing-room.*

Unhappy Shakespeare! Hadst thou made Rosencrantz inform his compeer, Guildenstern, of the iconography of the palace of Copenhagen, instead of presenting us with a moral dialogue between the Prince of Denmark and the gravedigger, the illuminated pit of Paris would have been instructed *a second time* to adore thy talents.

The result of all I have said, is, to shelter my own daring under the canon of the brightest genius this country, at least, has produced. I might have pleaded that, having created a new species of romance, I was at liberty to lay down what rules I thought fit for the conduct of it: but I should be more proud of having imitated, however faintly, weakly, and at a distance, so masterly a pattern, than to enjoy the entire merit of invention, unless I could have marked my work with genius, as well as with originality. Such as it is, the public have honoured it sufficiently, whatever rank their suffrages allot to it.

—*Horace Walpole.*

Chapter I.

MANFRED, Prince of Otranto,* had one son and one daughter: the latter, a most beautiful virgin, aged eighteen, was called Matilda. Conrad, the son, was three years younger, a homely youth, sickly, and of no promising disposition; yet he was the darling of his father, who never showed any symptoms of affection to Matilda. Manfred had contracted a marriage for his son with the Marquis of Vicenza's† daughter, Isabella; and she had already been delivered by her guardians into the hands of Manfred, that he might celebrate the wedding as soon as Conrad's infirm state of health would permit.

Manfred's impatience for this ceremonial was remarked by his family and neighbours. The former, indeed, apprehending the severity of their Prince's disposition, did not dare to utter their surmises on this precipitation. Hippolita, his wife, an amiable lady, did sometimes venture to represent the danger of marrying their only son so early, considering his great youth, and greater infirmities; but she never received any other answer than reflections on her own sterility, who had given him but one heir. His tenants

---

* A town in southern Italy's Apulia region. It was not a principality during the reign of the Aragonese kings.

† Vicenza is a city in northeastern Italy, in the region of Venice.

and subjects were less cautious in their discourses: they attributed this hasty wedding to the Prince's dread of seeing accomplished an ancient prophecy, which was said to have pronounced that *the castle and lordship of Otranto should pass from the present family, whenever the real owner should be grown too large to inhabit it.* It was difficult to make any sense of this prophecy; and still less easy to conceive what it had to do with the marriage in question. Yet these mysteries, or contradictions, did not make the populace adhere the less to their opinion.

Young Conrad's birthday was fixed for his espousals. The company was assembled in the chapel of the Castle, and everything ready for beginning the divine office, when Conrad himself was missing. Manfred, impatient of the least delay, and who had not observed his son retire, dispatched one of his attendants to summon the young Prince. The servant, who had not stayed long enough to have crossed the court to Conrad's apartment, came running back breathless, in a frantic manner, his eyes staring, and foaming at the mouth. He said nothing, but pointed to the court.

The company were struck with terror and amazement. The Princess Hippolita, without knowing what was the matter, but anxious for her son, swooned away. Manfred, less apprehensive than enraged at the procrastination of the nuptials, and at the folly of his domestic, asked imperiously, "What was the matter?" The fellow made no answer, but continued pointing towards the courtyard; and at last, after repeated questions put to him, cried out, "Oh! The helmet! The helmet!"

In the meantime, some of the company had run into the court, from whence was heard a confused noise of shrieks, horror, and surprise. Manfred, who began to be alarmed at not seeing his son, went himself to get information of what occasioned this strange confusion. Matilda remained endeavouring to assist her mother, and Isabella stayed for the same purpose, and to avoid showing any impatience for the bridegroom, for whom, in truth, she had conceived little affection.

The first thing that struck Manfred's eyes was a group of his servants endeavouring to raise something that appeared to him a mountain of sable plumes. He gazed without believing his sight.

"What are ye doing?" cried Manfred, wrathfully. "Where is my son?"

A volley of voices replied, "Oh! My Lord! The Prince! The Prince! The helmet! The helmet!"

Shocked with these lamentable sounds, and dreading he knew not what, he advanced hastily,—but what a sight for a father's eyes!—he beheld his child dashed to pieces, and almost buried under an enormous helmet, a hundred times more large than any casque ever made for human being, and shaded with a proportionable quantity of black feathers.

The horror of the spectacle, the ignorance of all around how this misfortune had happened, and above all, the tremendous phenomenon before him, took away the Prince's speech. Yet his silence lasted longer than even grief could occasion. He fixed his eyes on what he wished in vain to believe a vision; and seemed less attentive to his loss, than buried in meditation on the stupendous object that had occasioned it. He touched, he examined the fatal casque; nor could even the bleeding mangled remains of the young Prince divert the eyes of Manfred from the portent before him.

All who had known his partial fondness for young Conrad, were as much surprised at their Prince's insensibility, as thunderstruck themselves at the miracle of the helmet. They conveyed the disfigured corpse into the hall, without receiving the least direction from Manfred. As little was he attentive to the ladies who remained in the chapel; on the contrary, without mentioning the unhappy princesses, his wife and daughter, the first sounds that dropped from Manfred's lips were, "Take care of the Lady Isabella."

The domestics, without observing the singularity of this direction, were guided by their affection to their mistress, to consider it as peculiarly addressed to her situation, and flew to her assistance. They conveyed her to her chamber more dead than alive, and indifferent to all the strange circumstances she heard, except the death of her son.

Matilda, who doted on her mother, smothered her own grief and amazement, and thought of nothing but assisting and comforting her afflicted parent. Isabella, who had been treated by Hippolita like a daughter, and who returned that tenderness with equal duty and affection, was scarce less assiduous about the Princess; at the same time endeavouring to partake and lessen the weight of sorrow which she saw Matilda strove to suppress, for whom she had conceived the warmest sympathy of friendship. Yet her own situation could not help finding its place in her thoughts. She felt no concern for the death of young Conrad, except commiseration; and she was not sorry to be delivered from a marriage which had promised her little felicity, either from her destined bridegroom, or from the severe temper of Manfred, who, though he had distinguished her by great indulgence, had imprinted her mind with terror, from his causeless rigour to such amiable princesses as Hippolita and Matilda.

While the ladies were conveying the wretched mother to her bed, Manfred remained in the court, gazing on the ominous casque, and regardless of the crowd which the strangeness of the event had now assembled around him. The few words he articulated, tended solely to inquiries, whether any man knew from whence it could have come? Nobody could give him the least information. However, as it seemed to be the sole object of his curiosity, it soon became so to the rest of the spectators, whose conjectures were as absurd and improbable, as the catastrophe itself was unprecedented. In the midst of their senseless guesses, a young peasant, whom rumour had drawn thither from a neighbouring village, observed that the miraculous helmet was exactly like that on the figure in black marble of Alfonso the Good, one of their former princes, in the church of St. Nicholas.

"Villain! What sayest thou?" cried Manfred, starting from his trance in a tempest of rage, and seizing the young man by the collar. "How darest thou utter such treason? Thy life shall pay for it."

The spectators, who as little comprehended the cause of the Prince's fury as all the rest they had seen, were at a loss to unravel this new circumstance. The young peasant himself was still more astonished, not conceiving how he had offended the Prince. Yet recollecting himself, with a mixture of grace and humility, he disengaged himself from Manfred's grip, and then with an obeisance, which discovered more jealousy of innocence than dismay, he asked, with respect, of what he was guilty? Manfred, more enraged at the vigour, however decently exerted, with which the young man had shaken off his hold, than appeased by his submission, ordered his attendants to seize him, and, if he had not been withheld by his friends whom he had invited to the nuptials, would have poignarded* the peasant in their arms.

During this altercation, some of the vulgar spectators had run to the great church, which stood near the castle, and came back open-mouthed, declaring that the helmet was missing from Alfonso's statue. Manfred, at this news, grew perfectly frantic; and, as if he sought a subject on which to vent the tempest within him, he rushed again on the young peasant, crying, "Villain! Monster! Sorcerer! 'Tis thou hast done this! 'Tis thou hast slain my son!"

The mob, who wanted some object within the scope of their capacities, on whom they might discharge their bewildered reasoning, caught the words from the mouth of their lord, and re-echoed, "Ay, ay; 'tis he, 'tis he: He has stolen the helmet from good Alfonso's tomb, and dashed out the brains of our young Prince with it,"—never reflecting how enormous the disproportion was between the marble helmet that had been in the church, and that of steel before their eyes; nor how impossible it was for a youth seemingly not twenty, to wield a piece of armour of so prodigious a weight.

---

* Stabbed with a poignard, a dagger.

The folly of these ejaculations brought Manfred to himself: yet whether provoked at the peasant having observed the resemblance between the two helmets, and thereby led to the farther discovery of the absence of that in the church, or wishing to bury any such rumour under so impertinent a supposition, he gravely pronounced that the young man was certainly a necromancer, and that till the Church could take cognisance of the affair, he would have the Magician, whom they had thus detected, kept prisoner under the helmet itself, which he ordered his attendants to raise, and place the young man under it; declaring he should be kept there without food, with which his own infernal art might furnish him.

It was in vain for the youth to represent against this preposterous sentence: in vain did Manfred's friends endeavour to divert him from this savage and ill-grounded resolution. The generality were charmed with their lord's decision, which, to their apprehensions, carried great appearance of justice, as the Magician was to be punished by the very instrument with which he had offended: nor were they struck with the least compunction at the probability of the youth being starved, for they firmly believed that, by his diabolic skill, he could easily supply himself with nutriment.

Manfred thus saw his commands even cheerfully obeyed; and appointing a guard with strict orders to prevent any food being conveyed to the prisoner, he dismissed his friends and attendants, and retired to his own chamber, after locking the gates of the castle, in which he suffered none but his domestics to remain.

In the meantime, the care and zeal of the young Ladies had brought the Princess Hippolita to herself, who amidst the transports of her own sorrow frequently demanded news of her lord, would have dismissed her attendants to watch over him, and at last enjoined Matilda to leave her, and visit and comfort her father. Matilda, who wanted no affectionate duty to Manfred, though she trembled at his austerity, obeyed the orders of Hippolita, whom she tenderly recommended to Isabella; and inquiring of the domestics for her father, was informed that he was retired to his chamber, and had commanded that nobody should have admittance to him. Concluding that he was immersed in sorrow for the death of her brother, and fearing to renew his tears by the sight of his sole remaining child, she hesitated whether she should break in upon his affliction; yet solicitude for him, backed by the commands of her mother, encouraged her to venture disobeying the orders he had given; a fault she had never been guilty of before.

The gentle timidity of her nature made her pause for some minutes at his door. She heard him traverse his chamber backwards, and forwards with disordered steps; a mood which increased her apprehensions. She was, however, just going to beg admittance, when Manfred suddenly opened the door; and as it was now twilight, concurring with the disorder of his mind, he did not distinguish the person, but asked angrily, who it was?

Matilda replied, trembling, "My dearest father, it is I, your daughter."

Manfred, stepping back hastily, cried, "Begone! I do not want a daughter;" and flinging back abruptly, clapped the door against the terrified Matilda.

She was too well acquainted with her father's impetuosity to venture a second intrusion. When she had a little recovered the shock of so bitter a reception, she wiped away her tears to prevent the additional stab that the knowledge of it would give to Hippolita, who questioned her in the most anxious terms on the health of Manfred, and how he bore his loss. Matilda assured her he was well, and supported his misfortune with manly fortitude.

"But will he not let me see him?" said Hippolita mournfully. "Will he not permit me to blend my tears with his, and shed a mother's sorrows in the bosom of her Lord? Or do you deceive me, Matilda? I know how Manfred doted on his son: is not the stroke too heavy for him? Has he not sunk under it? You do not answer me—alas! I dread the worst!—Raise me, my maidens; I will, I will see my Lord. Bear me to him instantly: he is dearer to me even than my children."

Matilda made signs to Isabella to prevent Hippolita's rising; and both those lovely young women were using their gentle violence to stop and calm the Princess, when a servant, on the part of Manfred, arrived and told Isabella that his Lord demanded to speak with her.

"With me!" cried Isabella.

"Go," said Hippolita, relieved by a message from her Lord. "Manfred cannot support the sight of his own family. He thinks you less disordered than we are, and dreads the shock of my grief. Console him, dear Isabella, and tell him I will smother my own anguish rather than add to his."

As it was now evening the servant who conducted Isabella bore a torch before her. When they came to Manfred, who was walking impatiently about the gallery, he started, and said hastily, "Take away that light, and begone."

Then shutting the door impetuously, he flung himself upon a bench against the wall, and bade Isabella sit by him. She obeyed trembling.

"I sent for you, Lady," said he,—and then stopped under great appearance of confusion.

"My Lord!"

"Yes, I sent for you on a matter of great moment," resumed he. "Dry your tears, young Lady—you have lost your bridegroom. Yes, cruel fate! And I have lost the hopes of my race! But Conrad was not worthy of your beauty."

"How, my Lord!" said Isabella. "Sure you do not suspect me of not feeling the concern I ought: my duty and affection would have always—"

"Think no more of him," interrupted Manfred. "He was a sickly, puny child, and Heaven has perhaps taken him away, that I might not trust the honours of my house on so frail a foundation. The line of Manfred calls for numerous supports. My foolish fondness for that boy blinded the eyes of my prudence—but it is better as it is. I hope, in a few years, to have reason to rejoice at the death of Conrad."

Words cannot paint the astonishment of Isabella. At first she apprehended that grief had disordered Manfred's understanding. Her next thought suggested that this strange discourse was designed to ensnare her: she feared that Manfred had perceived her indifference for his son: and in consequence of that idea she replied, "Good my Lord, do not doubt my tenderness: my heart would have accompanied my hand. Conrad would have engrossed all my care; and wherever fate shall dispose of me, I shall always cherish his memory, and regard your Highness and the virtuous Hippolita as my parents."

"Curse on Hippolita!" cried Manfred. "Forget her from this moment, as I do. In short, Lady, you have missed a husband undeserving of your charms: they shall now be better disposed of. Instead of a sickly boy, you shall have a husband in the prime of his age, who will know how to value your beauties, and who may expect a numerous offspring."

"Alas, my Lord!" said Isabella. "My mind is too sadly engrossed by the recent catastrophe in your family to think of another marriage. If ever my father returns, and it shall be his pleasure, I shall obey, as I did when I consented to give my hand to your son: but until his return, permit me to remain under your hospitable roof, and employ the melancholy hours in assuaging yours, Hippolita's, and the fair Matilda's affliction."

"I desired you once before," said Manfred angrily, "not to name that woman: from this hour she must be a stranger to you, as she must be to me. In short, Isabella, since I cannot give you my son, I offer you myself."

"Heavens!" cried Isabella, waking from her delusion. "What do I hear? You! My Lord! You! My father-in-law! The father of Conrad! The husband of the virtuous and tender Hippolita!"

"I tell you," said Manfred imperiously, "Hippolita is no longer my wife; I divorce her from this hour. Too long has she cursed me by her unfruitfulness. My fate depends on having sons, and this night I trust will give a new date to my hopes."

At those words he seized the cold hand of Isabella, who was half dead with fright and horror. She shrieked, and started from him, Manfred rose to pursue her, when the moon, which was now up, and gleamed in at the opposite casement, presented to his sight the plumes of the fatal helmet, which rose to the height of the windows, waving backwards and forwards in a tempestuous manner, and accompanied with a hollow and rustling sound. Isabella, who gathered courage from her situation, and who dreaded nothing so much as Manfred's pursuit of his declaration, cried, "Look, my Lord! See, Heaven itself declares against your impious intentions!"

"Heaven nor Hell shall impede my designs," said Manfred, advancing again to seize the Princess.

At that instant the portrait of his grandfather, which hung over the bench where they had been sitting, uttered a deep sigh, and heaved its breast.

Isabella, whose back was turned to the picture, saw not the motion, nor knew whence the sound came, but started, and said, "Hark, my Lord! What sound was that?" and at the same time made towards the door.

Manfred, distracted between the flight of Isabella, who had now reached the stairs, and yet unable to keep his eyes from the picture, which began to move, had, however, advanced some steps after her, still looking backwards on the portrait, when he saw it quit its panel, and descend on the floor with a grave and melancholy air.

"Do I dream?" cried Manfred, returning. "Or are the devils themselves in league against me? Speak, internal spectre! Or, if thou art my grandsire, why dost thou too conspire against thy wretched descendant, who too dearly pays for—"

Ere he could finish the sentence, the vision sighed again, and made a sign to Manfred to follow him.

"Lead on!" cried Manfred. "I will follow thee to the gulf of perdition."

The spectre marched sedately, but dejected, to the end of the gallery, and turned into a chamber on the right hand. Manfred accompanied him at a little distance, full of anxiety and horror, but resolved. As he would have entered the chamber, the door was clapped to with violence by an invisible hand. The Prince, collecting courage from this delay, would have forcibly burst open the door with his foot, but found that it resisted his utmost efforts.

"Since Hell will not satisfy my curiosity," said Manfred, "I will use the human means in my power for preserving my race; Isabella shall not escape me."

That lady, whose resolution had given way to terror the moment she had quitted Manfred, continued her flight to the bottom of the principal staircase. There she stopped, not knowing whither to direct her steps, nor how to escape from the impetuosity of the Prince. The gates of the castle, she knew, were locked, and guards placed in the court. Should she, as her heart prompted her, go and prepare Hippolita for the cruel destiny that awaited her, she did not doubt but Manfred would seek her there, and that his violence would incite him to double the injury he meditated, without leaving room for them to avoid the impetuosity of his passions. Delay might give him time to reflect on the horrid measures he had conceived, or produce some circumstance in her favour, if she could—for that night, at least—avoid his odious purpose. Yet where conceal herself? How avoid the pursuit he would infallibly make throughout the castle?

As these thoughts passed rapidly through her mind, she recollected a subterraneous passage which led from the vaults of the castle to the church of St. Nicholas. Could she reach the altar before she was overtaken, she knew even Manfred's violence would not dare to profane the sacredness of the place; and she determined, if no other means of deliverance offered, to shut herself up for ever among the holy virgins whose convent was contiguous to the cathedral. In this resolution, she seized a lamp that burned at the foot of the staircase, and hurried towards the secret passage.

The lower part of the castle was hollowed into several intricate cloisters; and it was not easy for one under so much anxiety to find the door that opened into the cavern. An awful silence reigned throughout those subterraneous regions, except now and then some blasts of wind that shook the doors she had passed, and which, grating on the rusty hinges, were re-echoed through that long labyrinth of darkness. Every murmur struck her with new terror; yet more she dreaded to hear the wrathful voice of Manfred urging his domestics to pursue her.

She trod as softly as impatience would give her leave, yet frequently stopped and listened to hear if she was followed. In one of those moments she thought she heard a sigh. She shuddered, and recoiled a few paces. In a moment she thought she heard the step of some person. Her blood curdled; she concluded it was Manfred. Every suggestion that horror could inspire rushed into her mind. She condemned her rash flight, which had thus exposed her to his rage in a place where her cries were not likely to draw anybody to her assistance. Yet the sound seemed not to come from behind. If Manfred knew where she was, he must have followed her. She was still in one of the cloisters, and the steps she had heard were too distinct to proceed from the way she had come. Cheered with this reflection, and hoping to find a friend in whoever was not the Prince, she was going to advance, when a door that stood ajar, at some distance to the left, was opened gently: but ere her lamp, which she held up, could discover who opened it, the person retreated precipitately on seeing the light.

Isabella, whom every incident was sufficient to dismay, hesitated whether she should proceed. Her dread of Manfred soon outweighed every other terror. The very circumstance of the person avoiding her gave her a sort of courage. It could only be, she thought, some domestic belonging to the castle. Her gentleness had never raised her an enemy, and conscious innocence made her hope that, unless sent by the Prince's order to seek her, his servants would rather assist than prevent her flight. Fortifying herself with these reflections, and believing by what she could observe that she was near the mouth of the subterraneous cavern, she approached the door that had been opened; but a sudden gust of wind that met her at the door extinguished her lamp, and left her in total darkness.

Words cannot paint the horror of the Princess's situation. Alone in so dismal a place, her mind imprinted with all the terrible events of the day, hopeless of escaping, expecting every moment the arrival of Manfred, and far from tranquil on knowing she was within reach of somebody, she knew not whom, who for some cause seemed concealed thereabouts; all these thoughts crowded on her distracted mind, and she was ready to sink under her apprehensions. She addressed herself to every saint in Heaven, and inwardly implored their assistance. For a considerable time she remained in an agony of despair.

At last, as softly as was possible, she felt for the door, and having found it, entered trembling into the vault from whence she had heard the sigh and steps. It gave her a kind of momentary joy to perceive an imperfect ray of clouded moonshine gleam from the roof of the vault, which seemed to be fallen in, and from whence hung a fragment of earth or building, she could not distinguish which, that appeared to have been crushed inwards. She advanced eagerly towards this chasm, when she discerned a human form standing close against the wall.

She shrieked, believing it the ghost of her betrothed Conrad. The figure, advancing, said, in a submissive voice, "Be not alarmed, Lady; I will not injure you."

Isabella, a little encouraged by the words and tone of voice of the stranger, and recollecting that this must be the person who had opened the door, recovered her spirits enough to reply, "Sir, whoever you are, take pity on a wretched Princess, standing on the brink of destruction. Assist me to escape from this fatal castle, or in a few moments I may be made miserable for ever."

"Alas!" said the stranger. "What can I do to assist you? I will die in your defence; but I am unacquainted with the castle, and want—"

"Oh!" said Isabella, hastily interrupting him. "Help me but to find a trap-door that must be hereabout, and it is the greatest service you can do me, for I have not a minute to lose."

Saying these words, she felt about on the pavement, and directed the stranger to search likewise, for a smooth piece of brass enclosed in one of the stones.

"That," said she, "is the lock, which opens with a spring, of which I know the secret. If we can find that, I may escape—if not, alas! Courteous stranger, I fear I shall have involved you in my misfortunes: Manfred will suspect you for the accomplice of my flight, and you will fall a victim to his resentment."

"I value not my life," said the stranger, "and it will be some comfort to lose it in trying to deliver you from his tyranny."

"Generous youth," said Isabella, "how shall I ever requite—"

As she uttered those words, a ray of moonshine, streaming through a cranny of the ruin above, shone directly on the lock they sought.

"Oh! Transport!" said Isabella. "Here is the trap-door!" And, taking out the key, she touched the spring, which, starting aside, discovered an iron ring. "Lift up the door," said the Princess.

The stranger obeyed, and beneath appeared some stone steps descending into a vault totally dark.

"We must go down here," said Isabella. "Follow me; dark and dismal as it is, we cannot miss our way; it leads directly to the church of St. Nicholas. But, perhaps," added the Princess modestly, "you have no reason to leave the castle, nor have I farther occasion for your service; in a few minutes I shall be safe from Manfred's rage—only let me know to whom I am so much obliged."

"I will never quit you," said the stranger eagerly, "until I have placed you in safety—nor think me, Princess, more generous than I am; though you are my principal care—"

The stranger was interrupted by a sudden noise of voices that seemed approaching, and they soon distinguished these words—

"Talk not to me of necromancers; I tell you she must be in the castle; I will find her in spite of enchantment."

"Oh, heavens!" cried Isabella. "It is the voice of Manfred! Make haste, or we are ruined! And shut the trap-door after you."

Saying this, she descended the steps precipitately; and as the stranger hastened to follow her, he let the door slip out of his hands; it fell, and the spring closed over it. He tried in vain to open it, not having observed Isabella's method of touching the spring; nor had he many moments to make an essay.* The noise of the falling door had been heard by Manfred, who, directed by the sound, hastened thither, attended by his servants with torches.

"It must be Isabella," cried Manfred, before he entered the vault. "She is escaping by the subterraneous passage, but she cannot have got far."

What was the astonishment of the Prince when, instead of Isabella, the light of the torches discovered to him the young peasant whom he thought confined under the fatal helmet!

"Traitor!" said Manfred. "How camest thou here? I thought thee in durance above in the court."

"I am no traitor," replied the young man boldly, "nor am I answerable for your thoughts."

"Presumptuous villain!" cried Manfred. "Dost thou provoke my wrath? Tell me, how hast thou escaped from above? Thou hast corrupted thy guards, and their lives shall answer it."

"My poverty," said the peasant calmly, "will disculpate† them:

* To try, to make an attempt.

† Prove their innocence. The peasant says that he is too poor to have bribed them.

though the ministers of a tyrant's wrath, to thee they are faithful, and but too willing to execute the orders which you unjustly imposed upon them."

"Art thou so hardy as to dare my vengeance?" said the Prince. "But tortures shall force the truth from thee. Tell me; I will know thy accomplices."

"There was my accomplice!" said the youth, smiling, and pointing to the roof.

Manfred ordered the torches to be held up, and perceived that one of the cheeks of the enchanted casque had forced its way through the pavement of the court, as his servants had let it fall over the peasant, and had broken through into the vault, leaving a gap, through which the peasant had pressed himself some minutes before he was found by Isabella.

"Was that the way by which thou didst descend?" said Manfred.

"It was," said the youth.

"But what noise was that," said Manfred, "which I heard as I entered the cloister?"

"A door clapped," said the peasant. "I heard it as well as you."

"What door?" said Manfred hastily.

"I am not acquainted with your castle," said the peasant. "This is the first time I ever entered it, and this vault the only part of it within which I ever was."

"But I tell thee," said Manfred (wishing to find out if the youth had discovered the trap-door), "it was this way I heard the noise. My servants heard it too."

"My Lord," interrupted one of them officiously, "to be sure it was the trap-door, and he was going to make his escape."

"Peace, blockhead!" said the Prince angrily. "If he was going to escape, how should he come on this side? I will know from his own mouth what noise it was I heard. Tell me truly; thy life depends on thy veracity."

"My veracity is dearer to me than my life," said the peasant. "Nor would I purchase the one by forfeiting the other."

"Indeed, young philosopher!" said Manfred contemptuously. "Tell me, then, what was the noise I heard?"

"Ask me what I can answer," said he, "and put me to death instantly if I tell you a lie."

Manfred, growing impatient at the steady valour and indifference of the youth, cried, "Well, then, thou man of truth, answer! Was it the fall of the trap-door that I heard?"

"It was," said the youth.

"It was!" said the Prince. "And how didst thou come to know there was a trap-door here?"

"I saw the plate of brass by a gleam of moonshine," replied he.

"But what told thee it was a lock?" said Manfred. "How didst thou discover the secret of opening it?"

"Providence, that delivered me from the helmet, was able to direct me to the spring of a lock," said he.

"Providence should have gone a little farther, and have placed thee out of the reach of my resentment," said Manfred. "When Providence had taught thee to open the lock, it abandoned thee for a fool, who did not know how to make use of its favours. Why didst thou not pursue the path pointed out for thy escape? Why didst thou shut the trap-door before thou hadst descended the steps?"

"I might ask you, my Lord," said the peasant, "how I, totally unacquainted with your castle, was to know that those steps led to any outlet? But I scorn to evade your questions. Wherever those steps lead to, perhaps I should have explored the way—I could not be in a worse situation than I was. But the truth is, I let the trap-door fall: your immediate arrival followed. I had given the alarm—what imported it to me whether I was seized a minute sooner or a minute later?"

"Thou art a resolute villain for thy years," said Manfred. "Yet on reflection I suspect thou dost but trifle with me. Thou hast not yet told me how thou didst open the lock."

"That I will show you, my Lord," said the peasant; and, taking up a fragment of stone that had fallen from above, he laid himself on the trap-door, and began to beat on the piece of brass that covered it, meaning to gain time for the escape of the Princess. This presence of mind, joined to the frankness of the youth, staggered Manfred. He even felt a disposition towards pardoning one who had been guilty of no crime. Manfred was not one of those savage tyrants who wanton in cruelty unprovoked. The circumstances of his fortune had given an asperity to his temper, which was naturally humane; and his virtues were always ready to operate, when his passions did not obscure his reason.

While the Prince was in this suspense, a confused noise of voices echoed through the distant vaults. As the sound approached, he distinguished the clamours of some of his domestics, whom he had dispersed through the castle in search of Isabella, calling out, "Where is my Lord? Where is the Prince?"

"Here I am," said Manfred, as they came nearer. "Have you found the Princess?"

The first that arrived, replied, "Oh, my Lord! I am glad we have found you."

"Found me!" said Manfred. "Have you found the Princess?"

"We thought we had, my Lord," said the fellow, looking terrified, "but—"

"But, what?" cried the Prince. "Has she escaped?"

"Jaquez and I, my Lord—"

"Yes, I and Diego," interrupted the second, who came up in still greater consternation.

"Speak one of you at a time," said Manfred. "I ask you, where is the Princess?"

"We do not know," said they both together. "But we are frightened out of our wits."

"So I think, blockheads," said Manfred. "What is it has scared you thus?"

"Oh! My Lord," said Jaquez, "Diego has seen such a sight! Your Highness would not believe our eyes."

"What new absurdity is this?" cried Manfred. "Give me a direct answer, or, by Heaven—"

"Why, my Lord, if it please your Highness to hear me," said the poor fellow, "Diego and I—"

"Yes, I and Jaquez—" cried his comrade.

"Did not I forbid you to speak both at a time?" said the Prince. "You, Jaquez, answer; for the other fool seems more distracted than thou art; what is the matter?"

"My gracious Lord," said Jaquez, "if it please your Highness to hear me; Diego and I, according to your Highness's orders, went to search for the young Lady; but being comprehensive that we might meet the ghost of my young Lord, your Highness's son, God rest his soul, as he has not received Christian burial—"

"Sot!" cried Manfred in a rage. "Is it only a ghost, then, that thou hast seen?"

"Oh! Worse! Worse! my Lord," cried Diego. "I had rather have seen ten whole ghosts."

"Grant me patience!" said Manfred. "These blockheads distract me. Out of my sight, Diego! And thou, Jaquez, tell me in one word, art thou sober? Art thou raving? Thou wast wont to have some sense: has the other sot frightened himself and thee too? Speak; what is it he fancies he has seen?"

"Why, my Lord," replied Jaquez, trembling, "I was going to tell your Highness, that since the calamitous misfortune of my young Lord, God rest his precious soul! Not one of us your Highness's faithful servants—indeed we are, my Lord, though poor men—I say, not one of us has dared to set a foot about the castle, but two together: so Diego and I, thinking that my young Lady might be in the great gallery, went up there to look for her, and tell her your Highness wanted something to impart to her."

"O blundering fools!" cried Manfred. "And in the meantime, she has made her escape, because you were afraid of goblins!—Why, thou knave! She left me in the gallery; I came from thence myself."

"For all that, she may be there still for aught I know," said Jaquez. "But the devil shall have me before I seek her there again—poor Diego! I do not believe he will ever recover it."

"Recover what?" said Manfred. "Am I never to learn what it is has terrified these rascals? But I lose my time; follow me, slave; I will see if she is in the gallery."

"For Heaven's sake, my dear, good Lord," cried Jaquez, "do not go to the gallery. Satan himself I believe is in the chamber next to the gallery."

Manfred, who hitherto had treated the terror of his servants as an idle panic, was struck at this new circumstance. He recollected the apparition of the portrait, and the sudden closing of the door at the end of the gallery. His voice faltered, and he asked with disorder, "What is in the great chamber?"

"My Lord," said Jaquez, "when Diego and I came into the gallery, he went first, for he said he had more courage than I. So when we came into the gallery we found nobody. We looked under every bench and stool; and still we found nobody."

"Were all the pictures in their places?" said Manfred.

"Yes, my Lord," answered Jaquez, "but we did not think of looking behind them."

"Well, well!" said Manfred. "Proceed."

"When we came to the door of the great chamber," continued Jaquez, "we found it shut."

"And could not you open it?" said Manfred.

"Oh! Yes, my Lord; would to Heaven we had not!" replied he. "Nay, it was not I neither; it was Diego: he was grown foolhardy, and would go on, though I advised him not—if ever I open a door that is shut again—"

"Trifle not," said Manfred, shuddering, "but tell me what you saw in the great chamber on opening the door."

"I! My Lord!" said Jaquez. "I was behind Diego; but I heard the noise."

"Jaquez," said Manfred, in a solemn tone of voice, "tell me, I adjure thee by the souls of my ancestors, what was it thou sawest? What was it thou heardest?"

"It was Diego saw it, my Lord, it was not I," replied Jaquez. "I only heard the noise. Diego had no sooner opened the door, than he cried out, and ran back. I ran back too, and said, 'Is it the ghost?' 'The ghost! No, no,' said Diego, and his hair stood on end—'it is a giant, I believe; he is all clad in armour, for I saw his foot and part of his leg, and they are as large as the helmet below in the court.' As he said these words, my Lord, we heard a violent motion and the rattling of armour, as if the giant was rising, for Diego has told me since that he believes the giant was lying down, for the foot and leg were stretched at length on the floor. Before we could get to the end of the gallery, we heard the door of the great chamber clap behind us, but we did not dare turn back to see if the giant was following us—yet, now I think on it, we must have heard him if he had pursued us—but for Heaven's sake, good my Lord, send for the chaplain, and have the castle exorcised, for, for certain, it is enchanted."

"Ay, pray do, my Lord," cried all the servants at once, "or we must leave your Highness's service."

"Peace, dotards!" said Manfred. "And follow me; I will know what all this means."

"We! My Lord!" cried they with one voice. "We would not go up to the gallery for your Highness's revenue."

The young peasant, who had stood silent, now spoke. "Will your Highness," said he, "permit me to try this adventure? My life is of consequence to nobody; I fear no bad angel, and have offended no good one."

"Your behaviour is above your seeming," said Manfred, viewing him with surprise and admiration—"hereafter I will reward your bravery—but now," continued he with a sigh, "I am so circumstanced, that I dare trust no eyes but my own. However, I give you leave to accompany me."

Manfred, when he first followed Isabella from the gallery, had gone directly to the apartment of his wife, concluding the Princess had retired thither. Hippolita, who knew his step, rose with anxious fondness to meet her Lord, whom she had not seen since the death of their son. She would have flown in a transport mixed of joy and grief to his bosom, but he pushed her rudely off, and said, "Where is Isabella?"

"Isabella! My Lord!" said the astonished Hippolita.

"Yes, Isabella," cried Manfred imperiously. "I want Isabella."

"My Lord," replied Matilda, who perceived how much his behaviour had shocked her mother, "she has not been with us since your Highness summoned her to your apartment."

"Tell me where she is," said the Prince. "I do not want to know where she has been."

"My good Lord," says Hippolita, "your daughter tells you the truth: Isabella left us by your command, and has not returned since;—but, my good Lord, compose yourself: retire to your rest: this dismal day has disordered you. Isabella shall wait your orders in the morning."

"What, then, you know where she is!" cried Manfred. "Tell me directly, for I will not lose an instant—and you, woman," speaking to his wife, "order your chaplain to attend me forthwith."

"Isabella," said Hippolita calmly, "is retired, I suppose, to her chamber: she is not accustomed to watch at this late hour. Gracious my Lord," continued she, "let me know what has disturbed you. Has Isabella offended you?"

"Trouble me not with questions," said Manfred, "but tell me where she is."

"Matilda shall call her," said the Princess. "Sit down, my Lord, and resume your wonted fortitude."

"What, art thou jealous of Isabella?" replied he, "that you wish to be present at our interview!"

"Good heavens! My Lord," said Hippolita, "what is it your Highness means?"

"Thou wilt know ere many minutes are passed," said the cruel Prince. "Send your chaplain to me, and wait my pleasure here."

At these words he flung out of the room in search of Isabella, leaving the amazed ladies thunderstruck with his words and frantic deportment, and lost in vain conjectures on what he was meditating.

Manfred was now returning from the vault, attended by the peasant and a few of his servants whom he had obliged to accompany him. He ascended the staircase without stopping till he arrived at the gallery, at the door of which he met Hippolita and her chaplain. When Diego had been dismissed by Manfred, he had gone directly to the Princess's apartment with the alarm of what he had seen. That excellent Lady, who no more than Manfred doubted of the reality of the vision, yet affected to treat it as a delirium of the servant. Willing, however, to save her Lord from any additional shock, and prepared by a series of griefs not to tremble at any accession to it, she determined to make herself the first sacrifice, if fate had marked the present hour for their destruction. Dismissing the reluctant Matilda to her rest, who in vain sued for leave to accompany her mother, and attended only by her chaplain, Hippolita had visited the gallery and great chamber; and now with more serenity of soul than she had felt for many hours, she met her Lord, and assured him that the vision of the gigantic leg and foot was all a fable; and no doubt an impression made by fear, and the dark and dismal hour of the night, on the minds of his servants. She and the chaplain had examined the chamber, and found everything in the usual order.

Manfred, though persuaded, like his wife, that the vision had been no work of fancy, recovered a little from the tempest of mind into which so many strange events had thrown him. Ashamed, too, of his inhuman treatment of a Princess who returned every injury with new marks of tenderness and duty, he felt returning love forcing itself into his eyes; but not less ashamed of feeling remorse towards one against whom he was inwardly meditating a yet more bitter outrage, he curbed the yearnings of his heart, and did not dare to lean even towards pity. The next transition of his soul was to exquisite villainy.

Presuming on the unshaken submission of Hippolita, he flattered himself that she would not only acquiesce with patience to a divorce, but would obey, if it was his pleasure, in endeavouring to persuade Isabella to give him her hand—but ere he could indulge his horrid hope, he reflected that Isabella was not to be found. Coming to himself, he gave orders that every avenue to the castle should be strictly guarded, and charged his domestics on pain of their lives to suffer nobody to pass out. The young peasant, to whom he spoke favourably, he ordered to remain in a small chamber on the stairs, in which there was a pallet-bed, and the key of which he took away himself, telling the youth he would talk with him in the morning. Then dismissing his attendants, and bestowing a sullen kind of half-nod on Hippolita, he retired to his own chamber.

Chapter II.

MATILDA, who by Hippolita's order had retired to her apartment, was ill-disposed to take any rest. The shocking fate of her brother had deeply affected her. She was surprised at not seeing Isabella; but the strange words which had fallen from her father, and his obscure menace to the Princess his wife, accompanied by the most furious behaviour, had filled her gentle mind with terror and alarm. She waited anxiously for the return of Bianca, a young damsel that attended her, whom she had sent to learn what was become of Isabella. Bianca soon appeared, and informed her mistress of what she had gathered from the servants, that Isabella was nowhere to be found. She related the adventure of the young peasant who had been discovered in the vault, though with many simple additions from the incoherent accounts of the domestics; and she dwelt principally on the gigantic leg and foot which had been seen in the gallery-chamber. This last circumstance had terrified Bianca so much, that she was rejoiced when Matilda told her that she would not go to rest, but would watch till the Princess should rise.

The young Princess wearied herself in conjectures on the flight of Isabella, and on the threats of Manfred to her mother. "But what business could he have so urgent with the chaplain?"

said Matilda. "Does he intend to have my brother's body interred privately in the chapel?"

"Oh, Madam!" said Bianca. "Now I guess. As you are become his heiress, he is impatient to have you married: he has always been raving for more sons; I warrant he is now impatient for grandsons. As sure as I live, Madam, I shall see you a bride at last.—Good madam, you won't cast off your faithful Bianca: you won't put Donna Rosara over me now you are a great Princess."

"My poor Bianca," said Matilda, "how fast your thoughts amble! I a great princess! What hast thou seen in Manfred's behaviour since my brother's death that bespeaks any increase of tenderness to me? No, Bianca; his heart was ever a stranger to me—but he is my father, and I must not complain. Nay, if Heaven shuts my father's heart against me, it overpays my little merit in the tenderness of my mother—O that dear mother! Yes, Bianca, 'tis there I feel the rugged temper of Manfred. I can support his harshness to me with patience; but it wounds my soul when I am witness to his causeless severity towards her."

"Oh! Madam," said Bianca, "all men use their wives so, when they are weary of them."

"And yet you congratulated me but now," said Matilda, "when you fancied my father intended to dispose of me!"

"I would have you a great Lady," replied Bianca, "come what will. I do not wish to see you moped* in a convent, as you would be if you had your will, and if my Lady, your mother, who knows that a bad husband is better than no husband at all, did not hinder you.—Bless me! What noise is that! St. Nicholas forgive me! I was but in jest."

"It is the wind," said Matilda, "whistling through the battlements in the tower above: you have heard it a thousand times."

"Nay," said Bianca, "there was no harm neither in what I said: it is no sin to talk of matrimony—and so, Madam, as I was saying,

---

* Confined or shut up. According to the Oxford English Dictionary, this is the first reported usage of the word to mean such.

if my Lord Manfred should offer you a handsome young Prince for a bridegroom, you would drop him a curtsey, and tell him you would rather take the veil?"

"Thank Heaven! I am in no such danger," said Matilda. "You know how many proposals for me he has rejected—"

"And you thank him, like a dutiful daughter, do you, Madam? But come, Madam; suppose, to-morrow morning, he was to send for you to the great council chamber, and there you should find at his elbow a lovely young Prince, with large black eyes, a smooth white forehead, and manly curling locks like jet; in short, Madam, a young hero resembling the picture of the good Alfonso in the gallery, which you sit and gaze at for hours together—"

"Do not speak lightly of that picture," interrupted Matilda sighing. "I know the adoration with which I look at that picture is uncommon—but I am not in love with a coloured panel. The character of that virtuous Prince, the veneration with which my mother has inspired me for his memory, the orisons* which, I know not why, she has enjoined me to pour forth at his tomb, all have concurred to persuade me that somehow or other my destiny is linked with something relating to him."

"Lord, Madam! How should that be?" said Bianca. "I have always heard that your family was in no way related to his: and I am sure I cannot conceive why my Lady, the Princess, sends you in a cold morning or a damp evening to pray at his tomb: he is no saint by the almanack. If you must pray, why does she not bid you address yourself to our great St. Nicholas? I am sure he is the saint I pray to for a husband."

"Perhaps my mind would be less affected," said Matilda, "if my mother would explain her reasons to me: but it is the mystery she observes, that inspires me with this—I know not what to call it. As she never acts from caprice, I am sure there is some fatal secret at bottom—nay, I know there is: in her agony of grief for my brother's death she dropped some words that intimated as much."

---

* Prayers.

"Oh! Dear Madam," cried Bianca, "what were they?"

"No," said Matilda, "if a parent lets fall a word, and wishes it recalled, it is not for a child to utter it."

"What! Was she sorry for what she had said?" asked Bianca. "I am sure, Madam, you may trust me—"

"With my own little secrets when I have any, I may," said Matilda. "But never with my mother's: a child ought to have no ears or eyes but as a parent directs."

"Well! To be sure, Madam, you were born to be a saint," said Bianca, "and there is no resisting one's vocation: you will end in a convent at last. But there is my Lady Isabella would not be so reserved to me: she will let me talk to her of young men: and when a handsome cavalier has come to the castle, she has owned to me that she wished your brother Conrad resembled him."

"Bianca," said the Princess, "I do not allow you to mention my friend disrespectfully. Isabella is of a cheerful disposition, but her soul is pure as virtue itself. She knows your idle babbling humour, and perhaps has now and then encouraged it, to divert melancholy, and enliven the solitude in which my father keeps us—"

"Blessed Mary!" said Bianca, starting. "There it is again! Dear Madam, do you hear nothing? This castle is certainly haunted!"

"Peace!" said Matilda. "And listen! I did think I heard a voice— but it must be fancy: your terrors, I suppose, have infected me."

"Indeed! Indeed! Madam," said Bianca, half-weeping with agony, "I am sure I heard a voice."

"Does anybody lie in the chamber beneath?" said the Princess.

"Nobody has dared to lie there," answered Bianca, "since the great astrologer, that was your brother's tutor, drowned himself. For certain, Madam, his ghost and the young Prince's are now met in the chamber below—for Heaven's sake let us fly to your mother's apartment!"

"I charge you not to stir," said Matilda. "If they are spirits in pain, we may ease their sufferings by questioning them. They can mean no hurt to us, for we have not injured them—and if they should, shall we be more safe in one chamber than in another? Reach me my beads; we will say a prayer, and then speak to them."

"Oh! Dear Lady, I would not speak to a ghost for the world!" cried Bianca. As she said those words they heard the casement of the little chamber below Matilda's open. They listened attentively, and in a few minutes thought they heard a person sing, but could not distinguish the words.

"This can be no evil spirit," said the Princess, in a low voice. "It is undoubtedly one of the family—open the window, and we shall know the voice."

"I dare not, indeed, Madam," said Bianca.

"Thou art a very fool," said Matilda, opening the window gently herself. The noise the Princess made was, however, heard by the person beneath, who stopped; and they concluded had heard the casement open.

"Is anybody below?" said the Princess. "If there is, speak."

"Yes," said an unknown voice.

"Who is it?" said Matilda.

"A stranger," replied the voice.

"What stranger?" said she. "And how didst thou come there at this unusual hour, when all the gates of the castle are locked?"

"I am not here willingly," answered the voice. "But pardon me, Lady, if I have disturbed your rest; I knew not that I was overheard. Sleep had forsaken me; I left a restless couch, and came to waste the irksome hours with gazing on the fair approach of morning, impatient to be dismissed from this castle."

"Thy words and accents," said Matilda, "are of melancholy cast; if thou art unhappy, I pity thee. If poverty afflicts thee, let me know it; I will mention thee to the Princess, whose beneficent soul ever melts for the distressed, and she will relieve thee."

"I am indeed unhappy," said the stranger, "and I know not what wealth is. But I do not complain of the lot which Heaven has cast for me; I am young and healthy, and am not ashamed of owing my support to myself—yet think me not proud, or that I disdain your generous offers. I will remember you in my orisons, and will pray for blessings on your gracious self and your noble mistress—if I sigh, Lady, it is for others, not for myself."

"Now I have it, Madam," said Bianca, whispering the Princess. "This is certainly the young peasant; and, by my conscience, he is in love—Well! This is a charming adventure!—Do, Madam, let us sift him. He does not know you, but takes you for one of my Lady Hippolita's women."

"Art thou not ashamed, Bianca!" said the Princess. "What right have we to pry into the secrets of this young man's heart? He seems virtuous and frank, and tells us he is unhappy. Are those circumstances that authorise us to make a property of him? How are we entitled to his confidence?"

"Lord, Madam! How little you know of love!" replied Bianca. "Why, lovers have no pleasure equal to talking of their mistress."

"And would you have *me* become a peasant's confidante?" said the Princess.

"Well, then, let me talk to him," said Bianca. "Though I have the honour of being your Highness's maid of honour, I was not always so great. Besides, if love levels ranks, it raises them too; I have a respect for any young man in love."

"Peace, simpleton!" said the Princess. "Though he said he was unhappy, it does not follow that he must be in love. Think of all that has happened to-day, and tell me if there are no misfortunes but what love causes.—Stranger," resumed the Princess, "if thy misfortunes have not been occasioned by thy own fault, and are within the compass of the Princess Hippolita's power to redress, I will take upon me to answer that she will be thy protectress. When thou art dismissed from this castle, repair to holy father Jerome, at the convent adjoining to the church of St. Nicholas, and make thy story known to him, as far as thou thinkest meet. He will not fail to inform the Princess, who is the mother of all that want her assistance. Farewell; it is not seemly for me to hold farther converse with a man at this unwonted hour."

"May the saints guard thee, gracious Lady!" replied the peasant. "But oh! If a poor and worthless stranger might presume to beg a minute's audience farther; am I so happy? The casement is not shut; might I venture to ask—"

"Speak quickly," said Matilda. "the morning dawns apace: should the labourers come into the fields and perceive us—What wouldst thou ask?"

"I know not how, I know not if I dare," said the young stranger, faltering. "Yet the humanity with which you have spoken to me emboldens—Lady! Dare I trust you?"

"Heavens!" said Matilda, "what dost thou mean? With what wouldst thou trust me? Speak boldly, if thy secret is fit to be entrusted to a virtuous breast."

"I would ask," said the peasant, recollecting himself, "whether what I have heard from the domestics is true, that the Princess is missing from the castle?"

"What imports it to thee to know?" replied Matilda. "Thy first words bespoke a prudent and becoming gravity. Dost thou come hither to pry into the secrets of Manfred? Adieu. I have been mistaken in thee." Saying these words she shut the casement hastily, without giving the young man time to reply.

"I had acted more wisely," said the Princess to Bianca, with some sharpness, "if I had let thee converse with this peasant; his inquisitiveness seems of a piece with thy own."

"It is not fit for me to argue with your Highness," replied Bianca. "But perhaps the questions I should have put to him would have been more to the purpose than those you have been pleased to ask him."

"Oh! No doubt," said Matilda, "you are a very discreet personage! May I know what *you* would have asked him?"

"A bystander often sees more of the game than those that play," answered Bianca. "Does your Highness think, Madam, that this question about my Lady Isabella was the result of mere curiosity? No, no, Madam, there is more in it than you great folks are aware of. Lopez told me that all the servants believe this young fellow contrived my Lady Isabella's escape; now, pray, Madam, observe you and I both know that my Lady Isabella never much fancied the Prince your brother. Well! he is killed just in a critical minute—I accuse nobody. A helmet falls from the moon—so, my Lord, your father says; but Lopez and all the servants say that this young spark is a magician, and stole it from Alfonso's tomb—"

"Have done with this rhapsody of impertinence," said Matilda.

"Nay, Madam, as you please," cried Bianca. "Yet it is very particular though, that my Lady Isabella should be missing the very same day, and that this young sorcerer should be found at the mouth of the trap-door. I accuse nobody; but if my young Lord came honestly by his death—"

"Dare not on thy duty," said Matilda, "to breathe a suspicion on the purity of my dear Isabella's fame."

"Purity, or not purity," said Bianca, "gone she is—a stranger is found that nobody knows; you question him yourself; he tells you he is in love, or unhappy, it is the same thing—nay, he owned he was unhappy about others; and is anybody unhappy about another, unless they are in love with them? And at the very next word, he asks innocently, pour soul! If my Lady Isabella is missing."

"To be sure," said Matilda, "thy observations are not totally without foundation—Isabella's flight amazes me. The curiosity of the stranger is very particular; yet Isabella never concealed a thought from me."

"So she told you," said Bianca, "to fish out your secrets; but who knows, Madam, but this stranger may be some Prince in disguise? Do, Madam, let me open the window, and ask him a few questions."

"No," replied Matilda, "I will ask him myself, if he knows aught of Isabella; he is not worthy I should converse farther with him."

She was going to open the casement, when they heard the bell ring at the postern-gate of the castle, which is on the right hand of the tower, where Matilda lay. This prevented the Princess from renewing the conversation with the stranger.

After continuing silent for some time, "I am persuaded," said she to Bianca, "that whatever be the cause of Isabella's flight it had no unworthy motive. If this stranger was accessory to it, she must be satisfied with his fidelity and worth. I observed, did not you, Bianca? That his words were tinctured with an uncommon infusion of piety. It was no ruffian's speech; his phrases were becoming a man of gentle birth."

"I told you, Madam," said Bianca, "that I was sure he was some Prince in disguise."

"Yet," said Matilda, "if he was privy to her escape, how will you account for his not accompanying her in her flight? Why expose himself unnecessarily and rashly to my father's resentment?"

"As for that, Madam," replied she, "if he could get from under the helmet, he will find ways of eluding your father's anger. I do not doubt but he has some talisman or other about him."

"You resolve everything into magic," said Matilda, "but a man who has any intercourse with infernal spirits, does not dare to make use of those tremendous and holy words which he uttered. Didst thou not observe with what fervour he vowed to remember *me* to Heaven in his prayers? Yes; Isabella was undoubtedly convinced of his piety."

"Commend me to the piety of a young fellow and a damsel that consult to elope!" said Bianca. "No, no, Madam, my Lady Isabella is of another guess mould than you take her for. She used indeed to sigh and lift up her eyes in your company, because she knows you are a saint; but when your back was turned—"

"You wrong her," said Matilda. "Isabella is no hypocrite; she has a due sense of devotion, but never affected a call she has not. On the contrary, she always combated my inclination for the cloister; and though I own the mystery she has made to me of her flight confounds me; though it seems inconsistent with the friendship between us; I cannot forget the disinterested warmth with which she always opposed my taking the veil. She wished to see me married, though my dower would have been a loss to her and my brother's children. For her sake I will believe well of this young peasant."

"Then you do think there is some liking between them," said Bianca. While she was speaking, a servant came hastily into the chamber and told the Princess that the Lady Isabella was found.

"Where?" said Matilda.

"She has taken sanctuary in St. Nicholas's church," replied the servant. "Father Jerome has brought the news himself; he is below with his Highness."

"Where is my mother?" said Matilda.

"She is in her own chamber, Madam, and has asked for you."

Manfred had risen at the first dawn of light, and gone to Hippolita's apartment, to inquire if she knew aught of Isabella. While he was questioning her, word was brought that Jerome demanded to speak with him. Manfred, little suspecting the cause of the Friar's arrival, and knowing he was employed by Hippolita in her charities, ordered him to be admitted, intending to leave them together, while he pursued his search after Isabella.

"Is your business with me or the Princess?" said Manfred.

"With both," replied the holy man. "The Lady Isabella—"

"What of her?" interrupted Manfred, eagerly.

"Is at St. Nicholas's altar," replied Jerome.

"That is no business of Hippolita," said Manfred with confusion. "Let us retire to my chamber, Father, and inform me how she came thither."

"No, my Lord," replied the good man, with an air of firmness and authority, that daunted even the resolute Manfred, who could not help revering the saint-like virtues of Jerome. "My commission is to both, and with your Highness's good-liking, in the presence of both I shall deliver it; but first, my Lord, I must interrogate the Princess, whether she is acquainted with the cause of the Lady Isabella's retirement from your castle."

"No, on my soul," said Hippolita. "Does Isabella charge me with being privy to it?"

"Father," interrupted Manfred, "I pay due reverence to your holy profession; but I am sovereign here, and will allow no meddling priest to interfere in the affairs of my domestic. If you have aught to say attend me to my chamber; I do not use to let my wife be acquainted with the secret affairs of my state; they are not within a woman's province."

"My Lord," said the holy man, "I am no intruder into the secrets of families. My office is to promote peace, to heal divisions, to preach repentance, and teach mankind to curb their headstrong passions. I forgive your Highness's uncharitable apostrophe; I know my duty, and am the minister of a mightier prince than Manfred. Hearken to him who speaks through my organs."

Manfred trembled with rage and shame. Hippolita's countenance declared her astonishment and impatience to know where this would end. Her silence more strongly spoke her observance of Manfred.

"The Lady Isabella," resumed Jerome, "commends herself to both your Highnesses; she thanks both for the kindness with which she has been treated in your castle: she deplores the loss of your son, and her own misfortune in not becoming the daughter of such wise and noble Princes, whom she shall always respect as Parents; she prays for uninterrupted union and felicity between you:" [Manfred's colour changed] "but as it is no longer possible for her to be allied to you, she entreats your consent to remain in sanctuary, till she can learn news of her father, or, by the certainty of his death, be at liberty, with the approbation of her guardians, to dispose of herself in suitable marriage."

"I shall give no such consent," said the Prince, "but insist on her return to the castle without delay: I am answerable for her person to her guardians, and will not brook her being in any hands but my own."

"Your Highness will recollect whether that can any longer be proper," replied the Friar.

"I want no monitor," said Manfred, colouring. "Isabella's conduct leaves room for strange suspicions—and that young villain, who was at least the accomplice of her flight, if not the cause of it—"

"The cause!" interrupted Jerome. "Was a *young* man the cause?"

"This is not to be borne!" cried Manfred. "Am I to be bearded in my own palace by an insolent Monk? Thou art privy, I guess, to their amours."

"I would pray to Heaven to clear up your uncharitable surmises," said Jerome, "if your Highness were not satisfied in your conscience how unjustly you accuse me. I do pray to Heaven to pardon that uncharitableness: and I implore your Highness to leave the Princess at peace in that holy place, where she is not liable to be disturbed by such vain and worldly fantasies as discourses of love from any man."

"Cant not to me," said Manfred, "but return and bring the Princess to her duty."

"It is my duty to prevent her return hither," said Jerome. "She is where orphans and virgins are safest from the snares and wiles of this world; and nothing but a parent's authority shall take her thence."

"I am her parent," cried Manfred, "and demand her."

"She wished to have you for her parent," said the Friar. "But Heaven that forbad that connection has for ever dissolved all ties betwixt you: and I announce to your Highness—"

"Stop! Audacious man," said Manfred, "and dread my displeasure."

"Holy Father," said Hippolita, "it is your office to be no respecter of persons: you must speak as your duty prescribes:

but it is my duty to hear nothing that it pleases not my Lord I should hear. Attend the Prince to his chamber. I will retire to my oratory, and pray to the blessed Virgin to inspire you with her holy counsels, and to restore the heart of my gracious Lord to its wonted peace and gentleness."

"Excellent woman!" said the Friar. "My Lord, I attend your pleasure."

Manfred, accompanied by the Friar, passed to his own apartment, where shutting the door, "I perceive, Father," said he, "that Isabella has acquainted you with my purpose. Now hear my resolve, and obey. Reasons of state, most urgent reasons, my own and the safety of my people, demand that I should have a son. It is in vain to expect an heir from Hippolita. I have made choice of Isabella. You must bring her back; and you must do more. I know the influence you have with Hippolita: her conscience is in your hands. She is, I allow, a faultless woman: her soul is set on Heaven, and scorns the little grandeur of this world: you can withdraw her from it entirely. Persuade her to consent to the dissolution of our marriage, and to retire into a monastery—she shall endow one if she will; and she shall have the means of being as liberal to your order as she or you can wish. Thus you will divert the calamities that are hanging over our heads, and have the merit of saying the principality of Otranto from destruction. You are a prudent man, and though the warmth of my temper betrayed me into some unbecoming expressions, I honour your virtue, and wish to be indebted to you for the repose of my life and the preservation of my family."

"The will of Heaven be done!" said the Friar. "I am but its worthless instrument. It makes use of my tongue to tell thee, Prince, of thy unwarrantable designs. The injuries of the virtuous Hippolita have mounted to the throne of pity. By me thou art reprimanded for thy adulterous intention of repudiating her: by me thou art warned not to pursue the incestuous design on thy contracted daughter. Heaven that delivered her from thy fury, when the judgments so recently fallen on thy house ought to have inspired thee with other thoughts, will continue to watch over her. Even I, a poor and despised Friar, am able to protect her from thy violence—I, sinner as I am, and uncharitably reviled by your Highness as an accomplice of I know not what amours, scorn the allurements with which it has pleased thee to tempt mine honesty. I love my order; I honour devout souls; I respect the piety of thy Princess—but I will not betray the confidence she reposes in me, nor serve even the cause of religion by foul and sinful compliances—but forsooth! the welfare of the state depends on your Highness having a son! Heaven mocks the short-sighted views of man. But yester-morn, whose house was so great, so flourishing as Manfred's?—Where is young Conrad now?—My Lord, I respect your tears—but I mean not to check them—let them flow, Prince! They will weigh more with Heaven toward the welfare of thy subjects, than a marriage, which, founded on lust or policy, could never prosper. The sceptre, which passed from the race of Alfonso to thine, cannot be preserved by a match which the church will never allow. If it is the will of the Most High that Manfred's name must perish, resign yourself, my Lord, to its decrees; and thus deserve a crown that can never pass away. Come, my Lord; I like this sorrow—let us return to the Princess: she is not apprised of your cruel intentions; nor did I mean more than to alarm you. You saw with what gentle patience, with what efforts of love, she heard, she rejected hearing, the extent of your guilt. I know she longs to fold you in her arms, and assure you of her unalterable affection."

"Father," said the Prince, "you mistake my compunction: true, I honour Hippolita's virtues; I think her a Saint; and wish it were for my soul's health to tie faster the knot that has united us— but alas! Father, you know not the bitterest of my pangs! It is some time that I have had scruples on the legality of our union: Hippolita is related to me in the fourth degree—it is true, we had a dispensation: but I have been informed that she had also been contracted to another.* This it is that sits heavy at my heart: to this state of unlawful wedlock I impute the visitation that has fallen on me in the death of Conrad!—Ease my conscience of this burden: dissolve our marriage, and accomplish the work of godliness—which your divine exhortations have commenced in my soul."

How cutting was the anguish which the good man felt, when he perceived this turn in the wily Prince! He trembled for Hippolita, whose ruin he saw was determined; and he feared if Manfred had no hope of recovering Isabella, that his impatience for a son would direct him to some other object, who might not be equally proof against the temptation of Manfred's rank. For some time the holy man remained absorbed in thought. At length, conceiving some hopes from delay, he thought the wisest conduct would be to prevent the Prince from despairing of recovering Isabella. Her the Friar knew he could dispose, from her affection to Hippolita, and from the aversion she had expressed to him for Manfred's addresses, to second his views, till the censures of the church could be fulminated against a divorce. With this intention, as if struck with the Prince's scruples, he at length said, "My Lord, I have been pondering on what your Highness has said; and if in truth it is delicacy of conscience that is the real motive of your repugnance to your virtuous Lady, far be it from me to endeavour to harden your heart. The church is an indulgent mother: unfold your griefs to her: she alone can administer comfort to your soul, either by satisfying your conscience, or upon examination of your scruples, by setting you at liberty, and indulging you in the lawful means of continuing your lineage. In the latter case, if the Lady Isabella can be brought to consent—"

Manfred, who concluded that he had either over-reached the good man, or that his first warmth had been but a tribute paid to appearance, was overjoyed at this sudden turn, and repeated the most magnificent promises, if he should succeed by the Friar's

---

* This was a ploy used by Henry VIII to free himself from his marriage to Ann of Cleves.

mediation. The well-meaning priest suffered him to deceive himself, fully determined to traverse his views, instead of seconding them.

"Since we now understand one another," resumed the Prince, "I expect, Father, that you satisfy me in one point. Who is the youth that I found in the vault? He must have been privy to Isabella's flight: tell me truly, is he her lover? Or is he an agent for another's passion? I have often suspected Isabella's indifference to my son: a thousand circumstances crowd on my mind that confirm that suspicion. She herself was so conscious of it, that while I discoursed her in the gallery, she outran my suspicious, and endeavoured to justify herself from coolness to Conrad."

The Friar, who knew nothing of the youth, but what he had learnt occasionally from the Princess, ignorant what was become of him, and not sufficiently reflecting on the impetuosity of Manfred's temper, conceived that it might not be amiss to sow the seeds of jealousy in his mind: they might be turned to some use hereafter, either by prejudicing the Prince against Isabella, if he persisted in that union or by diverting his attention to a wrong scent, and employing his thoughts on a visionary intrigue, prevent his engaging in any new pursuit. With this unhappy policy, he answered in a manner to confirm Manfred in the belief of some connection between Isabella and the youth. The Prince, whose passions wanted little fuel to throw them into a blaze, fell into a rage at the idea of what the Friar suggested.

"I will fathom to the bottom of this intrigue," cried he; and quitting Jerome abruptly, with a command to remain there till his return, he hastened to the great hall of the castle, and ordered the peasant to be brought before him.

"Thou hardened young impostor!" said the Prince, as soon as he saw the youth. "What becomes of thy boasted veracity now? It was Providence, was it, and the light of the moon, that discovered the lock of the trap-door to thee? Tell me, audacious boy, who thou art, and how long thou hast been acquainted with the

Princess—and take care to answer with less equivocation than thou didst last night, or tortures shall wring the truth from thee."

The young man, perceiving that his share in the flight of the Princess was discovered, and concluding that anything he should say could no longer be of any service or detriment to her, replied—

"I am no impostor, my Lord, nor have I deserved opprobrious language. I answered to every question your Highness put to me last night with the same veracity that I shall speak now: and that will not be from fear of your tortures, but because my soul abhors a falsehood. Please to repeat your questions, my Lord; I am ready to give you all the satisfaction in my power."

"You know my questions," replied the Prince, "and only want time to prepare an evasion. Speak directly; who art thou? And how long hast thou been known to the Princess?"

"I am a labourer at the next village," said the peasant. "My name is Theodore. The Princess found me in the vault last night: before that hour I never was in her presence."

"I may believe as much or as little as I please of this," said Manfred, "but I will hear thy own story before I examine into the truth of it. Tell me, what reason did the Princess give thee for making her escape? Thy life depends on thy answer."

"She told me," replied Theodore, "that she was on the brink of destruction, and that if she could not escape from the castle, she was in danger in a few moments of being made miserable for ever."

"And on this slight foundation, on a silly girl's report," said Manfred, "thou didst hazard my displeasure?"

"I fear no man's displeasure," said Theodore, "when a woman in distress puts herself under my protection."

During this examination, Matilda was going to the apartment of Hippolita. At the upper end of the hall, where Manfred sat, was a boarded gallery with latticed windows, through which Matilda and Bianca were to pass. Hearing her father's voice, and seeing the servants assembled round him, she stopped to learn the occasion. The prisoner soon drew her attention: the steady and composed manner in which he answered, and the gallantry of his last reply, which were the first words she heard distinctly, interested her in his flavour. His person was noble, handsome, and commanding, even in that situation: but his countenance soon engrossed her whole care.

"Heavens! Bianca," said the Princess softly, "do I dream? Or is not that youth the exact resemblance of Alfonso's picture in the gallery?"

She could say no more, for her father's voice grew louder at every word.

"This bravado," said he, "surpasses all thy former insolence. Thou shalt experience the wrath with which thou darest to trifle. Seize him," continued Manfred, "and bind him—the first news the Princess hears of her champion shall be, that he has lost his head for her sake."

"The injustice of which thou art guilty towards me," said Theodore, "convinces me that I have done a good deed in delivering the Princess from thy tyranny. May she be happy, whatever becomes of me!"

"This is a lover!" cried Manfred in a rage. "A peasant within sight of death is not animated by such sentiments. Tell me, tell me, rash boy, who thou art, or the rack shall force thy secret from thee."

"Thou hast threatened me with death already," said the youth, "for the truth I have told thee: if that is all the encouragement I am to expect for sincerity, I am not tempted to indulge thy vain curiosity farther."

"Then thou wilt not speak?" said Manfred.

"I will not," replied he.

"Bear him away into the courtyard," said Manfred. "I will see his head this instant severed from his body."

Matilda fainted at hearing those words. Bianca shrieked, and cried, "Help! Help! the Princess is dead!"

Manfred started at this ejaculation, and demanded what was the matter! The young peasant, who heard it too, was struck with horror, and asked eagerly the same question; but Manfred ordered him to be hurried into the court, and kept there for execution, till he had informed himself of the cause of Bianca's shrieks. When he learned the meaning, he treated it as a womanish panic, and ordering Matilda to be carried to her apartment, he rushed into the court, and calling for one of his guards, bade Theodore kneel down, and prepare to receive the fatal blow.

The undaunted youth received the bitter sentence with a resignation that touched every heart but Manfred's. He wished earnestly to know the meaning of the words he had heard relating to the Princess; but fearing to exasperate the tyrant more against her, he desisted. The only boon he deigned to ask was, that he might be permitted to have a confessor, and make his peace with Heaven. Manfred, who hoped by the confessor's means to come at the youth's history, readily granted his request; and being convinced that Father Jerome was now in his interest, he ordered him to be called and shrive the prisoner. The holy man, who had little foreseen the catastrophe that his imprudence occasioned, fell on his knees to the Prince, and adjured him in the most solemn manner not to shed innocent blood. He accused himself in the bitterest terms for his indiscretion, endeavoured to disculpate the youth, and left no method untried to soften the tyrant's rage. Manfred, more incensed than appeased by Jerome's intercession, whose retraction now made him suspect he had been imposed upon by both, commanded the Friar to do his duty, telling him he would not allow the prisoner many minutes for confession.

"Nor do I ask many, my Lord," said the unhappy young man. "My sins, thank Heaven, have not been numerous; nor exceed what might be expected at my years. Dry your tears, good Father, and let us despatch. This is a bad world; nor have I had cause to leave it with regret."

"Oh wretched youth!" said Jerome. "How canst thou bear the sight of me with patience? I am thy murderer! It is I have brought this dismal hour upon thee!"

"I forgive thee from my soul," said the youth, "as I hope Heaven will pardon me. Hear my confession, Father; and give me thy blessing."

"How can I prepare thee for thy passage as I ought?" said Jerome. "Thou canst not be saved without pardoning thy foes— and canst thou forgive that impious man there?"

"I can," said Theodore. "I do."

"And does not this touch thee, cruel Prince?" said the Friar.

"I sent for thee to confess him," said Manfred, sternly, "not to plead for him. Thou didst first incense me against him—his blood be upon thy head!"

"It will! It will!" said the good man, in an agony of sorrow. "Thou and I must never hope to go where this blessed youth is going!"

"Despatch!" said Manfred. "I am no more to be moved by the whining of priests than by the shrieks of women."

"What!" said the youth. "Is it possible that my fate could have occasioned what I heard! Is the Princess then again in thy power?"

"Thou dost but remember me of my wrath," said Manfred. "Prepare thee, for this moment is thy last."

The youth, who felt his indignation rise, and who was touched with the sorrow which he saw he had infused into all the spectators, as well as into the Friar, suppressed his emotions, and putting off his doublet, and unbuttoning, his collar, knelt down to his prayers. As he stooped, his shirt slipped down below his shoulder, and discovered the mark of a bloody arrow.

"Gracious Heaven!" cried the holy man, starting. "What do I see? It is my child! My Theodore!"

The passions that ensued must be conceived; they cannot be painted. The tears of the assistants were suspended by wonder, rather than stopped by joy. They seemed to inquire in the eyes of their Lord what they ought to feel. Surprise, doubt, tenderness, respect, succeeded each other in the countenance of the youth. He received with modest submission the effusion of the old man's tears and embraces. Yet afraid of giving a loose to hope, and suspecting from what had passed the inflexibility of Manfred's temper, he cast a glance towards the Prince, as if to say, canst thou be unmoved at such a scene as this?

Manfred's heart was capable of being touched. He forgot his anger in his astonishment; yet his pride forbad his owning himself affected. He even doubted whether this discovery was not a contrivance of the Friar to save the youth.

"What may this mean?" said he. "How can he be thy son? Is it consistent with thy profession or reputed sanctity to avow a peasant's offspring for the fruit of thy irregular amours!"

"Oh, God!" said the holy man, "Dost thou question his being mine? Could I feel the anguish I do if I were not his father? Spare him! Good Prince! Spare him! And revile me as thou pleasest."

"Spare him! Spare him!" cried the attendants. "For this good man's sake!"

"Peace!" said Manfred, sternly. "I must know more ere I am disposed to pardon. A Saint's bastard may be no saint himself."

"Injurious Lord!" said Theodore, "Add not insult to cruelty. If I am this venerable man's son, though no Prince, as thou art, know the blood that flows in my veins—"

"Yes," said the Friar, interrupting him, "his blood is noble; nor is he that abject thing, my Lord, you speak him. He is my lawful son, and Sicily can boast of few houses more ancient than that of Falconara.* But alas! My Lord, what is blood! What is nobility! We are all reptiles, miserable, sinful creatures. It is piety alone that can distinguish us from the dust whence we sprung, and whither we must return."

"Truce to your sermon," said Manfred. "You forget you are no longer Friar Jerome, but the Count of Falconara. Let me know your history; you will have time to moralise hereafter, if you should not happen to obtain the grace of that sturdy criminal there."

"Mother of God!" said the Friar, "Is it possible my Lord can refuse a father the life of his only, his long-lost, child! Trample

---

* There is indeed a medieval Castle Falconara in Butera, Sicily.

me, my Lord, scorn, afflict me, accept my life for his, but spare my son!"

"Thou canst feel, then," said Manfred, "what it is to lose an only son! A little hour ago thou didst preach up resignation to me: *my* house, if fate so pleased, must perish—but the Count of Falconara—"

"Alas! My Lord," said Jerome, "I confess I have offended; but aggravate not an old man's sufferings! I boast not of my family, nor think of such vanities—it is nature, that pleads for this boy; it is the memory of the dear woman that bore him. Is she, Theodore, is she dead?"

"Her soul has long been with the blessed," said Theodore.

"Oh! How?" cried Jerome, "Tell me—no—she is happy! Thou art all my care now!—Most dread Lord! Will you—will you grant me my poor boy's life?"

"Return to thy convent," answered Manfred. "Conduct the Princess hither; obey me in what else thou knowest; and I promise thee the life of thy son."

"Oh! My Lord," said Jerome, "is my honesty the price I must pay for this dear youth's safety?"

"For me!" cried Theodore. "Let me die a thousand deaths, rather than stain thy conscience. What is it the tyrant would exact of thee? Is the Princess still safe from his power? Protect her, thou venerable old man; and let all the weight of his wrath fall on me."

Jerome endeavoured to check the impetuosity of the youth; and ere Manfred could reply, the trampling of horses was heard, and a brazen trumpet, which hung without the gate of the castle, was suddenly sounded. At the same instant the sable plumes on the enchanted helmet, which still remained at the other end of the court, were tempestuously agitated, and nodded thrice, as if bowed by some invisible wearer.

Chapter III.

MANFRED'S heart misgave him when he beheld the plumage on the miraculous casque shaken in concert with the sounding of the brazen trumpet.

"Father!" said he to Jerome, whom he now ceased to treat as Count of Falconara, "What mean these portents? If I have offended—" the plumes were shaken with greater violence than before.

"Unhappy Prince that I am," cried Manfred. "Holy Father! will you not assist me with your prayers?"

"My Lord," replied Jerome, "Heaven is no doubt displeased with your mockery of its servants. Submit yourself to the church; and cease to persecute her ministers. Dismiss this innocent youth; and learn to respect the holy character I wear. Heaven will not be trifled with: you see—" the trumpet sounded again.

"I acknowledge I have been too hasty," said Manfred. "Father, do you go to the wicket, and demand who is at the gate."

"Do you grant me the life of Theodore?" replied the Friar.

"I do," said Manfred. "But inquire who is without!"

Jerome, falling on the neck of his son, discharged a flood of tears, that spoke the fulness of his soul.

"You promised to go to the gate," said Manfred.

"I thought," replied the Friar, "your Highness would excuse my thanking you first in this tribute of my heart."

"Go, dearest, Sir," said Theodore. "Obey the Prince. I do not deserve that you should delay his satisfaction for me."

Jerome, inquiring who was without, was answered, "A Herald."

"From whom?" said he.

"From the Knight of the Gigantic Sabre," said the Herald. "And I must speak with the usurper of Otranto."

Jerome returned to the Prince, and did not fail to repeat the message in the very words it had been uttered. The first sounds struck Manfred with terror; but when he heard himself styled usurper, his rage rekindled, and all his courage revived.

"Usurper!—Insolent villain!" cried he. "Who dares to question my title? Retire, Father; this is no business for Monks: I will meet this presumptuous man myself. Go to your convent and prepare the Princess's return. Your son shall be a hostage for your fidelity: his life depends on your obedience."

"Good Heaven! My Lord," cried Jerome. "Your Highness did but this instant freely pardon my child—have you so soon forgot the interposition of Heaven?"

"Heaven," replied Manfred, "does not send Heralds to question the title of a lawful Prince. I doubt whether it even notifies its will through Friars—but that is your affair, not mine. At present you know my pleasure; and it is not a saucy Herald that shall save your son, if you do not return with the Princess."

It was in vain for the holy man to reply. Manfred commanded him to be conducted to the postern-gate, and shut out from the castle. And he ordered some of his attendants to carry Theodore to the top of the black tower, and guard him strictly; scarce permitting the father and son to exchange a hasty embrace at parting. He then withdrew to the hall, and seating himself in princely state, ordered the Herald to be admitted to his presence.

"Well! Thou insolent!" said the Prince. "What wouldst thou with me?"

"I come," replied he, "to thee, Manfred, usurper of the principality of Otranto, from the renowned and invincible Knight, the
Knight of the Gigantic Sabre: in the name of his Lord, Frederic,
Marquis of Vicenza, he demands the Lady Isabella, daughter
of that Prince, whom thou hast basely and traitorously got into
thy power, by bribing her false guardians during his absence;
and he requires thee to resign the principality of Otranto, which
thou hast usurped from the said Lord Frederic, the nearest of
blood to the last rightful Lord, Alfonso the Good. If thou dost
not instantly comply with these just demands, he defies thee to
single combat to the last extremity." And so saying the Herald
cast down his warder.*

"And where is this braggart who sends thee?" said Manfred.

"At the distance of a league," said the Herald. "He comes to
make good his Lord's claim against thee, as he is a true knight,
and thou an usurper and ravisher."

Injurious as this challenge was, Manfred reflected that it was not
his interest to provoke the Marquis. He knew how well founded the
claim of Frederic was; nor was this the first time he had heard of it.
Frederic's ancestors had assumed the style of Princes of Otranto,
from the death of Alfonso the Good without issue; but Manfred,
his father, and grandfather, had been too powerful for the house
of Vicenza to dispossess them. Frederic, a martial and amorous
young Prince, had married a beautiful young lady, of whom he was
enamoured, and who had died in childbed of Isabella. Her death
affected him so much that he had taken the cross and gone to the
Holy Land, where he was wounded in an engagement against
the infidels, made prisoner, and reported to be dead. When the
news reached Manfred's ears, he bribed the guardians of the Lady
Isabella to deliver her up to him as a bride for his son Conrad, by
which alliance he had proposed to unite the claims of the two
houses. This motive, on Conrad's death, had co-operated to make
him so suddenly resolve on espousing her himself; and the same

* A baton or truncheon.

reflection determined him now to endeavour at obtaining the consent of Frederic to this marriage. A like policy inspired him with the thought of inviting Frederic's champion into the castle, lest he should be informed of Isabella's flight, which he strictly enjoined his domestics not to disclose to any of the Knight's retinue.

"Herald," said Manfred, as soon as he had digested these reflections, "return to thy master, and tell him, ere we liquidate our differences by the sword, Manfred would hold some converse with him. Bid him welcome to my castle, where by my faith, as I am a true Knight, he shall have courteous reception, and full security for himself and followers. If we cannot adjust our quarrel by amicable means, I swear he shall depart in safety, and shall have full satisfaction according to the laws of arms: So help me God and His holy Trinity!"

The Herald made three obeisances and retired.

During this interview Jerome's mind was agitated by a thousand contrary passions. He trembled for the life of his son, and his first thought was to persuade Isabella to return to the castle. Yet he was scarce less alarmed at the thought of her union with Manfred. He dreaded Hippolita's unbounded submission to the will of her Lord; and though he did not doubt but he could alarm her piety not to consent to a divorce, if he could get access to her; yet should Manfred discover that the obstruction came from him, it might be equally fatal to Theodore. He was impatient to know whence came the Herald, who with so little management had questioned the title of Manfred: yet he did not dare absent himself from the convent, lest Isabella should leave it, and her flight be imputed to him. He returned disconsolately to the monastery, uncertain on what conduct to resolve.

A Monk, who met him in the porch and observed his melancholy air, said, "Alas! brother, is it then true that we have lost our excellent Princess Hippolita?"

The holy man started, and cried, "What meanest thou, brother? I come this instant from the castle, and left her in perfect health."

"Martelli," replied the other Friar, "passed by the convent but a quarter of an hour ago on his way from the castle, and reported that her Highness was dead. All our brethren are gone to the chapel to pray for her happy transit to a better life, and willed me to wait thy arrival. They know thy holy attachment to that good Lady, and are anxious for the affliction it will cause in thee—indeed we have all reason to weep; she was a mother to our house. But this life is but a pilgrimage; we must not murmur—we shall all follow her! May our end be like hers!"

"Good brother, thou dreamest," said Jerome. "I tell thee I come from the castle, and left the Princess well. Where is the Lady Isabella?"

"Poor Gentlewoman!" replied the Friar. "I told her the sad news, and offered her spiritual comfort. I reminded her of the transitory condition of mortality, and advised her to take the veil: I quoted the example of the holy Princess Sanchia of Arragon."

"Thy zeal was laudable," said Jerome, impatiently, "but at present it was unnecessary: Hippolita is well—at least I trust in the Lord she is; I heard nothing to the contrary—yet, methinks, the Prince's earnestness—Well, brother, but where is the Lady Isabella?"

"I know not," said the Friar. "She wept much, and said she would retire to her chamber."

Jerome left his comrade abruptly, and hastened to the Princess, but she was not in her chamber. He inquired of the domestics of the convent, but could learn no news of her. He searched in vain throughout the monastery and the church, and despatched messengers round the neighbourhood, to get intelligence if she had been seen; but to no purpose. Nothing could equal the good man's perplexity. He judged that Isabella, suspecting Manfred of having precipitated his wife's death, had taken the alarm, and withdrawn herself to some more secret place of concealment. This new flight would probably carry the Prince's fury to the height. The report of Hippolita's death, though it seemed almost incredible, increased his consternation; and though Isabella's escape bespoke her aversion of Manfred for a husband, Jerome could feel no comfort from it, while it endangered the life of his son. He determined to return to the castle, and made several of his brethren accompany him to attest his innocence to Manfred, and, if necessary, join their intercession with his for Theodore.

The Prince, in the meantime, had passed into the court, and ordered the gates of the castle to be flung open for the reception of the stranger Knight and his train. In a few minutes the cavalcade arrived. First came two harbingers with wands. Next a herald, followed by two pages and two trumpets. Then a hundred foot-guards. These were attended by as many horse. After them fifty footmen, clothed in scarlet and black, the colours of the Knight. Then a led horse. Two heralds on each side of a gentleman on horseback bearing a banner with the arms of Vicenza and Otranto quarterly—a circumstance that much offended Manfred—but he stifled his resentment. Two more pages. The Knight's confessor telling his beads. Fifty more footmen clad as before. Two Knights habited in complete armour, their beavers down, comrades to the principal Knight. The squires of the two Knights, carrying their shields and devices. The Knight's own squire. A hundred gentlemen bearing an enormous sword, and seeming to faint under the weight of it. The Knight himself on a chestnut steed, in complete armour, his lance in the rest, his face entirely concealed by his vizor, which was surmounted by a large plume of scarlet and black feathers. Fifty foot-guards with drums and trumpets closed the procession, which wheeled off to the right and left to make room for the principal Knight.

As soon as he approached the gate he stopped; and the herald advancing, read again the words of the challenge. Manfred's eyes were fixed on the gigantic sword, and he scarce seemed to attend to the cartel: but his attention was soon diverted by a tempest of wind that rose behind him. He turned and beheld the Plumes of the enchanted helmet agitated in the same extraordinary manner as before. It required intrepidity like Manfred's not to sink under a concurrence of circumstances that seemed to announce his fate. Yet scorning in the presence of strangers to betray the courage he had always manifested, he said boldly, "Sir Knight, whoever thou art, I bid thee welcome. If thou art of mortal mould, thy valour shall meet its equal: and if thou art a true Knight, thou wilt scorn to employ sorcery to carry thy point. Be these omens from Heaven or Hell, Manfred trusts to the righteousness of his cause and to the aid of St. Nicholas, who has ever protected his house. Alight, Sir Knight, and repose thyself. To-morrow thou shalt have a fair field, and Heaven befriend the juster side!"

The Knight made no reply, but dismounting, was conducted by Manfred to the great hall of the castle. As they traversed the court, the Knight stopped to gaze on the miraculous casque; and kneeling down, seemed to pray inwardly for some minutes. Rising, he made a sign to the Prince to lead on. As soon as they entered the hall, Manfred proposed to the stranger to disarm, but the Knight shook his head in token of refusal.

"Sir Knight," said Manfred, "this is not courteous, but by my good faith I will not cross thee, nor shalt thou have cause to complain of the Prince of Otranto. No treachery is designed on my part; I hope none is intended on thine; here take my gage:" (giving him his ring) "your friends and you shall enjoy the laws of hospitality. Rest here until refreshments are brought. I will but give orders for the accommodation of your train, and return to you." The three Knights bowed as accepting his courtesy. Manfred directed the stranger's retinue to be conducted to an adjacent hospital, founded by the Princess Hippolita for the reception of pilgrims. As they made the circuit of the court to return towards the gate, the gigantic sword burst from the supporters, and falling to the ground opposite to the helmet, remained immovable. Manfred, almost hardened to preternatural appearances, surmounted the shock of this new prodigy; and returning to the hall, where by this time the feast was ready, he invited his silent guests to take their places. Manfred, however ill his heart was at ease, endeavoured to inspire the company with mirth. He put several questions to them, but was answered only by signs. They raised their vizors but sufficiently to feed themselves, and that sparingly.

"Sirs," said the Prince, "ye are the first guests I ever treated within these walls who scorned to hold any intercourse with me: nor has it oft been customary, I ween, for princes to hazard their state and dignity against strangers and mutes. You say you come in the name of Frederic of Vicenza; I have ever heard that he was a gallant and courteous Knight; nor would he, I am bold to say, think it beneath him to mix in social converse with a Prince that is his equal, and not unknown by deeds in arms. Still ye are silent— well! be it as it may—by the laws of hospitality and chivalry ye are masters under this roof: ye shall do your pleasure. But come, give me a goblet of wine; ye will not refuse to pledge me to the healths of your fair mistresses."

The principal Knight sighed and crossed himself, and was rising from the board.

"Sir Knight," said Manfred, "what I said was but in sport. I shall constrain you in nothing: use your good liking. Since mirth is not your mood, let us be sad. Business may hit your fancies better. Let us withdraw, and hear if what I have to unfold may be better relished than the vain efforts I have made for your pastime."

Manfred then conducting the three Knights into an inner chamber, shut the door, and inviting them to be seated, began thus, addressing himself to the chief personage, "You come, Sir Knight, as I understand, in the name of the Marquis of Vicenza, to re-demand the Lady Isabella, his daughter, who has been contracted in the face of Holy Church to my son, by the consent of her legal guardians; and to require me to resign my dominions to your Lord, who gives himself for the nearest of blood to Prince Alfonso, whose soul God rest! I shall speak to the latter article of your demands first. You must know, your Lord knows, that I enjoy the principality of Otranto from my father, Don Manuel, as he received it from his father, Don Ricardo. Alfonso, their predecessor, dying childless in the Holy Land, bequeathed his estates to my grandfather, Don Ricardo, in consideration of his faithful services."

The stranger shook his head.

"Sir Knight," said Manfred, warmly, "Ricardo was a valiant and upright man; he was a pious man; witness his munificent foundation of the adjoining church and two convents. He was peculiarly patronised by St. Nicholas—my grandfather was incapable—I say, Sir, Don Ricardo was incapable—excuse me, your interruption has disordered me. I venerate the memory of my grandfather. Well, Sirs, he held this estate; he held it by his good sword and by the favour of St. Nicholas—so did my father; and so, Sirs, will I, come what come will. But Frederic, your Lord, is nearest in blood. I have consented to put my title to the issue of the sword. Does that imply a vicious title? I might have asked, where is Frederic your Lord? Report speaks him dead in captivity. You say, your actions say, he lives—I question it not—I might, Sirs, I might—but I do not. Other Princes would bid Frederic take his inheritance by force, if he can: they would not stake their dignity on a single combat: they would not submit it to the decision of unknown mutes!—pardon me, gentlemen, I am too warm: but suppose yourselves in my situation: as ye are stout Knights, would it not move your choler to have your own and the honour of your ancestors called in question?"

"But to the point. Ye require me to deliver up the Lady Isabella. Sirs, I must ask if ye are authorised to receive her?"

The Knight nodded.

"Receive her," continued Manfred. "Well, you are authorised to receive her, but, gentle Knight, may I ask if you have full powers?"

The Knight nodded.

"'Tis well," said Manfred. "Then hear what I have to offer. Ye see, gentlemen, before you, the most unhappy of men!" (He began to weep). "Afford me your compassion; I am entitled to it, indeed I am. Know, I have lost my only hope, my joy, the support of my house—Conrad died yester morning."

The Knights discovered signs of surprise.

"Yes, Sirs, fate has disposed of my son. Isabella is at liberty."

"Do you then restore her?" cried the chief Knight, breaking silence.

"Afford me your patience," said Manfred. "I rejoice to find, by this testimony of your goodwill, that this matter may be adjusted without blood. It is no interest of mine dictates what little I have farther to say. Ye behold in me a man disgusted with the world: the loss of my son has weaned me from earthly cares. Power and greatness have no longer any charms in my eyes. I wished to transmit the sceptre I had received from my ancestors with honour to my son—but that is over! Life itself is so indifferent to me, that I accepted your defiance with joy. A good Knight cannot go to the grave with more satisfaction than when falling in his vocation: whatever is the will of Heaven, I submit; for alas! Sirs, I am a man of many sorrows. Manfred is no object of envy, but no doubt you are acquainted with my story."

The Knight made signs of ignorance, and seemed curious to have Manfred proceed.

"Is it possible, Sirs," continued the Prince, "that my story should be a secret to you? Have you heard nothing relating to me and the Princess Hippolita?"

They shook their heads.

"No! Thus, then, Sirs, it is. You think me ambitious: ambition, alas! is composed of more rugged materials. If I were ambitious, I should not for so many years have been a prey to all the hell of conscientious scruples. But I weary your patience: I will be brief. Know, then, that I have long been troubled in mind on my union with the Princess Hippolita. Oh! Sirs, if ye were acquainted with that excellent woman! If ye knew that I adore her like a mistress, and cherish her as a friend—but man was not born for perfect happiness! She shares my scruples, and with her consent I have brought this matter before the church, for we are related within the forbidden degrees. I expect every hour the definitive sentence that must separate us for ever—I am sure you feel for me—I see you do—pardon these tears!"

The Knights gazed on each other, wondering where this would end.

Manfred continued, "The death of my son betiding while my soul was under this anxiety, I thought of nothing but resigning my dominions, and retiring for ever from the sight of mankind. My only difficulty was to fix on a successor, who would be tender of my people, and to dispose of the Lady Isabella, who is dear to me as my own blood. I was willing to restore the line of Alfonso, even in his most distant kindred. And though, pardon me, I am satisfied it was his will that Ricardo's lineage should take place of his own relations; yet where was I to search for those relations? I knew of none but Frederic, your Lord; he was a captive to the infidels, or dead; and were he living, and at home, would he quit the flourishing State of Vicenza for the inconsiderable principality of Otranto? If he would not, could I bear the thought of seeing a hard, unfeeling, Viceroy set over my poor faithful people? For, Sirs, I love my people, and thank Heaven am beloved by them. But ye will ask whither tends this long discourse? Briefly, then, thus, Sirs. Heaven in your arrival seems to point out a remedy for these difficulties and my misfortunes. The Lady Isabella is at liberty; I shall soon be so. I would submit to anything for the good of my people. Were it not the best, the only way to extinguish the feuds between our families, if I was to take the Lady Isabella to wife? You start. But though Hippolita's virtues will ever be dear to me, a Prince must not consider himself; he is born for his people."

A servant at that instant entering the chamber apprised Manfred that Jerome and several of his brethren demanded immediate access to him.

The Prince, provoked at this interruption, and fearing that the Friar would discover to the strangers that Isabella had taken sanctuary, was going to forbid Jerome's entrance. But recollecting that he was certainly arrived to notify the Princess's return, Manfred began to excuse himself to the Knights for leaving them for a few moments, but was prevented by the arrival of the Friars. Manfred angrily reprimanded them for their intrusion, and would have forced them back from the chamber; but Jerome was too much agitated to be repulsed. He declared aloud the flight of Isabella, with protestations of his own innocence.

Manfred, distracted at the news, and not less at its coming to the knowledge of the strangers, uttered nothing but incoherent sentences, now upbraiding the Friar, now apologising to the Knights, earnest to know what was become of Isabella, yet equally afraid of their knowing; impatient to pursue her, yet dreading to have them join in the pursuit. He offered to despatch messengers in quest of her, but the chief Knight, no longer keeping silence, reproached Manfred in bitter terms for his dark and ambiguous dealing, and demanded the cause of Isabella's first absence from the castle. Manfred, casting a stern look at Jerome, implying a command of silence, pretended that on Conrad's death he had placed her in sanctuary until he could determine how to dispose of her. Jerome, who trembled for his son's life, did not dare contradict this falsehood, but one of his brethren, not under the same anxiety, declared frankly that she had fled to their church in the preceding night. The Prince in vain endeavoured to stop this discovery, which overwhelmed him with shame and confusion. The principal stranger, amazed at the contradictions he heard, and more than half persuaded that Manfred had secreted the Princess, notwithstanding the concern he expressed at her flight, rushing to the door, said, "Thou traitor Prince! Isabella shall be found."

Manfred endeavoured to hold him, but the other Knights assisting their comrade, he broke from the Prince, and hastened into the court, demanding his attendants. Manfred, finding it vain to divert him from the pursuit, offered to accompany him and summoning his attendants, and taking Jerome and some of the Friars to guide them, they issued from the castle; Manfred privately giving orders to have the Knight's company secured, while to the knight he affected to despatch a messenger to require their assistance.

The company had no sooner quitted the castle than Matilda, who felt herself deeply interested for the young peasant, since she had seen him condemned to death in the hall, and whose thoughts had been taken up with concerting measures to save him, was informed by some of the female attendants that Manfred had despatched all his men various ways in pursuit of Isabella. He had in his hurry given this order in general terms, not meaning to extend it to the guard he had set upon Theodore, but forgetting it. The domestics, officious to obey so peremptory a Prince, and urged by their own curiosity and love of novelty to join in any precipitate chase, had to a man left the castle. Matilda disengaged herself from her women, stole up to the black tower, and unbolting the door, presented herself to the astonished Theodore.

"Young man," said she, "though filial duty and womanly modesty condemn the step I am taking, yet holy charity, surmounting all other ties, justifies this act. Fly; the doors of thy prison are open: my father and his domestics are absent; but they may soon return. Be gone in safety; and may the angels of Heaven direct thy course!"

"Thou art surely one of those angels!" said the enraptured Theodore. "None but a blessed saint could speak, could act— could look—like thee. May I not know the name of my divine protectress? Methought thou namedst thy father. Is it possible? Can Manfred's blood feel holy pity! Lovely Lady, thou answerest not. But how art thou here thyself? Why dost thou neglect thy own safety, and waste a thought on a wretch like Theodore? Let us fly together: the life thou bestowest shall be dedicated to thy defence."

"Alas! Thou mistakest," said Matilda, signing. "I am Manfred's daughter, but no dangers await me."

"Amazement!" said Theodore. "But last night I blessed myself for yielding thee the service thy gracious compassion so charitably returns me now."

"Still thou art in an error," said the Princess. "But this is no time for explanation. Fly, virtuous youth, while it is in my power to save thee: should my father return, thou and I both should indeed have cause to tremble."

"How!" said Theodore. "Thinkest thou, charming maid, that I will accept of life at the hazard of aught calamitous to thee? Better I endured a thousand deaths."

"I run no risk," said Matilda, "but by thy delay. Depart; it cannot be known that I have assisted thy flight."

"Swear by the saints above," said Theodore, "that thou canst not be suspected; else here I vow to await whatever can befall me."

"Oh! Thou art too generous," said Matilda. "But rest assured that no suspicion can alight on me."

"Give me thy beauteous hand in token that thou dost not deceive me," said Theodore, "and let me bathe it with the warm tears of gratitude."

"Forbear!" said the Princess. "This must not be."

"Alas!" said Theodore, "I have never known but calamity until this hour—perhaps shall never know other fortune again: suffer the chaste raptures of holy gratitude: 'tis my soul would print its effusions on thy hand."

"Forbear, and be gone," said Matilda. "How would Isabella approve of seeing thee at my feet?"

"Who is Isabella?" said the young man with surprise.

"Ah, me! I fear," said the Princess, "I am serving a deceitful one. Hast thou forgot thy curiosity this morning?"

"Thy looks, thy actions, all thy beauteous self seem an emanation of divinity," said Theodore, "but thy words are dark and mysterious. Speak, Lady; speak to thy servant's comprehension."

"Thou understandest but too well!" said Matilda. "But once more I command thee to be gone: thy blood, which I may preserve, will be on my head, if I waste the time in vain discourse."

"I go, Lady," said Theodore, "because it is thy will, and because I would not bring the grey hairs of my father with sorrow to the grave. Say but, adored Lady, that I have thy gentle pity."

"Stay," said Matilda. "I will conduct thee to the subterraneous vault by which Isabella escaped; it will lead thee to the church of St. Nicholas, where thou mayst take sanctuary."

"What!" said Theodore. "Was it another, and not thy lovely self that I assisted to find the subterraneous passage?"

"It was," said Matilda, "but ask no more; I tremble to see thee still abide here; fly to the sanctuary."

"To sanctuary," said Theodore. "No, Princess; sanctuaries are for helpless damsels, or for criminals. Theodore's soul is free from guilt, nor will wear the appearance of it. Give me a sword, Lady, and thy father shall learn that Theodore scorns an ignominious flight."

"Rash youth!" said Matilda. "Thou wouldst not dare to lift thy presumptuous arm against the Prince of Otranto?"

"Not against thy father; indeed, I dare not," said Theodore. "Excuse me, Lady; I had forgotten. But could I gaze on thee, and remember thou art sprung from the tyrant Manfred! But he is thy father, and from this moment my injuries are buried in oblivion."

A deep and hollow groan, which seemed to come from above, startled the Princess and Theodore.

"Good Heaven! We are overheard!" said the Princess. They listened; but perceiving no further noise, they both concluded it the effect of pent-up vapours. And the Princess, preceding Theodore softly, carried him to her father's armoury, where, equipping him with a complete suit, he was conducted by Matilda to the postern-gate.

"Avoid the town," said the Princess, "and all the western side of the castle. 'Tis there the search must be making by Manfred and the strangers; but hie thee to the opposite quarter. Yonder behind that forest to the east is a chain of rocks, hollowed into a labyrinth of caverns that reach to the sea coast. There thou mayst lie concealed, till thou canst make signs to some vessel to put on shore, and take thee off. Go! Heaven be thy guide!—And sometimes in thy prayers remember—Matilda!"

Theodore flung himself at her feet, and seizing her lily hand, which with struggles she suffered him to kiss, he vowed on the earliest opportunity to get himself knighted, and fervently entreated her permission to swear himself eternally her knight. Ere the Princess could reply, a clap of thunder was suddenly heard that shook the battlements. Theodore, regardless of the tempest, would have urged his suit: but the Princess, dismayed, retreated hastily into the castle, and commanded the youth to be gone with an air that would not be disobeyed. He sighed, and retired, but with eyes fixed on the gate, until Matilda, closing it, put an end to an interview, in which the hearts of both had drunk so deeply of a passion, which both now tasted for the first time.

Theodore went pensively to the convent, to acquaint his father with his deliverance. There he learned the absence of Jerome, and the pursuit that was making after the Lady Isabella, with some particulars of whose story he now first became acquainted. The generous gallantry of his nature prompted him to wish to assist her; but the Monks could lend him no lights to guess at the route she had taken. He was not tempted to wander far in search of her, for the idea of Matilda had imprinted itself so strongly on his heart, that he could not bear to absent himself at much distance from her abode. The tenderness Jerome had expressed for him concurred to confirm this reluctance; and he even persuaded himself that filial affection was the chief cause of his hovering between the castle and monastery.

Until Jerome should return at night, Theodore at length determined to repair to the forest that Matilda had pointed out to him. Arriving there, he sought the gloomiest shades, as best suited to the pleasing melancholy that reigned in his mind. In this mood he roved insensibly to the caves which had formerly served as a retreat to hermits, and were now reported round the country to be haunted by evil spirits. He recollected to have heard this tradition; and being of a brave and adventurous disposition, he willingly indulged his curiosity in exploring the secret recesses of this labyrinth. He had not penetrated far before he thought he heard the steps of some person who seemed to retreat before him.

Theodore, though firmly grounded in all our holy faith enjoins to be believed, had no apprehension that good men were abandoned without cause to the malice of the powers of darkness. He thought the place more likely to be infested by robbers than by those infernal agents who are reported to molest and bewilder travellers. He had long burned with impatience to approve his valour. Drawing his sabre, he marched sedately onwards, still directing his steps as the imperfect rustling sound before him led the way. The armour he wore was a like indication to the person who avoided him. Theodore, now convinced that he was not mistaken, redoubled his pace, and evidently gained on the person that fled, whose haste increasing, Theodore came up just as a woman fell breathless before him. He hasted to raise her, but her terror was so great that he apprehended she would faint in his arms. He used every gentle word to dispel her alarms, and assured her that far from injuring, he would defend her at the peril of his life.

The Lady recovering her spirits from his courteous demeanour, and gazing on her protector, said, "Sure, I have heard that voice before!"

"Not to my knowledge," replied Theodore. "Unless, as I conjecture, thou art the Lady Isabella."

"Merciful Heaven!" cried she. "Thou art not sent in quest of me, art thou?" And saying those words, she threw herself at his feet, and besought him not to deliver her up to Manfred.

"To Manfred!" cried Theodore. "No, Lady; I have once already delivered thee from his tyranny, and it shall fare hard with me now, but I will place thee out of the reach of his daring."

"Is it possible," said she, "that thou shouldst be the generous unknown whom I met last night in the vault of the castle? Sure thou art not a mortal, but my guardian angel. On my knees, let me thank—"

"Hold! Gentle Princess," said Theodore, "nor demean thyself before a poor and friendless young man. If Heaven has selected me for thy deliverer, it will accomplish its work, and strengthen my arm in thy cause. But come, Lady, we are too near the mouth of the cavern; let us seek its inmost recesses. I can have no tranquillity till I have placed thee beyond the reach of danger."

"Alas! What mean you, sir?" said she. "Though all your actions are noble, though your sentiments speak the purity of your soul, is it fitting that I should accompany you alone into these perplexed retreats? Should we be found together, what would a censorious world think of my conduct?"

"I respect your virtuous delicacy," said Theodore. "Nor do you harbour a suspicion that wounds my honour. I meant to conduct you into the most private cavity of these rocks, and then at the hazard of my life to guard their entrance against every living thing. Besides, Lady," continued he, drawing a deep sigh, "beauteous and all perfect as your form is, and though my wishes are not guiltless of aspiring, know, my soul is dedicated to another; and although—" A sudden noise prevented Theodore from proceeding. They soon distinguished these sounds—

"Isabella! What, ho! Isabella!" The trembling Princess relapsed into her former agony of fear. Theodore endeavoured to encourage her, but in vain. He assured her he would die rather than suffer her to return under Manfred's power; and begging her to remain concealed, he went forth to prevent the person in search of her from approaching.

At the mouth of the cavern he found an armed Knight, discoursing with a peasant, who assured him he had seen a lady enter the passes of the rock. The Knight was preparing to seek her, when Theodore, placing himself in his way, with his sword drawn, sternly forbad him at his peril to advance.

"And who art thou, who darest to cross my way?" said the Knight, haughtily.

"One who does not dare more than he will perform," said Theodore.

"I seek the Lady Isabella," said the Knight, "and understand she has taken refuge among these rocks. Impede me not, or thou wilt repent having provoked my resentment."

"Thy purpose is as odious as thy resentment is contemptible," said Theodore. "Return whence thou camest, or we shall soon know whose resentment is most terrible."

The stranger, who was the principal Knight that had arrived from the Marquis of Vicenza, had galloped from Manfred as he was busied in getting information of the Princess, and giving various orders to prevent her falling into the power of the three Knights. Their chief had suspected Manfred of being privy to the Princess's absconding, and this insult from a man, who he concluded was stationed by that Prince to secrete her, confirming his suspicions, he made no reply, but discharging a blow with his sabre at Theodore, would soon have removed all obstruction, if Theodore, who took him for one of Manfred's captains, and who had no sooner given the provocation than prepared to support it, had not received the stroke on his shield. The valour that had so long been smothered in his breast broke forth at once; he rushed impetuously on the Knight, whose pride and wrath were not less powerful incentives to hardy deeds. The combat was furious, but not long. Theodore wounded the Knight in three several places, and at last disarmed him as he fainted by the loss of blood.

The peasant, who had fled on the first onset, had given the alarm to some of Manfred's domestics, who, by his orders, were dispersed through the forest in pursuit of Isabella. They came up as the Knight fell, whom they soon discovered to be the noble stranger. Theodore, notwithstanding his hatred to Manfred, could not behold the victory he had gained without emotions of pity and generosity. But he was more touched when he learned the quality of his adversary, and was informed that he was no retainer, but an enemy, of Manfred. He assisted the servants of the latter in disarming the Knight, and in endeavouring to stanch the blood that flowed from his wounds. The Knight recovering his speech, said, in a faint and faltering voice—

"Generous foe, we have both been in an error. I took thee for an instrument of the tyrant; I perceive thou hast made the like mistake. It is too late for excuses. I faint. If Isabella is at hand— call her—I have important secrets to—"

"He is dying!" said one of the attendants. "Has nobody a crucifix about them? Andrea, do thou pray over him."

"Fetch some water," said Theodore, "and pour it down his throat, while I hasten to the Princess."

Saying this, he flew to Isabella, and in few words told her modestly that he had been so unfortunate by mistake as to wound a gentleman from her father's court, who wished, ere he died, to impart something of consequence to her.

The Princess, who had been transported at hearing the voice of Theodore, as he called to her to come forth, was astonished at what she heard. Suffering herself to be conducted by Theodore, the new proof of whose valour recalled her dispersed spirits, she came where the bleeding Knight lay speechless on the ground. But her fears returned when she beheld the domestics of Manfred. She would again have fled if Theodore had not made her observe that they were unarmed, and had not threatened them with instant death if they should dare to seize the Princess.

The stranger, opening his eyes, and beholding a woman, said, "Art thou—pray tell me truly—art thou Isabella of Vicenza?"

"I am," said she. "Good Heaven restore thee!"

"Then thou—then thou"—said the Knight, struggling for utterance—"seest—thy father. Give me one—"

"Oh! Amazement! Horror! What do I hear! What do I see!" cried Isabella. "My father! You my father! How came you here, Sir? For Heaven's sake, speak! Oh! Run for help, or he will expire!"

"'Tis most true," said the wounded Knight, exerting all his force. "I am Frederic thy father. Yes, I came to deliver thee. It will not be. Give me a parting kiss, and take—"

"Sir," said Theodore, "do not exhaust yourself; suffer us to convey you to the castle."

"To the castle!" said Isabella. "Is there no help nearer than the castle? Would you expose my father to the tyrant? If he goes thither, I dare not accompany him; and yet, can I leave him!"

"My child," said Frederic, "it matters not for me whither I am carried. A few minutes will place me beyond danger; but while I have eyes to dote on thee, forsake me not, dear Isabella! This brave Knight—I know not who he is—will protect thy innocence. Sir, you will not abandon my child, will you?"

Theodore, shedding tears over his victim, and vowing to guard the Princess at the expense of his life, persuaded Frederic to suffer himself to be conducted to the castle. They placed him on a horse belonging to one of the domestics, after binding up his wounds as well as they were able. Theodore marched by his side; and the afflicted Isabella, who could not bear to quit him, followed mournfully behind.

Chapter IV.

THE sorrowful troop no sooner arrived at the castle, than they were met by Hippolita and Matilda, whom Isabella had sent one of the domestics before to advertise of their approach. The ladies causing Frederic to be conveyed into the nearest chamber, retired, while the surgeons examined his wounds. Matilda blushed at seeing Theodore and Isabella together; but endeavoured to conceal it by embracing the latter, and condoling with her on her father's mischance. The surgeons soon came to acquaint Hippolita that none of the Marquis's wounds were dangerous; and that he was desirous of seeing his daughter and the Princesses.

Theodore, under pretence of expressing his joy at being freed from his apprehensions of the combat being fatal to Frederic, could not resist the impulse of following Matilda. Her eyes were so often cast down on meeting his, that Isabella, who regarded Theodore as attentively as he gazed on Matilda, soon divined who the object was that he had told her in the cave engaged his affections. While this mute scene passed, Hippolita demanded of Frederic the cause of his having taken that mysterious course for reclaiming his daughter; and threw in various apologies to excuse her Lord for the match contracted between their children.

Frederic, however incensed against Manfred, was not insensible to the courtesy and benevolence of Hippolita: but he was still more struck with the lovely form of Matilda. Wishing to detain them by his bedside, he informed Hippolita of his story. He told her that, while prisoner to the infidels, he had dreamed that his daughter, of whom he had learned no news since his captivity, was detained in a castle, where she was in danger of the most dreadful misfortunes: and that if he obtained his liberty, and repaired to a wood near Joppa, he would learn more. Alarmed at this dream, and incapable of obeying the direction given by it, his chains became more grievous than ever. But while his thoughts were occupied on the means of obtaining his liberty, he received the agreeable news that the confederate Princes who were warring in Palestine had paid his ransom. He instantly set out for the wood that had been marked in his dream.

For three days he and his attendants had wandered in the forest without seeing a human form: but on the evening of the third they came to a cell, in which they found a venerable hermit in the agonies of death. Applying rich cordials, they brought the fainting man to his speech.

"My sons," said he, "I am bounden to your charity—but it is in vain—I am going to my eternal rest—yet I die with the satisfaction of performing the will of Heaven. When first I repaired to this solitude, after seeing my country become a prey to unbelievers—it is alas! above fifty years since I was witness to that dreadful scene! St. Nicholas appeared to me, and revealed a secret, which he bade me never disclose to mortal man, but on my death-bed. This is that tremendous hour, and ye are no doubt the chosen warriors to whom I was ordered to reveal my trust. As soon as ye have done the last offices to this wretched corse, dig under the seventh tree on the left hand of this poor cave, and your pains will—Oh! good Heaven receive my soul!" With those words the devout man breathed his last.

"By break of day," continued Frederic, "when we had committed the holy relics to earth, we dug according to direction. But what was our astonishment when about the depth of six feet we discovered an enormous sabre—the very weapon yonder in the court. On the blade, which was then partly out of the scabbard, though since closed by our efforts in removing it, were written the following lines—no; excuse me, Madam," added the Marquis, turning to Hippolita, "if I forbear to repeat them: I respect your sex and rank, and would not be guilty of offending your ear with sounds injurious to aught that is dear to you."

He paused. Hippolita trembled. She did not doubt but Frederic was destined by Heaven to accomplish the fate that seemed to threaten her house. Looking with anxious fondness at Matilda, a silent tear stole down her cheek: but recollecting herself, she said, "Proceed, my Lord; Heaven does nothing in vain; mortals must receive its divine behests with lowliness and submission. It is our part to deprecate its wrath, or bow to its decrees. Repeat the sentence, my Lord; we listen resigned."

Frederic was grieved that he had proceeded so far. The dignity and patient firmness of Hippolita penetrated him with respect, and the tender silent affection with which the Princess and her daughter regarded each other, melted him almost to tears. Yet apprehensive that his forbearance to obey would be more alarming, he repeated in a faltering and low voice the following lines:

"Where'er a casque that suits this sword is found,
With perils is thy daughter compass'd round;
Alfonso's blood alone can save the maid,
And quiet a long restless Prince's shade."

"What is there in these lines," said Theodore impatiently, "that affects these Princesses? Why were they to be shocked by a mysterious delicacy, that has so little foundation?"

"Your words are rude, young man," said the Marquis, "and though fortune has favoured you once—"

"My honoured Lord," said Isabella, who resented Theodore's warmth, which she perceived was dictated by his sentiments for Matilda, "discompose not yourself for the glosing of a peasant's son: he forgets the reverence he owes you; but he is not accustomed—"

Hippolita, concerned at the heat that had arisen, checked Theodore for his boldness, but with an air acknowledging his zeal; and changing the conversation, demanded of Frederic where he had left her Lord? As the Marquis was going to reply, they heard a noise without, and rising to inquire the cause, Manfred, Jerome, and part of the troop, who had met an imperfect rumour of what had happened, entered the chamber. Manfred advanced hastily towards Frederic's bed to condole with him on his misfortune, and to learn the circumstances of the combat, when starting in an agony of terror and amazement, he cried—

"Ha! What art thou? Thou dreadful spectre! Is my hour come?"

"My dearest, gracious Lord," cried Hippolita, clasping him in her arms, "what is it you see! Why do you fix your eye-balls thus?"

"What!" cried Manfred breathless. "Dost thou see nothing, Hippolita? Is this ghastly phantom sent to me alone—to rue, who did not—"

"For mercy's sweetest self, my Lord," said Hippolita, "resume your soul, command your reason. There is none here, but us, your friends."

"What, is not that Alfonso?" cried Manfred. "Dost thou not see him? Can it be my brain's delirium?"

"This! My Lord," said Hippolita. "This is Theodore, the youth who has been so unfortunate."

"Theodore!" said Manfred mournfully, and striking his forehead. "Theodore or a phantom, he has unhinged the soul of Manfred. But how comes he here? And how comes he in armour?"

"I believe he went in search of Isabella," said Hippolita.

"Of Isabella!" said Manfred, relapsing into rage. "Yes, yes, that is not doubtful—. But how did he escape from durance in which I left him? Was it Isabella, or this hypocritical old Friar, that procured his enlargement?"

"And would a parent be criminal, my Lord," said Theodore, "if he meditated the deliverance of his child?"

Jerome, amazed to hear himself in a manner accused by his son, and without foundation, knew not what to think. He could not comprehend how Theodore had escaped, how he came to be armed, and to encounter Frederic. Still he would not venture to ask any questions that might tend to inflame Manfred's wrath against his son. Jerome's silence convinced Manfred that he had contrived Theodore's release.

"And is it thus, thou ungrateful old man," said the Prince, addressing himself to the Friar, "that thou repayest mine and Hippolita's bounties? And not content with traversing my heart's nearest wishes, thou armest thy bastard, and bringest him into my own castle to insult me!"

"My Lord," said Theodore, "you wrong my father: neither he nor I are capable of harbouring a thought against your peace. Is it insolence thus to surrender myself to your Highness's pleasure?" added he, laying his sword respectfully at Manfred's feet. "Behold my bosom; strike, my Lord, if you suspect that a disloyal thought is lodged there. There is not a sentiment engraven on my heart that does not venerate you and yours."

The grace and fervour with which Theodore uttered these words interested every person present in his favour. Even Manfred was touched—yet still possessed with his resemblance to Alfonso, his admiration was dashed with secret horror.

"Rise," said he. "Thy life is not my present purpose. But tell me thy history, and how thou camest connected with this old traitor here."

"My Lord," said Jerome eagerly.

"Peace! Impostor!" said Manfred. "I will not have him prompted."

"My Lord," said Theodore, "I want no assistance; my story

is very brief. I was carried at five years of age to Algiers with my mother, who had been taken by corsairs from the coast of Sicily. She died of grief in less than a twelvemonth." The tears gushed from Jerome's eyes, on whose countenance a thousand anxious passions stood expressed. "Before she died," continued Theodore, "she bound a writing about my arm under my garments, which told me I was the son of the Count Falconara."

"It is most true," said Jerome. "I am that wretched father."

"Again I enjoin thee silence," said Manfred. "Proceed."

"I remained in slavery," said Theodore, "until within these two years, when attending on my master in his cruises, I was delivered by a Christian vessel, which overpowered the pirate; and discovering myself to the captain, he generously put me on shore in Sicily; but alas! Instead of finding a father, I learned that his estate, which was situated on the coast, had, during his absence, been laid waste by the Rover who had carried my mother and me into captivity: that his castle had been burnt to the ground, and that my father on his return had sold what remained, and was retired into religion in the kingdom of Naples, but where no man could inform me. Destitute and friendless, hopeless almost of attaining the transport of a parent's embrace, I took the first opportunity of setting sail for Naples, from whence, within these six days, I wandered into this province, still supporting myself by the labour of my hands; nor until yester-morn did I believe that Heaven had reserved any lot for me but peace of mind and contented poverty. This, my Lord, is Theodore's story. I am blessed beyond my hope in finding a father; I am unfortunate beyond my desert in having incurred your Highness's displeasure."

He ceased. A murmur of approbation gently arose from the audience.

"This is not all," said Frederic. "I am bound in honour to add what he suppresses. Though he is modest, I must be generous; he is one of the bravest youths on Christian ground. He is warm too; and from the short knowledge I have of him, I will pledge myself for his veracity: if what he reports of himself were not true, he would not utter it—and for me, youth, I honour a frankness which becomes thy birth; but now, and thou didst offend me: yet the noble blood which flows in thy veins, may well be allowed to boil out, when it has so recently traced itself to its source. Come, my Lord," (turning to Manfred), "if I can pardon him, surely you may; it is not the youth's fault, if you took him for a spectre."

This bitter taunt galled the soul of Manfred.

"If beings from another world," replied he haughtily, "have power to impress my mind with awe, it is more than living man can do; nor could a stripling's arm."

"My Lord," interrupted Hippolita, "your guest has occasion for repose: shall we not leave him to his rest?" Saying this, and taking Manfred by the hand, she took leave of Frederic, and led the company forth.

The Prince, not sorry to quit a conversation which recalled to mind the discovery he had made of his most secret sensations, suffered himself to be conducted to his own apartment, after permitting Theodore, though under engagement to return to the castle on the morrow (a condition the young man gladly accepted), to retire with his father to the convent. Matilda and Isabella were too much occupied with their own reflections, and too little content with each other, to wish for farther converse that night. They separated each to her chamber, with more expressions of ceremony and fewer of affection than had passed between them since their childhood.

If they parted with small cordiality, they did but meet with greater impatience, as soon as the sun was risen. Their minds were in a situation that excluded sleep, and each recollected a thousand questions which she wished she had put to the other overnight. Matilda reflected that Isabella had been twice delivered by Theodore in very critical situations, which she could not believe accidental. His eyes, it was true, had been fixed on her in Frederic's chamber; but that might have been to disguise his passion for Isabella from the fathers of both. It were better to clear this up. She wished to know the truth, lest she should wrong her friend by entertaining a passion for Isabella's lover. Thus jealousy prompted, and at the same time borrowed an excuse from friendship to justify its curiosity.

Isabella, not less restless, had better foundation for her suspicions. Both Theodore's tongue and eyes had told her his heart was engaged; it was true—yet, perhaps, Matilda might not correspond to his passion; she had ever appeared insensible to love: all her thoughts were set on Heaven.

"Why did I dissuade her?" said Isabella to herself. "I am punished for my generosity; but when did they meet? Where? It cannot be; I have deceived myself; perhaps last night was the first time they ever beheld each other; it must be some other object that has prepossessed his affections—if it is, I am not so unhappy as I thought; if it is not my friend Matilda—how! Can I stoop to wish for the affection of a man, who rudely and unnecessarily acquainted me with his indifference? And that at the very moment in which common courtesy demanded at least expressions of civility. I will go to my dear Matilda, who will confirm me in this becoming pride. Man is false—I will advise with her on taking the veil: she will rejoice to find me in this disposition; and I will acquaint her that I no longer oppose her inclination for the cloister."

In this frame of mind, and determined to open her heart entirely to Matilda, she went to that Princess's chamber, whom she found already dressed, and leaning pensively on her arm. This attitude, so correspondent to what she felt herself, revived Isabella's suspicions, and destroyed the confidence she had purposed to place in her friend. They blushed at meeting, and were too much novices to disguise their sensations with address. After some unmeaning questions and replies, Matilda demanded of Isabella the cause of her flight?

The latter, who had almost forgotten Manfred's passion, so

entirely was she occupied by her own, concluding that Matilda referred to her last escape from the convent, which had occasioned the events of the preceding evening, replied, "Martelli brought word to the convent that your mother was dead."

"Oh!" said Matilda, interrupting her. "Bianca has explained that mistake to me: on seeing me faint, she cried out, 'The Princess is dead!' and Martelli, who had come for the usual dole to the castle—"

"And what made you faint?" said Isabella, indifferent to the rest.

Matilda blushed and stammered, "My father—he was sitting in judgment on a criminal—"

"What criminal?" said Isabella eagerly.

"A young man," said Matilda. "I believe—"

"I think it was that young man that—"

"What, Theodore?" said Isabella.

"Yes," answered she. "I never saw him before; I do not know how he had offended my father, but as he has been of service to you, I am glad my Lord has pardoned him."

"Served me!" replied Isabella. "Do you term it serving me, to wound my father, and almost occasion his death? Though it is but since yesterday that I am blessed with knowing a parent, I hope Matilda does not think I am such a stranger to filial tenderness as not to resent the boldness of that audacious youth, and that it is impossible for me ever to feel any affection for one who dared to lift his arm against the author of my being. No, Matilda, my heart abhors him; and if you still retain the friendship for me that you have vowed from your infancy, you will detest a man who has been on the point of making me miserable for ever."

Matilda held down her head and replied, "I hope my dearest Isabella does not doubt her Matilda's friendship: I never beheld that youth until yesterday; he is almost a stranger to me: but as the surgeons have pronounced your father out of danger, you ought not to harbour uncharitable resentment against one, who I am persuaded did not know the Marquis was related to you."

"You plead his cause very pathetically," said Isabella, "considering he is so much a stranger to you! I am mistaken, or he returns your charity."

"What mean you?" said Matilda.

"Nothing," said Isabella, repenting that she had given Matilda a hint of Theodore's inclination for her. Then changing the discourse, she asked Matilda what occasioned Manfred to take Theodore for a spectre?

"Bless me," said Matilda, "did not you observe his extreme resemblance to the portrait of Alfonso in the gallery? I took notice of it to Bianca even before I saw him in armour; but with the helmet on, he is the very image of that picture."

"I do not much observe pictures," said Isabella. "Much less have I examined this young man so attentively as you seem to have done. Ah? Matilda, your heart is in danger, but let me warn you as a friend, he has owned to me that he is in love; it cannot be with you, for yesterday was the first time you ever met—was it not?"

"Certainly," replied Matilda. "But why does my dearest Isabella conclude from anything I have said, that"—she paused—then continuing, "he saw you first, and I am far from having the vanity to think that my little portion of charms could engage a heart devoted to you; may you be happy, Isabella, whatever is the fate of Matilda!"

"My lovely friend," said Isabella, whose heart was too honest to resist a kind expression, "it is you that Theodore admires; I saw it; I am persuaded of it; nor shall a thought of my own happiness suffer me to interfere with yours."

This frankness drew tears from the gentle Matilda; and jealousy that for a moment had raised a coolness between these amiable maidens soon gave way to the natural sincerity and candour of their souls. Each confessed to the other the impression that Theodore had made on her; and this confidence was followed by a struggle of generosity, each insisting on yielding her claim to her friend. At length the dignity of Isabella's virtue reminding her of the preference which Theodore had almost declared for her rival, made her determine to conquer her passion, and cede the beloved object to her friend.

During this contest of amity, Hippolita entered her daughter's chamber.

"Madam," said she to Isabella, "you have so much tenderness for Matilda, and interest yourself so kindly in whatever affects our wretched house, that I can have no secrets with my child which are not proper for you to hear."

The princesses were all attention and anxiety.

"Know then, Madam," continued Hippolita, "and you my dearest Matilda, that being convinced by all the events of these two last ominous days, that Heaven purposes the sceptre of Otranto should pass from Manfred's hands into those of the Marquis Frederic, I have been perhaps inspired with the thought of averting our total destruction by the union of our rival houses. With this view I have been proposing to Manfred, my Lord, to tender this dear, dear child to Frederic, your father."

"Me to Lord Frederic!" cried Matilda. "Good heavens! My gracious mother—and have you named it to my father?"

"I have," said Hippolita. "He listened benignly to my proposal, and is gone to break it to the Marquis."

"Ah! Wretched princess!" cried Isabella. "What hast thou done! What ruin has thy inadvertent goodness been preparing for thyself, for me, and for Matilda!"

"Ruin from me to you and to my child!" said Hippolita "what can this mean?"

"Alas!" said Isabella, "the purity of your own heart prevents your seeing the depravity of others. Manfred, your lord, that impious man—"

"Hold," said Hippolita. "You must not in my presence, young

lady, mention Manfred with disrespect: he is my Lord and husband, and—"

"Will not long be so," said Isabella, "if his wicked purposes can be carried into execution."

"This language amazes me," said Hippolita. "Your feeling, Isabella, is warm; but until this hour I never knew it betray you into intemperance. What deed of Manfred authorises you to treat him as a murderer, an assassin?"

"Thou virtuous, and too credulous Princess!" replied Isabella. "It is not thy life he aims at—it is to separate himself from thee! To divorce thee! To—"

"To divorce me!" "To divorce my mother!" cried Hippolita and Matilda at once.

"Yes," said Isabella, "and to complete his crime, he meditates—I cannot speak it!"

"What can surpass what thou hast already uttered?" said Matilda.

Hippolita was silent. Grief choked her speech; and the recollection of Manfred's late ambiguous discourses confirmed what she heard.

"Excellent, dear lady! Madam! Mother!" cried Isabella, flinging herself at Hippolita's feet in a transport of passion. "Trust me, believe me, I will die a thousand deaths sooner than consent to injure you, than yield to so odious—oh!—"

"This is too much!" cried Hippolita. "What crimes does one crime suggest! Rise, dear Isabella; I do not doubt your virtue. Oh! Matilda, this stroke is too heavy for thee! Weep not, my child; and not a murmur, I charge thee. Remember, he is thy father still!"

"But you are my mother too," said Matilda fervently, "and you are virtuous, you are guiltless!—Oh! Must not I, must not I complain?"

"You must not," said Hippolita. "Come, all will yet be well. Manfred, in the agony for the loss of thy brother, knew not what he said; perhaps Isabella misunderstood him; his heart is good—and, my child, thou knowest not all! There is a destiny hangs over us; the hand of Providence is stretched out; oh! Could I but save thee from the wreck! Yes," continued she in a firmer tone, "perhaps the sacrifice of myself may atone for all; I will go and offer myself to this divorce—it boots not what becomes of me. I will withdraw into the neighbouring monastery, and waste the remainder of life in prayers and tears for my child and—the Prince!"

"Thou art as much too good for this world," said Isabella, "as Manfred is execrable; but think not, lady, that thy weakness shall determine for me. I swear, hear me all ye angels—"

"Stop, I adjure thee," cried Hippolita. "Remember thou dost not depend on thyself; thou hast a father."

"My father is too pious, too noble," interrupted Isabella, "to command an impious deed. But should he command it; can a father enjoin a cursed act? I was contracted to the son, can I wed the father? No, madam, no; force should not drag me to Manfred's hated bed. I loathe him, I abhor him: divine and human laws forbid—and my friend, my dearest Matilda! Would I wound her tender soul by injuring her adored mother? My own mother—I never have known another"—

"Oh! She is the mother of both!" cried Matilda. "Can we, can we, Isabella, adore her too much?"

"My lovely children," said the touched Hippolita, "your tenderness overpowers me—but I must not give way to it. It is not ours to make election for ourselves: Heaven, our fathers, and our husbands must decide for us. Have patience until you hear what Manfred and Frederic have determined. If the Marquis accepts Matilda's hand, I know she will readily obey. Heaven may interpose and prevent the rest. What means my child?" continued she, seeing Matilda fall at her feet with a flood of speechless tears— "But no; answer me not, my daughter: I must not hear a word against the pleasure of thy father."

"Oh! Doubt not my obedience, my dreadful obedience to him

and to you!" said Matilda. "But can I, most respected of women, can I experience all this tenderness, this world of goodness, and conceal a thought from the best of mothers?"

"What art thou going to utter?" said Isabella trembling. "Recollect thyself, Matilda."

"No, Isabella," said the Princess, "I should not deserve this incomparable parent, if the inmost recesses of my soul harboured a thought without her permission—nay, I have offended her; I have suffered a passion to enter my heart without her avowal— but here I disclaim it; here I vow to Heaven and her—"

"My child! My child," said Hippolita, "what words are these! What new calamities has fate in store for us! Thou, a passion? Thou, in this hour of destruction—"

"Oh! I see all my guilt!" said Matilda. "I abhor myself, if I cost my mother a pang. She is the dearest thing I have on earth—Oh! I will never, never behold him more!"

"Isabella," said Hippolita, "thou art conscious to this unhappy secret, whatever it is. Speak!"

"What!" cried Matilda. "Have I so forfeited my mother's love, that she will not permit me even to speak my own guilt? Oh! Wretched, wretched Matilda!"

"Thou art too cruel," said Isabella to Hippolita. "Canst thou behold this anguish of a virtuous mind, and not commiserate it?"

"Not pity my child!" said Hippolita, catching Matilda in her arms. "Oh! I know she is good, she is all virtue, all tenderness, and duty. I do forgive thee, my excellent, my only hope!"

The princesses then revealed to Hippolita their mutual inclination for Theodore, and the purpose of Isabella to resign him to Matilda. Hippolita blamed their imprudence, and showed them the improbability that either father would consent to bestow his heiress on so poor a man, though nobly born. Some comfort it gave her to find their passion of so recent a date, and that Theodore had had but little cause to suspect it in either. She strictly enjoined them to avoid all correspondence with him. This

Matilda fervently promised: but Isabella, who flattered herself that she meant no more than to promote his union with her friend, could not determine to avoid him; and made no reply.

"I will go to the convent," said Hippolita, "and order new masses to be said for a deliverance from these calamities."

"Oh! My mother," said Matilda, "you mean to quit us: you mean to take sanctuary, and to give my father an opportunity of pursuing his fatal intention. Alas! On my knees I supplicate you to forbear; will you leave me a prey to Frederic? I will follow you to the convent."

"Be at peace, my child," said Hippolita. "I will return instantly. I will never abandon thee, until I know it is the will of Heaven, and for thy benefit."

"Do not deceive me," said Matilda. "I will not marry Frederic until thou commandest it. Alas! What will become of me?"

"Why that exclamation?" said Hippolita. "I have promised thee to return—"

"Ah! My mother," replied Matilda, "stay and save me from myself. A frown from thee can do more than all my father's severity. I have given away my heart, and you alone can make me recall it."

"No more," said Hippolita. "Thou must not relapse, Matilda."

"I can quit Theodore," said she, "but must I wed another? Let me attend thee to the altar, and shut myself from the world for ever."

"Thy fate depends on thy father," said Hippolita. "I have ill-bestowed my tenderness, if it has taught thee to revere aught beyond him. Adieu! My child: I go to pray for thee."

Hippolita's real purpose was to demand of Jerome, whether in conscience she might not consent to the divorce. She had oft urged Manfred to resign the principality, which the delicacy of her conscience rendered an hourly burthen to her. These scruples concurred to make the separation from her husband appear less dreadful to her than it would have seemed in any other situation.

Jerome, at quitting the castle overnight, had questioned Theodore severely why he had accused him to Manfred of being privy to his escape. Theodore owned it had been with design to prevent Manfred's suspicion from alighting on Matilda; and added, the holiness of Jerome's life and character secured him from the tyrant's wrath. Jerome was heartily grieved to discover his son's inclination for that princess; and leaving him to his rest, promised in the morning to acquaint him with important reasons for conquering his passion.

Theodore, like Isabella, was too recently acquainted with parental authority to submit to its decisions against the impulse of his heart. He had little curiosity to learn the Friar's reasons, and less disposition to obey them. The lovely Matilda had made stronger impressions on him than filial affection. All night he pleased himself with visions of love; and it was not till late after the morning-office, that he recollected the Friar's commands to attend him at Alfonso's tomb.

"Young man," said Jerome, when he saw him, "this tardiness does not please me. Have a father's commands already so little weight?"

Theodore made awkward excuses, and attributed his delay to having overslept himself.

"And on whom were thy dreams employed?" said the Friar sternly. His son blushed. "Come, come," resumed the Friar, "inconsiderate youth, this must not be; eradicate this guilty passion from thy breast—"

"Guilty passion!" cried Theodore. "Can guilt dwell with innocent beauty and virtuous modesty?"

"It is sinful," replied the Friar, "to cherish those whom Heaven has doomed to destruction. A tyrant's race must be swept from the earth to the third and fourth generation."

"Will Heaven visit the innocent for the crimes of the guilty?" said Theodore. "The fair Matilda has virtues enough—"

"To undo thee," interrupted Jerome. "Hast thou so soon

forgotten that twice the savage Manfred has pronounced thy sentence?"

"Nor have I forgotten, sir," said Theodore, "that the charity of his daughter delivered me from his power. I can forget injuries, but never benefits."

"The injuries thou hast received from Manfred's race," said the Friar, "are beyond what thou canst conceive. Reply not, but view this holy image! Beneath this marble monument rest the ashes of the good Alfonso; a prince adorned with every virtue: the father of his people! The delight of mankind! Kneel, headstrong boy, and list, while a father unfolds a tale of horror that will expel every sentiment from thy soul, but sensations of sacred vengeance— Alfonso! Much injured prince! Let thy unsatisfied shade sit awful on the troubled air, while these trembling lips—Ha! Who comes there?—"

"The most wretched of women!" said Hippolita, entering the choir. "Good Father, art thou at leisure?—But why this kneeling youth? What means the horror imprinted on each countenance? Why at this venerable tomb—alas! Hast thou seen aught?"

"We were pouring forth our orisons to Heaven," replied the Friar, with some confusion, "to put an end to the woes of this deplorable province. Join with us, Lady! Thy spotless soul may obtain an exemption from the judgments which the portents of these days but too speakingly denounce against thy house."

"I pray fervently to Heaven to divert them," said the pious Princess. "Thou knowest it has been the occupation of my life to wrest a blessing for my Lord and my harmless children.—One alas! Is taken from me! Would Heaven but hear me for my poor Matilda! Father! Intercede for her!"

"Every heart will bless her," cried Theodore with rapture.

"Be dumb, rash youth!" said Jerome. "And thou, fond Princess, contend not with the Powers above! The Lord giveth, and the Lord taketh away: bless His holy name, and submit to his decrees."

"I do most devoutly," said Hippolita. "But will He not spare my only comfort? Must Matilda perish too?—Ah! Father, I came—but dismiss thy son. No ear but thine must hear what I have to utter."

"May Heaven grant thy every wish, most excellent Princess!" said Theodore retiring. Jerome frowned.

Hippolita then acquainted the Friar with the proposal she had suggested to Manfred, his approbation of it, and the tender of Matilda that he was gone to make to Frederic. Jerome could not conceal his dislike of the notion, which he covered under pretence of the improbability that Frederic, the nearest of blood to Alfonso, and who was come to claim his succession, would yield to an alliance with the usurper of his right. But nothing could equal the perplexity of the Friar, when Hippolita confessed her readiness not to oppose the separation, and demanded his opinion on the legality of her acquiescence. The Friar caught eagerly at her request of his advice, and without explaining his aversion to the proposed marriage of Manfred and Isabella, he painted to Hippolita in the most alarming colours the sinfulness of her consent, denounced judgments against her if she complied, and enjoined her in the severest terms to treat any such proposition with every mark of indignation and refusal.

Manfred, in the meantime, had broken his purpose to Frederic, and proposed the double marriage. That weak Prince, who had been struck with the charms of Matilda, listened but too eagerly to the offer. He forgot his enmity to Manfred, whom he saw but little hope of dispossessing by force; and flattering himself that no issue might succeed from the union of his daughter with the tyrant, he looked upon his own succession to the principality as facilitated by wedding Matilda. He made faint opposition to the proposal; affecting, for form only, not to acquiesce unless Hippolita should consent to the divorce. Manfred took that upon himself.

Transported with his success, and impatient to see himself in a situation to expect sons, he hastened to his wife's apartment, determined to extort her compliance. He learned with indignation that she was absent at the convent. His guilt suggested to him that she had probably been informed by Isabella of his purpose. He doubted whether her retirement to the convent did not import an intention of remaining there, until she could raise obstacles to their divorce; and the suspicions he had already entertained of Jerome, made him apprehend that the Friar would not only traverse his views, but might have inspired Hippolita with the resolution of talking sanctuary. Impatient to unravel this clue, and to defeat its success, Manfred hastened to the convent, and arrived there as the Friar was earnestly exhorting the Princess never to yield to the divorce.

"Madam," said Manfred, "what business drew you hither? Why did you not await my return from the Marquis?"

"I came to implore a blessing on your councils," replied Hippolita.

"My councils do not need a Friar's intervention," said Manfred. "And of all men living is that hoary traitor the only one whom you delight to confer with?"

"Profane Prince!" said Jerome. "Is it at the altar that thou choosest to insult the servants of the altar?—But, Manfred, thy impious schemes are known. Heaven and this virtuous lady know them—nay, frown not, Prince. The Church despises thy menaces. Her thunders will be heard above thy wrath. Dare to proceed in thy cursed purpose of a divorce, until her sentence be known, and here I lance her anathema at thy head."

"Audacious rebel!" said Manfred, endeavouring to conceal the awe with which the Friar's words inspired him. "Dost thou presume to threaten thy lawful Prince?"

"Thou art no lawful Prince," said Jerome. "Thou art no Prince—go, discuss thy claim with Frederic; and when that is done—"

"It is done," replied Manfred. "Frederic accepts Matilda's hand, and is content to waive his claim, unless I have no male issue"—as he spoke those words three drops of blood fell from the nose of

Alfonso's statue. Manfred turned pale, and the Princess sank on her knees.

"Behold!" said the Friar. "Mark this miraculous indication that the blood of Alfonso will never mix with that of Manfred!"

"My gracious Lord," said Hippolita, "let us submit ourselves to Heaven. Think not thy ever obedient wife rebels against thy authority. I have no will but that of my Lord and the Church. To that revered tribunal let us appeal. It does not depend on us to burst the bonds that unite us. If the Church shall approve the dissolution of our marriage, be it so—I have but few years, and those of sorrow, to pass. Where can they be worn away so well as at the foot of this altar, in prayers for thine and Matilda's safety?"

"But thou shalt not remain here until then," said Manfred. "Repair with me to the castle, and there I will advise on the proper measures for a divorce;—but this meddling Friar comes not thither; my hospitable roof shall never more harbour a traitor— and for thy Reverence's offspring," continued he, "I banish him from my dominions. He, I ween, is no sacred personage, nor under the protection of the Church. Whoever weds Isabella, it shall not be Father Falconara's started-up son."

"They start up," said the Friar, "who are suddenly beheld in the seat of lawful Princes; but they wither away like the grass, and their place knows them no more."

Manfred, casting a look of scorn at the Friar, led Hippolita forth; but at the door of the church whispered one of his attendants to remain concealed about the convent, and bring him instant notice, if any one from the castle should repair thither.

Chapter V.

EVERY reflection which Manfred made on the Friar's behaviour, conspired to persuade him that Jerome was privy to an amour between Isabella and Theodore. But Jerome's new presumption, so dissonant from his former meekness, suggested still deeper apprehensions. The Prince even suspected that the Friar depended on some secret support from Frederic, whose arrival, coinciding with the novel appearance of Theodore, seemed to bespeak a correspondence. Still more was he troubled with the resemblance of Theodore to Alfonso's portrait. The latter he knew had unquestionably died without issue. Frederic had consented to bestow Isabella on him. These contradictions agitated his mind with numberless pangs.

He saw but two methods of extricating himself from his difficulties. The one was to resign his dominions to the Marquis—pride, ambition, and his reliance on ancient prophecies, which had pointed out a possibility of his preserving them to his posterity, combated that thought. The other was to press his marriage with Isabella. After long ruminating on these anxious thoughts, as he marched silently with Hippolita to the castle, he at last discoursed with that Princess on the subject of his disquiet, and used every insinuating and plausible argument to extract her consent to, even her promise of promoting the divorce. Hippolita needed little persuasions to bend her to his pleasure. She endeavoured to win him over to the measure of resigning his dominions; but finding her exhortations fruitless, she assured him, that as far as her conscience would allow, she would raise no opposition to a separation, though without better founded scruples than what he yet alleged, she would not engage to be active in demanding it.

This compliance, though inadequate, was sufficient to raise Manfred's hopes. He trusted that his power and wealth would easily advance his suit at the court of Rome, whither he resolved to engage Frederic to take a journey on purpose. That Prince had discovered so much passion for Matilda, that Manfred hoped to obtain all he wished by holding out or withdrawing his daughter's charms, according as the Marquis should appear more or less disposed to co-operate in his views. Even the absence of Frederic would be a material point gained, until he could take further measures for his security.

Dismissing Hippolita to her apartment, he repaired to that of the Marquis; but crossing the great hall through which he was to pass he met Bianca. The damsel he knew was in the confidence of both the young ladies. It immediately occurred to him to sift her on the subject of Isabella and Theodore. Calling her aside into the recess of the oriel window of the hall, and soothing her with many fair words and promises, he demanded of her whether she knew aught of the state of Isabella's affections.

"I! My Lord! No my Lord—yes my Lord—poor Lady! She is wonderfully alarmed about her father's wounds; but I tell her he will do well; don't your Highness think so?"

"I do not ask you," replied Manfred, "what she thinks about her father; but you are in her secrets. Come, be a good girl and tell me; is there any young man—ha!—you understand me."

"Lord bless me! understand your Highness? No, not I. I told her a few vulnerary herbs and repose—"

"I am not talking," replied the Prince, impatiently, "about her father; I know he will do well."

"Bless me, I rejoice to hear your Highness say so; for though I thought it not right to let my young Lady despond, methought his greatness had a wan look, and a something—I remember when young Ferdinand was wounded by the Venetian—"

"Thou answerest from the point," interrupted Manfred. "But here, take this jewel, perhaps that may fix thy attention—nay, no reverences; my favour shall not stop here—come, tell me truly; how stands Isabella's heart?"

"Well! your Highness has such a way!" said Bianca. "to be sure—but can your Highness keep a secret? If it should ever come out of your lips—"

"It shall not, it shall not," cried Manfred.

"Nay, but swear, your Highness."

"By my halidame,* if it should ever be known that I said it—"

"Why, truth is truth, I do not think my Lady Isabella ever much affectioned my young Lord your son; yet he was a sweet youth as one should see; I am sure, if I had been a Princess—but bless me! I must attend my Lady Matilda; she will marvel what is become of me."

"Stay," cried Manfred. "Thou hast not satisfied my question. Hast thou ever carried any message, any letter?"

"I! Good gracious!" cried Bianca. "I carry a letter? I would not to be a Queen. I hope your Highness thinks, though I am poor, I am honest. Did your Highness never hear what Count Marsigli offered me, when he came a wooing to my Lady Matilda?"

"I have not leisure," said Manfred, "to listen to thy tale. I do not question thy honesty. But it is thy duty to conceal nothing from me. How long has Isabella been acquainted with Theodore?"

"Nay, there is nothing can escape your Highness!" said Bianca. "Not that I know any thing of the matter. Theodore, to be sure,

---

* A "halidame" was a holy relic. This was a common oath of the day.

is a proper young man, and, as my Lady Matilda says, the very image of good Alfonso. Has not your Highness remarked it?"

"Yes, yes,—No—thou torturest me," said Manfred. "Where did they meet? When?"

"Who! My Lady Matilda?" said Bianca.

"No, no, not Matilda: Isabella; when did Isabella first become acquainted with this Theodore!"

"Virgin Mary!" said Bianca. "how should I know?"

"Thou dost know," said Manfred, "and I must know; I will—"

"Lord! your Highness is not jealous of young Theodore!" said Bianca.

"Jealous! no, no. Why should I be jealous? Perhaps I mean to unite them—If I were sure Isabella would have no repugnance."

"Repugnance! No, I'll warrant her," said Bianca, "he is as comely a youth as ever trod on Christian ground. We are all in love with him; there is not a soul in the castle but would be rejoiced to have him for our Prince—I mean, when it shall please Heaven to call your Highness to itself."

"Indeed!" said Manfred. "has it gone so far! oh! this cursed Friar!—but I must not lose time—go, Bianca, attend Isabella; but I charge thee, not a word of what has passed. Find out how she is affected towards Theodore; bring me good news, and that ring has a companion. Wait at the foot of the winding staircase: I am going to visit the Marquis, and will talk further with thee at my return."

Manfred, after some general conversation, desired Frederic to dismiss the two Knights, his companions, having to talk with him on urgent affairs.

As soon as they were alone, he began in artful guise to sound the Marquis on the subject of Matilda; and finding him disposed to his wish, he let drop hints on the difficulties that would attend the celebration of their marriage, unless—At that instant Bianca burst into the room with a wildness in her look and gestures that spoke the utmost terror.

"Oh! My Lord, My Lord!" cried she. "We are all undone! it is come again! it is come again!"

"What is come again?" cried Manfred amazed.

"Oh! the hand! the Giant! the hand!—support me! I am terrified out of my senses," cried Bianca. "I will not sleep in the castle to-night. Where shall I go? My things may come after me to-morrow—would I had been content to wed Francesco! this comes of ambition!"

"What has terrified thee thus, young woman?" said the Marquis. "Thou art safe here; be not alarmed."

"Oh! your Greatness is wonderfully good," said Bianca, "but I dare not—no, pray let me go—I had rather leave everything behind me, than stay another hour under this roof."

"Go to, thou hast lost thy senses," said Manfred. "Interrupt us not; we were communing on important matters—My Lord, this wench is subject to fits—Come with me, Bianca."

"Oh! the Saints! No," said Bianca, "for certain it comes to warn your Highness; why should it appear to me else? I say my prayers morning and evening—oh! if your Highness had believed Diego! 'Tis the same hand that he saw the foot to in the gallery-chamber—Father Jerome has often told us the prophecy would be out one of these days—'Bianca,' said he, 'mark my words—'"

"Thou ravest," said Manfred, in a rage. "Be gone, and keep these fooleries to frighten thy companions."

"What! my Lord," cried Bianca, "do you think I have seen nothing? Go to the foot of the great stairs yourself—as I live I saw it."

"Saw what? Tell us, fair maid, what thou hast seen," said Frederic.

"Can your Highness listen," said Manfred, "to the delirium of a silly wench, who has heard stories of apparitions until she believes them?"

"This is more than fancy," said the Marquis. "Her terror is too natural and too strongly impressed to be the work of imagination. Tell us, fair maiden, what it is has moved thee thus?"

"Yes, my Lord, thank your Greatness," said Bianca. "I believe I look very pale; I shall be better when I have recovered myself—I was going to my Lady Isabella's chamber, by his Highness's order—"

"We do not want the circumstances," interrupted Manfred. "Since his Highness will have it so, proceed; but be brief."

"Lord! your Highness thwarts one so!" replied Bianca. "I fear my hair—I am sure I never in my life—well! as I was telling your Greatness, I was going by his Highness's order to my Lady Isabella's chamber; she lies in the watchet-coloured* chamber, on the right hand, one pair of stairs: so when I came to the great stairs—I was looking on his Highness's present here—"

"Grant me patience!" said Manfred. "Will this wench never come to the point? What imports it to the Marquis, that I gave thee a bauble for thy faithful attendance on my daughter? We want to know what thou sawest."

"I was going to tell your Highness," said Bianca, "if you would permit me. So as I was rubbing the ring—I am sure I had not gone up three steps, but I heard the rattling of armour; for all the world such a clatter as Diego says he heard when the Giant turned him about in the gallery-chamber."

"What Giant is this, my Lord?" said the Marquis. "Is your castle haunted by giants and goblins?"

"Lord! What, has not your Greatness heard the story of the Giant in the gallery-chamber?" cried Bianca. "I marvel his Highness has not told you; mayhap you do not know there is a prophecy—"

"This trifling is intolerable," interrupted Manfred. "Let us dismiss this silly wench, my Lord! We have more important affairs to discuss."

"By your favour," said Frederic, "these are no trifles. The enormous sabre I was directed to in the wood, yon casque, its fellow—are these visions of this poor maiden's brain?"

---

* Light blue.

"So Jaquez thinks, may it please your Greatness," said Bianca. "He says this moon will not be out without our seeing some strange revolution. For my part, I should not be surprised if it was to happen to-morrow; for, as I was saying, when I heard the clattering of armour, I was all in a cold sweat. I looked up, and, if your Greatness will believe me, I saw upon the uppermost banister of the great stairs a hand in armour as big as big. I thought I should have swooned. I never stopped until I came hither—would I were well out of this castle. My Lady Matilda told me but yester-morning that her Highness Hippolita knows something."

"Thou art an insolent!" cried Manfred. "Lord Marquis, it much misgives me that this scene is concerted to affront me. Are my own domestics suborned to spread tales injurious to my honour? Pursue your claim by manly daring; or let us bury our feuds, as was proposed, by the intermarriage of our children. But trust me, it ill becomes a Prince of your bearing to practise on mercenary wenches."

"I scorn your imputation," said Frederic. "Until this hour I never set eyes on this damsel: I have given her no jewel. My Lord, my Lord, your conscience, your guilt accuses you, and would throw the suspicion on me; but keep your daughter, and think no more of Isabella. The judgments already fallen on your house forbid me matching into it."

Manfred, alarmed at the resolute tone in which Frederic delivered these words, endeavoured to pacify him. Dismissing Bianca, he made such submissions to the Marquis, and threw in such artful encomiums on Matilda, that Frederic was once more staggered. However, as his passion was of so recent a date, it could not at once surmount the scruples he had conceived. He had gathered enough from Bianca's discourse to persuade him that Heaven declared itself against Manfred. The proposed marriages too removed his claim to a distance; and the principality of Otranto was a stronger temptation than the contingent reversion of it with Matilda. Still he would not absolutely recede from his engagements; but purposing to gain time, he demanded of Manfred if it was true in fact that Hippolita consented to the divorce. The Prince, transported to find no other obstacle, and depending on his influence over his wife, assured the Marquis it was so, and that he might satisfy himself of the truth from her own mouth.

As they were thus discoursing, word was brought that the banquet was prepared. Manfred conducted Frederic to the great hall, where they were received by Hippolita and the young Princesses. Manfred placed the Marquis next to Matilda, and seated himself between his wife and Isabella. Hippolita comported herself with an easy gravity; but the young ladies were silent and melancholy. Manfred, who was determined to pursue his point with the Marquis in the remainder of the evening, pushed on the feast until it waxed late; affecting unrestrained gaiety, and plying Frederic with repeated goblets of wine. The latter, more upon his guard than Manfred wished, declined his frequent challenges, on pretence of his late loss of blood; while the Prince, to raise his own disordered spirits, and to counterfeit unconcern, indulged himself in plentiful draughts, though not to the intoxication of his senses.

The evening being far advanced, the banquet concluded. Manfred would have withdrawn with Frederic; but the latter pleading weakness and want of repose, retired to his chamber, gallantly telling the Prince that his daughter should amuse his Highness until himself could attend him. Manfred accepted the party, and to the no small grief of Isabella, accompanied her to her apartment. Matilda waited on her mother to enjoy the freshness of the evening on the ramparts of the castle.

Soon as the company were dispersed their several ways, Frederic, quitting his chamber, inquired if Hippolita was alone, and was told by one of her attendants, who had not noticed her going forth, that at that hour she generally withdrew to her oratory, where he probably would find her. The Marquis, during the repast, had beheld Matilda with increase of passion. He now wished to find Hippolita in the disposition her Lord had promised. The portents that had alarmed him were forgotten in his desires. Stealing softly and unobserved to the apartment of Hippolita, he entered it with a resolution to encourage her acquiescence to the divorce, having perceived that Manfred was resolved to make the possession of Isabella an unalterable condition, before he would grant Matilda to his wishes.

The Marquis was not surprised at the silence that reigned in the Princess's apartment. Concluding her, as he had been advertised, in her oratory, he passed on. The door was ajar; the evening gloomy and overcast. Pushing open the door gently, he saw a person kneeling before the altar. As he approached nearer, it seemed not a woman, but one in a long woollen weed, whose back was towards him. The person seemed absorbed in prayer. The Marquis was about to return, when the figure, rising, stood some moments fixed in meditation, without regarding him. The Marquis, expecting the holy person to come forth, and meaning to excuse his uncivil interruption, said,

"Reverend Father, I sought the Lady Hippolita."

"Hippolita!" replied a hollow voice. "Camest thou to this castle to seek Hippolita?" and then the figure, turning slowly round, discovered to Frederic the fleshless jaws and empty sockets of a skeleton, wrapt in a hermit's cowl.

"Angels of grace protect me!" cried Frederic, recoiling.

"Deserve their protection!" said the Spectre. Frederic, falling on his knees, adjured the phantom to take pity on him.

"Dost thou not remember me?" said the apparition. "Remember the wood of Joppa!"

"Art thou that holy hermit?" cried Frederic, trembling. "Can I do aught for thy eternal peace?"

"Wast thou delivered from bondage," said the spectre, "to pursue carnal delights? Hast thou forgotten the buried sabre, and the behest of Heaven engraven on it?"

"I have not, I have not," said Frederic. "But say, blest spirit, what is thy errand to me? What remains to be done?"

"To forget Matilda!" said the apparition; and vanished.

Frederic's blood froze in his veins. For some minutes he remained motionless. Then falling prostrate on his face before the altar, he besought the intercession of every saint for pardon. A flood of tears succeeded to this transport; and the image of the beauteous Matilda rushing in spite of him on his thoughts, he lay on the ground in a conflict of penitence and passion. Ere he could recover from this agony of his spirits, the Princess Hippolita with a taper in her hand entered the oratory alone. Seeing a man without motion on the floor, she gave a shriek, concluding him dead. Her fright brought Frederic to himself. Rising suddenly, his face bedewed with tears, he would have rushed from her presence; but Hippolita stopping him, conjured him in the most plaintive accents to explain the cause of his disorder, and by what strange chance she had found him there in that posture.

"Ah, virtuous Princess!" said the Marquis, penetrated with grief, and stopped.

"For the love of Heaven, my Lord," said Hippolita, "disclose the cause of this transport! What mean these doleful sounds, this alarming exclamation on my name? What woes has Heaven still in store for the wretched Hippolita? Yet silent! By every pitying angel, I adjure thee, noble Prince," continued she, falling at his feet, "to disclose the purport of what lies at thy heart. I see thou feelest for me; thou feelest the sharp pangs that thou inflictest— speak, for pity! Does aught thou knowest concern my child?"

"I cannot speak," cried Frederic, bursting from her. "Oh, Matilda!"

Quitting the Princess thus abruptly, he hastened to his own apartment. At the door of it he was accosted by Manfred, who flushed by wine and love had come to seek him, and to propose to waste some hours of the night in music and revelling. Frederic, offended at an invitation so dissonant from the mood of his soul, pushed him rudely aside, and entering his chamber, flung the door intemperately against Manfred, and bolted it inwards.

The haughty Prince, enraged at this unaccountable behaviour, withdrew in a frame of mind capable of the most fatal excesses. As he crossed the court, he was met by the domestic whom he had planted at the convent as a spy on Jerome and Theodore. This man, almost breathless with the haste he had made, informed his Lord that Theodore, and some lady from the castle were, at that instant, in private conference at the tomb of Alfonso in St. Nicholas's church. He had dogged Theodore thither, but the gloominess of the night had prevented his discovering who the woman was.

Manfred, whose spirits were inflamed, and whom Isabella had driven from her on his urging his passion with too little reserve, did not doubt but the inquietude she had expressed had been occasioned by her impatience to meet Theodore. Provoked by this conjecture, and enraged at her father, he hastened secretly to the great church. Gliding softly between the aisles, and guided by an imperfect gleam of moonshine that shone faintly through the illuminated windows, he stole towards the tomb of Alfonso, to which he was directed by indistinct whispers of the persons he sought. The first sounds he could distinguish were, "Does it, alas! Depend on me? Manfred will never permit our union."

"No, this shall prevent it!" cried the tyrant, drawing his dagger, and plunging it over her shoulder into the bosom of the person that spoke.

"Ah, me, I am slain!" cried Matilda, sinking. "Good Heaven, receive my soul!"

"Savage, inhuman monster, what hast thou done!" cried Theodore, rushing on him, and wrenching his dagger from him.

"Stop, stop thy impious hand!" cried Matilda. "It is my father!"

Manfred, waking as from a trance, beat his breast, twisted his hands in his locks, and endeavoured to recover his dagger from Theodore to despatch himself. Theodore, scarce less distracted, and only mastering the transports of his grief to assist Matilda, had now by his cries drawn some of the monks to his aid. While part of them endeavoured, in concert with the afflicted Theodore, to stop the blood of the dying Princess, the rest prevented Manfred from laying violent hands on himself.

Matilda, resigning herself patiently to her fate, acknowledged with looks of grateful love the zeal of Theodore. Yet oft as her faintness would permit her speech its way, she begged the assistants to comfort her father. Jerome, by this time, had learnt the fatal news, and reached the church. His looks seemed to reproach Theodore, but turning to Manfred, he said,

"Now, tyrant! Behold the completion of woe fulfilled on thy impious and devoted head! The blood of Alfonso cried to Heaven for vengeance; and Heaven has permitted its altar to be polluted by assassination, that thou mightest shed thy own blood at the foot of that Prince's sepulchre!"

"Cruel man!" cried Matilda, "To aggravate the woes of a parent; may Heaven bless my father, and forgive him as I do! My Lord, my gracious Sire, dost thou forgive thy child? Indeed, I came not hither to meet Theodore. I found him praying at this tomb, whither my mother sent me to intercede for thee, for her—dearest father, bless your child, and say you forgive her."

"Forgive thee! Murderous monster!" cried Manfred. "Can assassins forgive? I took thee for Isabella; but Heaven directed my bloody hand to the heart of my child. Oh, Matilda!—I cannot utter it—canst thou forgive the blindness of my rage?"

"I can, I do; and may Heaven confirm it!" said Matilda. "But while I have life to ask it—oh! My mother! What will she feel? Will you comfort her, my Lord? Will you not put her away? Indeed she loves you! Oh, I am faint! Bear me to the castle. Can I live to have her close my eyes?"

Theodore and the monks besought her earnestly to suffer herself to be borne into the convent; but her instances were so pressing to be carried to the castle, that placing her on a litter, they conveyed her thither as she requested. Theodore, supporting her head with his arm, and hanging over her in an agony of despairing love, still endeavoured to inspire her with hopes of life. Jerome, on the other side, comforted her with discourses of Heaven, and holding a crucifix before her, which she bathed with innocent tears, prepared her for her passage to immortality. Manfred, plunged in the deepest affliction, followed the litter in despair.

Ere they reached the castle, Hippolita, informed of the dreadful catastrophe, had flown to meet her murdered child; but when she saw the afflicted procession, the mightiness of her grief deprived her of her senses, and she fell lifeless to the earth in a swoon. Isabella and Frederic, who attended her, were overwhelmed in almost equal sorrow. Matilda alone seemed insensible to her own situation: every thought was lost in tenderness for her mother.

Ordering the litter to stop, as soon as Hippolita was brought to herself, she asked for her father. He approached, unable to speak. Matilda, seizing his hand and her mother's, locked them in her own, and then clasped them to her heart. Manfred could not support this act of pathetic piety. He dashed himself on the ground, and cursed the day he was born. Isabella, apprehensive that these struggles of passion were more than Matilda could support, took upon herself to order Manfred to be borne to his apartment, while she caused Matilda to be conveyed to the nearest chamber. Hippolita, scarce more alive than her daughter, was regardless of everything but her; but when the tender Isabella's care would have likewise removed her, while the surgeons examined Matilda's wound, she cried,

"Remove me! Never, never! I lived but in her, and will expire with her."

Matilda raised her eyes at her mother's voice, but closed them again without speaking. Her sinking pulse and the damp coldness of her hand soon dispelled all hopes of recovery. Theodore followed the surgeons into the outer chamber, and heard them pronounce the fatal sentence with a transport equal to frenzy.

"Since she cannot live mine," cried he, "at least she shall be mine in death! Father! Jerome! Will you not join our hands?"

cried he to the Friar, who, with the Marquis, had accompanied the surgeons.

"What means thy distracted rashness?" said Jerome. "Is this an hour for marriage?"

"It is, it is," cried Theodore. "Alas! There is no other!"

"Young man, thou art too unadvised," said Frederic. "Dost thou think we are to listen to thy fond transports in this hour of fate? What pretensions hast thou to the Princess?"

"Those of a Prince," said Theodore, "of the sovereign of Otranto. This reverend man, my father, has informed me who I am."

"Thou ravest," said the Marquis. "There is no Prince of Otranto but myself, now Manfred, by murder, by sacrilegious murder, has forfeited all pretensions."

"My Lord," said Jerome, assuming an air of command, "he tells you true. It was not my purpose the secret should have been divulged so soon, but fate presses onward to its work. What his hot-headed passion has revealed, my tongue confirms. Know, Prince, that when Alfonso set sail for the Holy Land—"

"Is this a season for explanations?" cried Theodore. "Father, come and unite me to the Princess; she shall be mine! In every other thing I will dutifully obey you. My life! my adored Matilda!" continued Theodore, rushing back into the inner chamber. "Will you not be mine? Will you not bless your—"

Isabella made signs to him to be silent, apprehending the Princess was near her end.

"What, is she dead?" cried Theodore. "Is it possible!"

The violence of his exclamations brought Matilda to herself. Lifting up her eyes, she looked round for her mother.

"Life of my soul, I am here!" cried Hippolita. "Think not I will quit thee!"

"Oh! you are too good," said Matilda. "But weep not for me, my mother! I am going where sorrow never dwells—Isabella, thou hast loved me; wouldst thou not supply my fondness to this dear, dear woman? Indeed I am faint!"

"Oh! my child! my child!" said Hippolita in a flood of tears, "can I not withhold thee a moment?"

"It will not be," said Matilda. "Commend me to Heaven— Where is my father? forgive him, dearest mother—forgive him my death; it was an error. Oh! I had forgotten—dearest mother, I vowed never to see Theodore more—perhaps that has drawn down this calamity—but it was not intentional—can you pardon me?"

"Oh! wound not my agonising soul!" said Hippolita. "Thou never couldst offend me—Alas! she faints! help! help!"

"I would say something more," said Matilda, struggling, "but it cannot be—Isabella—Theodore—for my sake—Oh!—" she expired.

Isabella and her women tore Hippolita from the corse; but Theodore threatened destruction to all who attempted to remove him from it. He printed a thousand kisses on her clay-cold hands, and uttered every expression that despairing love could dictate.

Isabella, in the meantime, was accompanying the afflicted Hippolita to her apartment; but, in the middle of the court, they were met by Manfred, who, distracted with his own thoughts, and anxious once more to behold his daughter, was advancing to the chamber where she lay. As the moon was now at its height, he read in the countenances of this unhappy company the event he dreaded.

"What! Is she dead?" cried he in wild confusion. A clap of thunder at that instant shook the castle to its foundations; the earth rocked, and the clank of more than mortal armour was heard behind. Frederic and Jerome thought the last day was at hand. The latter, forcing Theodore along with them, rushed into the court. The moment Theodore appeared, the walls of the castle behind Manfred were thrown down with a mighty force, and the form of Alfonso, dilated to an immense magnitude, appeared in the centre of the ruins.

"Behold in Theodore the true heir of Alfonso!" said the vision:

And having pronounced those words, accompanied by a clap of thunder, it ascended solemnly towards Heaven, where the clouds parting asunder, the form of St. Nicholas was seen, and receiving Alfonso's shade, they were soon wrapt from mortal eyes in a blaze of glory.

The beholders fell prostrate on their faces, acknowledging the divine will. The first that broke silence was Hippolita.

"My Lord," said she to the desponding Manfred, "behold the vanity of human greatness! Conrad is gone! Matilda is no more! In Theodore we view the true Prince of Otranto. By what miracle he is so I know not—suffice it to us, our doom is pronounced! Shall we not, can we but dedicate the few deplorable hours we have to live, in deprecating the further wrath of Heaven? Heaven ejects us—whither can we fly, but to yon holy cells that yet offer us a retreat."

"Thou guiltless but unhappy woman! unhappy by my crimes!" replied Manfred. "My heart at last is open to thy devout admonitions. Oh! Could—but it cannot be—ye are lost in wonder—let me at last do justice on myself! To heap shame on my own head is all the satisfaction I have left to offer to offended Heaven. My story has drawn down these judgments: Let my confession atone—but, ah! What can atone for usurpation and a murdered child? A child murdered in a consecrated place? List, sirs, and may this bloody record be a warning to future tyrants!"

"Alfonso, ye all know, died in the Holy Land—ye would interrupt me; ye would say he came not fairly to his end—it is most true—why else this bitter cup which Manfred must drink to the dregs. Ricardo, my grandfather, was his chamberlain—I would draw a veil over my ancestor's crimes—but it is in vain! Alfonso died by poison. A fictitious will declared Ricardo his heir. His crimes pursued him—yet he lost no Conrad, no Matilda! I pay the price of usurpation for all! A storm overtook him. Haunted by his guilt he vowed to St. Nicholas to found a church and two convents, if he lived to reach Otranto. The sacrifice was accepted:

the saint appeared to him in a dream, and promised that Ricardo's posterity should reign in Otranto until the rightful owner should be grown too large to inhabit the castle, and as long as issue male from Ricardo's loins should remain to enjoy it—alas! Alas! Nor male nor female, except myself, remains of all his wretched race! I have done—the woes of these three days speak the rest. How this young man can be Alfonso's heir I know not—yet I do not doubt it. His are these dominions; I resign them—yet I knew not Alfonso had an heir—I question not the will of Heaven—poverty and prayer must fill up the woeful space, until Manfred shall be summoned to Ricardo."

"What remains is my part to declare," said Jerome. "When Alfonso set sail for the Holy Land he was driven by a storm to the coast of Sicily. The other vessel, which bore Ricardo and his train, as your Lordship must have heard, was separated from him."

"It is most true," said Manfred, "and the title you give me is more than an outcast can claim—well! Be it so—proceed."

Jerome blushed, and continued. "For three months Lord Alfonso was wind-bound in Sicily. There he became enamoured of a fair virgin named Victoria. He was too pious to tempt her to forbidden pleasures. They were married. Yet deeming this amour incongruous with the holy vow of arms by which he was bound, he determined to conceal their nuptials until his return from the Crusade, when he purposed to seek and acknowledge her for his lawful wife. He left her pregnant. During his absence she was delivered of a daughter. But scarce had she felt a mother's pangs ere she heard the fatal rumour of her Lord's death, and the succession of Ricardo. What could a friendless, helpless woman do? Would her testimony avail?—Yet, my Lord, I have an authentic writing—"

"It needs not," said Manfred. "The horrors of these days, the vision we have but now seen, all corroborate thy evidence beyond a thousand parchments. Matilda's death and my expulsion—"

"Be composed, my Lord," said Hippolita. "This holy man did not mean to recall your griefs." Jerome proceeded.

"I shall not dwell on what is needless. The daughter of which Victoria was delivered, was at her maturity bestowed in marriage on me. Victoria died; and the secret remained locked in my breast. Theodore's narrative has told the rest."

The Friar ceased. The disconsolate company retired to the remaining part of the castle. In the morning Manfred signed his abdication of the principality, with the approbation of Hippolita, and each took on them the habit of religion in the neighbouring convents. Frederic offered his daughter to the new Prince, which Hippolita's tenderness for Isabella concurred to promote. But Theodore's grief was too fresh to admit the thought of another love; and it was not until after frequent discourses with Isabella of his dear Matilda, that he was persuaded he could know no happiness but in the society of one with whom he could for ever indulge the melancholy that had taken possession of his soul.

FINIS.

The Old English Baron

by Clara Reeve

PREFACE.

AS this Story is of a species which, though not new, is out of the common track, it has been thought necessary to point out some circumstances to the reader, which will elucidate the design, and, it is hoped, will induce him to form a favourable, as well as a right judgment of the work before him.

This Story is the literary offspring of *The Castle of Otranto*, written upon the same plan, with a design to unite the most attractive and interesting circumstances of the ancient Romance and modern Novel, at the same time it assumes a character and manner of its own, that differs from both; it is distinguished by the appellation of a Gothic Story, being a picture of Gothic times and manners. Fictitious stories have been the delight of all times and all countries, by oral tradition in barbarous, by writing in more civilized ones; and although some persons of wit and learning have condemned them indiscriminately, I would venture to affirm, that even those who so much affect to despise them under one form, will receive and embrace them under another.

Thus, for instance, a man shall admire and almost adore the Epic poems of the Ancients, and yet despise and execrate the ancient Romances, which are only Epics in prose.

History represents human nature as it is in real life, alas, too often a melancholy retrospect! Romance displays only the amiable side of the picture; it shews the pleasing features, and throws a veil over the blemishes: Mankind are naturally pleased with what gratifies their vanity; and vanity, like all other passions of the human heart, may be rendered subservient to good and useful purposes.

I confess that it may be abused, and become an instrument to corrupt the manners and morals of mankind; so may poetry, so may plays, so may every kind of composition; but that will prove nothing more than the old saying lately revived by the philosophers the most in fashion, "that every earthly thing has two handles."

The business of Romance is, first, to excite the attention; and secondly, to direct it to some useful, or at least innocent, end: Happy the writer who attains both these points, like Richardson! And not unfortunate, or undeserving praise, he who gains only the latter, and furnishes out an entertainment for the reader!

Having, in some degree, opened my design, I beg leave to conduct my reader back again, till he comes within view of The Castle of Otranto; a work which, as already has been observed, is an attempt to unite the various merits and graces of the ancient Romance and modern Novel. To attain this end, there is required a sufficient degree of the marvellous, to excite the attention; enough of the manners of real life, to give an air of probability to the work; and enough of the pathetic, to engage the heart in its behalf.

The book we have mentioned is excellent in the two last points, but has a redundancy in the first; the opening excites the attention very strongly; the conduct of the story is artful and judicious; the characters are admirably drawn and supported; the diction polished and elegant; yet, with all these brilliant advantages, it palls upon the mind (though it does not upon the ear); and the reason is obvious, the machinery is so violent, that it destroys the effect it is intended to excite. Had the story been kept within the utmost *verge* of probability, the effect had been preserved, without losing the least circumstance that excites or detains the attention.

For instance; we can conceive, and allow of, the appearance of a ghost; we can even dispense with an enchanted sword and helmet; but then they must keep within certain limits of credibility: A sword so large as to require an hundred men to lift it; a helmet that by its own weight forces a passage through a court-yard into an arched vault, big enough for a man to go through; a picture that walks out of its frame; a skeleton ghost in a hermit's cowl:— When your expectation is wound up to the highest pitch, these circumstances take it down with a witness, destroy the work of imagination, and, instead of attention, excite laughter. I was both surprised and vexed to find the enchantment dissolved, which I wished might continue to the end of the book; and several of its readers have confessed the same disappointment to me: The beauties are so numerous, that we cannot bear the defects, but want it to be perfect in all respects.

In the course of my observations upon this singular book, it seemed to me that it was possible to compose a work upon the same plan, wherein these defects might be avoided; and the *keeping*, as in *painting*, might be preserved.

But then I began to fear it might happen to me as to certain translators, and imitators of Shakespeare; the unities may be preserved, while the spirit is evaporated. However, I ventured to attempt it; I read the beginning to a circle of friends of approved judgment, and by their approbation was encouraged to proceed, and to finish it.

By the advice of the same friends I printed the First Edition in the country, where it circulated chiefly, very few copies being sent to London, and being thus encouraged, I have determined to offer a second Edition to that public which has so often rewarded the efforts of those, who have endeavoured to contribute to its entertainment.

The work has lately undergone a revision and correction, the

former Edition being very incorrect; and by the earnest solici-
tation of several friends, for whose judgment I have the greatest
deference, I have consented to a change of the title from the
Champion of Virtue to *The Old English Baron*:—as that character
is thought to be the principal one in the story.

I have also been prevailed upon, though with extreme reluctance, to suffer my name to appear in the title-page; and I do now,
with the utmost respect and diffidence, submit the whole to the
candour of the Public.

—*Clara Reeve.*

THE OLD ENGLISH BARON:
A GOTHIC STORY.

IN the minority of Henry the Sixth, King of England, when the renowned John, Duke of Bedford was Regent of France, and Humphrey, the good Duke of Gloucester, was Protector of England, a worthy knight, called Sir Philip Harclay, returned from his travels to England, his native country. He had served under the glorious King Henry the Fifth[*] with distinguished valour, had acquired an honourable fame, and was no less esteemed for Christian virtues than for deeds of chivalry. After the death of his prince, he entered into the service of the Greek emperor,[†] and distinguished his courage against the encroachments of the Saracens. In a battle there, he took prisoner a certain gentleman, by name M. Zadisky, of Greek extraction, but brought up by a Saracen officer; this man he converted to the Christian faith; after which he bound him to himself by the ties of friendship and gratitude, and he resolved to continue with his benefactor. After thirty years travel and warlike service, he determined to return to his native land, and to spend the remainder

---

[*] Henry V died in 1422.

[†] Sir Philip's service would have been to Manuel II Palaiologos (1350–1425), who was the Byzantine emperor from 1391 until his death. The Byzantine empire was constantly at war with the Ottoman empire (the "Saracens"), and characteristically Manuel II died at the hands of the Turks.

of his life in peace; and, by devoting himself to works of piety and charity, prepare for a better state hereafter.

This noble knight had, in his early youth, contracted a strict friendship with the only son of the Lord Lovel, a gentleman of eminent virtues and accomplishments. During Sir Philip's residence in foreign countries, he had frequently written to his friend, and had for a time received answers; the last informed him of the death of old Lord Lovel, and the marriage of the young one; but from that time he had heard no more from him. Sir Philip imputed it not to neglect or forgetfulness, but to the difficulties of intercourse, common at that time to all travellers and adventurers. When he was returning home, he resolved, after looking into his family affairs, to visit the Castle of Lovel, and enquire into the situation of his friend. He landed in Kent, attended by his Greek friend and two faithful servants, one of which was maimed by the wounds he had received in the defence of his master.

Sir Philip went to his family seat in Yorkshire. He found his mother and sister were dead, and his estates sequestered in the hands of commissioners appointed by the Protector.* He was obliged to prove the reality of his claim, and the identity of his person (by the testimony of some of the old servants of his family), after which every thing was restored to him. He took possession of his own house, established his household, settled the old servants in their former stations, and placed those he brought home in the upper offices of his family. He then left his friend to superintend his domestic affairs; and, attended by only one of his old servants, he set out for the Castle of Lovel, in the west of England. They travelled by easy journeys; but, towards the evening of the second day, the servant was so ill and fatigued he could go no further; he stopped at an inn where he grew worse every hour, and the next day expired. Sir Philip was under great concern for the loss of his servant, and some for himself, being

---

* Henry VI ascended to the throne at the age of 9 months. The "Protectors" were regents who served until his sixteenth birthday.

alone in a strange place; however he took courage, ordered his servant's funeral, attended it himself, and, having shed a tear of humanity over his grave, proceeded alone on his journey.

As he drew near the estate of his friend, he began to enquire of every one he met, whether the Lord Lovel resided at the seat of his ancestors? He was answered by one, he did not know; by another, he could not tell; by a third, that he never heard of such a person. Sir Philip thought it strange that a man of Lord Lovel's consequence should be unknown in his own neighbourhood, and where his ancestors had usually resided. He ruminated on the uncertainty of human happiness. "This world," said he, "has nothing for a wise man to depend upon. I have lost all my relations, and most of my friends; and am even uncertain whether any are remaining. I will, however, be thankful for the blessings that are spared to me; and I will endeavour to replace those that I have lost. If my friend lives, he shall share my fortune with me; his children shall have the reversion of it; and I will share his comforts in return. But perhaps my friend may have met with troubles that have made him disgusted with the world; perhaps he has buried his amiable wife, or his promising children; and, tired of public life, he is retired into a monastery. At least, I will know what all this silence means."

When he came within a mile of the Castle of Lovel, he stopped at a cottage and asked for a draught of water; a peasant, master of the house, brought it, and asked if his honour would alight and take a moment's refreshment. Sir Philip accepted his offer, being resolved to make farther enquiry before he approached the castle. He asked the same questions of him, that he had before of others.

"Which Lord Lovel," said the man, "does your honour enquire after?"

"The man whom I knew was called Arthur," said Sir Philip.

"Ay," said the Peasant, "he was the only surviving son of Richard, Lord Lovel, as I think?"

"Very true, friend, he was so."

"Alas, sir," said the man, "he is dead! He survived his father but a short time."

"Dead! Say you? How long since?"

"About fifteen years, to the best of my remembrance."

Sir Philip sighed deeply.

"Alas!" said he. "What do we, by living long, but survive all our friends! But pray tell me how he died?"

"I will, sir, to the best of my knowledge. An't please your honour, I heard say, that he attended the King when he went against the Welch rebels, and he left his lady big with child; and so there was a battle fought, and the King got the better of the rebels. There came first a report that none of the officers were killed; but a few days after there came a messenger with an account very different, that several were wounded, and that the Lord Lovel was slain; which sad news overset us all with sorrow, for he was a noble gentleman, a bountiful master, and the delight of all the neighbourhood."

"He was indeed," said Sir Philip, "all that is amiable and good; he was my dear and noble friend, and I am inconsolable for his loss. But the unfortunate lady, what became of her?"

"Why, a'nt please your honour, they said she died of grief for the loss of her husband; but her death was kept private for a time, and we did not know it for certain till some weeks afterwards."

"The will of Heaven be obeyed!" said Sir Philip. "But who succeeded to the title and estate?"

"The next heir," said the peasant, "a kinsman of the deceased, Sir Walter Lovel by name."

"I have seen him," said Sir Philip, "formerly; but where was he when these events happened?"

"At the Castle of Lovel, sir; he came there on a visit to the lady, and waited there to receive my Lord, at his return from Wales; when the news of his death arrived, Sir Walter did every thing in his power to comfort her, and some said he was to marry her; but she refused to be comforted, and took it so to heart that she died."

"And does the present Lord Lovel reside at the castle?"

"No, sir."

"Who then?"

"The Lord Baron Fitz-Owen."

"And how came Sir Walter to leave the seat of his ancestors?"

"Why, sir, he married his sister to this said Lord; and so he sold the Castle to him, and went away, and built himself a house in the north country, as far as Northumberland, I think they call it."

"That is very strange!" said Sir Philip.

"So it is, please your honour; but this is all I know about it."

"I thank you, friend, for your intelligence; I have taken a long journey to no purpose, and have met with nothing but cross accidents. This life is, indeed, a pilgrimage! Pray direct me the nearest way to the next monastery."

"Noble sir," said the peasant, "it is full five miles off, the night is coming on, and the ways are bad; I am but a poor man, and cannot entertain your honour as you are used to; but if you will enter my poor cottage, that, and every thing in it, are at your service."

"My honest friend, I thank you heartily," said Sir Philip. "Your kindness and hospitality might shame many of higher birth and breeding; I will accept your kind offer;—but pray let me know the name of my host?"

"John Wyatt, sir; an honest man though a poor one, and a Christian man, though a sinful one."

"Whose cottage is this?"

"It belongs to the Lord Fitz-Owen."

"What family have you?"

"A wife, two sons and a daughter, who will all be proud to wait upon your honour; let me hold your honour's stirrup whilst you alight."

He seconded these words by the proper action, and having assisted his guest to dismount, he conducted him into his house, called his wife to attend him, and then led his horse under a poor shed, that served him as a stable. Sir Philip was fatigued in body and mind, and was glad to repose himself anywhere. The courtesy of his host engaged his attention, and satisfied his wishes. He soon after returned, followed by a youth of about eighteen years.

"Make haste, John," said the father, "and be sure you say neither more nor less than what I have told you."

"I will, father," said the lad; and immediately set off, ran like a buck across the fields, and was out of sight in an instant.

"I hope, friend," said Sir Philip, "you have not sent your son to provide for my entertainment; I am a soldier, used to lodge and fare hard; and, if it were otherwise, your courtesy and kindness would give a relish to the most ordinary food."

"I wish heartily," said Wyatt, "it was in my power to entertain your honour as you ought to be; but, as I cannot do so, I will, when my son returns, acquaint you with the errand I sent him on."

After this they conversed together on common subjects, like fellow-creatures of the same natural form and endowments, though different kinds of education had given a conscious superiority to the one, a conscious inferiority to the other; and the due respect was paid by the latter, without being exacted by the former. In about half an hour young John returned.

"Thou hast made haste," said the father.

"Not more than good speed," quoth the son.

"Tell us, then, how you speed?"

"Shall I tell all that passed?" said John.

"All," said the father. "I don't want to hide any thing."

John stood with his cap in his hand, and thus told his tale—

"I went straight to the castle as fast as I could run; it was my hap to light on young Master Edmund first, so I told him just as you had me, that a noble gentleman was come a long journey from foreign parts to see the Lord Lovel, his friend; and, having lived abroad many years, he did not know that he was dead, and that the castle was fallen into other hands; that upon hearing these tidings he was much grieved and disappointed, and wanting a night's lodging, to rest himself before he returned to his own home, he was fain to take up with one at our cottage; that my father thought my Lord would be angry with him, if he were not told of the stranger's journey and intentions, especially to let such a man lie at our cottage, where he could neither be lodged nor entertained according to his quality."

Here John stopped, and his father exclaimed, "A good lad! you did your errand very well; and tell us the answer."

John proceeded. "Master Edmund ordered me some beer, and went to acquaint my Lord of the message; he stayed a while, and then came back to me.—'John,' said he, 'tell the noble stranger that the Baron Fitz-Owen greets him well, and desires him to rest assured, that though Lord Lovel is dead, and the castle fallen into other hands, his friends will always find a welcome there; and my Lord desires that he will accept of a lodging there, while he remains in this country.'—So I came away directly, and made haste to deliver my errand."

Sir Philip expressed some dissatisfaction at this mark of old Wyatt's respect.

"I wish," said he, "that you had acquainted me with your intention before you sent to inform the Baron I was here. I choose rather to lodge with you; and I propose to make amends for the trouble I shall give you."

"Pray, sir, don't mention it," said the peasant, "you are as welcome as myself; I hope no offence; the only reason of my sending was, because I am both unable and unworthy to entertain your honour."

"I am sorry," said Sir Philip, "you should think me so dainty; I am a Christian soldier; and him I acknowledge for my Prince and Master, accepted the invitations of the poor, and washed the feet of his disciples. Let us say no more on this head; I am resolved to stay this night in your cottage, tomorrow I will wait on the Baron, and thank him for his hospitable invitation."

"That shall be as your honour pleases, since you will condescend to stay here. John, do you run back and acquaint my Lord of it."

"Not so," said Sir Philip, "it is now almost dark."

"'Tis no matter," said John, "I can go it blindfold."

Sir Philip then gave him a message to the Baron in his own name, acquainting him that he would pay his respects to him in the morning. John flew back the second time, and soon returned with new commendations from the Baron, and that he would expect him on the morrow. Sir Philip gave him an angel of gold, and praised his speed and abilities.

He supped with Wyatt and his family upon new-laid eggs and rashers of bacon, with the highest relish. They praised the Creator for His gifts, and acknowledged they were unworthy of the least of His blessings. They gave the best of their two lofts up to Sir Philip, the rest of the family slept in the other, the old woman and her daughter in the bed, the father and his two sons upon clean straw. Sir Philip's bed was of a better kind, and yet much inferior to his usual accommodations; nevertheless the good knight slept as well in Wyatt's cottage, as he could have done in a palace.

During his sleep, many strange and incoherent dreams arose to his imagination. He thought he received a message from his friend Lord Lovel, to come to him at the castle; that he stood at the gate and received him, that he strove to embrace him, but could not; but that he spoke to this effect:—"Though I have been dead these fifteen years, I still command here, and none can enter these gates without my permission; know that it is I that invite, and bid you welcome; the hopes of my house rest upon you." Upon this he bid Sir Philip follow him; he led him through many rooms, till at last he sunk down, and Sir Philip thought he still followed him, till he came into a dark and frightful cave, where he disappeared, and in his stead he beheld a complete suit of armour stained with blood, which belonged to his friend, and he thought he heard dismal groans from beneath. Presently after, he thought he was hurried away by an invisible hand, and led into a wild heath, where the people were inclosing the ground, and making preparations for two combatants; the trumpet sounded, and a voice called out still louder, "Forbear! It is not permitted to be revealed till the time is ripe for the event; wait with patience on the decrees of heaven." He was then transported to his own house, where, going into an unfrequented room, he was again met by his friend, who was living, and in all the bloom of youth, as when he first knew him: He started at the sight, and awoke. The sun shone upon his curtains, and, perceiving it was day, he sat up, and recollected where he was. The images that impressed his sleeping fancy remained strongly on his mind waking; but his reason strove to disperse them; it was natural that the story he had heard should create these ideas, that they should wait on him in his sleep, and that every dream should bear some relation to his deceased friend. The sun dazzled his eyes, the birds serenaded him and diverted his attention, and a woodbine forced its way through the window, and regaled his sense of smelling with its fragrance. He arose, paid his devotions to Heaven, and then carefully descended the narrow stairs, and went out at the door of the cottage. There he saw the industrious wife and daughter of old Wyatt at their morning work, the one milking her cow, the other feeding her poultry. He asked for a draught of milk, which, with a slice of rye bread, served to break his fast. He walked about the fields alone; for old Wyatt and his two sons were gone out to their daily labour. He was soon called back by the good woman, who told him that a servant from the Baron waited to conduct him to the Castle. He took leave of Wyatt's wife, telling her he would see her again before he left the country. The daughter fetched his horse, which he mounted, and set forward with the servant, of whom he asked many questions concerning his master's family.

"How long have you lived with the Baron?"

"Ten years."

"Is he a good master?"

"Yes, Sir, and also a good husband and father."

"What family has he?"

"Three sons and a daughter."

"What age are they of?"

"The eldest son is in his seventeenth year, the second in his sixteenth, the others several years younger; but beside these my Lord has several young gentlemen brought up with his own sons, two of which are his nephews; he keeps in his house a learned clerk to teach them languages; and as for all bodily exercises, none come near them; there is a fletcher to teach them the use of the cross-bow; a master to teach them to ride; another the use of the sword; another learns them to dance; and then they wrestle and run, and have such activity in all their motions, that it does one good to see them; and my Lord thinks nothing too much to bestow on their education."

"Truly," says Sir Philip, "he does the part of a good parent, and I honour him greatly for it; but are the young gentlemen of a promising disposition?"

"Yes indeed, Sir," answered the servant, "the young gentlemen, my Lord's sons, are hopeful youths; but yet there is one who is thought to exceed them all, though he is the son of a poor labourer."

"And who is he?" said the knight.

"One Edmund Twyford, the son of a cottager in our village; he is to be sure as fine a youth as ever the sun shone upon, and of so sweet a disposition that nobody envies his good fortune."

"What good fortune does he enjoy?"

"Why, Sir, about two years ago, my Lord, at his sons request, took him into his own family, and gives him the same education as his own children; the young Lords doat upon him, especially Master William, who is about his own age: It is supposed that he will attend the young Lords when they go to the wars, which my Lord intends they shall by and by."

"What you tell me," said Sir Philip, "increases every minute my respect for your Lord; he is an excellent father and master, he seeks out merit in obscurity; he distinguishes and rewards it,—I honour him with all my heart."

In this manner they conversed together till they came within view of the castle. In a field near the house they saw a company of youths, with crossbows in their hands, shooting at a mark.

"There," said the servant, "are our young gentlemen at their exercises."

Sir Philip stopped his horse to observe them; he heard two or three of them cry out, "Edmund is the victor! He wins the prize!"

"I must," said Sir Philip, "take a view of this Edmund."

He jumped off his horse, gave the bridle to the servant, and walked into the field. The young gentlemen came up, and paid their respects to him; he apologized for intruding upon their sports, and asked which was the victor? Upon which the youth he spoke to beckoned to another, who immediately advanced, and made his obeisance; As he drew near, Sir Philip fixed his eyes upon him, with so much attention, that he seemed not to observe his courtesy and address. At length he recollected himself, and said, "What is your name, young man?"

"Edmund Twyford," replied the youth, "and I have the honour to attend upon the Lord Fitz-Owen's sons."

"Pray, noble sir," said the youth who first addressed Sir Philip, "are not you the stranger who is expected by my father?"

"I am, sir," answered he, "and I go to pay my respects to him."

"Will you excuse our attendance, Sir? We have not yet finished our exercises."

"My dear youth," said Sir Philip, "no apology is necessary; but will you favour me with your proper name, that I may know to whose courtesy I am obliged?"

"My name is William Fitz-Owen; that gentleman is my eldest brother, Master Robert; that other my kinsman, Master Richard Wenlock."

"Very well; I thank you, gentle Sir; I beg you not to stir another step, your servant holds my horse."

"Farewell, Sir," said Master William. "I hope we shall have the pleasure of meeting you at dinner."

The youths returned to their sports, and Sir Philip mounted his horse and proceeded to the castle; he entered it with a deep sigh, and melancholy recollections. The Baron received him with the utmost respect and courtesy. He gave a brief account of the principal events that had happened in the family of Lovel during his absence; he spoke of the late Lord Lovel with respect, of the present with the affection of a brother. Sir Philip, in return, gave a brief recital of his own adventures abroad, and of the disagreeable circumstances he had met with since his return home; he pathetically lamented the loss of all his friends, not forgetting that of his faithful servant on the way; saying he could be contented to give up the world, and retire to a religious house, but that he was withheld by the consideration, that some who depended entirely upon him, would want his presence and assistance; and, beside that, he thought he might be of service to many others. The Baron agreed with him in opinion, that a man was of much more service to the world who continued in it, than one who retired from it, and gave his fortune to the Church, whose servants did not always make the best use of it. Sir Philip then turned the conversation, and congratulated the Baron on his hopeful family; he praised their persons and address, and warmly applauded the care he bestowed on their education. The Baron listened with pleasure to the honest approbation of a worthy heart, and enjoyed the true happiness of a parent.

Sir Philip then made further enquiry concerning Edmund, whose appearance had struck him with an impression in his favour.

"That boy," said the Baron, "is the son of a cottager in this neighbourhood; his uncommon merit, and gentleness of manners, distinguish him from those of his own class; from his childhood he attracted the notice and affection of all that knew him; he was beloved everywhere but at his father's house, and there it should seem that his merits were his crimes; for the peasant, his father, hated him, treated him severely, and at length threatened to turn him out of doors; he used to run here and there on errands for my people, and at length they obliged me to take notice of him; my sons earnestly desired I would take him into my family; I did so about two years ago, intending to make him their servant; but his extraordinary genius and disposition have obliged me to look upon him in a superior light; perhaps I may incur the censure of many people, by giving him so many advantages, and treating him as the companion of my children; his merit must justify or condemn my partiality for him; however, I trust that I have secured to my children a faithful servant of the upper kind, and a useful friend to my family."

Sir Philip warmly applauded his generous host, and wished to be a sharer in his bounty to that fine youth, whose appearance indicated all the qualities that had endeared him to his companions.

At the hour of dinner the young men presented themselves before their Lord, and his guest. Sir Philip addressed himself to Edmund; he asked him many questions, and received modest and intelligent answers, and he grew every minute more pleased with him. After dinner the youths withdrew with their tutor to pursue their studies. Sir Philip sat for some time wrapt up in meditation. After some minutes, the Baron asked him, if he might not be favoured with the fruits of his contemplations?

"You shall, my Lord," answered he, "for you have a right to them. I was thinking, that when many blessings are lost, we should cherish those that remain, and even endeavour to replace the others. My Lord, I have taken a strong liking to that youth whom you call Edmund Twyford; I have neither children nor relations to claim my fortune, nor share my affections; your Lordship has many demands upon your generosity: I can provide for this promising youth without doing injustice to any one; will you give him to me?"

"He is a fortunate boy," said the Baron, "to gain your favour so soon."

"My Lord," said the knight, "I will confess to you, that the first thing that touched my heart in his favour, is a strong resemblance he bears to a certain dear friend I once had, and his manner resembles him as much as his person; his qualities deserve that he should be placed in a higher rank; I will adopt him for my son, and introduce him into the world as my relation, if you will resign him to me; What say you?"

"Sir," said the Baron, "you have made a noble offer, and I am too much the young man's friend to be a hindrance to his preferment. It is true that I intended to provide for him in my own family; but I cannot do it so effectually as by giving him to you, whose generous affection being unlimited by other ties, may in time prefer him to a higher station as he shall deserve it. I have only one condition to make; that the lad shall have his option; for I would not oblige him to leave my service against his inclination."

"You say well," replied Sir Philip, "nor would I take him upon other terms."

"Agreed then," said the Baron, "let us send for Edmund hither."

A servant was sent to fetch him; he came immediately, and his Lord thus bespoke him.

"Edmund, you owe eternal obligations to this gentleman, who, perceiving in you a certain resemblance to a friend of his, and liking your behaviour, has taken a great affection for you, insomuch that he desires to receive you into his family: I cannot better provide for you than by disposing of you to him; and, if you have no objection, you shall return home with him when he goes from hence."

The countenance of Edmund underwent many alterations during this proposal of his Lord; it expressed tenderness, gratitude, and sorrow, but the last was predominant; he bowed respectfully to the Baron and Sir Philip, and, after some hesitation, spoke as follows:—

"I feel very strongly the obligations I owe to this gentleman, for his noble and generous offer; I cannot express the sense I have of his goodness to me, a peasant boy, only known to him by my Lord's kind and partial mention; this uncommon bounty claims my eternal gratitude. To you, my honoured Lord, I owe every thing, even this gentleman's good opinion; you distinguished me when nobody else did; and, next to you, your sons are my best and dearest benefactors; they introduced me to your notice. My heart is unalterably attached to this house and family, and my utmost ambition is to spend my life in your service; but if you have perceived any great and grievous faults in me, that make you wish to put me out of your family, and if you have recommended me to this gentleman in order to be rid of me, in that case I will submit to your pleasure, as I would if you should sentence me to death."

During this speech the tears made themselves channels down Edmund's cheeks; and his two noble auditors, catching the tender inflection, wiped their eyes at the conclusion.

"My dear child," said the Baron, "you overcome me by your tenderness and gratitude! I know of no faults you have committed, that I should wish to be rid of you. I thought to do you the best service by promoting you to that of Sir Philip Harclay, who is both able and willing to provide for you; but if you prefer my service to his, I will not part with you."

Upon this Edmund kneeled to the Baron; he embraced his knees. "My dear Lord! I am, and will be your servant, in preference to any man living; I only ask your permission to live and die in your service."

"You see, Sir Philip," said the Baron, "how this boy engages the heart; how can I part with him?"

"I cannot ask you any more," answered Sir Philip, "I see it is impossible; but I esteem you both still higher than ever; the youth for his gratitude, and your Lordship for your noble mind and true generosity; blessings attend you both!"

"Oh, sir," said Edmund, pressing the hand of Sir Philip, "do not think me ungrateful to you; I will ever remember your goodness, and pray to Heaven to reward it: the name of Sir Philip Harclay shall be engraven upon my heart, next to my Lord and his family, for ever."

Sir Philip raised the youth and embraced him, saying, "If ever you want a friend, remember me; and depend upon my protection, so long as you continue to deserve it."

Edmund bowed low, and withdrew, with his eyes full of tears of sensibility and gratitude. When he was gone, Sir Philip said, "I am thinking, that though young Edmund wants not my assistance at present, he may hereafter stand in need of my friendship. I should not wonder if such rare qualities as he possesses, should one day create envy, and raise him enemies; in which case he might come to lose your favour, without any fault of yours or his own."

"I am obliged to you for the warning," said the Baron, "I hope it will be unnecessary; but if ever I part with Edmund, you shall have the refusal of him."

"I thank your Lordship for all your civilities to me," said the knight. "I leave my best wishes with you and your hopeful family, and I humbly take my leave."

"Will you not stay one night in the castle?" returned my Lord. "You shall be as welcome a guest as ever."

"I acknowledge your goodness and hospitality, but this house fills me with melancholy recollections; I came hither with a heavy heart, and it will not be lighter while I remain here. I shall always remember your Lordship with the highest respect and esteem; and I pray God to preserve you, and increase your blessings!"

After some further ceremonies, Sir Philip departed, and returned to old Wyatt's, ruminating on the vicissitude of human affairs, and thinking on the changes he had seen.

At his return to Wyatt's cottage, he found the family assembled together. He told them he would take another night's lodging there, which they heard with great pleasure;—for he had familiarised himself to them in the last evening's conversation, insomuch that they began to enjoy his company. He told Wyatt of the misfortune he had sustained by losing his servant on the way, and wished he could get one to attend him home in his place. Young John looked earnestly at his father, who returned a look of approbation.

"I perceive one in this company," said he, "that would be proud to serve your honour; but I fear he is not brought up well enough."

John coloured with impatience; he could not forbear speaking.

"Sir, I can answer for an honest heart, a willing mind, and a light pair of heels; and though I am somewhat awkward, I shall be proud to learn, to please my noble master, if he will but try me."

"You say well," said Sir Philip, "I have observed your qualifications, and if you are desirous to serve me, I am equally pleased with you; if your father has no objection I will take you."

"Objection, sir!" said the old man. "It will be my pride to prefer him to such a noble gentleman; I will make no terms for him, but leave it to your honour to do for him as he shall deserve."

"Very well," said Sir Philip, "you shall be no loser by that; I will charge myself with the care of the young man."

The bargain was struck, and Sir Philip purchased a horse for John of the old man. The next morning they set out; the knight left marks of his bounty with the good couple, and departed, laden with their blessing and prayers. He stopped at the place where his faithful servant was buried, and caused masses to be said for the repose of his soul; then, pursuing his way by easy journeys, arrived in safety at home. His family rejoiced at his return; he settled his new servant in attendance upon his person; he then looked round his neighbourhood for objects of his charity; when he saw merit in distress, it was his delight to raise and support it; he spent his time in the service of his Creator, and glorified him in doing good to his creatures. He reflected frequently upon every thing that had befallen him in his late journey to the west; and, at his leisure, took down all the particulars in writing.

Here follows an interval of four years, as by the manuscript; and this omission seems intended by the writer. What follows is in a different hand, and the character is more modern.

About this time the prognostics of Sir Philip Harclay began to be verified, that Edmund's good qualities might one day excite envy and create him enemies. The sons and kinsmen of his patron began to seek occasion to find fault with him, and to depreciate him with others. The Baron's eldest son and heir, Master Robert, had several contests with Master William, the second son, upon his account: This youth had a warm affection for Edmund, and whenever his brother and kinsmen treated him slightly, he supported him against their malicious insinuations. Mr. Richard Wenlock, and Mr. John Markham, were the sisters sons of the Lord Fitz-Owen; and there were several other more distant relations, who, with them, secretly envied Edmund's fine qualities, and strove to lessen him in the esteem of the Baron and his family. By degrees they excited a dislike in Master Robert, that in time was fixed into habit, and fell little short of aversion.

Young Wenlock's hatred was confirmed by an additional circumstance: He had a growing passion for the Lady Emma, the Baron's only daughter; and, as love is eagle-eyed, he saw, or fancied he saw her cast an eye of preference on Edmund. An accidental service that she received from him, had excited her grateful regards and attentions towards him. The incessant view of his fine person and qualities, had perhaps improved her esteem into a still softer sensation, though she was yet ignorant of it, and thought it only the tribute due to gratitude and friendship.

One Christmas time, the Baron and all his family went to visit a family in Wales; crossing a ford, the horse that carried the Lady Emma, who rode behind her cousin Wenlock, stumbled and fell down, and threw her off into the water: Edmund dismounted in a moment, and flew to her assistance; he took her out so quick, that the accident was not known to some part of the company. From this time Wenlock strove to undermine Edmund in her esteem, and she conceived herself obliged in justice and gratitude to defend him against the malicious insinuations of his enemies. She one day asked Wenlock, why he in particular should endeavour to recommend himself to her favour, by speaking against Edmund, to whom she was under great obligations? He made but little reply; but the impression sunk deep into his rancorous heart; every word in Edmund's behalf was like a poisoned arrow that rankled in the wound, and grew every day more inflamed. Sometimes he would pretend to extenuate Edmund's supposed faults, in order to load him with the sin of ingratitude upon other occasions. Rancour works deepest in the heart that strives to conceal it; and, when covered by art, frequently puts on the appearance of candour. By these means did Wenlock and Markham impose upon the credulity of Master Robert and their other relations: Master William only stood proof against all their insinuations.

The same autumn that Edmund completed his eighteenth year, the Baron declared his intention of sending the young men of his house to France the following spring, to learn the art of war, and signalize their courage and abilities.

Their ill-will towards Edmund was so well concealed, that his patron had not discovered it; but it was whispered among the servants, who are generally close observers of the manners of their principals. Edmund was a favourite with them all, which was a strong presumption that he deserved to be so, for they seldom shew much regard to dependents, or to superiour domestics, who are generally objects of envy and dislike. Edmund was courteous, but not familiar with them; and, by this means, gained their affections without soliciting them. Among them was an old serving man, called Joseph Howel; this man had formerly served the old Lord Lovel, and his son; and when the young Lord died, and Sir Walter sold the castle to his brother-in-law, the Lord Fitz-Owen, he only of all the old servants was left in the house, to take care of it, and to deliver it into the possession of the new proprietor, who retained him in his service: He was a man of few words, but much reflection: and, without troubling himself about other people's affairs, went silently and properly about his own business; more solicitous to discharge his duty, than to recommend himself to notice, and not seeming to aspire to any higher office than that of a serving man. This old man would fix his eyes upon Edmund, whenever he could do it without observation; sometimes he would sigh deeply, and a tear would start from his eye, which he strove to conceal from observation. One day Edmund surprised him in this tender emotion, as he was wiping his eyes with the back of his hand. "Why," said he, "my good friend, do you look at me so earnestly and affectionately?"

"Because I love you, Master Edmund," said he. "Because I wish you well."

"I thank you kindly," answered Edmund, "I am unable to repay your love, otherwise than by returning it, which I do sincerely."

"I thank you, sir," said the old man, "that is all I desire, and more than I deserve."

"Do not say so," said Edmund, "if I had any better way to thank you, I would not say so much about it; but words are all my inheritance."

Upon this he shook hands with Joseph, who withdrew hastily to conceal his emotion, saying, "God bless you, master, and make your fortune equal to your deserts! I cannot help thinking you were born to a higher station than what you now hold."

"You know to the contrary," said Edmund; but Joseph was gone out of sight and hearing.

The notice and observation of strangers, and the affection of individuals, together with that inward consciousness that always attends superiour qualities, would sometimes kindle the flames of ambition in Edmund's heart; but he checked them presently by reflecting upon his low birth and dependant station. He was modest, yet intrepid; gentle and courteous to all; frank and unreserved to those that loved him, discreet and complaisant to those who hated him; generous and compassionate to the distresses of his fellow-creatures in general; humble, but not servile, to his patron and superiors. Once, when he with a manly spirit justified himself against a malicious imputation, his young Lord, Robert, taxed him with pride and arrogance to his kinsmen. Edmund denied the charge against him with equal spirit and modesty.

Master Robert answered him sharply, "How dare you contradict my cousins? Do you mean to give them the lie?"

"Not in words, Sir," said Edmund, "but I will behave so as that you shall not believe them."

Master Robert haughtily bid him be silent and know himself, and not presume to contend with men so much his superiors in every respect. These heart-burnings in some degree subsided by their preparations for going to France. Master Robert was to be presented at court before his departure, and it was expected that he should be knighted. The Baron designed Edmund to be his esquire; but this was frustrated by his old enemies, who persuaded Robert to make choice of one of his own domestics, called Thomas Hewson; him did they set up as a rival to Edmund, and he took every occasion to affront him. All that Master Robert gained by this step was the contempt of those, who saw Edmund's merit, and thought it want of discernment in him not to distinguish and reward it. Edmund requested of his Lord that he might be Master William's attendant; "and when," said he, "my patron shall be knighted, as I make no doubt he will one day be, he has promised that I shall be his esquire." The Baron granted Edmund's request; and, being freed from servitude to the rest, he was devoted to that of his beloved Master William, who treated him in public as his principal domestic, but in private as his chosen friend and brother.

The whole cabal of his enemies consulted together in what manner they should vent their resentment against him; and it was agreed that they should treat him with indifference and neglect, till they should arrive in France; and when there, they should contrive to render his courage suspected, and by putting him upon some desperate enterprize, rid themselves of him for ever. About this time died the great Duke of Bedford, to the irreparable loss of the English nation.* He was succeeded by Richard Plantagenet, Duke of York, as Regent of France, of which great part had revolted to Charles the Dauphin. Frequent actions ensued. Cities were lost and won; and continual occasions offered to exercise the courage, and abilities, of the youths of both nations.

The young men of Baron Fitz-Owen's house were recommended particularly to the Regent's notice. Master Robert was knighted, with several other young men of family, who distinguished themselves by their spirit and activity upon every occasion. The youth were daily employed in warlike exercises, and frequent actions; and made their first essay in arms in such a manner as to bring into notice all that deserved it. Various arts were used by Edmund's enemies to expose him to danger; but all their contrivances recoiled upon themselves, and brought increase of honour upon Edmund's head; he distinguished himself upon so many occasions, that Sir Robert himself began to pay him more than ordinary regard, to the infinite mortification of his kinsmen and relations. They laid many schemes against him, but none took effect.

From this place the characters in the manuscript are effaced by time and damp. Here and there some sentences are legible, but not sufficient to pursue the thread of the story. Mention is made of several actions in which the young men were engaged—that Edmund distinguished himself by intrepidity in action; by gentleness, humanity and modesty in the cessations—that he attracted the notice of every person of observation, and also that he received personal commendation from the Regent.

---

* This occurred in 1435.

*The following incidents are clear enough to be tran-
scribed; but the beginning of the next succeeding pages is
obliterated. However, we may guess at the beginning by
what remains.*

——

As soon as the cabal met in Sir Robert's tent, Mr. Wenlock thus
began:—"You see, my friends, that every attempt we make to
humble this upstart, turns into applause, and serves only to raise
his pride still higher. Something must be done, or his praise will
go home before us, at our own expence; and we shall seem only
soils to set off his glories. Any thing would I give to the man who
should execute our vengeance upon him."

"Stop there, cousin Wenlock," said Sir Robert, "though I think
Edmund proud and vain-glorious, and would join in any scheme
to humble him, and make him know himself, I will not suffer
any man to use such base methods to effect it. Edmund is brave;
and it is beneath an Englishman to revenge himself by unworthy means; if any such are used, I will be the first man to bring
the guilty to justice; and if I hear another word to this purpose,
I will inform my brother William, who will acquaint Edmund
with your mean intentions." Upon this the cabal drew back, and
Mr. Wenlock protested that he meant no more than to mortify
his pride, and make him know his proper station. Soon after Sir
Robert withdrew, and they resumed their deliberations.

Then spoke Thomas Hewson: "There is a party to be sent out
to-morrow night, to intercept a convoy of provisions for the relief
of Rouen; I will provoke Mr. Edmund to make one of this party,
and when he is engaged in the action, I and my companions will
draw off, and leave him to the enemy, who I trust will so handle
him, that you shall no more be troubled with him."

"This will do," said Mr. Wenlock, "but let it be kept from my
two cousins, and only known to ourselves; if they offer to be of

the party, I will persuade them off it. And you, Thomas, if you bring this scheme to a conclusion, may depend upon my eternal gratitude."

"And mine," said Markham; and so said all. The next day the affair was publicly mentioned; and Hewson, as he promised, provoked Edmund to the trial. Several young men of family offered themselves; among the rest, Sir Robert, and his brother William. Mr. Wenlock persuaded them not to go, and set the danger of the enterprize in the strongest colours. At last Sir Robert complained of the tooth-ache, and was confined to his tent. Edmund waited on him; and judging by the ardour of his own courage of that of his patron, thus bespoke him:—"I am greatly concerned, dear Sir, that we cannot have your company at night; but as I know what you will suffer in being absent, I would beg the favour of you to let me use your arms and device, and I will promise not to disgrace them."

"No, Edmund, I cannot consent to that: I thank you for your noble offer, and will remember it to your advantage; but I cannot wear honours of another man's getting. You have awakened me to a sense of my duty: I will go with you, and contend with you for glory; and William shall do the same."

In a few hours they were ready to set out. Wenlock and Markham, and their dependants, found themselves engaged in honour to go upon an enterprize they never intended; and set out, with heavy hearts, to join the party. They marched in silence in the horrors of a dark night, and wet roads; they met the convoy where they expected, and a sharp engagement ensued. The victory was some time doubtful; but the moon rising on the backs of the English, gave them the advantage. They saw the disposition of their enemies, and availed themselves of it. Edmund advanced the foremost of the party; he drew out the leader on the French side; he slew him. Mr. William pressed forward to assist his friend; Sir Robert, to defend his brother; Wenlock, and Markham, from shame to stay behind.

Thomas Hewson and his associates drew back on their side; the French perceived it, and pursued the advantage. Edmund pushed them in front; the young nobles all followed him; they broke through the detachment, and stopped the waggons. The officer who commanded the party, encouraged them to go on; the defeat was soon complete, and the provisions carried in triumph to the English camp.

Edmund was presented to the Regent as the man to whom the victory was chiefly owing. Not a tongue presumed to move itself against him; even malice and envy were silenced.

"Approach, young man," said the Regent, "that I may confer upon you the honour of knighthood, which you have well deserved."

Mr. Wenlock could no longer forbear speaking—"Knighthood," said he, "is an order belonging to gentlemen, it cannot be conferred on a peasant."

"What say you, sir!" returned the Regent. "Is this youth a peasant?"

"He is," said Wenlock, "let him deny it if he can."

Edmund, with a modest bow, replied, "It is true indeed I am a peasant, and this honour is too great for me; I have only done my duty."

The Duke of York, whose pride of birth equalled that of any man living or dead, sheathea his sword immediately. "Though," said he, "I cannot reward you as I intended, I will take care that you shall have a large share in the spoils of this night; and, I declare publicly, that you stand first in the list of gallant men in this engagement."

Thomas Hewson and his associates made a poor figure in their return; they were publicly reproved for their backwardness. Hewson was wounded in body and more in mind, for the bad success of his ill-laid design. He could not hold up his head before Edmund; who, unconscious of their malice, administered every kind of comfort to them. He spoke in their behalf to the commanding officer, imputing their conduct to unavoidable accidents. He visited them privately; he gave them a part of the spoils allotted to himself; by every act of valour and courtesy he strove to engage those hearts that hated, envied, and maligned him: But where hatred arises from envy of superior qualities, every display of those qualities increases the cause from whence it arises.

Another pause ensues here.

The young nobles and gentlemen who distinguished Edmund were prevented from raising him to preferment by the insinuations of Wenlock and his associates, who never failed to set before them his low descent, and his pride and arrogance in presuming to rank with gentlemen.

Here the manuscript is not legible for several pages. There is mention, about this time, of the death of the Lady Fitz-Owen, but not the cause.

Wenlock rejoiced to find that his schemes took effect, and that they should be recalled at the approach of winter. The Baron was glad of a pretence to send for them home; for he could no longer endure the absence of his children, after the loss of their mother.

The manuscript is again defaced for many leaves; at length the letters become more legible, and the remainder of it is quite perfect.

———

From the time the young men returned from France, the enemies of Edmund employed their utmost abilities to ruin him in the Baron's opinion, and get him dismissed from the family.

They insinuated a thousand things against him, that happened, as they said, during his residence in France, and therefore could not be known to his master; but when the Baron privately enquired of his two elder sons, he found there was no truth in their reports. Sir Robert, though he did not love him, scorned to join in untruths against him. Mr. William spoke of him with the warmth of fraternal affection. The Baron perceived that his kinsmen disliked Edmund; but his own good heart hindered him from seeing the baseness of theirs. It is said, that continual dropping will wear away a stone; so did their incessant reports, by insensible degrees, produce a coolness in his patron's behaviour towards him. If he behaved with manly spirit, it was misconstrued into pride and arrogance; his generosity was imprudence; his humility was hypocrisy, the better to cover his ambition. Edmund bore patiently all the indignities that were thrown upon him; and, though he felt them severely in his bosom, scorned to justify his conduct at the expence even of his enemies. Perhaps his gentle spirit might at length have sunk under this treatment, but providence interposed in his behalf; and, by seemingly accidental circumstances, conducted him imperceptibly towards the crisis of his fate.

Father Oswald, who had been preceptor to the young men, had a strong affection for Edmund, from a thorough knowledge of his heart; he saw through the mean artifices that were used to undermine him in his patron's favour; he watched their machinations, and strove to frustrate their designs.

This good man used frequently to walk out with Edmund; they conversed upon various subjects; and the youth would lament to him the unhappiness of his situation, and the peculiar circumstances that attended him. The father, by his wholesome advice, comforted his drooping heart, and confirmed him in his resolution of bearing unavoidable evils with patience and fortitude, from the consciousness of his own innocence, and the assurance of a future and eternal reward.

One day, as they were walking in a wood near the castle, Edmund asked the father, what meant those preparations for building, the cutting down trees, and burning of bricks?

"What," said Oswald, "have you not heard that my Lord is going to build a new apartment on the west side of the castle?"

"And why," said Edmund, "should my Lord be at that expence when there is one on the east side that is never occupied?"

"That apartment," said the friar, "you must have observed is always shut up."

"I have observed it often," said Edmund, "but I never presumed to ask any questions about it."

"You had then," said Oswald, "less curiosity, and more discretion, than is common at your age."

"You have raised my curiosity," said Edmund, "and, if it be not improper, I beg of you to gratify it."

"We are alone," said Oswald, "and I am so well assured of your prudence, that I will explain this mystery in some degree to you."

"You must know, that apartment was occupied by the last Lord Lovel when he was a batchelor. He married in his father's lifetime, who gave up his own apartment to him, and offered to retire to this himself; but the son would not permit him; he chose to sleep here, rather than in any other. He had been married about three months, when his father, the old lord, died of a fever. About twelve months after his marriage, he was called upon to attend the King, Henry the Fourth, on an expedition into Wales, whither he was attended by many of his dependants. He left his lady big with child, and full of care and anxiety for his safety and return.

"After the King had chastised the rebels, and obtained the victory, the Lord Lovel was expected home every day; various reports were sent home before him; one messenger brought an account of his health and safety; soon after another came with bad news, that he was slain in battle. His kinsman, Sir Walter Lovel, came here on a visit to comfort the Lady; and he waited to receive his kinsman at his return. It was he that brought the news of the sad event of the battle to the Lady Lovel.

"She fainted away at the relation; but, when she revived, exerted the utmost resolution; saying, it was her duty to bear this dreadful stroke with Christian fortitude and patience, especially in regard to the child she went with, the last remains of her beloved husband, and the undoubted heir of a noble house. For several days she seemed an example of patience and resignation; but then, all at once, she renounced them, and broke out into passionate and frantic exclamations; she said, that her dear Lord was basely murdered; that his ghost had appeared to her, and revealed his fate. She called upon Heaven and earth to revenge her wrongs; saying, she would never cease complaining to God, and the King, for vengeance and justice.

"Upon this, Sir Walter told the servants that Lady Lovel was distracted, from grief for the death of her Lord; that his regard for her was as strong as ever; and that, if she recovered, he would himself be her comforter, and marry her. In the mean time she was confined in this very apartment, and in less than a month the poor Lady died. She lies buried in the family vault in St. Austin's church in the village. Sir Walter took possession of the castle, and all the other estates, and assumed the title of Lord Lovel.

"Soon after, it was reported that the castle was haunted, and that the ghosts of Lord and Lady Lovel had been seen by several of the servants. Whoever went into this apartment were terrified by uncommon noises, and strange appearances; at length this apartment was wholly shut up, and the servants were forbid to enter it, or to talk of any thing relating to it: However, the story did not stop here; it was whispered about, that the new Lord Lovel was so disturbed every night, that he could not sleep in quiet; and, being at last tired of the place, he sold the castle and estate of his ancestors, to his brother-in-law the Lord Fitz-Owen, who now enjoys it, and left this country."

"All this is news to me," said Edmund, "but, father, tell me what grounds there were for the lady's suspicion that her Lord died unfairly?"

"Alas!" said Oswald. "That is only known to God. There were strange thoughts in the minds of many at that time; I had mine; but I will not disclose them, not even to you. I will not injure those who may be innocent; and I leave it to Providence, who will doubtless, in its own best time and manner, punish the guilty. But let what I have told you be as if you had never heard it."

"I thank you for these marks of your esteem and confidence," said Edmund, "be assured that I will not abuse them; nor do I desire to pry into secrets not proper to be revealed. I entirely approve your discretion, and acquiesce in your conclusion, that Providence will in its own time vindicate its ways to man; if it were not for that trust, my situation would be insupportable. I strive earnestly to deserve the esteem and favour of good men; I endeavour to regulate my conduct so as to avoid giving offence to any man; but I see, with infinite pain, that it is impossible for me to gain these points."

"I see it too, with great concern," said Oswald, "and every thing that I can say and do in your favour is misconstrued; and, by seeking to do you service, I lose my own influence. But I will never give my sanction to acts of injustice, nor join to oppress innocence. My dear child, put your trust in God: He who brought light out of darkness, can bring good out of evil."

"I hope and trust so," said Edmund, "but, father, if my enemies should prevail—if my Lord should believe their stories against me, and I should be put out of the house with disgrace, what will become of me? I have nothing but my character to depend upon; if I lose that, I lose every thing; and I see they seek no less than my ruin."

"Trust in my Lord's honour and justice," replied Oswald, "he knows your virtue, and he is not ignorant of their ill-will towards you."

"I know my Lord's justice too well to doubt it," said Edmund, "but would it not be better to rid him of this trouble, and his family of an incumbrance? I would gladly do something for myself, but cannot without my Lord's recommendation; and, such is my situation, that I fear the asking for a dismission would be accounted base ingratitude; beside, when I think of leaving this house, my heart saddens at the thought, and tells me I cannot be happy out of it; yet I think I could return to a peasant's life with cheerfulness, rather than live in a palace under disdain and contempt."

"Have patience a little longer, my son," said Oswald. "I will think of some way to serve you, and to represent your grievances to my Lord, without offence to either—perhaps the causes may be removed. Continue to observe the same irreproachable conduct; and be assured that Heaven will defend your innocence, and defeat the unjust designs of your enemies. Let us now return home."

About a week after this conference, Edmund walked out in the fields ruminating on the disagreeable circumstances of his situation. Insensible of the time, he had been out several hours without perceiving how the day wore away, when he heard himself called by name several times; looking backward, he saw his friend Mr. William, and hallooed to him. He came running towards him; and, leaping over the style, stood still a while to recover his breath.

"What is the matter, sir?" said Edmund. "Your looks bespeak some tidings of importance."

With a look of tender concern and affection, the youth pressed his hand and spoke—

"My dear Edmund, you must come home with me directly; your old enemies have united to ruin you with my father; my brother Robert has declared that he thinks there will be no peace in our family till you are dismissed from it, and told my father, he hoped he would not break with his kinsmen rather than give up Edmund."

"But what do they lay to my charge?" said Edmund.

"I cannot rightly understand," answered William, "for they

make a great mystery of it; something of great consequence, they say; but they will not tell me what: However, my father has told them that they must bring their accusation before your face, and he will have you answer them publicly. I have been seeking you this hour, to inform you of this, that you might be prepared to defend yourself against your accusers."

"God reward you, sir," said Edmund, "for all your goodness to me! I see they are determined to ruin me if possible: I shall be compelled to leave the castle; but, whatever becomes of me, be assured you shall have no cause to blush for your kindness and partiality to your Edmund."

"I know it, I am sure of it," said William, "and here I swear to you, as Jonathan did to David, I beseech Heaven to bless me, as my friendship to you shall be steady and inviolable!"

"Only so long as I shall deserve so great a blessing," interrupted Edmund.

"I know your worth and honour," continued William, "and such is my confidence in your merit, that I firmly believe Heaven designs you for something extraordinary; and I expect that some great and unforeseen event will raise you to the rank and station to which you appear to belong: Promise me, therefore, that whatever may be your fate you will preserve the same friendship for me that I bear to you."

Edmund was so much affected that he could not answer but in broken sentences.

"Oh my friend, my master! I vow, I promise, my heart promises!"

He kneeled down with clasped hands, and uplifted eyes. William kneeled by him, and they invoked the Supreme to witness to their friendship, and implored His blessing upon it. They then rose up and embraced each other, while tears of cordial affection bedewed their cheeks.

As soon as they were able to speak, Edmund conjured his friend not to expose himself to the displeasure of his family out of kindness to him.

"I submit to the will of Heaven," said he. "I wait with patience its disposal of me; if I leave the castle, I will find means to inform you of my fate and fortunes."

"I hope," said William, "that things may yet be accommodated; but do not take any resolution, let us act as occasions arise."

In this manner these amiable youths conferred, till they arrived at the castle. The Baron was sitting in the great hall, on a high chair with a footstep before, with the state and dignity of a judge; before him stood Father Oswald, as pleading the cause for himself and Edmund. Round the Baron's chair stood his eldest son and his kinsmen, with their principal domestics. The old servant, Joseph, at some distance, with his head leaning forward, as listening with the utmost attention to what passed. Mr. William approached the chair. "My Lord, I have found Edmund, and brought him to answer for himself."

"You have done well," said the Baron. "Edmund, come hither; you are charged with some indiscretions, for I cannot properly call them crimes: I am resolved to do justice between you and your accusers; I shall therefore hear you as well as them; for no man ought to be condemned unheard."

"My Lord," said Edmund, with equal modesty and intrepidity, "I demand my trial; if I shall be found guilty of any crimes against my Benefactor, let me be punished with the utmost rigour; But if, as I trust, no such charge can be proved against me, I know your goodness too well to doubt that you will do justice to me, as well as to others; and if it should so happen that by the misrepresentations of my enemies (who have long sought my ruin privately, and now avow it publicly), if by their artifices your Lordship should be induced to think me guilty, I would submit to your sentence in silence, and appeal to another tribunal."

"See," said Mr. Wenlock, "the confidence of the fellow! He already supposes that my Lord must be in the wrong if he condemns him; and then this meek creature will appeal to another tribunal. To whose will he appeal? I desire he may be made to explain himself."

"That I will immediately," said Edmund, "without being compelled. I only meant to appeal to Heaven that best knows my innocence."

"'Tis true," said the Baron, "and no offence to any one; man can only judge by appearances, but Heaven knows the heart; Let every one of you bear this in mind, that you may not bring a false accusation, nor justify yourselves by concealing the truth. Edmund, I am informed that Oswald and you have made very free with me and my family, in some of your conversations; you were heard to censure me for the absurdity of building a new apartment on the west side of the castle, when there was one on the east side uninhabited. Oswald said, that apartment was shut up because it was haunted; that some shocking murder had been committed there; adding many particulars concerning Lord Lovel's family, such as he could not know the truth of, and, if he had known, was imprudent to reveal. But, further, you complained of ill-treatment here; and mentioned an intention to leave the castle, and seek your fortune elsewhere. I shall examine into all these particulars in turn. At present I desire you, Edmund, to relate all that you can remember of the conversation that passed between you and Oswald in the wood last Monday."

"Good God!" said Edmund, "is it possible that any person could put such a construction upon so innocent a conversation?"

"Tell me then," said the Baron, "the particulars of it."

"I will, my Lord, as nearly as my memory will allow me." Accordingly he related most of the conversation that passed in the wood; but, in the part that concerned the family of Lovel, he abbreviated as much as possible. Oswald's countenance cleared up, for he had done the same before Edmund came. The Baron called to his eldest son.

"You hear, Sir Robert, what both parties say; I have questioned them separately; neither of them knew what the other would answer, yet their accounts agree almost to a word."

"I confess they do so," answered Sir Robert, "but, sir, it is very bold and presuming for them to speak of our family affairs in such a manner; if my uncle, Lord Lovel, should come to know it, he would punish them severely; and, if his honour is reflected upon, it becomes us to resent and to punish it." Here Mr. Wenlock broke out into passion, and offered to swear to the truth of his accusation.

"Be silent, Dick," said the Baron, "I shall judge for myself. I protest," said he to Sir Robert, "I never heard so much as Oswald has now told me concerning the deaths of Lord and Lady Lovel; I think it is best to let such stories alone till they die away of themselves. I had, indeed, heard of an idle story of the east apartment's being haunted, when first I came hither, and my brother advised me to shut it up till it should be forgotten; but what has now been said, has suggested a thought that may make that apartment useful in future. I have thought of a punishment for Edmund that will stop the mouth of his accusers for the present; and, as I hope, will establish his credit with every body. Edmund, will you undertake this adventure for me?"

"What adventure, my Lord?" said Edmund. "There is nothing I would not undertake to shew my gratitude and fidelity to you. As to my courage, I would shew that at the expence of my malicious accusers, if respect to my Lord's blood did not tie up my hands; as I am situated, I beg it may be put to the proof in whatever way is most for my master's service."

"That is well said," cried the Baron, "as to your enemies, I am thinking how to separate you from them effectually; of that I shall speak hereafter. I am going to try Edmund's courage; he shall sleep three nights in the east apartment, that he may testify to all whether it be haunted or not; afterwards I will have that apartment set in order, and my eldest son shall take it for his own; it will spare me some expence, and answer my purpose as well, or better; Will you consent, Edmund?"

"With all my heart, my Lord," said Edmund, "I have not wilfully offended God or man; I have, therefore, nothing to fear."

"Brave boy!" said my Lord. "I am not deceived in you, nor shall you be deceived in your reliance on me. You shall sleep in that apartment to-night, and to-morrow I will have some private talk with you. Do you, Oswald, go with me; I want to have some conversation with you. The rest of you, retire to your studies and business; I will meet you at dinner."

Edmund retired to his own chamber, and Oswald was shut up with the Baron; he defended Edmund's cause and his own, and laid open as much as he knew of the malice and designs of his enemies. The Baron expressed much concern at the untimely deaths of Lord and Lady Lovel, and desired Oswald to be circumspect in regard to what he had to say of the circumstances attending them; adding, that he was both innocent and ignorant of any treachery towards either of them. Oswald excused himself for his communications to Edmund, saying, they fell undesignedly into the subject, and that he mentioned it in confidence to him only.

The Baron sent orders to the young men to come to dinner; but they refused to meet Edmund at table; accordingly he ate in the steward's apartment. After dinner, the Baron tried to reconcile his kinsmen to Edmund; but found it impossible. They saw their designs were laid open; and, judging of him by themselves, thought it impossible to forgive or be forgiven. The Baron ordered them to keep in separate apartments; he took his eldest son for his own companion, as being the most reasonable of the malcontents; and ordered his kinsmen to keep their own apartment, with a servant to watch their motions. Mr. William had Oswald for his companion. Old Joseph was bid to attend on Edmund; to serve him at supper; and, at the hour of nine, to conduct him to the haunted apartment. Edmund desired that he might have a light and his sword, lest his enemies should endeavour to surprise him. The Baron thought his request reasonable, and complied with it.

There was a great search to find the key of the apartment; at last it was discovered by Edmund, himself, among a parcel of old rusty keys in a lumber room. The Baron sent the young men their suppers to their respective apartments. Edmund declined eating, and desired to be conducted to his apartment. He was accompanied by most of the servants to the door of it; they wished him success, and prayed for him as if he had been going to execution.

The door was with great difficulty unlocked, and Joseph gave Edmund a lighted lamp, and wished him a good night; he returned his good wishes to them all with the utmost cheerfulness, took the key on the inside of the door, and dismissed them.

He then took a survey of his chamber; the furniture, by long neglect, was decayed and dropping to pieces; the bed was devoured by the moths, and occupied by the rats, who had built their nests there with impunity for many generations. The bedding was very damp, for the rain had forced its way through the ceiling; he determined, therefore, to lie down in his clothes. There were two doors on the further side of the room, with keys in them; being not at all sleepy, he resolved to examine them; he attempted one lock, and opened it with ease; he went into a large dining-room, the furniture of which was in the same tattered condition; out of this was a large closet* with some books in it, and hung round with coats of arms, with genealogies and alliances of the house of Lovel; he amused himself here some minutes, and then returned into the bed-chamber.

He recollected the other door, and resolved to see where it led to; the key was rusted into the lock, and resisted his attempts; he set the lamp on the ground, and, exerting all his strength, opened the door, and at the same instant the wind of it blew out the lamp, and left him in utter darkness. At the same moment he heard a hollow rustling noise, like that of a person coming through a narrow passage. Till this moment not one idea of fear had approached the mind of Edmund; but, just then, all the concurrent circumstances of his situation struck upon his heart, and gave him a new and disagreeable sensation. He paused a while; and, recollecting himself, cried out aloud. "What should I fear? I

---

* A small chamber.

have not wilfully offended God or man; why then should I doubt protection? But I have not yet implored the divine assistance; how then can I expect it!" Upon this, he kneeled down and prayed earnestly, resigning himself wholly to the will of heaven; while he was yet speaking, his courage returned, and he resumed his usual confidence; again he approached the door from whence the noise proceeded; he thought he saw a glimmering light upon a staircase before him. "If," said he, "this apartment is haunted, I will use my endeavours to discover the cause of it; and if the spirit appears visibly, I will speak to it."

He was preparing to descend the staircase, when he heard several knocks at the door by which he first entered the room; and, stepping backward, the door was clapped to with great violence. Again fear attacked him, but he resisted it, and boldly cried out, "Who is there?"

A voice at the outer door answered, "It's I; Joseph, your friend!"

"What do you want?" said Edmund.

"I have brought you some wood to make a fire," said Joseph.

"I thank you kindly," said Edmund, "but my lamp is gone out; I will try to find the door, however."

After some trouble he found, and opened it; and was not sorry to see his friend Joseph, with a light in one hand, a flagon of beer in the other, and a fagot upon his shoulder. "I come," said the good old man, "to bring you something to keep up your spirits; the evening is cold; I know this room wants airing; and beside that, my master, I think your present undertaking requires a little assistance."

"My good friend," said Edmund, "I never shall be able to deserve or requite your kindness to me."

"My dear sir, you always deserved more than I could do for you; and I think I shall yet live to see you defeat the designs of your enemies, and acknowledge the services of your friends."

"Alas!" said Edmund, "I see little prospect of that!"

"I see," said Joseph, "something that persuades me you are

designed for great things; and I perceive that things are working about to some great end: have courage, my Master, my heart beats strangely high upon your account!"

"You make me smile," said Edmund.

"I am glad to see it, sir; may you smile all the rest of your life!"

"I thank your honest affection," returned Edmund, "though it is too partial to me. You had better go to bed, however; if it is known that you visit me here, it will be bad for us both."

"So I will presently; but, please God, I will come here again to-morrow night, when all the family are a-bed; and I will tell you some things that you never yet heard."

"But pray tell me," said Edmund, "where does that door lead to?"

"Upon a passage that ends in a staircase that leads to the lower rooms; and there is likewise a door out of that passage into the dining-room."

"And what rooms are there below stairs," said Edmund?

"The same as above," replied he.

"Very well; then I wish you a good night, we will talk further to-morrow."

"Aye, to-morrow night; and in this place, my dear master."

"Why do you call me your master? I never was, nor ever can be, your master."

"God only knows that," said the good old man. "Good-night, and heaven bless you!"

"Good-night, my worthy friend!"

Joseph withdrew, and Edmund returned to the other door, and attempted several times to open it in vain; his hands were benumbed and tired; at length he gave over. He made a fire in the chimney, placed the lamp on a table, and opened one of the window-shutters to admit the day-light; he then recommended himself to the Divine protection, and threw himself upon the bed; he presently fell asleep, and continued in that state, till the sun saluted him with his orient beams through the window he had opened.

As soon as he was perfectly awake, he strove to recollect his dreams. He thought that he heard people coming up the stair-case that he had a glimpse of; that the door opened, and there entered a warrior, leading a lady by the hand, who was young and beautiful, but pale and wan; The man was dressed in com-plete armour, and his helmet down. They approached the bed; they undrew the curtains. He thought the man said, "Is this our child?" The woman replied, "It is; and the hour approaches that he shall be known for such." They then separated, and one stood on each side of the bed; their hands met over his head, and they gave him a solemn benediction. He strove to rise and pay them his respects, but they forbad him; and the lady said, "Sleep in peace, oh my Edmund! for those who are the true possessors of this apartment are employed in thy preservation; sleep on, sweet hope of a house that is thought past hope!"

Upon this, they withdrew, and went out at the same door by which they entered, and he heard them descend the stairs. After this, he followed a funeral as chief mourner; he saw the whole procession, and heard the ceremonies performed. He was snatched away from this mournful scene to one of a contrary kind, a stately feast, at which he presided; and he heard himself congratulated as a husband, and a father; his friend William sat by his side; and his happiness was complete. Every succeeding idea was happiness without allay; and his mind was not idle a moment till the morning sun awakened him. He perfectly remembered his dreams, and meditated on what all these things should portend. "Am I then," said he, "not Edmund Twyford, but somebody of consequence in whose fate so many people are interested? Vain thought, that must have arisen from the partial suggestion of my two friends, Mr. William and old Joseph."

He lay thus reflecting, when a servant knocked at his door, and told him it was past six o'clock, and that the Baron expected him to breakfast in an hour. He rose immediately; paid his tribute of thanks to heaven for its protection, and went from his chamber in high health and spirits. He walked in the garden till the hour of breakfast, and then attended the Baron.

"Good morrow, Edmund!" said he. "How have you rested in your new apartment?"

"Extremely well, my Lord," answered he.

"I am glad to hear it," said the Baron, "but I did not know your accommodations were so bad, as Joseph tells me they are."

"'Tis of no consequence," said Edmund, "if they were much worse, I could dispense with them for three nights."

"Very well," said the Baron, "you are a brave lad; I am satisfied with you, and will excuse the other two nights."

"But, my Lord, I will not be excused; no one shall have reason to suspect my courage; I am determined to go through the remaining nights upon many accounts."

"That shall be as you please," said my Lord. "I think of you as you deserve; so well, that I shall ask your advice by and by in some affairs of consequence."

"My life and services are yours, my Lord; command them freely."

"Let Oswald be called in," said my Lord. "He shall be one of our consultation." He came; the servants were dismissed; and the Baron spoke as follows:

"Edmund, when first I took you into my family, it was at the request of my sons and kinsmen; I bear witness to your good behaviour, you have not deserved to lose their esteem; but, nevertheless, I have observed for some years past, that all but my son William have set their faces against you; I see their meanness, and I perceive their motives: but they are, and must be, my relations; and I would rather govern them by love, than fear. I love and esteem your virtues: I cannot give you up to gratify their humours. My son William has lost the affections of the rest, for that he bears to you; but he has increased my regard for him; I think myself bound in honour to him and you to provide for you; I cannot do it, as I wished, under my own roof. If you stay here,

I see nothing but confusion in my family; yet I cannot put you out of it disgracefully. I want to think of some way to prefer you, that you may leave this house with honour; and I desire both of you to give me your advice in this matter. If Edmund will tell me in what way I can employ him to his own honour and my advantage, I am ready to do it; let him propose it, and Oswald shall moderate between us."

Here he stopped; and Edmund, whose sighs almost choked him, threw himself at the Baron's feet, and wet his hand with his tears. "Oh, my noble, generous benefactor! Do you condescend to consult such a one as me upon the state of your family? Does your most amiable and beloved son incur the ill-will of his brothers and kinsmen for my sake? What am I, that I should disturb the peace of this noble family? Oh, my Lord, send me away directly! I should be unworthy to live, if I did not earnestly endeavour to restore your happiness. You have given me a noble education, and I trust I shall not disgrace it. If you will recommend me, and give me a character, I fear not to make my own fortune."

The Baron wiped his eyes. "I wish to do this, my child, but in what way?"

"My Lord," said Edmund, "I will open my heart to you. I have served with credit in the army, and I should prefer a soldier's life."

"You please me well," said the Baron. "I will send you to France, and give you a recommendation to the Regent; he knows you personally, and will prefer you, for my sake, and for your own merit."

"My Lord, you overwhelm me with your goodness! I am but your creature, and my life shall be devoted to your service."

"But," said the Baron, "how to dispose of you till the spring?"

"That," said Oswald, "may be thought of at leisure; I am glad that you have resolved, and I congratulate you both." The Baron put an end to the conversation by desiring Edmund to go with him into the menage to see his horses. He ordered Oswald to acquaint his son William with all that had passed, and to try to persuade the young men to meet Edmund and William at dinner.

The Baron took Edmund with him into his menage to see some horses he had lately purchased; while they were examining the beauties and defects of these noble and useful animals, Edmund declared that he preferred Caradoc, a horse he had broke himself, to any other in my Lord's stables. "Then," said the Baron, "I will give him to you; and you shall go upon him to seek your fortune." He made new acknowledgments for this gift, and declared he would prize it highly for the giver's sake. "But I shall not part with you yet," said my Lord. "I will first carry all my points with these saucy boys, and oblige them to do you justice."

"You have already done that," said Edmund, "and I will not suffer any of your Lordship's blood to undergo any farther humiliation upon my account. I think, with humble submission to your better judgment, the sooner I go hence the better."

While they were speaking, Oswald came to them, and said, that the young men had absolutely refused to dine at the table, if Edmund was present.

"'Tis well," said the Baron. "I shall find a way to punish their contumacy hereafter; I will make them know that I am the master here. Edmund and you, Oswald, shall spend the day in my apartment above stairs. William shall dine with me alone; and I will acquaint him with our determination; my son Robert, and his cabal, shall be prisoners in the great parlour. Edmund shall, according to his own desire, spend this and the following night in the haunted apartment; and this for his sake, and my own; for if I should now contradict my former orders, it would subject us both to their impertinent reflections."

He then took Oswald aside, and charged him not to let Edmund go out of his sight; for if he should come in the way of those implacable enemies, he trembled for the consequences. He then walked back to the stables, and the two friends returned into the house.

They had a long conversation on various subjects; in the course of it, Edmund acquainted Oswald with all that had passed between him and Joseph the preceding night, the curiosity he had raised in him, and his promise to gratify it the night following.

"I wish," said Oswald, "you would permit me to be one of your party."

"How can that be?" said Edmund. "We shall be watched, perhaps; and, if discovered, what excuse can you make for coming there? Beside, if it were known, I shall be branded with the imputation of cowardice; and, though I have borne much, I will not promise to bear that patiently."

"Never fear," replied Oswald, "I will speak to Joseph about it; and, after prayers are over and the family gone to bed, I will steal away from my own chamber and come to you. I am strongly interested in your affairs; and I cannot be easy unless you will receive me into your company; I will bind myself to secrecy in any manner you shall enjoin."

"Your word is sufficient," said Edmund. "I have as much reason to trust you, father, as any man living; I should be ungrateful to refuse you any thing in my power to grant; But suppose the apartment should really be haunted, would you have resolution enough to pursue the adventure to a discovery?"

"I hope so," said Oswald, "but have you any reason to believe it is?"

"I have," said Edmund, "but I have not opened my lips upon this subject to any creature but yourself. This night I purpose, if Heaven permit, to go all over the rooms; and, though I had formed this design, I will confess that your company will strengthen my resolution. I will have no reserves to you in any respect; but I must put a seal upon your lips."

Oswald swore secrecy till he should be permitted to disclose the mysteries of that apartment; and both of them waited, in solemn expectation, the event of the approaching night.

In the afternoon Mr. William was allowed to visit his friend. An affecting interview passed between them. He lamented the necessity of Edmund's departure; and they took a solemn leave of each other, as if they foreboded it would be long ere they should meet again.

About the same hour as the preceding evening, Joseph came to conduct Edmund to his apartment.

"You will find better accommodations than you had last night," said he, "and all by my Lord's own order."

"I every hour receive some new proof of his goodness," said Edmund.

When they arrived, he found a good fire in the chamber, and a table covered with cold meats, and a flagon of strong beer.

"Sit down and get your supper, my dear Master," said Joseph. "I must attend my Lord; but as soon as the family are gone to bed, I will visit you again."

"Do so," said Edmund, "but first, see Father Oswald; he has something to say to you. You may trust him, for I have no reserves to him."

"Well, Sir, I will see him if you desire it; and I will come to you as soon as possible." So saying, he went his way, and Edmund sat down to supper.

After a moderate refreshment, he kneeled down, and prayed with the greatest fervency. He resigned himself to the disposal of Heaven. "I am nothing," said he, "I desire to be nothing but what thou, O Lord, pleasest to make me. If it is thy will that I should return to my former obscurity, be it obeyed with cheerfulness; and, if thou art pleased to exalt me, I will look up to thee, as the only fountain of honour and dignity." While he prayed, he felt an enlargement of heart beyond what he had ever experienced before; all idle fears were dispersed, and his heart glowed with divine love and affiance;—he seemed raised above the world and all its pursuits. He continued wrapt up in mental devotion, till a knocking at the door obliged him to rise, and let in his two friends, who came without shoes, and on tiptoe, to visit him.

"Save you, my son!" said the friar. "You look cheerful and happy."

"I am so, father," said Edmund. "I have resigned myself to the disposal of Heaven, and I find my heart strengthened above what I can express."

"Heaven be praised!" said Oswald. "I believe you are designed for great things, my son."

"What! Do you too encourage my ambition?" says Edmund. "Strange concurrence of circumstances!—Sit down, my friends; and do you, my good Joseph, tell me the particulars you promised last night."

They drew their chairs round the fire, and Joseph began as follows:

"You have heard of the untimely death of the late Lord Lovel, my noble and worthy master; perhaps you may have also heard that, from that time, this apartment was haunted. What passed the other day, when my Lord questioned you both on this head, brought all the circumstances fresh into my mind. You then said, there were suspicions that he came not fairly to his end. I trust you both, and will speak what I know of it. There was a person suspected of this murder; and whom do you think it was?"

"You must speak out," said Oswald.

"Why then," said Joseph, "it was the present Lord Lovel."

"You speak my thoughts," said Oswald, "but proceed to the proofs."

"I will," said Joseph.

"From the time that my Lord's death was reported, there were strange whisperings and consultations between the new Lord and some of the servants; there was a deal of private business carried on in this apartment. Soon after, they gave out that my poor lady was distracted; but she threw out strong expressions that savoured nothing of madness. She said, that the ghost of her departed Lord had appeared to her, and revealed the circumstances of this murder. None of the servants, but one, were permitted to see her. At this very time, Sir Walter, the new Lord, had the cruelty to offer love to her; he urged her to marry him; and one of her women overheard her say, she would sooner die than give her hand to the man who caused the death of her Lord; Soon after this, we were told my Lady was dead. The Lord Lovel made a public and sumptuous funeral for her."

"That is true," said Oswald, "for I was a novice, and assisted at it."

"Well," says Joseph, "now comes my part of the story. As I was coming home from the burial, I overtook Roger our ploughman. Said he, What think you of this burying?—'What should I think,' said I, 'but that we have lost the best Master and Lady that we shall ever know?' 'God, He knows,' quoth Roger, 'whether they be living or dead; but if ever I saw my Lady in my life, I saw her alive the night they say she died.' I tried to convince him that he was mistaken; but he offered to take his oath, that the very night they said she died, he saw her come out at the garden gate into the fields; that she often stopped, like a person in pain, and then went forward again until he lost sight of her. Now it is certain that her time was out, and she expected to lie down every day; and they did not pretend that she died in child-bed. I thought upon what I heard, but nothing I said. Roger told the same story to another servant; so he was called to an account, the story was hushed up, and the foolish fellow said, he was verily persuaded it was her ghost that he saw. Now you must take notice that, from this time, they began to talk about, that this apartment was troubled; and not only this, but at last the new Lord could not sleep in quiet in his own room; and this induced him to sell the castle to his brother-in-law, and get out of this country as fast as possible. He took most of the servants away with him, and Roger among the rest. As for me, they thought I knew nothing, and so they left me behind; but I was neither blind nor deaf, though I could hear, and see, and say nothing."

"This is a dark story," said Oswald.

"It is so," said Edmund, "but why should Joseph seem to think it concerns me in particular?"

"Ah, dear Sir," said Joseph, "I must tell you, though I never uttered it to mortal man before; the striking resemblance this young man bears to my dear Lord, the strange dislike his reputed father took to him, his gentle manners, his generous heart, his noble qualities so uncommon in those of his birth and breeding, the sound of his voice—you may smile at the strength of my fancy, but I cannot put it out of my mind but that he is my own master's son."

At these words Edmund changed colour and trembled; he clapped his hand upon his breast, and looked up to Heaven in silence; his dream recurred to his memory, and struck upon his heart. He related it to his attentive auditors.

"The ways of Providence are wonderful," said Oswald. "If this be so, Heaven in its own time will make it appear."

Here a silence of several minutes ensued; when, suddenly, they were awakened from their reverie by a violent noise in the rooms underneath them. It seemed like the clashing of arms, and something seemed to fall down with violence.

They started, and Edmund rose up with a look full of resolution and intrepidity.

"I am called!" said he. "I obey the call!"

He took up a lamp, and went to the door that he had opened the night before. Oswald followed with his rosary in his hand, and Joseph last with trembling steps. The door opened with ease, and they descended the stairs in profound silence.

The lower rooms answered exactly to those above; there were two parlours and a large closet. They saw nothing remarkable in these rooms, except two pictures, that were turned with their faces to the wall. Joseph took the courage to turn them. "These," said he, "are the portraits of my Lord and Lady. Father, look at this face; do you know who is like it?"

"I should think," said Oswald, "it was done for Edmund!"

"I am," said Edmund, "struck with the resemblance myself; but let us go on; I feel myself inspired with unusual courage. Let us open the closet door."

Oswald stopped him short.

"Take heed," said he, "lest the wind of the door put out the lamp. I will open this door."

He attempted it without success; Joseph did the same, but to no purpose; Edmund gave the lamp to Joseph; he approached the door, tried the key, and it gave way to his hand in a moment.

"This adventure belongs," said he, "to me only; that is plain— bring the lamp forward."

Oswald repeated the paternoster, in which they all joined, and then entered the closet.

The first thing that presented itself to their view, was a complete suit of armour, that seemed to have fallen down on an heap.

"Behold!" said Edmund. "This made the noise we heard above."

They took it up, and examined it piece by piece; the inside of the breast plate was stained with blood.

"See here!" said Edmund. "What think you of this?"

"'Tis my Lord's armour," said Joseph. "I know it well—here has been bloody work in this closet!"

Going forward, he stumbled over something; it was a ring with the arms of Lovel engraved upon it.

"This is my Lord's ring," said Joseph. "I have seen him wear it; I give it to you, sir, as the right owner; and most religiously do I believe you his son."

"Heaven only knows that," said Edmund, "and, if it permits, I will know who was my father before I am a day older."

While he was speaking, he shifted his ground, and perceived that the boards rose up on the other side of the closet; upon farther examination they found that the whole floor was loose, and a table that stood over them concealed the circumstance from a casual observer.

"I perceive," said Oswald, "that some great discovery is at hand."

"God defend us!" said Edmund. "But I verily believe that the person that owned this armour lies buried under us."

Upon this, a dismal hollow groan was heard, as if from under-neath. A solemn silence ensued, and marks of fear were visible upon all three; the groan was thrice heard; Oswald made signs for them to kneel, and he prayed audibly, that Heaven would direct them how to act; he also prayed for the soul of the departed, that it might rest in peace. After this, he arose; but Edmund continued kneeling—he vowed solemnly to devote himself to the discovery of this secret, and the avenging the death of the person there bur-ied. He then rose up. "It would be to no purpose," said he, "for us to examine further now; when I am properly authorised, I will have this place opened; I trust that time is not far off."

"I believe it," said Oswald, "you are designed by Heaven to be its instrument in bringing this deed of darkness to light. We are your creatures; only tell us what you would have us do, and we are ready to obey your commands."

"I only demand your silence," said Edmund, "till I call for your evidence; and then, you must speak all you know, and all you suspect."

"Oh," said Joseph, "that I may but live to see that day, and I shall have lived long enough!"

"Come," said Edmund, "let us return up stairs, and we will consult further how I shall proceed."

So saying, he went out of the closet, and they followed him. He locked the door, and took the key out—"I will keep this," said he, "till I have power to use it to purpose, lest any one should presume to pry into the secret of this closet. I will always carry it about me, to remind me of what I have undertaken."

Upon this, they returned up stairs into the bed-chamber; all was still, and they heard nothing more to disturb them. "How," said Edmund, "is it possible that I should be the son of Lord Lovel? for, however circumstances have seemed to encourage such a notion, what reason have I to believe it?"

"I am strangely puzzled about it," said Oswald. "It seems unlikely that so good a man as Lord Lovel should corrupt the wife of a peasant, his vassal; and, especially, being so lately married to a lady with whom he was passionately in love."

"Hold there!" said Joseph. "My Lord was incapable of such an action; If Master Edmund is the son of my Lord, he is also the son of my lady."

"How can that be," said Edmund?

"I don't know how," said Joseph, "but there is a person who can tell if she will; I mean Margery Twyford, who calls herself your mother."

"You meet my thoughts," said Edmund. "I had resolved, before you spoke, to visit her, and to interrogate her on the subject; I will ask my Lord's permission to go this very day."

"That is right," said Oswald, "but be cautious and prudent in your enquiries."

"If you," said Edmund, "would bear me company, I should do better; she might think herself obliged to answer your questions; and, being less interested in the event, you would be more discreet in your interrogations."

"That I will most readily," said he, "and I will ask my Lord's permission for us both."

"This point is well determined," said Joseph. "I am impatient for the result; and I believe my feet will carry me to meet you whether I consent or not."

"I am as impatient as you," said Oswald, "but let us be silent as the grave, and let not a word or look indicate any thing knowing or mysterious."

The daylight began to dawn upon their conference; and Edmund, observing it, begged his friends to withdraw in silence. They did so, and left Edmund to his own recollections. His thoughts were too much employed for sleep to approach him; he threw himself upon the bed, and lay meditating how he should proceed; a thousand schemes offered themselves and were rejected; But he resolved, at all events, to leave Baron Fitz-Owen's family the first opportunity that presented itself.

He was summoned, as before, to attend my Lord at break-fast; during which, he was silent, absent, and reserved. My Lord observed it, and rallied him; enquiring how he had spent the night?

"In reflecting upon my situation, my Lord; and in laying plans for my future conduct." Oswald took the hint, and asked permission to visit Edmund's mother in his company, and acquaint her with his intentions of leaving the country soon. He consented freely; but seemed unresolved about Edmund's departure.

They set out directly, and Edmund went hastily to old Twyford's cottage, declaring that every field seemed a mile to him. "Restrain your warmth, my son," said Oswald, "compose your mind, and recover your breath, before you enter upon a business of such consequence." Margery met them at the door, and asked Edmund, what wind blew him thither?

"Is it so very surprising," said he, "that I should visit my parents?"

"Yes, it is," said she, "considering the treatment you have met with from us; but since Andrew is not in the house, I may say I am glad to see you; Lord bless you, what a fine youth you be grown! 'Tis a long time since I saw you; but that is not my fault; many a cross word, and many a blow, have I had on your account; but I may now venture to embrace my dear child."

Edmund came forward and embraced her fervently; the starting tears, on both sides, evinced their affection. "And why," said he, "should my father forbid you to embrace your child? what have I ever done to deserve his hatred?"

"Nothing, my dear boy! You were always good and tender-hearted, and deserved the love of every body."

"It is not common," said Edmund, "for a parent to hate his first-born son without his having deserved it."

"That is true," said Oswald. "It is uncommon, it is unnatural; nay, I am of opinion it is almost impossible. I am so convinced of this truth, that I believe the man who thus hates and abuses

Edmund, cannot be his father." In saying this, he observed her countenance attentively; she changed colour apparently. "Come," said he, "let us sit down; and do you, Margery, answer to what I have said."

"Blessed Virgin!" said Margery. "What does your reverence mean? what do you suspect?"

"I suspect," said he, "that Edmund is not the son of Andrew your husband."

"Lord bless me!" said she. "What is it you do suspect?"

"Do not evade my question, woman! I am come here by authority to examine you upon this point."

The woman trembled every joint. "Would to Heaven!" said she. "That Andrew was at home!"

"It is much better as it is," said Oswald. "You are the person we are to examine."

"Oh, father," said she, "do you think that I—that I—that I am to blame in this matter? what have I done?"

"Do you, sir," said he, "ask your own questions."

Upon this, Edmund threw himself at her feet, and embraced her knees. "O my mother!" said he, "for as such my heart owns you, tell me for the love of Heaven! Tell me, who was my father?"

"Gracious Heaven!" said she. "What will become of me?"

"Woman!" said Oswald. "Confess the truth, or you shall be compelled to do it; by whom had you this youth?"

"Who, I?" said she. "I had him! No, father, I am not guilty of the black crime of adultery; God, He knows my innocence; I am not worthy to be the mother of such a sweet youth as that is."

"You are not his mother, then, nor Andrew his father?"

"Oh, what shall I do?" said Margery. "Andrew will be the death of me!"

"No, he shall not," said Edmund. "You shall be protected and rewarded for the discovery."

"Goody,"* said Oswald, "confess the whole truth, and I will

---

* An abbreviation for "good woman."

protect you from harm and from blame; you may be the means of making Edmund's fortune, in which case he will certainly provide for you; on the other hand, by an obstinate silence you will deprive yourself of all advantages you might receive from the discovery; and, beside, you will soon be examined in a different manner, and be obliged to confess all you know, and nobody will thank you for it."

"Ah," said she, "but Andrew beat me the last time I spoke to Edmund; and told me he would break every bone in my skin, if ever I spoke to him again."

"He knows it then?" said Oswald.

"He know it! Lord help you, it was all his own doing."

"Tell us then," said Oswald, "for Andrew shall never know it, till it is out of his power to punish you."

"'Tis a long story," said she, "and cannot be told in a few words."

"It will never be told at this rate," said he. "Sit down and begin it instantly."

"My fate depends upon your words," said Edmund. "My soul is impatient of the suspense! If ever you loved me and cherished me, shew it now, and tell while I have breath to ask it."

He sat in extreme agitation of mind; his words and actions were equally expressive of his inward emotions.

"I will," said she, "but I must try to recollect all the circumstances. You must know, young man, that you are just one-and-twenty years of age."

"On what day was he born," said Oswald?

"The day before yesterday," said she, "the 21st of September."

"A remarkable era," said he.

"'Tis so, indeed," said Edmund, "Oh, that night! That apartment!"

"Be silent," said Oswald, "and do you, Margery, begin your story."

"I will," said she. "Just one-and-twenty years ago, on that very day, I lost my first-born son; I got a hurt by over-reaching myself, when I was near my time, and so the poor child died. And so, as I was sitting all alone, and very melancholy, Andrew came home from work; 'See, Margery,' said he, 'I have brought you a child instead of that you have lost.' So he gave me a bundle, as I thought; but sure enough it was a child; a poor helpless babe just born, and only rolled up in a fine handkerchief, and over that a rich velvet cloak, trimmed with gold lace. 'And where did you find this?' says I. 'Upon the foot-bridge,' says he, 'just below the clayfield. This child,' said he, 'belongs to some great folk, and perhaps it may be enquired after one day, and may make our fortunes; take care of it,' said he, 'and bring it up as if it was your own.' The poor infant was cold, and it cried, and looked up at me so pitifully, that I loved it; beside, my milk was troublesome to me, and I was glad to be eased of it; so I gave it the breast, and from that hour I loved the child as if it were my own, and so I do still if I dared to own it."

"And this is all you know of Edmund's birth?" said Oswald.

"No, not all," said Margery, "but pray look out and see whether Andrew is coming, for I am all over in a twitter."

"He is not," said Oswald. "Go on, I beseech you!"

"This happened," said she, "as I told you, on the 21st. On the morrow, my Andrew went out early to work, along with one Robin Rouse, our neighbour; they had not been gone above an hour, when they both came back seemingly very much frightened. Says Andrew, 'Go you, Robin, and borrow a pickaxe at neighbour Styles's.' What is the matter now?' said I. 'Matter enough!' quoth Andrew. 'We may come to be hanged, perhaps, as many an innocent man has before us.' 'Tell me what is the matter,' said I. 'I will,' said he, 'but if ever you open your mouth about it, woe be to you!' 'I never will,' said I, but he made me swear by all the blessed saints in the Calendar; and then he told me, that, as Robin and he were going over the foot-bridge, where he found the child the evening before, they saw something floating upon the water; so they followed it, till it stuck against a stake, and found it to be the dead body of a woman; 'as sure as you are alive, Madge,' said he, 'this was the mother of the child I brought home.'"

"Merciful God!" said Edmund. "Am I the child of that hapless mother?"

"Be composed," said Oswald. "Proceed, good woman, the time is precious."

"And so," continued she, "Andrew told me they dragged the body out of the river, and it was richly dressed, and must be somebody of consequence. 'I suppose,' said he, 'when the poor Lady had taken care of her child, she went to find some help; and, the night being dark, her foot slipped, and she fell into the river, and was drowned.'

"'Lord have mercy!' said Robin. 'What shall we do with the dead body? We may be taken up for the murder; what had we to do to meddle with it?' 'Ay, but,' says Andrew, 'we must have something to do with it now; and our wisest way is to bury it.' Robin was sadly frightened, but at last they agreed to carry it into the wood, and bury it there; so they came home for a pickaxe and shovel. 'Well,' said I, 'Andrew, but will you bury all the rich clothes you speak of?' 'Why,' said he, 'it would be both a sin and a shame to strip the dead.' 'So it would,' said I; 'but I will give you a sheet to wrap the body in, and you may take off her upper garments, and any thing of value; but do not strip her to the skin for any thing.' 'Well said, wench!' said he; 'I will do as you say.' So I fetched a sheet, and by that time Robin was come back, and away they went together.

"They did not come back again till noon, and then they sat down and ate a morsel together. Says Andrew, 'Now we may sit down and eat in peace.' 'Aye,' says Robin, 'and sleep in peace too, for we have done no harm.' 'No, to be sure,' said I; 'but yet I am much concerned that the poor Lady had not Christian burial.' 'Never trouble thyself about that,' said Andrew; 'we have done the best we could for her; but let us see what we have got in our bags; we must divide them.' So they opened their bags, and took out a fine gown and a pair of rich shoes; but, besides these, there was a fine necklace with a golden locket, and a pair of earrings. Says Andrew, and winked at me, 'I will have these, and you may take the rest.' Robin said, he was satisfied, and so he went his way. When he was gone, 'Here, you fool,' says Andrew, 'take these, and keep them as safe as the bud of your eye; If ever young master is found, these will make our fortune.'"

"And have you them now?" said Oswald.

"Yes, that I have," answered she. "Andrew would have sold them long ago, but I always put him off it."

"Heaven be praised!" said Edmund.

"Hush," said Oswald, "let us not lose time; proceed, Goody!"

"Nay," said Margery, "I have not much more to say. We looked every day to hear some enquiries after the child, but nothing passed, nobody was missing."

"Did nobody of note die about that time?" said Oswald.

"Why yes," said Margery, "the widow Lady Lovel died that same week; by the same token, Andrew went to the funeral, and brought home a scutcheon, which I keep unto this day."

"Very well; go on."

"My husband behaved well enough to the boy, till such time as he had two or three children of his own; and then he began to grumble, and say, it was hard to maintain other folks' children, when he found it hard enough to keep his own; I loved the boy quite as well as my own; often and often have I pacified Andrew, and made him to hope that he should one day or other be paid for his trouble; but at last he grew out of patience, and gave over all hopes of that kind.

"As Edmund grew up, he grew sickly and tender, and could not bear hard labour; and that was another reason why my husband could not bear with him. 'If,' quoth he, 'the boy could earn his living, I did not care; but I must bear all the expence.' There came an old pilgrim into our parts; he was a scholar, and had been a soldier, and he taught Edmund to read; then he told him histories of wars, and knights, and lords, and great men; and Edmund took such delight in hearing him, that he would not take to any thing else.

"To be sure, Edwin was a pleasant companion; he would tell old stories, and sing old songs, that one could have sat all night to hear him; but, as I was a saying, Edmund grew more and more fond of reading, and less of work; however, he would run of errands, and do many handy turns for the neighbours; and he was so courteous a lad, that people took notice of him. Andrew once catched him alone reading, and then told him, that if he did not find some way to earn his bread, he would turn him out of doors in a very short time; and so he would have done, sure enough, if my Lord Fitz-Owen had not taken him into his service just in the nick."

"Very well, Goody," said Oswald, "you have told your story very well; I am glad, for Edmund's sake, that you can do it so properly. But now, can you keep a secret?"

"Why, an't please your reverence, I think I have shewed you that I can."

"But can you keep it from your husband?"

"Aye," said she, "surely I can; for I dare not tell it him."

"That is a good security," said he, "but I must have a better. You must swear upon this book not to disclose any thing that has passed between us three, till we desire you to do it. Be assured you will soon be called upon for this purpose; Edmund's birth is near the discovery; He is the son of parents of high degree; and it will be in his power to make your fortune, when he takes possession of his own."

"Holy Virgin! What is it you tell me? How you rejoice me to hear, that what I have so long prayed for will come to pass!"

She took the oath required, saying it after Oswald.

"Now," said he, "go and fetch the tokens you have mentioned."

When she was gone, Edmund's passions, long suppressed, broke out in tears and exclamations; he kneeled down, and, with his hands clasped together, returned thanks to Heaven for the discovery. Oswald begged him to be composed, lest Margery should perceive his agitation, and misconstrue the cause. She soon returned with the necklace and earrings; They were pearls of great value; and the necklace had a locket, on which the cypher of Lovel was engraved.

"This," said Oswald, "is indeed a proof of consequence. Keep it, sir, for it belongs to you."

"Must he take it away?" said she.

"Certainly," returned Oswald, "we can do nothing without it; but if Andrew should ask for it, you must put him off for the present, and hereafter he will find his account in it."

Margery consented reluctantly to part with the jewels; and, after some further conversation, they took leave of her.

Edmund embraced her affectionately. "I thank you with my whole heart," said he, "for all your goodness to me! Though I confess, I never felt much regard for your husband, yet for you I had always the tender affection of a son. You will, I trust, give your evidence in my behalf when called upon; and I hope it will one day be in my power to reward your kindness; In that case, I will own you as my foster-mother, and you shall always be treated as such."

Margery wept. "The Lord grant it!" said she, "and I pray him to have you in his holy keeping. Farewell, my dear child!"

Oswald desired them to separate for fear of intrusion; and they returned to the castle. Margery stood at the door of her cottage, looking every way to see if the coast was clear.

"Now, Sir," said Oswald, "I congratulate you as the son of Lord and Lady Lovel; the proofs are strong and indisputable."

"To us they are so," said Edmund, "but how shall we make them so to others? And what are we to think of the funeral of Lady Lovel?"

"As of a fiction," said Oswald, "the work of the present lord, to secure his title and fortune."

"And what means can we use to dispossess him?" said Edmund. "He is not a man for a poor youth like me to contend with."

"Doubt not," said Oswald, "but Heaven, who has evidently conducted you by the hand thus far, will complete its own work; for my part, I can only wonder and adore!"

"Give me your advice then," said Edmund, "for Heaven assists us by natural means."

"It seems to me," said Oswald, "that your first step must be to make a friend of some great man, of consequence enough to espouse your cause, and to get this affair examined into by authority."

Edmund started, and crossed himself; he suddenly exclaimed, "A friend! Yes, I have a friend! a powerful one too; one sent by Heaven to be my protector, but whom I have too long neglected."

"Who can that be?" said Oswald.

"Who should it be," said Edmund, "but that good Sir Philip Harclay, the chosen friend of him, whom I shall from henceforward call my father."

"'Tis true indeed," said Oswald, "and this is a fresh proof of what I before observed, that Heaven assists you, and will complete its own work."

"I think so myself," said Edmund, "and rely upon its direction. I have already determined on my future conduct, which I will communicate to you. My first step shall be to leave the castle; my Lord has this day given me a horse, upon which I purpose to set out this very night, without the knowledge of any of the family. I will go to Sir Philip Harclay; I will throw myself at his feet, relate my strange story, and implore his protection; With him I will consult on the most proper way of bringing this murderer to public justice; and I will be guided by his advice and direction in everything."

"Nothing can be better," said Oswald, "than what you propose; but give me leave to offer an addition to your scheme. You shall set off in the dead of night, as you intend; Joseph and I, will favour your departure in such a manner as to throw a mystery over the circumstances of it. Your disappearing at such a time from the haunted apartment will terrify and confound all the family; they will puzzle themselves in vain to account for it, and they will be afraid to pry into the secrets of that place."

"You say well, and I approve your addition," replied Edmund. "Suppose, likewise, there was a letter written in a mysterious manner, and dropt in my Lord's way, or sent to him afterwards; it would forward our design, and frighten them away from that apartment."

"That shall be my care," said Oswald, "and I will warrant you that they will not find themselves disposed to inhabit it presently."

"But how shall I leave my dear friend Mr. William, without a word of notice of this separation?"

"I have thought of that too," said Oswald, "and I will so manage, as to acquaint him with it in such a manner as he shall think out of the common course of things, and which shall make him wonder and be silent."

"How will you do that," said Edmund?

"I will tell you hereafter," said Oswald, "for here comes old Joseph to meet us."

He came, indeed, as fast as his age would permit him. As soon as he was within hearing, he asked them what news? They related all that had passed at Twyford's cottage; he heard them with the greatest eagerness of attention, and as soon as they came to the great event, "I knew it! I knew it!" exclaimed Joseph. "I was sure it would prove so! Thank God for it! But I will be the first to acknowledge my young Lord, and I will live and die his faithful servant!" Here Joseph attempted to kneel to him, but Edmund prevented him with a warm embrace.

"My friend! My dear friend!" said he. "I cannot suffer a man of your age to kneel to me; are you not one of my best and truest friends? I will ever remember your disinterested affection for me; and if heaven restores me to my rights, it shall be one of my first cares to render your old age easy and happy." Joseph wept over him, and it was some time before he could utter a word.

Oswald gave them both time to recover their emotion, by acquainting Joseph with Edmund's scheme for his departure.

Joseph wiped his eyes and spoke. "I have thought," said he, "of something that will be both agree and useful to my dear master. John Wyatt, Sir Philip Harclay's servant, is now upon a visit at his father's; I have heard that he goes home soon; now he would be both a guide and companion, on the way."

"That is, indeed, a happy circumstance," said Edmund, "but how shall we know certainly the time of his departure?"

"Why, Sir, I will go to him, and enquire; and bring you word directly."

"Do so," said Edmund, "and you will oblige me greatly."

"But, Sir," said Oswald, "I think it will be best not to let John Wyatt know who is to be his companion; only let Joseph tell him that a gentleman is going to visit his master, and, if possible, prevail upon him to set out this night."

"Do so, my good friend," said Edmund, "and tell him, further, that this person has business of great consequence to communicate to his master, and cannot delay his journey on any account."

"I will do this, you may depend," said Joseph, "and acquaint you with my success as soon as possible; but, sir, you must not go without a guide, at any rate."

"I trust I shall not," said Edmund, "though I go alone; he that has received such a call as I have, can want no other, nor fear any danger."

They conversed on these points till they drew near the castle, when Joseph left them to go on his errand, and Edmund attended his Lord at dinner. The Baron observed that he was silent and reserved; the conversation languished on both sides. As soon as dinner was ended, Edmund asked permission to go up into his own apartment; where he packed up some necessaries, and made a hasty preparation for his departure.

Afterwards he walked into the garden, revolving in his mind the peculiarity of his situation, and the uncertainty of his future prospects; lost in thought, he walked to and fro in a covered walk, with his arms crossed and his eyes cast down, without perceiving that he was observed by two females who stood at a distance watching his motions. It was the Lady Emma, and her attendant, who were thus engaged. At length, he lifted up his eyes and saw them; he stood still, and was irresolute whether to advance or retire. They approached him; and, as they drew near, fair Emma spoke.

"You have been so wrapt in meditation, Edmund, that I am apprehensive of some new vexation that I am yet a stranger to. Would it were in my power to lessen those you have already! But tell me if I guess truly?"

He stood still irresolute, he answered with hesitation. "O, lady—I am—I am grieved, I am concerned, to be the cause of so much confusion in this noble family, to which I am so much indebted; I see no way to lessen these evils but to remove the cause of them."

"Meaning yourself?" said she.

"Certainly, Madam; and I was meditating on my departure."

"But," said she, "by your departure you will not remove the cause."

"How so, madam?"

"Because you are not the cause, but those you will leave behind you."

"Lady Emma!"

"How can you affect this ignorance, Edmund? You know well enough it is that odious Wenlock, your enemy and my aversion, that has caused all this mischief among us, and will much more, if he is not removed."

"This, madam, is a subject that it becomes me to be silent upon. Mr. Wenlock is your kinsman; he is not my friend; and for that reason I ought not to speak against him, nor you to hear it from me. If he has used me ill, I am recompensed by the generous treatment of my Lord your father, who is all that is great and good; he has allowed me to justify myself to him, and he has restored me to his good opinion, which I prize among the best gifts of heaven. Your amiable brother William thinks well of me, and his esteem is infinitely dear to me; and you, excellent Lady, permit me to hope that you honour me with your good opinion. Are not these ample amends for the ill-will Mr. Wenlock bears me?"

"My opinion of you, Edmund," said she, "is fixed and settled. It is not founded upon events of yesterday, but upon long knowledge and experience; upon your whole conduct and character."

"You honour me, lady! Continue to think well of me, it will excite me to deserve it. When I am far distant from this place, the remembrance of your goodness will be a cordial to my heart."

"But why will you leave us, Edmund? Stay and defeat the designs of your enemy; you shall have my wishes and assistance."

"Pardon me, Madam, that is among the things I cannot do, even if it were in my power, which it is not. Mr. Wenlock loves you, lady, and if he is so unhappy as to be your aversion, that is a punishment severe enough. For the rest, I may be unfortunate by the wickedness of others, but if I am unworthy, it must be by my own fault."

"So then you think it is an unworthy action to oppose Mr. Wenlock! Very well, sir. Then I suppose you wish him success; you wish that I may be married to him?"

"I, Madam!" said Edmund, confused. "What am I that I should give my opinion on an affair of so much consequence? You distress me by the question. May you be happy! may you enjoy your own wishes!"

He sighed, he turned away. She called him back; he trembled, and kept silence.

She seemed to enjoy his confusion; she was cruel enough to repeat the question.

"Tell me, Edmund, and truly, do you wish to see me give my hand to Wenlock? I insist upon your answer."

All on a sudden he recovered both his voice and courage; he stepped forward, his person erect, his countenance assured, his voice resolute and intrepid.

"Since Lady Emma insists upon my answer, since she avows a dislike to Wenlock, since she condescends to ask my opinion, I will tell her my thoughts, my wishes."

The fair Emma now trembled in her turn; she blushed, looked down, and was ashamed to have spoken so freely.

Edmund went on. "My most ardent wishes are, that the fair Emma may reserve her heart and hand till a certain person, a friend of mine, is at liberty to solicit them; whose utmost ambition is, first to deserve, and then to obtain them."

"Your friend, Sir!" said Lady Emma, her brow clouded, her eye disdainful.

Edmund proceeded. "My friend is so particularly circumstanced that he cannot at present with propriety ask for Lady Emma's favour; but as soon as he has gained a cause that is yet in suspence, he will openly declare his pretensions, and if he is unsuccessful, he will then condemn himself to eternal silence."

Lady Emma knew not what to think of this declaration; she hoped, she feared, she meditated; but her attention was too strongly excited to be satisfied without some gratification; After a pause, she pursued the subject.

"And this friend of yours, sir, of what degree and fortune is he?"

Edmund smiled; but, commanding his emotion, he replied, "His birth is noble, his degree and fortune uncertain."

Her countenance fell, she sighed; he proceeded. "It is utterly impossible," said he, "for any man of inferior degree to aspire to Lady Emma's favour; her noble birth, the dignity of her beauty and virtues, must awe and keep at their proper distance, all men of inferior degree and merit; they may admire, they may revere;

but they must not presume to approach too near, lest their presumption should meet with its punishment."

"Well, sir," said she, suddenly, "and so this friend of yours has commissioned you to speak in his behalf?"

"He has, Madam."

"Then I must tell you, that I think his assurance is very great, and yours not much less."

"I am sorry for that, Madam."

"Tell him, that I shall reserve my heart and hand for the man to whom my father shall bid me give them."

"Very well, Lady; I am certain my Lord loves you too well to dispose of them against your inclination."

"How do you know that, sir? But tell him, that the man that hopes for my favour must apply to my Lord for his."

"That is my friend's intention—his resolution, I should say—as soon as he can do it with propriety; and I accept your permission for him to do so."

"My permission did you say? I am astonished at your assurance! Tell me no more of your friend; But perhaps you are pleading for Wenlock all this time; It is all one to me; only, say no more."

"Are you offended with me, madam?"

"No matter, sir."

"Yes, it is."

"I am surprised at you, Edmund."

"I am surprised at my own temerity; but, forgive me."

"It does not signify; good bye ty'e, sir."

"Don't leave me in anger, madam; I cannot bear that. Perhaps I may not see you again for a long time."

He looked afflicted; she turned back. "I do forgive you, Edmund; I was concerned for you; but, it seems, you are more concerned for every body than for yourself." She sighed. "Farewell!" said she.

Edmund gazed on her with tenderness; he approached her, he just touched her hand; his heart was rising to his lips, but he recollected his situation; he checked himself immediately; he retired back, he sighed deeply, bowed low, and hastily quitted her.

The lady turning into another walk, he reached the house first, and went up again to his chamber; he threw himself upon his knees; prayed for a thousand blessings upon every one of the family of his benefactor, and involuntarily wept at mentioning the name of the charming Emma, whom he was about to leave abruptly, and perhaps for ever. He then endeavoured to compose himself, and once more attended the Baron; wished him a good night; and withdrew to his chamber, till he was called upon to go again to the haunted apartment.

He came down equipped for his journey, and went hastily for fear of observation; he paid his customary devotions, and soon after Oswald tapped at the door. They conferred together upon the interesting subject that engrossed their attention, until Joseph came to them, who brought the rest of Edmund's baggage, and some refreshment for him before he set out. Edmund promised to give them the earliest information of his situation and success. At the hour of twelve they heard the same groans as the night before in the lower apartment; but, being somewhat familiarized to it, they were not so strongly affected. Oswald crossed himself, and prayed for the departed soul; he also prayed for Edmund, and recommended him to the Divine protection. He then arose, and embraced that young man; who, also, took a tender leave of his friend Joseph. They then went, with silence and caution, through a long gallery; they descended the stairs in the same manner; they crossed the hall in profound silence, and hardly dared to breathe, lest they should be overheard; they found some difficulty in opening one of the folding doors, which at last they accomplished; they were again in jeopardy at the outward gate. At length they conveyed him safely into the stables; there they again embraced him, and prayed for his prosperity.

He then mounted his horse, and set forward to Wyatt's cottage; he hallooed at the door, and was answered from within. In a few minutes John came out to him.

"What, is it you, Master Edmund?"

"Hush!" said he. "Not a word of who I am; I go upon private business, and would not wish to be known."

"If you will go forward, sir, I will soon overtake you." He did so; and they pursued their journey to the north. In the mean time, Oswald and Joseph returned in silence into the house; they retired to their respective apartments without hearing or being heard by any one.

About the dawn of day Oswald intended to lay his packets in the way of those to whom they were addressed; after much contrivance he determined to take a bold step, and, if he were discovered, to frame some excuse. Encouraged by his late success, he went on tip-toe into Master William's chamber, placed a letter upon his pillow, and withdrew unheard. Exulting in his heart, he attempted the Baron's apartment, but found it fastened within. Finding this scheme frustrated, he waited till the hour the Baron was expected down to breakfast, and laid the letter and the key of the haunted apartment upon the table. Soon after, he saw the Baron enter the breakfast room; he got out of sight, but staid within call, preparing himself for a summons. The Baron sat down to breakfast; he saw a letter directed to himself—he opened it, and to his great surprise, read as follows:

> "The guardian of the haunted apartment to Baron Fitz-Owen. To thee I remit the key of my charge, until the right owner shall come, who will both discover and avenge my wrongs; then, woe be to the guilty!—But let the innocent rest in peace. In the mean time, let none presume to explore the secrets of my apartment, lest they suffer for their temerity."

The Baron was struck with amazement at the letter. He took up the key, examined it, then laid it down, and took up the letter; he was in such confusion of thought, he knew not what to do or say for several minutes. At length he called his servants about him; the first question he asked was—

"Where is Edmund?"

"They could not tell."

"Has he been called?"

"Yes, my Lord, but nobody answered, and the key was not in the door."

"Where is Joseph?"

"Gone into the stables."

"Where is Father Oswald?"

"In his study."

"Seek him, and desire him to come hither."

By the time the Baron had read the letter over again, he came.

He had been framing a steady countenance to answer to all interrogatories. As he came in he attentively observed the Baron, whose features were in strong agitation; as soon as he saw Oswald, he spoke as one out of breath.

"Take that key, and read this letter!"

He did so, shrugged up his shoulders, and remained silent.

"Father," said my Lord, "what think you of this letter?"

"It is a very surprising one."

"The contents are alarming. Where is Edmund?"

"I do not know."

"Has nobody seen him?"

"Not that I know of."

"Call my sons, my kinsmen, my servants."

The servants came in.

"Have any of you seen or heard of Edmund?"

"No," was the answer.

"Father, step upstairs to my sons and kinsmen, and desire them to come down immediately."

Oswald withdrew; and went, first, to Mr. William's chamber. "My dear sir, you must come to my Lord now directly—he has something extraordinary to communicate to you."

"And so have I, father—see what I have found upon my pillow!"

"Pray, sir, read it to me before you shew it to any body; my Lord is alarmed too much already, and wants nothing to increase his consternation."

William read his letter, while Oswald looked as if he was an utter stranger to the contents, which were these:

"Whatever may be heard or seen, let the seal of friendship be upon thy lips. The peasant Edmund is no more; but there still lives a man who hopes to acknowledge, and repay, the Lord Fitz-Owen's generous care and protection; to return his beloved William's vowed affection, and to claim his friendship on terms of equality."

"What," said William, "can this mean?"

"It is not easy to say," replied Oswald.

"Can you tell what is the cause of this alarm?"

"I can tell you nothing, but that my Lord desires to see you directly—pray make haste down; I must go up to your brothers and kinsmen, nobody knows what to think, or believe."

Master William went down stairs, and Father Oswald went to the malcontents. As soon as he entered the outward door of their apartment, Mr. Wenlock called out. "Here comes the friend— now for some new proposal!"

"Gentlemen," said Oswald, "my Lord desires your company immediately in the breakfast parlour."

"What! To meet your favourite Edmund, I suppose?" said Mr. Wenlock.

"No, sir."

"What, then, is the matter?" said Sir Robert.

"Something very extraordinary has happened, gentlemen.

Edmund is not to be found—he disappeared from the haunted apartment, the key of which was conveyed to my Lord in a strange manner, with a letter from an unknown hand; my Lord is both surprised and concerned, and wishes to have your opinion and advice on the occasion."

"Tell him," said Sir Robert, "we will wait upon him immediately."

As Oswald went away, he heard Wenlock say, "So Edmund is gone, it is no matter how, or whither."

Another said, "I hope the ghost has taken him out of the way." The rest laughed at the conceit, as they followed Oswald down stairs. They found the Baron, and his son William, commenting upon the key and the letter. My Lord gave them to Sir Robert, who looked on them with marks of surprise and confusion.

The Baron addressed him—

"Is not this a very strange affair? Son Robert, lay aside your ill humours, and behave to your father with the respect and affection his tenderness deserves from you, and give me your advice and opinion on this alarming subject."

"My Lord," said Sir Robert, "I am as much confounded as yourself—I can give no advice—let my cousins see the letter— let us have their opinion."

They read it in turn—they were equally surprised; but when it came into Wenlock's hand, he paused and meditated some minutes.

At length—"I am indeed surprised, and still more concerned, to see my Lord and uncle the dupe of an artful contrivance; and, if he will permit me, I shall endeavour to unriddle it, to the confusion of all that are concerned in it."

"Do so, Dick," said my Lord, "and you shall have my thanks for it."

"This letter," said he, "I imagine to be the contrivance of Edmund, or some ingenious friend of his, to conceal some designs they have against the peace of this family, which has been too often disturbed upon that rascal's account."

"But what end could be proposed by it?" said the Baron.

"Why, one part of the scheme is to cover Edmund's departure, that is clear enough; for the rest, we can only guess at it—perhaps he may be concealed somewhere in that apartment, from whence he may rush out in the night, and either rob or murder us; or, at least, alarm and terrify the family."

The Baron smiled.

"You shoot beyond the mark, sir, and overshoot yourself, as you have done before now; you shew only your inveteracy against that poor lad, whom you cannot mention with temper. To what purpose should he shut himself up there, to be starved?"

"Starved! No, no! He has friends in this house (looking at Oswald), who will not suffer him to want anything; those who have always magnified his virtues, and extenuated his faults, will lend a hand to help him in time of need; and, perhaps, to assist his ingenious contrivances."

Oswald shrugged up his shoulders, and remained silent.

"This is a strange fancy of yours, Dick," said my Lord, "but I am willing to pursue it,—first, to discover what you drive at; and, secondly, to satisfy all that are here present of the truth or falsehood of it, that they may know what value to set upon your sagacity hereafter. Let us all go over that apartment together; and let Joseph be called to attend us thither."

Oswald offered to call him, but Wenlock stopped him. "No, father," said he, "you must stay with us; we want your ghostly counsel and advice; Joseph shall have no private conference with you."

"What mean you," said Oswald, "to insinuate to my Lord against me or Joseph? But your ill-will spares nobody. It will one day be known who is the disturber of the peace of this family; I wait for that time, and am silent."

Joseph came; when he was told whither they were going, he looked hard at Oswald. Wenlock observed them.

"Lead the way, father," said he, "and Joseph shall follow us."

Oswald smiled.

"We will go where Heaven permits us," said he. "Alas! The wisdom of man can neither hasten, nor retard, its decrees."

They followed the father up stairs, and went directly to the haunted apartment. The Baron unlocked the door; he bid Joseph open the shutters, and admit the daylight, which had been excluded for many years. They went over the rooms above stairs, and then descended the staircase, and through the lower rooms in the same manner. However, they overlooked the closet, in which the fatal secret was concealed; the door was covered with tapestry, the same as the room, and united so well that it seemed but one piece. Wenlock tauntingly desired Father Oswald to introduce them to the ghost. The father, in reply, asked them where they should find Edmund. "Do you think," said he, "that he lies hid in my pocket, or in Joseph's?"

"'Tis no matter," answered he. "Thoughts are free."

"My opinion of you, Sir," said Oswald, "is not founded upon thoughts—I judge of men by their actions,—a rule, I believe, it will not suit you to be tried by."

"None of your insolent admonitions, father!" returned Wenlock. "This is neither the time nor the place for them."

"That is truer than you are aware of, sir; I meant not to enter into the subject just now."

"Be silent," said my Lord.

"I shall enter into this subject with you hereafter—then look you be prepared for it. In the mean time, do you, Dick Wenlock, answer to my questions:—Do you think Edmund is concealed in this apartment?"

"No, sir."

"Do you think there is any mystery in it?"

"No, my Lord."

"Is it haunted, think you?"

"No, I think not."

"Should you be afraid to try?"

"In what manner, my Lord?"

"Why, you have shewn your wit upon the subject, and I mean to shew your courage;—you, and Jack Markham your confident, shall sleep here three nights, as Edmund has done before."

"Sir," said Sir Robert, "for what purpose? I should be glad to understand why."

"I have my reasons, sir, as well as your kinsmen there. No reply, Sirs! I insist upon being obeyed in this point. Joseph, let the beds be well aired, and every thing made agreeable to the gentlemen; If there is any contrivance to impose upon me, they, I am sure, will have pleasure in detecting it; and, if not, I shall obtain my end in making these rooms habitable. Oswald, come with me; and the rest may go where they list till dinner-time."

The Baron went with Oswald into the parlour.

"Now tell me, father," said he, "do you disapprove what I have done?"

"Quite the contrary, my Lord," said he. "I entirely approve it."

"But you do not know all my reasons for it. Yesterday Edmund's behaviour was different from what I have ever seen it—he is naturally frank and open in all his ways; but he was then silent, thoughtful, absent; he sighed deeply, and once I saw tears stand in his eyes. Now, I do suspect there is something uncommon in that apartment—that Edmund has discovered the secret; and, fearing to disclose it, he is fled away from the house. As to this letter, perhaps he may have written it to hint that there is more than he dares reveal; I tremble at the hints contained in it, though I shall appear to make light of it. But I and mine are innocent; and if Heaven discloses the guilt of others, I ought to adore and submit to its decrees."

"That is prudently and piously resolved, my Lord; let us do our duty, and leave events to Heaven."

"But, father, I have a further view in obliging my kinsmen to sleep there:—if any thing should appear to them, it is better that it should only be known to my own family; if there is nothing in it, I shall put to the proof the courage and veracity of my two kinsmen, of whom I think very indifferently. I mean shortly to enquire into many things I have heard lately to their disadvantage; and, if I find them guilty, they shall not escape with impunity."

"My Lord," said Oswald, "you judge like yourself; I wish you to make enquiry concerning them, and believe the result will be to their confusion, and your Lordship will be enabled to re-establish the peace of your family."

During this conversation, Oswald was upon his guard, lest any thing should escape that might create suspicion. He withdrew as soon as he could with decency, and left the Baron meditating what all these things should mean; he feared there was some misfortune impending over his house, though he knew not from what cause.

He dined with his children and kinsmen, and strove to appear cheerful; but a gloom was perceivable through his deportment. Sir Robert was reserved and respectful; Mr. William was silent and attentive; the rest of the family dutifully assiduous to my Lord; only Wenlock and Markham were sullen and chagrined. The Baron detained the young men the whole afternoon; he strove to amuse and to be amused; he shewed the greatest affection and parental regard to his children, and endeavoured to conciliate their affections, and engage their gratitude by kindness. Wenlock and Markham felt their courage abate as the night approached; At the hour of nine, old Joseph came to conduct them to the haunted apartment; they took leave of their kinsmen, and went up stairs with heavy hearts.

They found the chamber set in order for them, and a table spread with provision and good liquor to keep up their spirits.

"It seems," said Wenlock, "that your friend Edmund was obliged to you for his accommodations here."

"Sir," said Joseph, "his accommodations were bad enough the first night; but, afterwards, they were bettered by my Lord's orders."

"Owing to your officious cares?" said Wenlock.

"I own it," said Joseph, "and I am not ashamed of it."

"Are you not anxious to know what is become of him?" said Markham.

"Not at all, sir; I trust he is in the best protection; so good a young man as he is, is safe everywhere."

"You see, cousin Jack," said Wenlock, "how this villain has stole the hearts of my uncle's servants; I suppose this canting old fellow knows where he is, if the truth were known."

"Have you any further commands for me, gentlemen?" said the old man.

"No, not we."

"Then I am ordered to attend my Lord, when you have done with me."

"Go, then, about your business."

Joseph went away, glad to be dismissed.

"What shall we do, cousin Jack," said Wenlock, "to pass away the time?—it is plaguy dull sitting here."

"Dull enough," said Markham, "I think the best thing we can do, is to go to bed and sleep it away."

"Faith!" says Wenlock. "I am in no disposition to sleep. Who would have thought the old man would have obliged us to spend the night here?"

"Don't say us, I beg of you; it was all your own doing," replied Markham.

"I did not intend he should have taken me at my word."

"Then you should have spoken more cautiously. I have always been governed by you, like a fool as I am; you play the braggart, and I suffer for it; But they begin to see through your fine-spun arts and contrivances, and I believe you will meet with your deserts one day or other."

"What now? do you mean to affront me, Jack? Know, that some are born to plan, others to execute; I am one of the former, thou of the latter. Know your friend, or—"

"Or what?" replied Markham. "Do you mean to threaten me? If you do!"

"What then?" said Wenlock.

"Why, then, I will try which of us two is the best man, sir!"

Upon this Markham arose, and put himself into a posture of defence. Wenlock perceiving he was serious in his anger, began to soothe him; he persuaded, he flattered, he promised great things if he would be composed. Markham was sullen, uneasy, resentful; whenever he spoke, it was to upbraid Wenlock with his treachery and falsehood. Wenlock tried all his eloquence to get him into a good humour, but in vain; he threatened to acquaint his uncle with all that he knew, and to exculpate himself at the other's expence. Wenlock began to find his choler rise; they were both almost choaked with rage; and, at length, they both rose with a resolution to fight.

As they stood with their fists clenched, on a sudden they were alarmed with a dismal groan from the room underneath. They stood like statues petrified by fear, yet listening with trembling expectation. A second groan increased their consternation; and, soon after, a third completed it. They staggered to a seat, and sunk down upon it, ready to faint. Presently, all the doors flew open, a pale glimmering light appeared at the door, from the staircase, and a man in complete armour entered the room. He stood, with one hand extended, pointing to the outward door; they took the hint, and crawled away as fast as fear would let them; they staggered along the gallery, and from thence to the Baron's apartment, where Wenlock sunk down in a swoon, and Markham had just strength enough to knock at the door.

The servant who slept in the outward room alarmed his Lord. Markham cried out, "For Heaven's sake, let us in!"

Upon hearing his voice, the door was opened, and Markham approached his Uncle in such an attitude of fear, as excited a degree of it in the Baron. He pointed to Wenlock, who was with some difficulty recovered from the fit he was fallen into; the servant was terrified, he rung the alarm-bell; the servants came running from all parts to their Lord's apartment; The young gentlemen came likewise, and presently all was confusion, and the terror was universal. Oswald, who guessed the business, was the only one that could question them. He asked several times,

"What is the matter?"

Markham, at last, answered him, "We have seen the ghost!"

All regard to secrecy was now at an end; the echo ran through the whole family—"They have seen the ghost!"

The Baron desired Oswald to talk to the young men, and endeavour to quiet the disturbance. He came forward; he comforted some, he rebuked others; he had the servants retire into the outward room. The Baron, with his sons and kinsmen, remained in the bed-chamber.

"It is very unfortunate," said Oswald, "that this affair should be made so public; surely these young men might have related what they had seen, without alarming the whole family. I am very much concerned upon my Lord's account."

"I thank you, father," said the Baron, "but prudence was quite overthrown here. Wenlock was half dead, and Markham half distracted; the family were alarmed without my being able to prevent it. But let us hear what these poor terrified creatures say."

Oswald demanded, "What have you seen, gentlemen?"

"The ghost!" said Markham.

"In what form did it appear?"

"A man in armour."

"Did it speak to you?"

"No."

"What did it do to terrify you so much?"

"It stood at the farthest door, and pointed to the outward door, as if to have us leave the room; we did not wait for a second notice, but came away as fast as we could."

"Did it follow you?"

"No."

"Then you need not have raised such a disturbance."

Wenlock lifted up his head, and spoke, "I believe, father, if you had been with us, you would not have stood upon ceremonies any more than we did. I wish my Lord would send you to parley with the ghost; for, without doubt, you are better qualified than we."

"My Lord," said Oswald, "I will go thither, with your permission; I will see that every thing is safe, and bring the key back to you; Perhaps this may help to dispel the fears that have been raised—at least, I will try to do it."

"I thank you, father, for your good offices—do as you please."

Oswald went into the outward room. "I am going," said he, "to shut up the apartment. The young gentlemen have been more frightened than they had occasion for; I will try to account for it. Which of you will go with me?"

They all drew back, except Joseph, who offered to bear him company. They went into the bedroom in the haunted apartment, and found every thing quiet there. They put out the fire, extinguished the lights, locked the door, and brought away the key. As they returned, "I thought how it would be," said Joseph.

"Hush! Not a word," said Oswald. "You find we are suspected of something, though they know not what. Wait till you are called upon, and then we will both speak to purpose." They carried the key to the Baron.

"All is quiet in the apartment," said Oswald, "as we can testify."

"Did you ask Joseph to go with you," said the Baron, "or did he offer himself?"

"My Lord, I asked if any body would go with me, and they all declined it but he; I thought proper to have a witness beside myself, for whatever might be seen or heard."

"Joseph, you were servant to the late Lord Lovel; what kind of man was he?"

"A very comely man, please your Lordship."

"Should you know him if you were to see him?"

"I cannot say, my Lord."

"Would you have any objection to sleep a night in that apartment?"

"I beg,"—"I hope,"—"I beseech your Lordship not to command me to do it!"

"You are then afraid; why did you offer yourself to go thither?"

"Because I was not so much frightened as the rest."

"I wish you would lie a night there; but I do not insist upon it."

"My Lord, I am a poor ignorant old man, not fit for such an undertaking; beside, if I should see the ghost, and if it should be the person of my master, and if it should tell me any thing, and bid me keep it secret, I should not dare to disclose it; and then, what service should I do your Lordship?"

"That is true, indeed," said the Baron.

"This speech," said Sir Robert, "is both a simple and an artful one. You see, however, that Joseph is not a man for us to depend upon; he regards the Lord Lovel, though dead, more than Lord Fitz-Owen, living; he calls him his master, and promises to keep his secrets. What say you, father, Is the ghost your master, or your friend? Are you under any obligation to keep his secrets?"

"Sir," said Oswald, "I answer as Joseph does; I would sooner die than discover a secret revealed in that manner."

"I thought as much," said Sir Robert, "there is a mystery in Father Oswald's behaviour, that I cannot comprehend."

"Do not reflect upon the father," said the Baron. "I have no cause to complain of him; perhaps the mystery may be too soon explained; but let us not anticipate evils. Oswald and Joseph have spoken like good men; I am satisfied with their answers; let us, who are innocent, rest in peace; and let us endeavour to restore peace in the family; and do you, father, assist us."

"With my best services," said Oswald. He called the servants in. "Let nothing be mentioned out of doors," said he, "of what has lately passed within, especially in the east apartment; the young gentlemen had not so much reason to be frightened as they apprehended; a piece of furniture fell down in the rooms underneath, which made the noise that alarmed them so much; but I can certify that all things in the rooms are in quiet, and there is nothing to fear. All of you attend me in the chapel in an hour; do your duties, put your trust in God, and obey your Lord, and you will find every thing go right as it used to do."

They dispersed; the sun rose, the day came on, and every thing went on in the usual course; but the servants were not so easily satisfied; they whispered that something was wrong, and expected the time that should set all right. The mind of the Baron was employed in meditating upon these circumstances, that seemed to him the forerunners of some great events; he sometimes thought of Edmund; he sighed for his expulsion, and lamented the uncertainty of his fate; but, to his family, he appeared easy and satisfied.

From the time of Edmund's departure, the fair Emma had many uneasy hours; she wished to enquire after him, but feared to shew any solicitude concerning him. The next day, when her brother William came into her apartment, she took courage to ask a question.

"Pray, brother, can you give any guess what is become of Edmund?"

"No," said he, with a sigh, "why do you ask me?"

"Because, my dear William, I should think if any body knew, it must be you; and I thought he loved you too well to leave you in ignorance. But don't you think he left the castle in a very strange manner?"

"I do, my dear; there is a mystery in every circumstance of his departure; Nevertheless (I will trust you with a secret), he did not leave the castle without making a distinction in my favour."

"I thought so," said she, "but you might tell me what you know about him."

"Alas, my dear Emma! I know nothing. When I saw him last, he seemed a good deal affected, as if he were taking leave of me; and I had a foreboding that we parted for a longer time than usual."

"Ah! So had I," said she, "when he parted from me in the garden."

"What leave did he take of you, Emma?"

She blushed, and hesitated to tell him all that passed between them; but he begged, persuaded, insisted; and, at length, under the strongest injunctions of secrecy, she told him all.

He said, "That Edmund's behaviour on that occasion was as mysterious as the rest of his conduct; but, now you have revealed your secret, you have a right to know mine."

He then gave her the letter he found upon his pillow; she read it with great emotion.

"Saint Winifred assist me!" said she. "What can I think? 'The peasant Edmund is no more, but there lives one,'—that is to my thinking, Edmund lives, but is no peasant."

"Go on, my dear," said William. "I like your explanation."

"Nay, brother, I only guess; but what think you?"

"I believe we think alike in more than one respect, that he meant to recommend no other person than himself to your favour; and, if he were indeed of noble birth, I would prefer him to a prince for a husband to my Emma!"

"Bless me!" said she. "Do you think it possible that he should be of either birth or fortune?"

"It is hard to say what is impossible! We have proof that the east apartment is haunted. It was there that Edmund was made acquainted with many secrets, I doubt not: and, perhaps, his own fate may be involved in that of others. I am confident that what he saw and heard there, was the cause of his departure. We must wait with patience the unravelling this intricate affair; I believe I need not enjoin your secrecy as to what I have said; your heart will be my security."

"What mean you, brother?"

"Don't affect ignorance, my dear; you love Edmund, so do I; it is nothing to be ashamed of. It would have been strange, if a girl of your good sense had not distinguished a swan among a flock of geese."

"Dear William, don't let a word of this escape you; but you

have taken a weight off my heart. You may depend that I will not dispose of my hand or heart till I know the end of this affair."

William smiled. "Keep them for Edmund's friend; I shall rejoice to see him in a situation to ask them."

"Hush, my brother! Not a word more; I hear footsteps."

They were her eldest brother's, who came to ask Mr. William to ride out with him, which finished the conference.

The fair Emma from this time assumed an air of satisfaction; and William frequently stole away from his companions to talk with his sister upon their favourite subject.

While these things passed at the Castle of Lovel, Edmund and his companion John Wyatt proceeded on their journey to Sir Philip Harclay's seat; they conversed together on the way, and Edmund found him a man of understanding, though not improved by education; he also discovered that John loved his master, and respected him even to veneration; from him he learned many particulars concerning that worthy knight. Wyatt told him, "That Sir Philip maintained twelve old soldiers who had been maimed and disabled in the wars, and had no provision made for them; also six old officers, who had been unfortunate, and were grown grey without preferment; he likewise mentioned the Greek gentleman, his master's captive and friend, as a man eminent for valour and piety; but, beside these," said Wyatt, "there are many others who eat of my master's bread and drink of his cup, and who join in blessings and prayers to Heaven for their noble benefactor; his ears are ever open to distress, his hand to relieve it, and he shares in every good man's joys and blessings."

"Oh, what a glorious character!" said Edmund. "How my heart throbs with wishes to imitate such a man! Oh, that I might resemble him, though at ever so great a distance!"

Edmund was never weary of hearing the actions of this truly great man, nor Wyatt with relating them; and, during three days journey, there were but few pauses in their conversation.

The fourth day, when they came within view of the house,

Edmund's heart began to raise doubts of his reception. "If," said he, "Sir Philip should not receive me kindly, if he should resent my long neglect, and disown my acquaintance, it would be no more than justice."

He sent Wyatt before, to notify his arrival to Sir Philip, while he waited at the gate, full of doubts and anxieties concerning his reception. Wyatt was met and congratulated on his return by most of his fellow-servants.

He asked, "Where is my master?"

"In the parlour."

"Are any strangers with him?"

"No, only his own family."

"Then I will shew myself to him."

He presented himself before Sir Philip.

"So, John," said he, "you are welcome home! I hope you left your parents and relations well?"

"All well, thank God! And send their humble duty to your honour, and they pray for you every day of their lives. I hope your honour is in good health."

"Very well."

"Thank God for that! But, sir, I have something further to tell you; I have had a companion all the way home, a person who comes to wait on your honour, on business of great consequence, as he says."

"Who is that, John?"

"It is Master Edmund Twyford, from the Castle of Lovel."

"Young Edmund!" says Sir Philip, surprised. "Where is he?"

"At the gate, sir."

"Why did you leave him there?"

"Because he bade me come before, and acquaint your honour, that he waits your pleasure."

"Bring him hither," said Sir Philip, "tell him I shall be glad to see him."

John made haste to deliver his message, and Edmund followed him in silence into Sir Philip's presence.

He bowed low, and kept at a distance. Sir Philip held out his hand, and bad him approach. As he drew near, he was seized with an universal trembling; he kneeled down, took his hand, kissed it, and pressed it to his heart in silence.

"You are welcome, young man!" said Sir Philip. "Take courage, and speak for yourself."

Edmund sighed deeply; he at length broke silence with difficulty. "I am come thus far, noble sir, to throw myself at your feet, and implore your protection. You are, under God, my only reliance."

"I receive you," said Sir Philip, "with all my heart! Your person is greatly improved since I saw you last, and I hope your mind is equally so; I have heard a great character of you from some that knew you in France. I remember the promise I made you long ago, and am ready now to fulfil it, upon condition that you have done nothing to disgrace the good opinion I formerly entertained of you; and am ready to serve you in any thing consistent with my own honour."

Edmund kissed the hand that was extended to raise him. "I accept your favour, sir, upon this condition only; and if ever you find me to impose upon your credulity, or incroach on your goodness, may you renounce me from that moment!"

"Enough," said Sir Philip. "Rise, then, and let me embrace you; You are truly welcome!"

"Oh, noble sir!" said Edmund. "I have a strange story to tell you; but it must be by ourselves, with only heaven to bear witness to what passes between us."

"Very well," said Sir Philip, "I am ready to hear you; but first, go and get some refreshment after your journey, and then come to me again. John Wyatt will attend you."

"I want no refreshment," said Edmund, "and I cannot eat or drink till I have told my business to your honour."

"Well then," said Sir Philip, "come along with me." He took the youth by the hand, and led him into another parlour, leaving his friends in great surprise, what this young man's errand could be; John Wyatt told them all that he knew relating to Edmund's birth, character, and situation.

When Sir Philip had seated his young friend, he listened in silence to the surprising tale he had to tell him. Edmund told him briefly the most remarkable circumstances of his life, from the time when he first saw and liked him, till his return from France; but from that era, he related at large every thing that had happened, recounting every interesting particular, which was imprinted on his memory in strong and lasting characters. Sir Philip grew every moment more affected by the recital; sometimes he clasped his hands together, he lifted them up to heaven, he smote his breast, he sighed, he exclaimed aloud; when Edmund related his dream, he breathed short, and seemed to devour him with attention; when he described the fatal closet, he trembled, sighed, sobbed, and was almost suffocated with his agitation. But when he related all that passed between his supposed mother and himself, and finally produced the jewels, the proofs of his birth, and the death of his unfortunate mother, he flew to him, he pressed him to his bosom, he strove to speak, but speech was for some minutes denied. He wept aloud; and, at length, his words found their way in broken exclamations.

"Son of my dearest friend! Dear and precious relic of a noble house! Child of Providence! The beloved of heaven! Welcome! Thrice welcome to my arms! To my heart! I will be thy parent from henceforward, and thou shalt be indeed my child, my heir! My mind told me from the first moment I beheld thee, that thou wert the image of my friend! My heart then opened itself to receive thee, as his offspring. I had a strange foreboding that I was to be thy protector. I would then have made thee my own; but heaven orders things for the best; it made thee the instrument of this discovery, and in its own time and manner conducted thee to my arms. Praise be to God for his wonderful doings towards the children of men! Every thing that has befallen thee is by his direction, and he will not leave his work unfinished; I trust that I shall be his instrument to do justice on the guilty, and to restore the orphan of my friend to his rights and title. I devote myself to this service, and will make it the business of my life to effect it."

Edmund gave vent to his emotions, in raptures of joy and gratitude. They spent several hours in this way, without thinking of the time that passed; the one enquiring, the other explaining, and repeating, every particular of the interesting story.

At length they were interrupted by the careful John Wyatt, who was anxious to know if any thing was likely to give trouble to his master.

"Sir," said John, "it grows dark—do you want a light?"

"We want no light but what heaven gives us," said Sir Philip. "I knew not whether it was dark or light."

"I hope," said John, "nothing has happened, I hope your honour has heard no bad tidings; I—I—I hope no offence."

"None at all," said the good knight. "I am obliged to your solicitude for me; I have heard some things that grieve me, and others that give me great pleasure; but the sorrows are past, and the joys remain."

"Thank God!" said John. "I was afraid something was the matter to give your honour trouble."

"I thank you, my good servant! You see this young gentleman; I would have you, John, devote yourself to his service; I give you to him for an attendant on his person, and would have you shew your affection to me by your attachment to him."

"Oh, Sir!" said John in a melancholy voice. "What have I done to be turned out of your service?"

"No such matter, John," said Sir Philip. "You will not leave my service."

"Sir," said John, "I would rather die than leave you."

"And, my lad, I like you too well to part with you; but in serving my friend you will serve me. Know, that this young man is my son."

"Your son, sir!" said John.

"Not my natural son, but my relation; my son by adoption, my heir!"

"And will he live with you, sir?"

"Yes, John; and I hope to die with him."

"Oh, then, I will serve him with all my heart and soul; and I will do my best to please you both."

"I thank you, John, and I will not forget your honest love and duty. I have so good an opinion of you, that I will tell you of some things concerning this gentleman that will entitle him to your respect."

"'Tis enough for me," said John, "to know that your honour respects him, to make me pay him as much duty as yourself."

"But, John, when you know him better, you will respect him still more; at present, I shall only tell you what he is not; for you think him only the son of Andrew Twyford."

"And is he not?" said John.

"No, but his wife nursed him, and he passed for her son."

"And does old Twyford know it, sir?"

"He does, and will bear witness to it; but he is the son of a near friend of mine, of quality superior to my own, and as such you must serve and respect him."

"I shall, to be sure, sir; but what name shall I call him?"

"You shall know that hereafter; in the mean time bring a light, and wait on us to the other parlour."

When John was withdrawn, Sir Philip said, "That is a point to be considered and determined immediately; It is proper that you should assume a name till you can take that of your father; for I choose you should drop that of your foster-father; and I would have you be called by one that is respectable."

"In that, and every other point, I will be wholly governed by you, sir," said Edmund.

"Well then, I will give you the name of Seagrave; I shall say that you are a relation of my own; and my mother was really of that family."

John soon returned, and attended them into the other parlour; Sir Philip entered, with Edmund in his hand.

"My friends," said he, "this gentleman is Mr. Edward Seagrave, the son of a dear friend and relation of mine. He was lost in his infancy, brought up by a good woman out of pure humanity, and is but lately restored to his own family. The circumstances shall be made known hereafter; In the meantime, I have taken him under my care and protection, and will use all my power and interest to see him restored to his fortune, which is enjoyed by the usurper who was the cause of his expulsion, and the death of his parents. Receive him as my relation, and friend; Zadisky, do you embrace him first. Edmund, you and this gentleman must love each other for my sake; hereafter you will do it for your own." They all rose; each embraced and congratulated the young man.

Zadisky said, "Sir, whatever griefs and misfortunes you may have endured, you may reckon them at an end, from the hour you are beloved and protected by Sir Philip Harclay."

"I firmly believe it, sir," replied Edmund, "and my heart enjoys, already, more happiness than I ever yet felt, and promises me all that I can wish in future; his friendship is the earnest Heaven gives me of its blessings hereafter."

They sat down to supper with mutual cheerfulness; and Edmund enjoyed the repast with more satisfaction than he had felt a long time. Sir Philip saw his countenance brighten up, and looked on him with heart-felt pleasure.

"Every time I look on you," said he, "reminds me of your father; you are the same person I loved twenty-three years ago—I rejoice to see you under my roof. Go to your repose early, and to-morrow we will consult farther."

Edmund withdrew, and enjoyed a night of sweet undisturbed repose.

The next morning Edmund arose in perfect health and spirits: he waited on his benefactor. They were soon after joined by Zadisky, who shewed great attention and respect to the youth, and offered him his best services without reserve. Edmund accepted them with equal respect and modesty; and finding himself at ease, began to display his amiable qualities. They breakfasted together; afterwards, Sir Philip desired Edmund to walk out with him.

As soon as they were out of hearing, Sir Philip said, "I could not sleep last night for thinking of your affairs; I laid schemes for you, and rejected them again. We must lay our plan before we begin to act. What shall be done with this treacherous kinsman! This inhuman monster! This assassin of his nearest relation? I will risk my life and fortune to bring him to justice. Shall I go to court, and demand justice of the King? Or shall I accuse him of the murder, and make him stand a public trial? If I treat him as a baron of the realm, he must be tried by his peers; if as a commoner, he must be tried at the county assize; but we must shew reason why he should be degraded from his title. Have you any thing to propose?"

"Nothing, sir; I have only to wish that it might be as private as possible, for the sake of my noble benefactor, the Lord Fitz-Owen, upon whom some part of the family disgrace would naturally fall; and that would be an ill return for all his kindness and generosity to me."

"That is a generous and grateful consideration on your part; but you owe still more to the memory of your injured parents. However, there is yet another way that suits me better than any hitherto proposed; I will challenge the traitor to meet me in the field; and, if he has spirit enough to answer my call, I will there bring him to justice; if not, I will bring him to a public trial."

"No, sir," said Edmund, "that is my province. Should I stand by and see my noble, gallant friend expose his life for me, I should be unworthy to bear the name of that friend whom you so much lament. It will become his son to vindicate his name, and revenge his death. I will be the challenger, and no other."

"And do you think he will answer the challenge of an unknown youth, with nothing but his pretensions to his name and title?

Certainly not. Leave this matter to me; I will think of a way that will oblige him to meet me at the house of a third person who is known to all the parties concerned, and where we will have authentic witnesses of all that passes between him and me. I will devise the time, place, and manner, and satisfy all your scruples."

Edmund offered to reply; but Sir Philip bad him be silent, and let him proceed in his own way.

He then led him over his estate, and shewed him every thing deserving his notice; he told him all the particulars of his domestic economy, and they returned home in time to meet their friends at dinner.

They spent several days in consulting how to bring Sir Walter to account, and in improving their friendship and confidence in each other. Edmund endeared himself so much to his friend and patron, that he declared him his adopted son and heir before all his friends and servants, and ordered them to respect him as such. He every day improved their love and regard for him, and became the darling of the whole family.

After much consideration, Sir Philip fixed his resolutions, and began to execute his purposes. He set out for the seat of the Lord Clifford, attended by Edmund, M. Zadisky, and two servants. Lord Clifford received them with kindness and hospitality.

Sir Philip presented Edmund to Lord Clifford and his family, as his near relation and presumptive heir; They spent the evening in the pleasures of convivial mirth and hospitable entertainment. The next day Sir Philip began to open his mind to Lord Clifford, informing him that both his young friend and himself had received great injuries from the present Lord Lovel, for which they were resolved to call him to account; but that, for many reasons, they were desirous to have proper witnesses of all that should pass between them, and begging the favour of his Lordship to be the principal one. Lord Clifford acknowledged the confidence placed in him; and besought Sir Philip to let him be the arbitrator between them. Sir Philip assured him, that their wrongs would not admit of arbitration, as he should hereafter judge; but that he was unwilling to explain them further till he knew certainly whether or not the Lord Lovel would meet him; for, if he refused, he must take another method with him.

Lord Clifford was desirous to know the grounds of the quarrel; but Sir Philip declined entering into particulars at present, assuring him of a full information hereafter. He then sent M. Zadisky, attended by John Wyatt, and a servant of Lord Clifford, with a letter to Lord Lovel; the contents were as follow:

"*My Lord Lovel,*

Sir Philip Harclay earnestly desires to see you at the house of Lord Clifford, where he waits to call you to account for the injuries done by you to the late Arthur Lord Lovel, your kinsman; If you accept his demand, he will make the Lord Clifford a witness and a judge of the cause; if not, he will expose you publicly as a traitor and a coward. Please to answer this letter, and he will acquaint you with the time, place, and manner of the meeting.

"PHILIP HARCLAY."

Zadisky presented the letter to Lord Lovel, informing him that he was the friend of Sir Philip Harclay. He seemed surprised and confounded at the contents; but, putting on an haughty air, "I know nothing," said he, "of the business this letter hints at; but wait a few hours, and I will give you an answer." He gave orders to treat Zadisky as a gentleman in every respect, except in avoiding his company; for the Greek had a shrewd and penetrating aspect, and he observed every turn of his countenance. The next day he came and apologized for his absence, and gave him the answer; sending his respects to the Lord Clifford. The messengers returned with all speed, and Sir Philip read the answer before all present.

"Lord Lovel knows not of any injuries done by him to the late Arthur Lord Lovel, whom he succeeded by just right of inheritance; nor of any right Sir Philip Harclay has, to call to account a man to whom he is barely known, having seen him only once, many years ago, at the house of his uncle, the old Lord Lovel: Nevertheless, Lord Lovel will not suffer any man to call his name and honour into question with impunity; for which reason he will meet Sir Philip Harclay at any time, place, and in what manner he shall appoint, bringing the same number of friends and dependents, that justice may be done to all parties.

"LOVEL."

"'Tis well," said Sir Philip. "I am glad to find he has the spirit to meet me; he is an enemy worthy of my sword."

Lord Clifford then proposed that both parties should pass the borders, and obtain leave of the warden of the Scottish marches to decide the quarrel in his jurisdiction, with a select number of friends on both sides. Sir Philip agreed to the proposal; and Lord Clifford wrote in his own name to ask permission of the Lord Graham, that his friends might come there; and obtained it, on condition that neither party should exceed a limited number of friends and followers.

Lord Clifford sent chosen messengers to Lord Lovel, acquainting him with the conditions, and appointing the time, place, and manner of their meeting, and that he had been desired to accept the office of judge of the field. Lord Lovel accepted the conditions, and promised to be there without fail. Lord Clifford notified the same to Lord Graham, warden of the marches, who caused a piece of ground to be inclosed for the lists, and made preparations against the day appointed.

In the interim, Sir Philip Harclay thought proper to settle his worldly affairs. He made Zadisky acquainted with every circumstance of Edmund's history, and the obligation that lay upon him to revenge the death of his friend, and see justice done to his heir. Zadisky entered into the cause with an ardour that spoke the affection he bore to his friend.

"Why," said he, "would you not suffer me to engage this traitor? Your life is of too much consequence to be staked against his; but though I trust that the justice of your cause must succeed, yet, if it should happen otherwise, I vow to revenge you; he shall never go back from us both. However, my hope and trust is, to see your arm the minister of justice."

Sir Philip then sent for a lawyer and made his will, by which he appointed Edmund his chief heir, by the name of Lovel, alias Seagrave, alias Twyford; he ordered that all his old friends, soldiers, and servants, should be maintained in the same manner during their lives; he left to Zadisky an annuity of an hundred a year, and a legacy of two hundred pounds; one hundred pounds to a certain monastery; the same sum to be distributed among disbanded soldiers, and the same to the poor and needy in his neighbourhood.

He appointed Lord Clifford joint executor with Edmund, and gave his will into that nobleman's care, recommending Edmund to his favour and protection.

"If I live," said he, "I will make him appear to be worthy of it; if I die, he will want a friend. I am desirous your Lordship, as a judge of the field, should be unprejudiced on either side, that you may judge impartially. If I die, Edmund's pretensions die with me; but my friend Zadisky will acquaint you with the foundation of them. I take these precautions, because I ought to be prepared for every thing; but my heart is warm with better hopes, and I trust I shall live to justify my own cause, as well as that of my friend, who is a person of more consequence than he appears to be."

Lord Clifford accepted the trust, and expressed the greatest reliance upon Sir Philip's honour and veracity.

While these preparations were making for the great event that was to decide the pretensions of Edmund, his enemies at the Castle of Lovel were brought to shame for their behaviour to him.

The disagreement between Wenlock and Markham had by degrees brought on an explanation of some parts of their conduct. Father Oswald had often hinted to the Baron, Wenlock's envy of Edmund's superior qualities, and the artifices by which he had obtained such an influence with Sir Robert, as to make him take his part upon all occasions. Oswald now took advantage of the breach between these two incendiaries, to persuade Markham to justify himself at Wenlock's expence, and to tell all he knew of his wickedness; at length, he promised to declare all he knew of Wenlock's conduct, as well in France as since their return, when he should be called upon; and, by him, Oswald was enabled to unravel the whole of his contrivances, against the honour, interest, and even life of Edmund.

He prevailed on Hewson, and Kemp, his associate, to add their testimony to the others. Hewson confessed that he was touched in his conscience, when he reflected on the cruelty and injustice of his behaviour to Edmund, whose behaviour towards him, after he had laid a snare for his life, was so noble and generous, that he was cut to the heart by it, and had suffered so much pain and remorse, that he longed for nothing so much as an opportunity to unburden his mind; but the dread of Mr. Wenlock's anger, and the effects of his resentment, had hitherto kept him silent, always hoping there would come a time, when he might have leave to declare the whole truth.

Oswald conveyed this information to the Baron's ear, who waited for an opportunity to make the proper use of it. Not long after, the two principal incendiaries came to an open rupture, and Markham threatened Wenlock that he would shew his uncle what a serpent he had harboured in his bosom. The Baron arrested his words, and insisted upon his telling all he knew; adding,—

"If you speak the truth, I will support you; but if you prove false, I will punish you severely. As to Mr. Wenlock, he shall have a fair trial; and, if all the accusations I have heard are made good, it is high time that I should put him out of my family."

The Baron, with a stern aspect, bade them follow him into the great hall; and sent for all the rest of the family together.

He then, with great solemnity, told them he was ready to hear all sides of the question. He declared the whole substance of his informations, and called upon the accusers to support the charge. Hewson and Kemp gave the same account they had done to Oswald, offering to swear to the truth of their testimony; several of the other servants related such circumstances as had come to their knowledge. Markham then spoke of every thing, and gave a particular account of all that had passed on the night they spent in the east apartment; he accused himself of being privy to Wenlock's villany, called himself fool and blockhead for being the instrument of his malignant disposition, and asked pardon of his uncle for concealing it so long.

The Baron called upon Wenlock to reply to the charge; who, instead of answering, flew into a passion, raged, swore, threatened, and finally denied every thing. The witnesses persisted in their assertions. Markham desired leave to make known the reason why they were all afraid of him.

"He gives it out," said he, "that he is to be my Lord's son-in-law; and they, supposing him to stand first in his favour, are afraid of his displeasure."

"I hope," said the Baron, "I shall not be at such a loss for a son-in-law, as to make choice of such a one as him; he never but once hinted at such a thing, and then I gave him no encouragement. I have long seen there was something very wrong in him; but I did not believe he was of so wicked a disposition; It is no wonder that princes should be so frequently deceived, when I, a private man, could be so much imposed upon within the circle of my own family. What think you, son Robert?"

"I, sir, have been much more imposed on; and I take shame to myself on the occasion."

"Enough, my son," said the Baron. "A generous confession is only a proof of growing wisdom. You are now sensible, that the best of us are liable to imposition. The artifices of this unworthy kinsman have set us at variance with each other, and driven away an excellent youth from this house, to go I know not whither; but he shall no longer triumph in his wickedness; he shall feel what it is to be banished from the house of his protector. He shall set out for his mother's this very day; I will write to her in such a manner as shall inform her that he has offended me, without particularising the nature of his faults; I will give him an opportunity of recovering his credit with his own family, and this shall be my security against his doing further mischief. May he repent, and be forgiven.

"Markham deserves punishment, but not in the same degree."

"I confess it," said he, "and will submit to whatever your Lordship shall enjoin."

"You shall only be banished for a time, but he for ever. I will send you abroad on a business that shall put you in a way to do credit to yourself, and service to me. Son Robert, have you any objection to my sentence?"

"My Lord," said he, "I have great reason to distrust myself; I am sensible of my own weakness, and your superior wisdom, as well as goodness; and I will henceforward submit to you in all things."

The Baron ordered two of his servants to pack up Wenlock's clothes and necessaries, and to set out with him that very day; he bade some others keep an eye upon him lest he should escape; As soon as they were ready, my Lord wished him a good journey, and gave him a letter for his mother. He departed without saying a word, in a sullen kind of resentment, but his countenance shewed the inward agitations of his mind.

As soon as he was gone, every mouth was opened against him; a thousand stories came out that they never heard before; The Baron and his sons were astonished that he should go on so long without detection. My Lord sighed deeply at the thoughts of Edmund's expulsion, and ardently wished to know what was become of him.

Sir Robert took the opportunity of coming to an explanation with his brother William; he took shame to himself for some part of his past behaviour. Mr. William owned his affection to Edmund, and justified it by his merit and attachment to him, which were such that he was certain no time or distance could alter them. He accepted his brother's acknowledgement, as a full amends for all that had passed, and begged that henceforward an entire love and confidence might ever subsist between them. These new regulations restored peace, confidence, and harmony, in the Castle of Lovel.

At length, the day arrived for the combatants to meet. The Lord Graham, with twelve followers gentlemen, and twelve servants, was ready at the dawn of day to receive them.

The first that entered the field, was Sir Philip Harclay, knight, armed completely, excepting his head-piece; Hugh Rugby, his esquire, bearing his lance; John Barnard, his page, carrying his helmet and spurs; and two servants in his proper livery. The next came Edmund, the heir of Lovel, followed by his servant John Wyatt; Zadisky, followed by his servant.

At a short distance came the Lord Clifford, as judge of the field, with his esquire, two pages, and two livery-servants; followed by his eldest son, his nephew, and a gentleman his friend, each attended by one servant; He also brought a surgeon of note to take care of the wounded.

The Lord Graham saluted them; and, by his order, they took their places without the lists, and the trumpet sounded for the challenger. It was answered by the defendant, who soon after appeared, attended by three gentlemen his friends, with each one servant, beside his own proper attendants.

A place was erected for the Lord Clifford, as judge of the field; he desired Lord Graham would share the office, who accepted it, on condition that the combatants should make no objection, and they agreed to it with the greatest courtesy and respect. They consulted together on many points of honour and ceremony between the two combatants.

They appointed a marshal of the field, and other inferior officers, usually employed on these occasions. The Lord Graham sent the marshal for the challenger, desiring him to declare the cause of his quarrel before his enemy. Sir Philip Harclay then advanced, and thus spoke:

"I, Philip Harclay, knight, challenge Walter, commonly called Lord Lovel, as a base, treacherous, and bloody man, who, by his wicked arts and devices, did kill, or cause to be killed, his kinsman, Arthur Lord Lovel, my dear and noble friend. I am called upon, in an extraordinary manner, to revenge his death; and I will prove the truth of what I have affirmed at the peril of my life."

Lord Graham then bade the defendant answer to the charge. Lord Lovel stood forth before his followers, and thus replied:

"I, Walter, Baron of Lovel, do deny the charge against me, and affirm it to be a base, false, and malicious accusation of this Sir Philip Harclay, which I believe to be invented by himself, or else framed by some enemy, and told to him for wicked ends; but, be that as it may, I will maintain my own honour, and prove him to be a false traitor, at the hazard of my own life, and to the punishment of his presumption."

Then said the Lord Graham, "will not this quarrel admit of arbitration?"

"No," replied Sir Philip, "when I have justified this charge, I have more to bring against him. I trust in God and the justice of my cause, and defy that traitor to the death!"

Lord Clifford then spoke a few words to Lord Graham, who immediately called to the marshal, and bade him open the lists, and deliver their weapons to the combatants.

While the marshal was arranging the combatants and their followers, Edmund approached his friend and patron; he put one knee to the ground, he embraced his knees with the strongest emotions of grief and anxiety. He was dressed in complete armour, with his visor down; his device was a hawthorn, with a graft of the rose upon it, the motto—*This is not my true parent*; but Sir Philip bade him take these words—*E fructu arbor cognoscitur.*[*]

Sir Philip embraced the youth with strong marks of affection. "Be composed, my child!" said he. "I have neither guilt, fear, nor doubt in me; I am so certain of success, that I bid you be prepared for the consequence."

Zadisky embraced his friend, he comforted Edmund, he suggested every thing that could confirm his hopes of success.

The marshal waited to deliver the spear to Sir Philip; he now presented it with the usual form.

"Sir, receive your lance, and God defend the right!"

Sir Philip answered, "Amen!" in a voice that was heard by all present.

He next presented his weapon to Lord Lovel with the same sentence, who likewise answered "Amen!" with a good courage. Immediately the lists were cleared, and the combatants began to fight.

They contended a long time with equal skill and courage; at length Sir Philip unhorsed his antagonist. The judges ordered, that either he should alight, or suffer his enemy to remount; he chose the former, and a short combat on foot ensued. The sweat ran off their bodies with the violence of the exercise. Sir Philip watched every motion of his enemy, and strove to weary him out, intending to wound, but not to kill him, unless obliged for his own safety.

He thrust his sword through his left arm, and demanded, whether he would confess the fact? Lord Lovel enraged, answered, he would die sooner. Sir Philip then passed the sword through his body twice, and Lord Lovel fell, crying out that he was slain.

"I hope not," said Sir Philip, "for I have a great deal of business for you to do before you die: confess your sins, and endeavour to atone for them, as the only ground to hope for pardon."

---

[*] Roughly, "by the fruit is the tree known."

Lord Lovel replied, "You are the victor, use your good fortune generously!"

Sir Philip took away his sword, and then waved it over his head, and beckoned for assistance. The judges sent to beg Sir Philip to spare the life of his enemy.

"I will," said he, "upon condition that he will make an honest confession."

Lord Lovel desired a surgeon and a confessor.

"You shall have both," said Sir Philip, "but you must first answer me a question or two. Did you kill your kinsman or not?"

"It was not my hand that killed him," answered the wounded man.

"It was done by your own order, however? You shall have no assistance till you answer this point."

"It was," said he, "and Heaven is just!"

"Bear witness all present," said Sir Philip, "he confesses the fact!"

He then beckoned Edmund, who approached.

"Take off your helmet," said he, "look on that youth, he is the son of your injured kinsman."

"It is himself!" said the Lord Lovel, and fainted away.

Sir Philip then called for a surgeon and a priest, both of which Lord Graham had provided; the former began to bind up his wounds, and his assistants poured a cordial into his mouth. "Preserve his life, if it be possible," said Sir Philip, "for much depends upon it."

He then took Edmund by the hand, and presented him to all the company. "In this young man," said he, "you see the true heir of the house of Lovel! Heaven has in its own way made him the instrument to discover the death of his parents. His father was assassinated by order of that wicked man, who now receives his punishment; his mother was, by his cruel treatment, compelled to leave her own house; she was delivered in the fields, and perished herself in seeking a shelter for her infant. I have sufficient proofs of every thing I say, which I am ready to communicate to every person who desires to know the particulars. Heaven, by my hand, has chastised him; he has confessed the fact I accuse him of, and it remains that he make restitution of the fortune and honours he hath usurped so long."

Edmund kneeled, and with uplifted hands returned thanks to Heaven, that his noble friend and champion was crowned with victory. The lords and gentlemen gathered round them, they congratulated them both; while Lord Lovel's friends and followers were employed in taking care of him. Lord Clifford took Sir Philip's hand.

"You have acted with so much honour and prudence, that it is presumptuous to offer you advice; but what mean you to do with the wounded man?"

"I have not determined," said he. "I thank you for the hint, and beg your advice how to proceed."

"Let us consult Lord Graham," replied he.

Lord Graham insisted upon their going all to his castle. "There," said he, "you will have impartial witnesses of all that passes." Sir Philip was unwilling to give so much trouble. The Lord Graham protested he should be proud to do any service to so noble a gentleman. Lord Clifford enforced his request, saying, it was better upon all accounts to keep their prisoner on this side the borders till they saw what turn his health would take, and to keep him safely till he had settled his worldly affairs.

This resolution being taken, Lord Graham invited the wounded man and his friends to his castle, as being the nearest place where he could be lodged and taken proper care of, it being dangerous to carry him further. They accepted the proposal with many acknowledgements; and, having made a kind of litter of boughs, they all proceeded to Lord Graham's castle, where they put Lord Lovel to bed, and the surgeon dressed his wounds, and desired he might be kept quiet, not knowing at present whether they were dangerous or not.

About an hour after, the wounded man complained of thirst; he asked for the surgeon, and enquired if his life was in danger? The surgeon answered him doubtfully. He asked—

"Where is Sir Philip Harclay?"

"In the castle."

"Where is that young man whom he calls the heir of Lovel?"

"He is here, too."

"Then I am surrounded with my enemies. I want to speak to one of my own servants, without witnesses; let one be sent to me."

The surgeon withdrew, and acquainted the gentlemen below. "He shall not speak to any man," said Sir Philip, "but in my presence." He went with him into the sick man's room. Upon the sight of Sir Philip, he seemed in great agitation.

"Am I not allowed to speak with my own servant?" said he.

"Yes, sir, you may; but not without witnesses."

"Then I am a prisoner, it seems?"

"No, not so, sir; but some caution is necessary at present. But compose yourself, I do not wish for your death."

"Then why did you seek it? I never injured you."

"Yes, you have, in the person of my friend, and I am only the instrument of justice in the hand of Heaven; endeavour to make atonement while life is spared to you. Shall I send the priest to you? perhaps he may convince you of the necessity of restitution, in order to obtain forgiveness of your sins."

Sir Philip sent for the priest and the surgeon, and obliged the servant to retire with him. "I leave you, sir, to the care of these gentlemen; and whenever a third person is admitted, I will be his attendant; I will visit you again within an hour."

He then retired, and consulted his friends below; they were of opinion that no time should be lost. "You will then," said he, "accompany me into the sick man's apartment in an hour's time."

Within the hour, Sir Philip, attended by Lord Clifford and Lord Graham, entered the chamber. Lord Lovel was in great emotion; the priest stood on one side of the bed, the surgeon on the other;

the former exhorted him to confess his sins, the other desired he might be left to his repose. Lord Lovel seemed in great anguish of mind; he trembled, and was in the utmost confusion. Sir Philip intreated him, with the piety of a confessor, to consider his soul's health before that of his body. He then asked Sir Philip, by what means he knew that he was concerned in the death of his kinsman?

"Sir," replied he, "it was not merely by human means this fact was discovered. There is a certain apartment in the Castle of Lovel, that has been shut up these one and twenty years, but has lately been opened and examined into."

"O Heaven!" exclaimed he. "Then Geoffry must have betrayed me!"

"No, sir, he has not; it was revealed in a very extraordinary manner to that youth whom it most concerns."

"How can he be the heir of Lovel?"

"By being the son of that unfortunate woman, whom you cruelly obliged to leave her own house, to avoid being compelled to wed the murderer of her husband: we are not ignorant, moreover, of the fictitious funeral you made for her. All is discovered, and you will not tell us any more than we know already; but we desire to have it confirmed by your confession."

"The judgments of Heaven are fallen upon me!" said Lord Lovel. "I am childless, and one is arisen from the grave to claim my inheritance."

"Nothing, then, hinders you to do justice and make restitution; it is for the ease of your conscience; and you have no other way of making atonement for all the mischief you have done."

"You know too much," said the criminal, "and I will relate what you do not know.

"You may remember," proceeded he, "that I saw you once at my uncle's house?"

"I well remember it."

"At that time my mind was disturbed by the baleful passion of envy; it was from that root all my bad actions sprung."

"Praise be to God!" said the good priest. "He hath touched your heart with true contrition, and you shew the effect of his mercies; you will do justice, and you will be rewarded by the gift of repentance unto salvation."

Sir Philip desired the penitent to proceed.

"My kinsman excelled me in every kind of merit, in the graces of person and mind, in all his exercises, and in every accomplishment. I was totally eclipsed by him, and I hated to be in his company; but what finished my aversion, was his addressing the lady upon whom I had fixed my affections. I strove to rival him there, but she gave him the preference that, indeed, was only his due; but I could not bear to see, or acknowledge, it.

"The most bitter hatred took possession of my breast, and I vowed to revenge the supposed injury as soon as opportunity should offer. I buried my resentment deep in my heart, and outwardly appeared to rejoice at his success. I made a merit of resigning my pretensions to him, but I could not bear to be present at his nuptials; I retired to my father's seat, and brooded over my revenge in secret. My father died this year, and soon after my uncle followed him; within another year my kinsman was summoned to attend the King on his Welch expedition.

"As soon as I heard he was gone from home, I resolved to prevent his return, exulting in the prospect of possessing his title, fortune, and his lady. I hired messengers, who were constantly going and coming to give me intelligence of all that passed at the castle; I went there soon after, under pretence of visiting my kinsman. My spies brought me an account of all that happened; one informed me of the event of the battle, but could not tell whether my rival was living or dead; I hoped the latter, that I might avoid the crime I meditated. I reported his death to his Lady, who took it very heavily.

"Soon after a messenger arrived with tidings that he was alive and well, and had obtained leave to return home immediately.

"I instantly dispatched my two emissaries to intercept him on the way. He made so much haste to return, that he was met within a mile of his own castle; he had out-rode his servants, and was alone. They killed him, and drew him aside out of the highway. They then came to me with all speed, and desired my orders; it was then about sunset. I sent them back to fetch the dead body, which they brought privately into the castle: they tied it neck and heels, and put it into a trunk, which they buried under the floor in the closet you mentioned. The sight of the body stung me to the heart; I then felt the pangs of remorse, but it was too late; I took every precaution that prudence suggested to prevent the discovery; but nothing can be concealed from the eye of Heaven.

"From that fatal hour I have never known peace, always in fear of something impending to discover my guilt, and to bring me to shame; at length I am overtaken by justice. I am brought to a severe reckoning here, and I dread to meet one more severe hereafter."

"Enough," said the priest, "you have done a good work, my son! Trust in the Lord; and, now this burden is off your mind, the rest will be made easy to you."

Lord Lovel took a minute's repose, and then went on.

"I hope by the hint you gave, Sir Philip, the poor lady is yet alive?"

"No, sir, she is not; but she died not till after she brought forth a son, whom Heaven made its instrument to discover and avenge the death of both his parents."

"They are well avenged!" said he. "I have no children to lament for me; all mine have been taken from me in the bloom of youth; only one daughter lived to be twelve years old; I intended her for a wife for one of my nephews, but within three months I have buried her." He sighed, wept, and was silent.

The gentlemen present lifted up their hands and eyes to Heaven in silence.

"The will of Heaven be obeyed!" said the priest. "My penitent hath confessed all; what more would you require?"

"That he make atonement," said Sir Philip, "that he surrender the title and estate to the right heir, and dispose of his own proper fortune to his nearest relations, and resign himself to penitence and preparation for a future state. For this time I leave him with you, father, and will join my prayers with yours for his repentance."

So saying, he left the room, and was followed by the Barons and the surgeon; the priest alone remaining with him. As soon as they were out of hearing, Sir Philip questioned the surgeon concerning his patient's situation; who answered, that at present he saw no signs of immediate danger, but he could not yet pronounce that there was none.

"If he were mortally wounded," said he, "he could not be so well, nor speak so long without faintness; and it is my opinion that he will soon recover, if nothing happens to retard the cure."

"Then," said Sir Philip, "keep this opinion from him; for I would suffer the fear of death to operate on him until he hath performed some necessary acts of justice. Let it only be known to these noblemen, upon whose honour I can rely, and I trust they will approve my request to you, sir."

"I join in it," said Lord Clifford, "from the same motives."

"I insist upon it," said Lord Graham, "and I can answer for my surgeon's discretion."

"My Lords," said the surgeon, "you may depend on my fidelity; and, after what I have just heard, my conscience is engaged in this noble gentleman's behalf, and I will do every thing in my power to second your intentions."

"I thank you, sir," said Sir Philip, "and you may depend on my gratitude in return. I presume you will sit up with him to-night; if any danger should arise, I desire to be called immediately; but, otherwise, I would suffer him to rest quietly, that he may be prepared for the business of the following day."

"I shall obey your directions, sir; my necessary attendance will give me a pretence not to leave him, and thus I shall hear all that passes between him and all that visit him."

"You will oblige me highly," said Sir Philip, "and I shall go to rest with confidence in your care."

The surgeon returned to the sick man's chamber, Sir Philip and the Barons to the company below: they supped in the great hall, with all the gentlemen that were present at the combat. Sir Philip and his Edmund retired to their repose, being heartily fatigued; and the company staid to a late hour, commenting upon the action of the day, praising the courage and generosity of the noble knight, and wishing a good event to his undertaking.

Most of Lord Lovel's friends went away as soon as they saw him safely lodged, being ashamed of him, and of their appearance in his behalf; and the few that stayed were induced by their desire of a further information of the base action he had committed, and to justify their own characters and conduct.

The next morning Sir Philip entered into consultation with the two Barons, on the methods he should take to get Edmund received, and acknowledged, as heir of the house of Lovel. They were all of opinion, that the criminal should be kept in fear till he had settled his worldly affairs, and they had resolved how to dispose of him. With this determination they entered his room, and enquired of the surgeon how he had passed the night. He shook his head, and said but little.

Lord Lovel desired that he might be removed to his own house. Lord Graham said, he could not consent to that, as there was evident danger in removing him; and appealed to the surgeon, who confirmed his opinion. Lord Graham desired he would make himself easy, and that he should have every kind of assistance there.

Sir Philip then proposed to send for the Lord Fitz-Owen, who would see that all possible care was taken of his brother-in-law, and would assist him in settling his affairs. Lord Lovel was against it; he was peevish and uneasy, and desired to be left with only his own servants to attend him. Sir Philip quitted the room with a significant look; and the two Lords endeavoured to reconcile him to his situation. He interrupted them. "It is easy for men in your situation to advise, but it is difficult for one in mine to practise; wounded in body and mind, it is natural that I should strive to avoid the extremes of shame and punishment; I thank you for your kind offices, and beg I may be left with my own servants."

"With them, and the surgeon, you shall," said Lord Graham; and they both retired.

Sir Philip met them below. "My Lords," said he, "I am desirous that my Lord Fitz-Owen should be sent for, and that he may hear his brother's confession; for I suspect that he may hereafter deny, what only the fear of death has extorted from him; with your permission I am determined to send messengers to-day."

They both expressed approbation, and Lord Clifford proposed to write to him, saying, a letter from an impartial person will have the more weight; I will send one of my principal domestics with your own. This measure being resolved upon, Lord Clifford retired to write, and Sir Philip to prepare his servants for instant departure. Edmund desired leave to write to Father Oswald, and John Wyatt was ordered to be the bearer of his letter. When the Lord Clifford had finished his letter, he read it to Sir Philip and his chosen friends, as follows:

"*RIGHT HON. MY GOOD LORD,*

I have taken upon me to acquaint your Lordship, that there has been a solemn combat at arms between your brother-in-law, the Lord Lovel, and Sir Philip Harclay, Knt. of Yorkshire. It was fought in the jurisdiction of the Lord Graham, who, with myself, was appointed judge of the field; it was fairly won, and Sir Philip is the conqueror. After he had gained the victory he declared at large the cause of the quarrel, and that he had revenged the death of Arthur Lord Lovel his friend, whom the present Lord Lovel had assassinated, that he might enjoy his title and estate. The wounded man confessed the fact; and Sir

Philip gave him his life, and only carried off his sword as
a trophy of his victory. Both the victor and the vanquished
were conveyed to Lord Graham's castle, where the Lord
Lovel now lies in great danger. He is desirous to settle his
worldly affairs, and to make his peace with God and man.
Sir Philip Harclay says there is a male heir of the house
of Lovel, for whom he claims the title and estate; but he is
very desirous that your Lordship should be present at the
disposal of your brother's property that of right belongs to
him, of which your children are the undoubted heirs. He
also wants to consult you in many other points of honour
and equity. Let me intreat you, on the receipt of this letter,
to set out immediately for Lord Graham's castle, where
you will be received with the utmost respect and hospital-
ity. You will hear things that will surprise you as much
as they do me; you will judge of them with that justice
and honour that speaks your character; and you will unite
with us in wondering at the ways of Providence, and sub-
mitting to its decrees, in punishing the guilty, and doing
justice to the innocent and oppressed. My best wishes and
prayers attend you and your hopeful family. My Lord, I
remain your humble servant,

"Clifford."

Every one present expressed the highest approbation of this
letter. Sir Philip gave orders to John Wyatt to be very circumspect in his behaviour, to give Edmund's letter privately to Father
Oswald, and to make no mention of him, or his pretensions to
Lovel Castle.

Lord Clifford gave his servant the requisite precautions. Lord
Graham added a note of invitation, and sent it by a servant of his
own. As soon as all things were ready, the messengers set out with
all speed for the Castle of Lovel.

They stayed no longer by the way than to take some refreshment, but rode night and day till they arrived there.

Lord Fitz-Owen was in the parlour with his children; Father Oswald was walking in the avenue before the house, when he saw three messengers whose horses seemed jaded, and the riders fatigued, like men come a long journey. He came up, just as the first had delivered his message to the porter. John Wyatt knew him; he dismounted, and made signs that he had something to say to him; he retired back a few steps, and John, with great dexterity, slipped a letter into his hand. The father gave him his blessing, and a welcome.

"Who do you come from?" said he aloud.

"From the Lords Graham and Clifford to the Lord Fitz-Owen; and we bring letters of consequence to the Baron."

Oswald followed the messengers into the hall; a servant announced their arrival. Lord Fitz-Owen received them in the parlour; Lord Clifford's servant delivered his master's letter, Lord Graham's his, and they said they would retire and wait his Lordship's answer. The Baron ordered them some refreshment. They retired, and he opened his letters. He read them with great agitations, he struck his hand upon his heart, he exclaimed, "My fears are all verified! The blow is struck, and it has fallen upon the guilty!"

Oswald came in a minute after.

"You are come in good time," said the Baron. "Read that letter, that my children may know the contents."

He read it, with faultering voice, and trembling limbs. They were all in great surprise. William looked down, and kept a studied silence. Sir Robert exclaimed—

"Is it possible? can my uncle be guilty of such an action?"

"You hear," said the Baron, "he has confessed it!"

"But to whom?" said Sir Robert.

His father replied, "Lord Clifford's honour is unquestionable, and I cannot doubt what he affirms."

Sir Robert leaned his head upon his hand, as one lost in thought; at length he seemed to awake.

"My Lord, I have no doubt that Edmund is at the bottom of this business. Do you not remember that Sir Philip Harclay long ago promised him his friendship? Edmund disappears; and, soon after, this man challenges my Uncle. You know what passed here before his departure; He has suggested this affair to Sir Philip, and instigated him to this action. This is the return he has made for the favours he has received from our family, to which he owes every thing!"

"Softly, my son!" said the Baron. "Let us be cautious of reflecting upon Edmund; there is a greater hand in this business. My conjecture was too true; It was in that fatal apartment that he was made acquainted with the circumstances of Lord Lovel's death; he was, perhaps, enjoined to reveal them to Sir Philip Harclay, the bosom friend of the deceased. The mystery of that apartment is disclosed, the woe to the guilty is accomplished! There is no reflection upon any one; Heaven effects its purposes in its own time and manner. I and mine are innocent; let us worship, and be silent!"

"But what do you propose to do?" said Sir Robert.

"To return with the messengers," answered the Baron. "I think it highly proper that I should see your Uncle, and hear what he has to say; my children are his heirs; in justice to them, I ought to be acquainted with every thing that concerns the disposal of his fortune."

"Your Lordship is in the right," answered Sir Robert, "it concerns us all. I have only to ask your permission to bear you company."

"With all my heart," said the Baron, "I have only to ask of you in return, that you will command yourself, and not speak your mind hastily; wait for the proofs before you give judgment, and take advice of your reason before you decide upon any thing; if you reflect upon the past, you will find reason to distrust yourself.

Leave all to me, and be assured I will protect your honour and my own."

"I will obey you in all things, my Lord; and will make immediate preparation for our departure." So saying, he left the room.

As soon as he was gone, Mr. William broke silence.

"My Lord," said he, "if you have no great objection, I beg leave also to accompany you both."

"You shall, my son, if you desire it; I think I can see your motives, and your brother's also; your coolness will be a good balance to his warmth; you shall go with us. My son Walter shall be his sister's protector in our absence, and he shall be master here till we return."

"I hope, my dear father, that will not be long; I shall not be happy till you come home," said the fair Emma.

"It shall be no longer, my dearest, than till this untoward affair is settled."

The Baron desired to know when the messengers were expected to return. Oswald took this opportunity to retire; he went to his own apartment, and read the letter, as follows:

"The Heir of Lovel, to his dear and reverend friend, Father Oswald.

"Let my friends at the Castle of Lovel know that I live in hopes one day to see them there. If you could by any means return with the messengers, your testimony would add weight to mine; perhaps you might obtain permission to attend the Baron; I leave it to you to manage this. John Wyatt will inform you of all that has passed here, and that hitherto my success has outrun my expectation, and, almost, my wishes. I am in the high road to my inheritance; and trust that the Power who hath conducted me thus far, will not leave his work unfinished. Tell my beloved William, that I live, and hope to embrace him before long. I recommend

myself to your holy prayers and blessing, and remain your
son and servant,

"EDMUND."

Oswald then went to the messengers; he drew John Wyatt to a distance from the rest, and got the information he wanted. He stayed with him till he was sent for by the Baron, to whom he went directly, and prevented his questions, by saying, "I have been talking with the messengers; I find they have travelled night and day to bring the letters with all speed; they only require one night's rest, and will be ready to set out with you to-morrow."

"'Tis well," said the Baron, "we will set out as soon as they are ready."

"My Lord," said Oswald, "I have a favour to beg of you; it is, that I may attend you; I have seen the progress of this wonderful discovery, and I have a great desire to see the conclusion of it; perhaps my presence may be of service in the course of your business."

"Perhaps it may," said the Baron. "I have no objection, if you desire to go."

They then separated, and went to prepare for their journey.

Oswald had a private interview with Joseph, whom he informed of all that he knew, and his resolution to attend the Baron in his journey to the north.

"I go," said he, "to bear witness in behalf of injured innocence. If it be needful, I shall call upon you; therefore hold yourself in readiness in case you should be sent for."

"That I will," said Joseph, "and spend my last remains of life and strength, to help my young Lord to his right and title. But do they not begin to suspect who is the heir of Lovel?"

"Not in the least," said Oswald. "They think him concerned in the discovery, but have no idea of his being interested in the event."

"Oh, father!" said Joseph. "I shall think every day a week till your return; but I will no longer keep you from your repose."

"Good night," said Oswald, "but I have another visit to pay before I go to rest."

He left Joseph, and went on tip-toe to Mr. William's room, and tapped at his door. He came and opened it. "What news, father?"

"Not much; I have only orders to tell you that Edmund is well, and as much your friend as ever."

"I guessed," said William, "that we should hear something of him. I have still another guess."

"What is that, my child?"

"That we shall see or hear of him where we are going."

"It is very likely," said Oswald, "and I would have you be prepared for it;—I am confident we shall hear nothing to his discredit."

"I am certain of that," said William, "and I shall rejoice to see him; I conclude that he is under the protection of Sir Philip Harclay."

"He is so," said Oswald. "I had my information from Sir Philip's servant, who is one of the messengers, and was guide to the others in their way hither."

After some farther conversation they separated, and each went to his repose.

The next morning the whole party set out on their journey; they travelled by easy stages on account of the Baron's health, which began to be impaired, and arrived in health and spirits at the castle of Lord Graham, where they were received with the utmost respect and kindness by the noble master.

The Lord Lovel had recovered his health and strength as much as possible in the time, and was impatient to be gone from thence to his own house. He was surprised to hear of the arrival of his brother and nephews, and expressed no pleasure at the thoughts of seeing them. When Sir Philip Harclay came to pay his respects to Baron Fitz-Owen, the latter received him with civility, but with a coldness that was apparent. Sir Robert left the room, doubting his resolution. Sir Philip advanced, and took the Baron by the hand.

"My Lord," said he, "I rejoice to see you here. I cannot be satisfied with the bare civilities of such a man as you. I aspire to your esteem, to your friendship, and I shall not be happy till I obtain them. I will make you the judge of every part of my conduct, and where you shall condemn me, I will condemn myself."

The Baron was softened, his noble heart felt its alliance with its counterpart, but he thought the situation of his brother demanded some reserve towards the man who sought his life; but, in spite of himself, it wore off every moment. Lord Clifford related all that had passed, with the due regard to Sir Philip's honour; he remarked how nobly he concealed the cause of his resentment against the Lord Lovel till the day of combat, that he might not prepossess the judges against him. He enlarged on his humanity to the vanquished, on the desire he expressed to have justice done to his heirs; finally, he mentioned his great respect for the Lord Fitz-Owen, and the solicitude he shewed to have him come to settle the estate of the sick man in favour of his children. Lord Clifford also employed his son to soften Sir Robert, and to explain to him every doubtful part of Sir Philip's behaviour.

After the travellers had taken some rest, the Lord Graham proposed that they should make a visit to the sick man's chamber. The lords sent to acquaint him they were coming to visit him, and they followed the messenger. The Lord Fitz-Owen went up to the bedside; he embraced his brother with strong emotions of concern. Sir Robert followed him; then Mr. William.

Lord Lovel embraced them, but said nothing; his countenance shewed his inward agitations. Lord Fitz-Owen first broke silence.

"I hope," said he, "I see my brother better than I expected?"

Lord Lovel bit his fingers, he pulled the bed-clothes, he seemed almost distracted; at length he broke out—

"I owe no thanks to those who sent for my relations! Sir Philip

Harclay, you have used ungenerously the advantage you have gained over me! You spared my life, only to take away my reputation. You have exposed me to strangers, and, what is worse, to my dearest friends; when I lay in a state of danger, you obliged me to say any thing, and now you take advantage of it, to ruin me in my friends' affection. But, if I recover, you may repent it!"

Sir Philip then came forward.

"My Lords, I shall take no notice of what this unhappy man has just now said; I shall appeal to you, as to the honourable witnesses of all that has passed; you see it was no more than necessary. I appeal to you for the motives of my treatment of him, before, at, and after our meeting. I did not take his life, as I might have done; I wished him to repent of his sins, and to make restitution of what he unjustly possesses. I was called out to do an act of justice; I had taken the heir of Lovel under my protection, my chief view was to see justice done to him;—what regarded this man was but a secondary motive. This was my end, and I will never, never lose sight of it."

Lord Lovel seemed almost choaked with passion, to see every one giving some mark of approbation and respect to Sir Philip. He called out—

"I demand to know who is this pretended heir, whom he brings out to claim my title and fortune?"

"My noble auditors," said Sir Philip, "I shall appeal to your judgment, in regard to the proofs of my ward's birth and family; every circumstance shall be laid before you, and you shall decide upon them.

"Here is a young man, supposed the son of a peasant, who, by a train of circumstances that could not have happened by human contrivance, discovers not only who were his real parents, but that they came to untimely deaths. He even discovers the different places where their bones are buried, both out of consecrated ground, and appeals to their ashes for the truth of his pretensions. He has also living proofs to offer, that will convince the most incredulous. I have deferred entering into particulars, till the arrival of Baron Fitz-Owen. I know his noble heart and honourable character, from one that has long been an eye-witness of his goodness; such is the opinion I have of his justice, that I will accept him as one of the judges in his brother's cause. I and my ward will bring our proofs before him, and the company here present; in the course of them, it will appear that he is the best qualified of any to judge of them, because he can ascertain many of the facts we shall have occasion to mention. I will rest our cause upon their decision."

Lord Graham applauded Sir Philip's appeal, affirming his own impartiality, and calling upon Lord Clifford and his son, and also his own nephews who were present. Lord Clifford said—

"Sir Philip offers fairly, and like himself; there can be no place nor persons more impartial than the present, and I presume the Lord Lovel can have no objection."

"No objection!" answered he. "What, to be tried like a criminal, to have judges appointed over me, to decide upon my right to my own estate and title? I will not submit to such a jurisdiction!"

"Then," said Sir Philip, "you had rather be tried by the laws of the land, and have them pronounce sentence upon you? Take your choice, sir; if you refuse the one, you shall be certain of the other."

Lord Clifford then said, "You will allow Lord Lovel to consider of the proposal; he will consult his friends, and be determined by their advice."

Lord Fitz-Owen said, "I am very much surprised at what I have heard. I should be glad to know all that Sir Philip Harclay has to say for his ward, that I may judge what my brother has to hope or fear; I will then give my best advice, or offer my mediation, as he may stand in need of them."

"You say well," replied Lord Graham, "and pray let us come directly to the point; Sir Philip, you will introduce your ward to this company, and enter upon your proofs."

Sir Philip bowed to the company; he went out and brought

in Edmund, encouraging him by the way; he presented him to Baron Fitz-Owen, who looked very serious.

"Edmund Twyford," said he, "are you the heir of the house of Lovel?"

"I am, my Lord," said Edmund, bowing to the ground. "The proofs will appear; but I am, at the same time, the most humble and grateful of all your servants, and the servant of your virtues."

Sir Robert rose up, and was going to leave the room.

"Son Robert, stay," said the Baron, "if there is any fraud, you will be pleased to detect it, and, if all that is affirmed be true, you will not shut your eyes against the light; you are concerned in this business; hear it in silence, and let reason be arbiter in your cause."

He bowed to his father, bit his lip, and retired to the window. William nodded to Edmund, and was silent. All the company had their eyes fixed on the young man, who stood in the midst, casting down his eyes with modest respect to the audience; while Sir Philip related all the material circumstances of his life, the wonderful gradation by which he came to the knowledge of his birth, the adventures of the haunted apartment, the discovery of the fatal closet, and the presumptive proofs that Lord Lovel was buried there. At this part of his narration, Lord Fitz-Owen interrupted him.

"Where is this closet you talk of? For I and my sons went over the apartment since Edmund's departure, and found no such place as you describe."

"My Lord," said Edmund, "I can account for it: the door is covered with tapestry, the same as the room, and you might easily overlook it; but I have a witness here," said he, and putting his hand into his bosom, he drew out the key. "If this is not the key of that closet, let me be deemed an impostor, and all I say a falsehood; I will risk my pretensions upon this proof."

"And for what purpose did you take it away?" said the Baron.

"To prevent any person from going into it," replied Edmund, "I have vowed to keep it till I shall open that closet before witnesses appointed for that purpose."

"Proceed, sir," said the Baron Fitz-Owen.

Sir Philip then related the conversation between Edmund and Margery Twyford, his supposed mother.

Lord Fitz-Owen seemed in the utmost surprise. He exclaimed, "Can this be true? Strange discovery! Unfortunate child!"

Edmund's tears bore witness to his veracity. He was obliged to hide his face, he lifted up his clasped hands to heaven, and was in great emotions during all this part of the relation; while Lord Lovel groaned, and seemed in great agitation.

Sir Philip then addressed himself to Lord Fitz-Owen.

"My Lord, there was another person present at the conversation between Edmund and his foster-mother, who can witness to all that passed; perhaps your Lordship can tell who that was?"

"It was Father Oswald," replied the Baron. "I well remember that he went with him at his request; let him be called in."

He was sent for, and came immediately. The Baron desired him to relate all that passed between Edmund and his mother.

Oswald then began—

"Since I am now properly called upon to testify what I know concerning this young man, I will speak the truth, without fear or favour of any one; and I will swear, by the rules of my holy order, to the truth of what I shall relate."

He then gave a particular account of all that passed on that occasion, and mentioned the tokens found on both the infant and his mother.

"Where are these tokens to be seen?" said the Lord Clifford.

"I have them here, my Lord," said Edmund, "and I keep them as my greatest treasures."

He then produced them before all the company.

"There is no appearance of any fraud or collusion," said Lord Graham. "If any man thinks he sees any, let him speak."

"Pray, my Lord, suffer me to speak a word," said Sir Robert.

"Do you remember that I hinted my suspicions concerning Father Oswald, the night our kinsmen lay in the east apartment?"

"I do," said the Baron.

"Well, sir, it now appears that he did know more than he would tell us; you find he is very deep in all Edmund's secrets, and you may judge what were his motives for undertaking this journey."

"I observe what you say," answered his father, "but let us hear all that Oswald has to say; I will be as impartial as possible."

"My Lord," returned Oswald, "I beg you also to recollect what I said, on the night your son speaks of, concerning secrecy in certain matters."

"I remember that also," said the Baron, "but proceed."

"My Lord," continued Oswald, "I knew more than I thought myself at liberty to disclose at that time; but I will now tell you every thing. I saw there was something more than common in the accidents that befell this young man, and in his being called out to sleep in the east apartment; I earnestly desired him to let me be with him on the second night, to which he consented reluctantly; we heard a great noise in the rooms underneath, we went down stairs together; I saw him open the fatal closet, I heard groans that pierced me to the heart, I kneeled down and prayed for the repose of the spirit departed; I found a seal, with the arms of Lovel engraven upon it, which I gave to Edmund, and he now has it in his possession. He enjoined me to keep secret what I had seen and heard, till the time should come to declare it. I conceived that I was called to be a witness of these things; besides, my curiosity was excited to know the event; I, therefore, desired to be present at the interview between him and his mother, which was affecting beyond expression. I heard what I have now declared as nearly as my memory permits me. I hope no impartial person will blame me for any part of my conduct; but if they should, I do not repent it. If I should forfeit the favour of the rich and great, I shall have acquitted myself to God and my conscience. I have no worldly ends to answer; I plead the cause of the injured orphan; and I think, also, that I second the designs of Providence."

"You have well spoken, father," said the Lord Clifford, "your testimony is indeed of consequence."

"It is amazing and convincing," said Lord Graham, "and the whole story is so well connected, that I can see nothing to make us doubt the truth of it; but let us examine the proofs."

Edmund gave into their hands the necklace and earrings; he shewed them the locket with the cypher of Lovel, and the seal with the arms; he told them the cloak, in which he was wrapped, was in the custody of his foster-mother, who would produce it on demand. He begged that some proper persons might be commissioned to go with him to examine whether or no the bodies of his parents were buried where he affirmed; adding, that he put his pretensions into their hands with pleasure, relying entirely upon their honour and justice.

During this interesting scene, the criminal covered his face, and was silent; but he sent forth bitter sighs and groans that denoted the anguish of his heart. At length, Lord Graham, in compassion to him, proposed that they should retire and consider of the proofs; adding, "Lord Lovel must needs be fatigued; we will resume the subject in his presence, when he is disposed to receive us."

Sir Philip Harclay approached the bed. "Sir," said he, "I now leave you in the hands of your own relations; they are men of strict honour, and I confide in them to take care of you and of your concerns."

They then went out of the room, leaving only the Lord Fitz-Owen and his sons with the criminal. They discoursed of the wonderful story of Edmund's birth, and the principal events of his life.

After dinner, Sir Philip requested another conference with the Lords, and their principal friends. There were present also Father Oswald, and Lord Graham's confessor, who had taken the Lord

Lovel's confession, Edmund, and Zadisky. "Now, gentlemen," said Sir Philip, "I desire to know your opinion of our proofs, and your advice upon them."

Lord Graham replied, "I am desired to speak for the rest. We think there are strong presumptive proofs that this young man is the true heir of Lovel; but they ought to be confirmed and authenticated. Of the murder of the late Lord there is no doubt; the criminal hath confessed it, and the circumstances confirm it; the proofs of his crime are so connected with those of the young man's birth, that one cannot be public without the other. We are desirous to do justice; and yet are unwilling, for the Lord Fitz-Owen's sake, to bring the criminal to public shame and punishment. We wish to find out a medium; we therefore desire Sir Philip to make proposals for his ward, and let Lord Fitz-Owen answer for himself and his brother, and we will be moderators between them."

Here every one expressed approbation, and called upon Sir Philip to make his demands.

"If," said he, "I were to demand strict justice, I should not be satisfied with any thing less than the life of the criminal; but I am a Christian soldier, the disciple of Him who came into the world to save sinners;—for His sake," continued he, crossing himself, "I forego my revenge, I spare the guilty. If Heaven gives him time for repentance, man should not deny it. It is my ward's particular request, that I will not bring shame upon the house of his benefactor, the Lord Fitz-Owen, for whom he hath a filial affection and profound veneration. My proposals are these:—First, that the criminal make restitution of the title and estate, obtained with so much injustice and cruelty, to the lawful heir, whom he shall acknowledge such before proper witnesses. Secondly, that he shall surrender his own lawful inheritance and personal estate into the hands of the Lord Fitz-Owen, in trust for his sons, who are his heirs of blood. Thirdly, that he shall retire into a religious house, or else quit the kingdom in three months time; and, in either case, those who enjoy his fortune shall allow him a decent annuity, that he may not want the comforts of life. By the last, I disable him from the means of doing further mischief, and enable him to devote the remainder of his days to penitence. These are my proposals, and I give him four-and-twenty hours to consider of them; if he refuses to comply with them, I shall be obliged to proceed to severer measures, and to a public prosecution. But the goodness of the Lord Fitz-Owen bids me expect, from his influence with his brother, a compliance with proposals made out of respect to his honourable character."

Lord Graham applauded the humanity, prudence, and piety of Sir Philip's proposals. He enforced them with all his influence and eloquence. Lord Clifford seconded him; and the rest gave tokens of approbation.

Sir Robert Fitz-Owen then rose up. "I beg leave to observe to the company, who are going to dispose so generously of another man's property, that my father purchased the castle and estate of the house of Lovel; who is to repay him the money for it?"

Sir Philip then said, "I have also a question to ask. Who is to pay the arrears of my ward's estate, which he has unjustly been kept out of these one-and-twenty years? Let Lord Clifford answer to both points, for he is not interested in either."

Lord Clifford smiled.

"I think," returned he, "the first question is answered by the second, and that the parties concerned should set one against the other, especially as Lord Fitz-Owen's children will inherit the fortune, which includes the purchase-money."

Lord Graham said, "This determination is both equitable and generous, and I hope will answer the expectations on all sides."

"I have another proposal to make to my Lord Fitz-Owen," said Sir Philip, "but I first wait for the acceptance of those already made."

Lord Fitz-Owen replied, "I shall report them to my brother, and acquaint the company with his resolution to-morrow."

They then separated; and the Baron, with his sons, returned to the sick man's chamber; there he exhorted his brother, with the piety of a confessor, to repent of his sins and make atonement for them. He made known Sir Philip's proposals, and observed on the wonderful discovery of his crime, and the punishment that followed it. "Your repentance," continued he, "may be accepted, and your crime may yet be pardoned. If you continue refractory, and refuse to make atonement, you will draw down upon you a severer punishment."

The criminal would not confess, and yet could not deny, the truth and justice of his observations. The Baron spent several hours in his brother's chamber. He sent for a priest, who took his confession; and they both sat up with him all night, advising, persuading, and exhorting him to do justice, and to comply with the proposals. He was unwilling to give up the world, and yet more so to become the object of public shame, disgrace, and punishment.

The next day, Lord Fitz-Owen summoned the company into his brother's chamber, and there declared, in his name, that he accepted Sir Philip Harclay's proposals; that, if the young man could, as he promised, direct them to the places where his parents were buried, and if his birth should be authenticated by his foster-parents, he should be acknowledged the heir of the house of Lovel. That to be certified of these things, they must commission proper persons to go with him for this purpose; and, in case the truth should be made plain, they should immediately put him in possession of the castle and estate, in the state it was. He desired Lord Graham and Lord Clifford to choose the commissioners, and gave Sir Philip and Edmund a right to add to them, each, another person. [sic]

Lord Graham named the eldest son of Lord Clifford, and the other, in return, named his nephew; they also chose the priest, Lord Graham's confessor, and the eldest son of Baron Fitz-Owen, to his great mortification. Sir Philip appointed Mr. William

Fitz-Owen, and Edmund named Father Oswald; they chose out
the servants to attend them, who were also to be witnesses of all
that should pass. Lord Clifford proposed to Baron Fitz-Owen,
that, as soon as the commissioners were set out, the remainder of
the company should adjourn to his seat in Cumberland, whither
Lord Graham should be invited to accompany them, and to stay
till this affair was decided. After some debate, this was agreed to;
and, at the same time, that the criminal should be kept with them
till every thing was properly settled.

Lord Fitz-Owen gave his son William the charge to receive and
entertain the commissioners at the castle; But, before they set out,
Sir Philip had a conference with Lord Fitz-Owen, concerning the
surrender of the castle; in which he insisted on the furniture and
stock of the farm, in consideration of the arrears. Lord Fitz-Owen
slightly mentioned the young man's education and expences. Sir
Philip answered, "You are right, my Lord; I had not thought of
this point; we owe you, in this respect, more than we can ever
repay. But you know not half the respect and affection Edmund
bears for you. When restitution of his title and fortune are fully
made, his happiness will still depend on you."

"How on me?" said the Baron.

"Why, he will not be happy unless you honour him with your
notice and esteem; but this is not all, I must hope that you will
do still more for him."

"Indeed," said the Baron, "he has put my regard for him to a
severe proof; what further can he expect from me?"

"My dear Lord, be not offended, I have only one more proposal to make to you; if you refuse it, I can allow for you; and I
confess it requires a greatness of mind, but not more than you
possess, to grant it."

"Well, sir, speak your demand."

"Say rather my request; it is this: Cease to look upon Edmund
as the enemy of your house; look upon him as a son, and make
him so indeed."

"How say you, Sir Philip? My son!"

"Yes, my Lord, give him your daughter. He is already your son in filial affection; your son William and he are sworn brothers; what remains but to make him yours? He deserves such a parent, you such a son; and you will, by this means, ingraft into your family, the name, title, and estate of Lovel, which will be entailed on your posterity for ever."

"This offer requires much consideration," returned the Baron.

"Suffer me to suggest some hints to you," said Sir Philip. "This match is, I think, verily pointed out by Providence, which hath conducted the dear boy through so many dangers, and brought him within view of his happiness; look on him as the precious relic of a noble house, the son of my dearest friend! Or look on him as my son and heir, and let me, as his father, implore you to consent to his marriage with your daughter."

The Baron's heart was touched, he turned away his face.

"Oh, Sir Philip Harclay, what a friend are you! Why should such a man be our enemy?"

"My Lord," said Sir Philip, "we are not, cannot be enemies; our hearts are already allied; and I am certain we shall one day be dear friends."

The Baron suppressed his emotions, but Sir Philip saw into his heart.

"I must consult my eldest son," returned he.

"Then," replied Sir Philip, "I foresee much difficulty; he is prejudiced against Edmund, and thinks the restitution of his inheritance an injury to your family. Hereafter he will see this alliance in a different light, and will rejoice that such a brother is added to the family; but, at present, he will set his face against it. However, we will not despair; virtue and resolution will surmount all obstacles. Let me call in young Lovel."

He brought Edmund to the Baron, and acquainted him with the proposal he had been making in his name, my Lord's answers, and the objections he feared on the part of Sir Robert.

Edmund kneeled to the Baron; he took his hand and pressed it to his lips.

"Best of men! Of parents! Of patrons!" said he. "I will ever be your son in filial affection, whether I have the honour to be legally so or not; not one of your own children can feel a stronger sense of love and duty."

"Tell me," said the Baron, "do you love my daughter?"

"I do, my Lord, with the most ardent affection; I never loved any woman but her; and, if I am so unfortunate as to be refused her, I will not marry at all. Oh, my Lord, reject not my honest suit! Your alliance will give me consequence with myself, it will excite me to act worthy of the station to which I am exalted; if you refuse me, I shall seem an abject wretch, disdained by those whom my heart claims relation to; your family are the whole world to me. Give me your lovely daughter! give me also your son, my beloved William; and let me share with them the fortune Providence bestows upon me. But what is title or fortune, if I am deprived of the society of those I love?"

"Edmund," said the Baron, "you have a noble friend; but you have a stronger in my heart, which I think was implanted there by Heaven to aid its own purposes. I feel a variety of emotions of different kinds, and am afraid to trust my own heart with you. But answer me a question: Are you assured of my daughter's consent? Have you solicited her favour? Have you gained her affections?"

"Never, my Lord. I am incapable of so base an action; I have loved her at an humble distance; but, in my situation, I should have thought it a violation of all the laws of gratitude and hospitality to have presumed to speak the sentiments of my heart."

"Then you have acted with unquestionable honour on this, and, I must say, on all other occasions."

"Your approbation, my Lord, is the first wish of my life; it is the seal of my honour and happiness."

Sir Philip smiled. "My Lord Fitz-Owen, I am jealous of Edmund's preferable regard for you; it is just the same now as formerly."

Edmund came to Sir Philip, he threw himself into his arms, he wept, he was overpowered with the feelings of his heart; he prayed to Heaven to strengthen his mind to support his inexpressible sensations.

"I am overwhelmed with obligation," said he. "Oh, best of friends, teach me, like you, to make my actions speak for me!"

"Enough, Edmund; I know your heart, and that is my security. My Lord, speak to him, and bring him to himself, by behaving coldly to him, if you can."

The Baron said, "I must not trust myself with you, you make a child of me. I will only add, gain my son Robert's favour, and be assured of mine; I owe some respect to the heir of my family; he is brave, honest, and sincere; your enemies are separated from him, you have William's influence in your behalf; make one effort, and let me know the result."

Edmund kissed his hand in transports of joy and gratitude.

"I will not lose a moment," said he. "I fly to obey your commands."

Edmund went immediately to his friend William, and related all that had passed between the Baron, Sir Philip, and himself. William promised him his interest in the warmest manner; he recapitulated all that had passed in the castle since his departure; but he guarded his sister's delicacy, till it should be resolved to give way to his address. They both consulted young Clifford, who had conceived an affection to Edmund for his amiable qualities, and to William for his generous friendship for him. He promised them his assistance, as Sir Robert seemed desirous to cultivate his friendship. Accordingly, they both attacked him with the whole artillery of friendship and persuasion. Clifford urged the merits of Edmund, and the advantages of his alliance. William enforced his arguments by a retrospect of Edmund's past life; and observed, that every obstacle thrown in his way had brought his enemies to shame, and increase of honour to himself. "I say nothing," continued he, "of his noble qualities and affectionate heart; those who have been so many years his companions, can want no proofs of it."

"We know your attachment to him, sir," said Sir Robert, "and, in consequence, your partiality."

"Nay," replied William, "you are sensible of the truth of my assertions; and, I am confident, would have loved him yourself, but for the insinuations of his enemies. But if he should make good his assertions, even you must be convinced of his veracity."

"And you would have my father give him your sister upon this uncertainty?"

"No, sir, but upon these conditions."

"But suppose he does not make them good?"

"Then I will be of your party, and give up his interest."

"Very well, sir; my father may do as he pleases; but I cannot agree to give my sister to one who has always stood in the way of our family, and now turns us out of our own house."

"I am sorry, brother, you see his pretensions in so wrong a light; but if you think there is any imposture in the case, go with us, and be a witness of all that passes."

"No, not I; if Edmund is to be master of the castle, I will never more set my foot in it."

"This matter," said Mr. Clifford, "must be left to time, which has brought stranger things to pass. Sir Robert's honour and good sense will enable him to subdue his prejudices, and to judge impartially."

They took leave, and went to make preparations for their journey. Edmund made his report of Sir Robert's inflexibility to his father, in presence of Sir Philip; who, again, ventured to urge the Baron on his favourite subject.

"It becomes me to wait for the further proofs," said he, "but, if they are as clear as I expect, I will not be inexorable to your wishes; Say nothing more on this subject till the return of the commissioners."

They were profuse in their acknowledgments of his goodness.

Edmund took a tender leave of his two paternal friends.

"When," said he, "I take possession of my inheritance, I must hope for the company of you both to complete my happiness."

"Of me," said Sir Philip, "you may be certain; and, as far as my influence reaches, of the Baron."

He was silent. Edmund assured them of his constant prayers for their happiness.

Soon after, the commissioners, with Edmund, set out for Lovel Castle; and the following day the Lord Clifford set out for his own house, with Baron Fitz-Owen and his son. The nominal Baron was carried with them, very much against his will. Sir Philip Harclay was invited to go with them by Lord Clifford, who declared his presence necessary to bring things to a conclusion. They all joined in acknowledging their obligations to Lord Graham's generous hospitality, and besought him to accompany them. At length he consented, on condition they would allow him to go to and fro, as his duty should call him.

Lord Clifford received them with the greatest hospitality, and presented them to his lady, and three daughters, who were in the bloom of youth and beauty. They spent their time very pleasantly, excepting the criminal, who continued gloomy and reserved, and declined company.

In the mean time, the commissioners proceeded on their journey. When they were within a day's distance from the castle, Mr. William and his servant put forward, and arrived several hours before the rest, to make preparations for their reception. His sister and brother received them with open arms, and enquired eagerly after the event of the journey to the North. He gave them a brief account of every thing that had happened to their uncle; adding, "But this is not all: Sir Philip Harclay has brought a young man who he pretends is the son of the late Lord Lovel, and claims his estate and title. This person is on his journey hither, with several others who are commissioned to enquire into certain particulars, to confirm his pretensions. If he make good his claim, my father will surrender the castle and estate into his hands. Sir Philip and my Lord have many points to settle; and he has proposed a compromise, that you, my sister, ought to know, because it nearly concerns you."

"Me! Brother William; pray explain yourself."

"Why, he proposes that, in lieu of arrears and other expectations, my father shall give his dear Emma to the heir of Lovel, in full of all demands."

She changed colour. "Holy Mary!" said she. "And does my father agree to this proposal?"

"He is not very averse to it; but Sir Robert refuses his consent. However, I have given him my interest with you."

"Have you indeed? What! A stranger, perhaps an impostor, who comes to turn us out of our dwelling?"

"Have patience, my Emma! See this young man without prejudice, and perhaps you will like him as well as I do."

"I am surprised at you, William."

"Dear Emma, I cannot bear to see you uneasy. Think of the man who of all others you would wish to see in a situation to ask you of your father, and expect to see your wishes realized."

"Impossible!" said she.

"Nothing is impossible, my dear; let us be prudent, and all will end happily. You must help me to receive and entertain these commissioners. I expect a very solemn scene; but when that is once got over, happier hours than the past will succeed. We shall first visit the haunted apartment; you, my sister, will keep in your own till I shall send for you. I go now to give orders to the servants."

He went and ordered them to be in waiting; and himself, and his youngest brother, stood in readiness to receive them.

The sound of the horn announced the arrival of the commissioners; at the same instant a sudden gust of wind arose, and the outward gates flew open. They entered the court-yard, and the great folding-doors into the hall were opened without any assistance. The moment Edmund entered the hall, every door in the house flew open; the servants all rushed into the hall, and fear was written on their countenances; Joseph only was undaunted. "These doors," said he, "open of their own accord to receive their master! This is he indeed!"

Edmund was soon apprized of what had happened.

"I accept the omen!" said he. "Gentlemen, let us go forward to the apartment! Let us finish the work of fate! I will lead the way." He went on to the apartment, followed by all present. "Open the shutters," said he, "the daylight shall no longer be excluded here; the deeds of darkness shall now be brought to light."

They descended the staircase; every door was open, till they came to the fatal closet. Edmund called to Mr. William, "Approach, my friend, and behold the door your family overlooked!"

They came forward; he drew the key out of his bosom, and unlocked the door; he made them observe that the boards were all loose; he then called to the servants, and bid them remove every thing out of the closet. While they were doing this, Edmund shewed them the breastplate all stained with blood. He then called to Joseph:—

"Do you know whose was this suit of armour?"

"It was my Lord's," said Joseph. "The late Lord Lovel; I have seen him wear it."

Edmund bade them bring shovels and remove the earth. While they were gone, he desired Oswald to repeat all that passed the night they sat up together in that apartment, which he did till the servants returned. They threw out the earth, while the by-standers in solemn silence waited the event. After some time and labour they struck against something. They proceeded till they discovered a large trunk, which with some difficulty they drew out. It had been corded round, but the cords were rotted to dust. They opened it, and found a skeleton which appeared to have been tied neck and heels together, and forced into the trunk.

"Behold," said Edmund, "the bones of him to whom I owe my birth!"

The priest from Lord Graham's advanced. "This is undoubtedly the body of the Lord Lovel; I heard his kinsman confess the manner in which he was interred. Let this awful spectacle be a lesson to all present, that though wickedness may triumph for a season, a day of retribution will come!"

Oswald exclaimed. "Behold the day of retribution! Of triumph to the innocent, of shame and confusion to the wicked!"

The young gentlemen declared that Edmund had made good his assertions.

"What then," said they, "remains?"

"I propose," said Lord Graham's priest, "that an account be written of this discovery, and signed by all the witnesses present; that an attested copy be left in the hands of this gentleman, and the original be sent to the Barons and Sir Philip Harclay, to convince them of the truth of it."

Mr. Clifford then desired Edmund to proceed in his own way.

"The first thing I propose to do," said he, "is to have a coffin made for these honoured remains. I trust to find the bones of my other parent, and to inter them all together in consecrated ground. Unfortunate pair! You shall at last rest together! Your son shall pay the last duties to your ashes!"

He stopped to shed tears, and none present but paid this tribute to their misfortunes. Edmund recovered his voice and proceeded.

"My next request is, that Father Oswald and this reverend father, with whoever else the gentlemen shall appoint, will send for Andrew and Margery Twyford, and examine them concerning the circumstances of my birth, and the death and burial of my unfortunate mother."

"It shall be done," said Mr. William, "but first let me intreat you to come with me and take some refreshment after your journey, for you must be fatigued; after dinner we will proceed in the enquiry."

They all followed him into the great hall, where they were

entertained with great hospitality, and Mr. William did the honours in his father's name. Edmund's heart was deeply affected, and the solemnity of his deportment bore witness to his sincerity; but it was a manly sorrow, that did not make him neglect his duty to his friends or himself. He enquired after the health of the Lady Emma.

"She is well," said William, "and as much your friend as ever." Edmund bowed in silence.

After dinner the commissioners sent for Andrew and his wife. They examined them separately, and found their accounts agreed together, and were in substance the same as Oswald and Edmund had before related, separately also. The commissioners observed, that there could be no collusion between them, and that the proofs were indisputable. They kept the foster parents all night; and the next day Andrew directed them to the place where the Lady Lovel was buried, between two trees which he had marked for a memorial. They collected the bones and carried them to the Castle, where Edmund caused a stately coffin to be made for the remains of the unfortunate pair. The two priests obtained leave to look in the coffin buried in the church, and found nothing but stones and earth in it. The commissioners then declared they were fully satisfied of the reality of Edmund's pretensions.

The two priests were employed in drawing up a circumstantial account of these discoveries, in order to make their report to the Barons at their return. In the mean time Mr. William took an opportunity to introduce Edmund to his sister.

"My Emma," said he, "the heir of Lovel is desirous to pay his respects to you."

They were both in apparent confusion; but Edmund's wore off, and Emma's increased.

"I have been long desirous," said he, "to pay my respects to the lady whom I most honour, but unavoidable duties have detained me; when these are fully paid, it is my wish to devote the remainder of my life to Lady Emma!"

"Are you, then, the heir of Lovel?"

"I am, madam; and am also the man in whose behalf I once presumed to speak."

"'Tis very strange indeed!"

"It is so, madam, to myself; but time that reconciles us to all things, will, I hope, render this change in my situation familiar to you."

William said, "You are both well acquainted with the wishes of my heart; but my advice is, that you do not encourage a farther intimacy till my Lord's determination be fully known."

"You may dispose of me as you please," said Edmund, "but I cannot help declaring my wishes; yet I will submit to my Lord's sentence, though he should doom me to despair."

From this period, the young pair behaved with solemn respect to each other, but with apparent reserve. The young lady sometimes appeared in company, but oftener chose to be in her own apartment, where she began to believe and hope for the completion of her wishes. The uncertainty of the Baron's determination, threw an air of anxiety over Edmund's face. His friend William, by the most tender care and attention, strove to dispel his fears, and encourage his hopes; but he waited with impatience for the return of the commissioners, and the decision of his fate.

While these things passed at the Castle of Lovel, the nominal Baron recovered his health and strength at the house of Lord Clifford. In the same proportion he grew more and more shy and reserved, avoided the company of his brother and nephew, and was frequently shut up with his two servants. Sir Robert Fitz-Owen made several attempts to gain his confidence, but in vain; he was equally shy to him as the rest. M. Zadisky observed his motions with the penetration for which his countrymen have been distinguished in all ages; he communicated his suspicions to Sir Philip and the Barons, giving it as his opinion, that the criminal was meditating an escape. They asked, what he thought was to be done? Zadisky offered to watch him in turn with another person, and to lie in wait for him; he also proposed, that horses should be kept in readiness, and men to mount them, without knowledge of the service they were to be employed in. The Barons agreed to leave the whole management of this affair to Zadisky. He took his measures so well, that he intercepted the three fugitives in the fields adjoining to the house, and brought them all back prisoner. They confined them separately, while the Lords and Gentlemen consulted how to dispose of them.

Sir Philip applied to Lord Fitz-Owen, who begged leave to be silent. "I have nothing," said he, "to offer in favour of this bad man; and I cannot propose harsher measures with so near a relation."

Zadisky then begged to be heard.

"You can no longer have any reliance upon the word of a man who has forfeited all pretensions to honour and sincerity. I have long wished to revisit once more my native country, and to enquire after some very dear friends I left there. I will undertake to convey this man to a very distant part of the world, where it will be out of his power to do further mischief, and free his relations from an ungrateful charge, unless you should rather choose to bring him to punishment here."

Lord Clifford approved of the proposal; Lord Fitz-Owen remained silent, but shewed no marks of disapprobation.

Sir Philip objected to parting with his friend; but Zadisky assured him he had particular reasons for returning to the Holy Land, of which he should be judge hereafter. Sir Philip desired the Lord Fitz-Owen to give him his company to the criminal's apartment, saying, "We will have one more conversation with him, and that shall decide his fate."

They found him silent and sullen, and he refused to answer their questions.

Sir Philip then bespoke him: "After the proofs you have given of your falsehood and insincerity, we can no longer have any reliance upon you, nor faith in your fulfilling the conditions of our agreement; I will, therefore, once more make you a proposal that shall still leave you indebted to our clemency. You shall banish yourself from England for ever, and go in pilgrimage to the Holy Land, with such companions as we shall appoint; or, secondly, you shall enter directly into a monastery, and there be shut up for life; or, thirdly, if you refuse both these offers, I will go directly to court, throw myself at the feet of my Sovereign, relate the whole story of your wicked life and actions, and demand vengeance on your head. The King is too good and pious to let such villany go unpunished; he will bring you to public shame and punishment; and be you assured, if I begin this prosecution, I will pursue it to the utmost. I appeal to your worthy brother for the justice of my proceeding. I reason no more with you, I only declare my resolution. I wait your answer one hour, and the next I put in execution whatever you shall oblige me to determine."

So saying, they retired, and left him to reflect and to resolve. At the expiration of the hour they sent Zadisky to receive his answer; he insinuated to him the generosity and charity of Sir Philip and the Lords, and the certainty of their resolutions, and begged him to take care what answer he returned, for that his fate depended on it. He kept silent several minutes, resentment and despair were painted on his visage. At length he spoke:—

"Tell my proud enemies that I prefer banishment to death, infamy, or a life of solitude."

"You have chosen well," said Zadisky. "To a wise man all countries are alike; it shall be my care to make mine agreeable to you."

"Are you, then, the person chosen for my companion?"

"I am, sir; and you may judge by that circumstance, that those whom you call your enemies, are not so in effect. Farewell, sir—I go to prepare for our departure."

Zadisky went and made his report, and then set immediately about his preparations. He chose two active young men for his attendants; and gave them directions to keep a strict eye upon their charge, for that they should be accountable if he should escape them.

In the meantime the Baron Fitz-Owen had several conferences with his brother; he endeavoured to make him sensible of his crimes, and of the justice and clemency of his conqueror; but he was moody and reserved to him as to the rest. Sir Philip Harclay obliged him to surrender his worldly estates into the hands of Lord Fitz-Owen. A writing was drawn up for that purpose, and executed in the presence of them all. Lord Fitz-Owen engaged to allow him an annual sum, and to advance money for the expences of his voyage. He spoke to him in the most affectionate manner, but he refused his embrace.

"You will have nothing to regret," said he, haughtily, "for the gain is yours."

Sir Philip conjured Zadisky to return to him again, who answered:

"I will either return, or give such reasons for my stay, as you shall approve. I will send a messenger to acquaint you with my arrival in Syria, and with such other particulars as I shall judge interesting to you and yours. In the meantime remember me in your prayers, and preserve for me those sentiments of friendship and esteem, that I have always deemed one of the chief honours and blessings of my life. Commend my love and duty to your adopted son; he will more than supply my absence, and be the comfort of your old age. Adieu, best and noblest of friends!"

They took a tender leave of each other, not without tears on both sides.

The travellers set out directly for a distant seaport where they heard of a ship bound for the Levant, in which they embarked and proceeded on their voyage.

The Commissioners arrived at Lord Clifford's a few days after the departure of the adventurers. They gave a minute account of their commission, and expressed themselves entirely satisfied of the justice of Edmund's pretensions; they gave an account in writing of all that they had been eyewitnesses to, and ventured to urge the Baron Fitz-Owen on the subject of Edmund's wishes.

The Baron was already disposed in his favour; his mind was employed in the future establishment of his family. During their residence at Lord Clifford's, his eldest son Sir Robert had cast his eye upon the eldest daughter of that nobleman, and he besought his father to ask her in marriage for him. The Baron was pleased with the alliance, and took the first opportunity to mention it to Lord Clifford; who answered him, pleasantly:

"I will give my daughter to your son, upon condition that you will give yours to the heir of Lovel." The Baron looked serious; Lord Clifford went on:

"I like that young man so well, that I would accept him for a son-in-law, if he asked me for my daughter; and if I have any influence with you, I will use it in his behalf."

"A powerful solicitor indeed!" said the Baron. "But you know my eldest son's reluctance to it; if he consents, so will I."

"He shall consent," said Lord Clifford, "or he shall have no daughter of mine. Let him subdue his prejudices, and then I will lay aside my scruples."

"But, my Lord," replied the Baron, "if I can obtain his free consent, it will be the best for all; I will try once more, and if he will not, I will leave it wholly to your management."

When the noble company were all assembled, Sir Philip Harclay revived the subject, and besought the Lord Fitz-Owen to put an end to the work he had begun, by confirming Edmund's happiness. The Baron rose up, and thus spoke:

"The proofs of Edmund's noble birth, the still stronger ones of his excellent endowments and qualities, the solicitations of so many noble friends in his behalf, have altogether determined me in his favour; and I hope to do justice to his merit, without detriment to my other children; I am resolved to make them all as happy as my power will allow me to do. Lord Clifford has been so gracious to promise his fair daughter to my son Robert, upon certain conditions, that I will take upon me to ratify, and which will render my son worthy of the happiness that awaits him. My children are the undoubted heirs of my unhappy brother, Lovel; you, my son, shall therefore immediately take possession of your uncle's house and estate, only obliging you to pay to each of your younger brothers, the sum of one thousand pounds; on this condition, I will secure that estate to you and your heirs for ever. I will by my own act and deed surrender the castle and estate of Lovel to the right owner, and at the same time marry him to my daughter. I will settle a proper allowance upon my two younger sons, and dispose of what remains by a will and testament; and then I shall have done all my business in this world, and shall have nothing to do but prepare for the next."

"Oh, my father!" said Sir Robert, "I cannot bear your generosity! You would give away all to others, and reserve nothing for yourself."

"Not so, my son," said the Baron, "I will repair my old castle in Wales, and reside there. I will visit my children, and be visited by them; I will enjoy their happiness, and by that means increase my own; whether I look backwards or forwards, I shall have nothing to do but rejoice, and be thankful to Heaven that has given me so many blessings; I shall have the comfortable reflection of having discharged my duties as a citizen, a husband, a father, a friend; and, whenever I am summoned away from this world, I shall die content."

Sir Robert came forward with tears on his cheeks; he kneeled to his father.

"Best of parents, and of men!" said he. "You have subdued a heart that has been too refractory to your will; you have this day made me sensible how much I owe to your goodness and forbearance with me. Forgive me all that is past, and from henceforward dispose of me; I will have no will but yours, no ambition but to be worthy of the name of your son."

"And this day," said the Baron, "do I enjoy the true happiness of a father! Rise, my son, and take possession of the first place in my affection without reserve." They embraced with tears on both sides; The company rose, and congratulated both father and son. The Baron presented his son to Lord Clifford, who embraced him, and said:

"You shall have my daughter, for I see that you deserve her."

Sir Philip Harclay approached—the Baron gave his son's hand to the knight.

"Love and respect that good man," said he, "deserve his friendship, and you will obtain it."

Nothing but congratulations were heard on all sides.

When their joy was in some degree reduced to composure, Sir Philip proposed that they should begin to execute the schemes of happiness they had planned. He proposed that my Lord Fitz-Owen should go with him to the Castle of Lovel, and settle the family there. The Baron consented; and both together invited such of the company, as liked it, to accompany them thither. It was agreed that a nephew of Lord Graham's, another of Lord Clifford's, two gentlemen, friends of Sir Philip Harclay, and Father Oswald, should be of the party; together with several of Sir Philip's dependants and domestics, and the attendants on the rest. Lord Fitz-Owen gave orders for their speedy departure. Lord Graham and his friends took leave of them, in order to return to his own home; but, before he went, he engaged his eldest nephew and heir to the second daughter of the Lord Clifford; Sir Robert offered himself to the eldest, who modestly received his address, and made no objection to his proposal. The fathers confirmed their engagement.

Lord Fitz-Owen promised to return to the celebration of the marriage; in the mean time he ordered his son to go and take possession of his uncle's house, and to settle his household; He invited young Clifford, and some other gentlemen, to go with him. The company separated with regret, and with many promises of friendship on all sides; and the gentlemen of the North were to cultivate the good neighbourhood on both sides of the borders.

Sir Philip Harclay and the Baron Fitz-Owen, with their friends and attendants, set forwards for the Castle of Lovel; a servant went before, at full speed, to acquaint the family of their approach. Edmund was in great anxiety of mind, now the crisis of his fate was near at hand; He enquired of the messenger, who were of the party? And finding that Sir Philip Harclay was there, and that Sir Robert Fitz-Owen stayed in the North, his hopes rose above his fears. Mr. William, attended by a servant, rode forward to meet them; he desired Edmund to stay and receive them. Edmund was under some difficulty with regard to his behaviour to the lovely Emma; a thousand times his heart rose to his lips, as often he suppressed his emotions; they both sighed frequently, said little, thought much, and wished for the event. Master Walter was too young to partake of their anxieties, but he wished for the arrival of his father to end them.

Mr. William's impatience spurred him on to meet his father; as soon as he saw him, he rode up directly to him.

"My dear father, you are welcome home!" said he.

"I think not, sir," said the Baron, and looked serious.

"Why so, my Lord?" said William.

"Because it is no longer mine, but another man's home," answered he, "and I must receive my welcome from him."

"Meaning Edmund?" said William.

"Whom else can it be?"

"Ah, my Lord! He is your creature, your servant; he puts his fate into your hands, and will submit to your pleasure in all things!"

"Why comes he not to meet us?" said the Baron.

"His fears prevent him," said William, "but speak the word, and I will fetch him."

"No," said the Baron, "we will wait on him."

William looked confused.

"Is Edmund so unfortunate," said he, "as to have incurred your displeasure?"

Sir Philip Harclay advanced, and laid his hand on William's saddle.

"Generous impatience! Noble youth!" said he. "Look round you, and see if you can discover in this company one enemy of your friend! Leave to your excellent father the time and manner of explaining himself; he only can do justice to his own sentiments."

The Baron smiled on Sir Philip; William's countenance cleared up; they went forward, and soon arrived at the Castle of Lovel.

Edmund was walking to and fro in the hall, when he heard the horn that announced their arrival; his emotions were so great that he could hardly support them. The Baron and Sir Philip entered the hall hand in hand; Edmund threw himself at their feet, and embraced their knees, but could not utter a word. They raised him between them, and strove to encourage him; but he threw himself into the arms of Sir Philip Harclay, deprived of strength, and almost of life. They supported him to a seat, where he recovered by degrees, but had no power to speak his feelings; he looked up to his benefactors in the most affecting manner, he laid his hand upon his bosom, but was still silent.

"Compose yourself, my dear son," said Sir Philip, "you are in the arms of your best friends. Look up to the happiness that awaits you—enjoy the blessings that Heaven sends you—lift up your heart in gratitude to the Creator, and think less of what you owe to the creature! You will have time enough to pay us your acknowledgments hereafter."

The company came round them, the servants flocked into the hall: shouts of joy were heard on all sides; the Baron came and took Edmund's hand.

"Rise, sir," said he, "and do the honours of your house! it is yours from this day: we are your guests, and expect from you our welcome!"

Edmund kneeled to the Baron, he spoke with a faltering voice:

"My Lord, I am yours! All that I have is at your devotion! Dispose of me as it pleases you best."

The Baron embraced him with the greatest affection.

"Look round you," said he, "and salute your friends; these gentlemen came hither to do you honour."

Edmund revived, he embraced and welcomed the gentlemen. Father Oswald received his embrace with peculiar affection, and gave him his benediction in a most affecting manner.

Edmund exclaimed, "Pray for me, father! That I may bear all these blessings with gratitude and moderation!"

He then saluted and shook hands with all the servants, not omitting the meanest; he distinguished Joseph by a cordial embrace; he called him his dear friend.

"Now," said he, "I can return your friendship, and I am proud to acknowledge it!"

The old man, with a faltering voice, cried out:

"Now I have lived long enough! I have seen my master's son acknowledged for the heir of Lovel!"

The hall echoed with his words, "Long live the heir of Lovel!"

The Baron took Edmund's hands in his own:

"Let us retire from this crowd," said he, "we have business of a more private nature to transact."

He led to the parlour, followed by Sir Philip and the other gentlemen.

"Where are my other children?" said he.

William retired, and presently returned with his brother and sister. They kneeled to their father, who raised and embraced them. He then called out, "William!—Edmund!—Come and receive my blessing also."

They approached hand in hand, they kneeled, and he gave them a solemn benediction.

"Your friendship deserves our praise, my children! Love each other always! And may Heaven pour down its choicest blessings upon your heads!"

They rose, and embraced in silent raptures of joy. Edmund presented his friend to Sir Philip.

"I understand you," said he, "this gentleman was my first

acquaintance of this family; he has a title to the second place in my heart; I shall tell him, at more leisure, how much I love and honour him for his own sake as well as yours."

He embraced the youth, and desired his friendship.

"Come hither, my Emma!" said the Baron.

She approached with tears on her check, sweetly blushing, like the damask rose wet with the dew of the morning.

"I must ask you a serious question, my child; answer me with the same sincerity you would to Heaven. You see this young man, the heir of Lovel! You have known him long; consult your own heart, and tell me whether you have any objection to receive him for your husband. I have promised to all this company to give you to him; but upon condition that you approve him: I think him worthy of you; and, whether you accept him or not, he shall ever be to me a son; but Heaven forbid that I should compel my child to give her hand, where she cannot bestow her heart! Speak freely, and decide this point for me and for yourself."

The fair Emma blushed, and was under some confusion; her virgin modesty prevented her speaking for some moments. Edmund trembled; he leaned upon William's shoulder to support himself. Emma cast her eye upon him, she saw his emotion, and hastened to relieve him; and thus spoke in a soft voice which gathered strength as she proceeded:

"My Lord and father's goodness has always prevented my wishes; I am the happiest of all children, in being able to obey his commands, without offering violence to my own inclinations. As I am called upon in this public manner, it is but justice to this gentleman's merit to declare, that, were I at liberty to choose a husband from all the world, he only should be my choice, who I can say, with joy, is my father's also."

Edmund bowed low, he advanced towards her; the Baron took his daughter's hand, and presented it to him; he kneeled upon one knee, he took her hand, kissed it, and pressed it to his bosom. The Baron embraced and blessed them; he presented them to Sir Philip Harclay—"Receive and acknowledge your children!" said he.

"I do receive them as the gift of Heaven!" said the noble knight. "They are as much mine as if I had begotten them: all that I have is theirs, and shall descend to their children for ever." A fresh scene of congratulation ensued; and the hearts of all the auditors were too much engaged to be able soon to return to the ease and tranquillity of common life.

After they had refreshed themselves, and recovered from the emotions they had sustained on this interesting occasion, Edmund thus addressed the Baron:

"On the brink of happiness I must claim your attention to a melancholy subject. The bones of both my parents lie unburied in this house; permit me, my honoured Lord, to perform my last duties to them, and the remainder of my life shall be devoted to you and yours."

"Certainly," said the Baron, "why have you not interred them?"

"My Lord, I waited for your arrival, that you might be certified of the reality, and that no doubts might remain."

"I have no doubts," said the Baron. "Alas! Both the crime and punishment of the offender leave no room for them!" He sighed. "Let us now put an end to this affair; and, if possible, forget it for ever."

"If it will not be too painful to you, my Lord, I would intreat you, with these gentlemen our friends, to follow me into the east apartment, the scene of my parents' woes, and yet the dawning of my better hopes."

They rose to attend him; he committed the Lady Emma to the care of her youngest brother, observing that the scene was too solemn for a lady to be present at it. They proceeded to the apartment; he shewed the Baron the fatal closet, and the place where the bones were found, also the trunk that contained them; he recapitulated all that passed before their arrival; he shewed them the coffin where the bones of the unfortunate pair were deposited: he then desired the Baron to give orders for their interment.

"No," replied he, "it belongs to you to order, and every one here is ready to perform it."

Edmund then desired Father Oswald to give notice to the friars of the monastery of St. Austin, that with their permission the funeral should be solemnized there, and the bones interred in the church. He also gave orders that the closet should be floored, the apartment repaired and put in order. He then returned to the other side of the Castle.

Preparations being made for the funeral, it was performed a few days after. Edmund attended in person as chief mourner, Sir Philip Harclay as the second; Joseph desired he might assist as servant to the deceased. They were followed by most people of the village. The story was now become public, and every one blessed Edmund for the piety and devotion with which he performed the last duties to his parents.—Edmund appeared in deep mourning; the week after, he assisted at a mass for the repose of the deceased.

Sir Philip Harclay ordered a monument to be erected to the memory of his friends, with the following inscription:

> *Praye for the soules of Arthur Lord Lovele and Marie his wife, who were cut off in the flowere of theire youthe, by the trecherye and crueltie of theire neare kinnesmanne. Edmunde theire onlie sonne, one and twentie yeares after theire deathe, by the direction of heavene, made the discoverye of the mannere of theire deathe, and at the same time proved his owne birthe. He collected theire bones together, and interred them in this place: A warning and proofe to late posteritie, of the justice of Providence, and the certaintie of Retribution.*

The Sunday after the funeral Edmund threw off his mourning, and appeared in a dress suitable to his condition. He received the compliments of his friends with ease and cheerfulness, and began to enjoy his happiness. He asked an audience of his fair mistress, and was permitted to declare the passion he had so long stifled in his own bosom. She gave him a favourable hearing, and in a short time confessed that she had suffered equally in that suspense that was so grievous to him. They engaged themselves by mutual vows to each other, and only waited the Baron's pleasure to complete their happiness; every cloud was vanished from their brows, and sweet tranquillity took possession of their bosoms. Their friends shared their happiness; William and Edmund renewed their vows of everlasting friendship, and promised to be as much together as William's other duties would permit.

The Baron once more summoned all his company together; he told Edmund all that had passed relating to his brother in-law, his exile, and the pilgrimage of Zadisky; he then related the circumstances of Sir Robert's engagement to Lord Clifford's daughter, his establishment in his uncle's seat, and his own obligations to return time enough to be present at the marriage. "But before I go," said he, "I will give my daughter to the heir of Lovel, and then I shall have discharged my duty to him, and my promise to Sir Philip Harclay."

"You have nobly performed both," said Sir Philip, "and whenever you depart I shall be your companion."

"What," said Edmund, "am I to be deprived of both my fathers at once? My honoured Lord, you have given away two houses—where do you intend to reside?"

"No matter," said the Baron. "I know I shall be welcome to both."

"My dear Lord," said Edmund, "stay here and be still the master; I shall be proud to be under your command, and to be your servant as well as your son!"

"No, Edmund," said the Baron, "that would not now be proper; this is your castle, you are its lord and master, and it is incumbent on you to shew yourself worthy of the great things Providence has done for you."

"How shall I, a young man, acquit myself of so many duties as will be upon me, without the advice and assistance of my two paternal friends? Oh, Sir Philip! Will you too leave me? Once you gave me hopes—"

He stopped greatly affected.

Sir Philip said, "Tell me truly, Edmund, do you really desire that I should live with you?"

"As truly, sir, as I desire life and happiness!"

"Then, my dear child, I will live and die with you!"

They embraced with tears of affection, and Edmund was all joy and gratitude.

"My good Lord," said Sir Philip, "you have disposed of two houses, and have none ready to receive you; will you accept of mine? It is much at your service, and its being in the same county with your eldest son, will be an inducement to you to reside there."

The Baron caught Sir Philip's hand.

"Noble sir, I thank you, and I will embrace your kind offer; I will be your tenant for the present; my castle in Wales shall be put in repair, in the meantime; if I do not reside there, it will be an establishment for one of my younger sons."

"But what will you do with your old soldiers and dependants?"

"My Lord, I will never cast them off. There is another house on my estate that has been shut up many years; I will have it repaired and furnished properly for the reception of my old men: I will endow it with a certain sum to be paid annually, and will appoint a steward to manage their revenue; I will continue it during the lives of the first inhabitants, and after that I shall leave it to my son here, to do as he pleases."

"Your son," said Edmund, "will make it the business of his life to act worthy of such a father."

"Enough," said Sir Philip, "I am satisfied that you will. I purpose to reside myself in that very apartment which my dear friend your father inhabited; I will tread in his footsteps, and think he sees me acting his part in his son's family. I will be attended by my own servants; and, whenever you desire it, I will give you my company; your joys, your griefs shall be mine; I shall hold your children in my arms, and their prattle shall amuse my old age; and, as my last earthly wish, your hands shall close my eyes."

"Long, very long," said Edmund, with eyes and hands lifted up, "may it be ere I perform so sad a duty!"

"Long and happily may you live together!" said the Baron. "I will hope to see you sometimes, and to claim a share in your blessings. But let us give no more tears to sorrow, the rest shall be those of joy and transport. The first step we take shall be to marry our Edmund; I will give orders for the celebration, and they shall be the last orders I shall give in this house." They then separated, and went to prepare for the approaching solemnity.

Sir Philip and the Baron had a private conference concerning Edmund's assuming the name and title of Lovel. "I am resolved," said Sir Philip, "to go to the King; to acquaint him briefly with Edmund's history; I will request that he may be called up to parliament by a writ, for there is no need of a new patent, he being the true inheritor; in the mean time he shall assume the name, arms, and title, and I will answer any one that shall dispute his right to them." Sir Philip then declared his resolution to set out with the Baron at his departure, and to settle all his other affairs before he returned to take up his residence at the Castle.

A few days after, the marriage was celebrated, to the entire satisfaction of all parties. The Baron ordered the doors to be thrown open, and the house free for all comers; with every other token of joy and festivity. Edmund appeared full of joy without levity, of mirth without extravagance; he received the congratulations of his friends, with ease, freedom, and vivacity. He sent for his foster father and mother, who began to think themselves neglected, as he had been so deeply engaged in affairs of more consequence that he had not been particularly attentive to them; he made them come into the great hall, and presented them to his lady.

"These," said he, "are the good people to whom I am, under God, indebted for my present happiness; they were my first benefactors; I was obliged to them for food and sustenance in my childhood, and this good woman nourished my infancy at her own breast." The lady received them graciously, and saluted Margery. Andrew kneeled down, and, with great humility, begged Edmund's pardon for his treatment of him in his childhood. "I heartily forgive you," said he, "and I will excuse you to yourself; it was natural for you to look upon me as an intruder that was eating your children's bread; you saved my life, and afterwards you sustained it by your food and raiment: I ought to have maintained myself, and to have contributed to your maintenance. But besides this, your treatment of me was the first of my preferment; it recommended me to the notice of this noble family. Everything that happened to me since, has been a step to my present state of honour and happiness. Never man had so many benefactors as myself; but both they, and myself, have been only instruments in the hands of Providence, to bring about its own purposes; let us praise God for all! I shared your poverty, and you will share my riches; I will give you the cottage where you dwell, and the ground about it; I will also pay you the annual sum of ten pounds for the lives of you both; I will put out your children to manual trades, and assist you to provide for them in their own station; and you are to look upon this as paying a debt, and not bestowing a gift; I owe you more than I can ever pay; and, if there be any thing further in my power that will contribute to your happiness, you can ask nothing in reason that I will deny you."

Andrew hid his face. "I cannot bear it!" said he. "Oh what a brute was I, to abuse such a child as this! I shall never forgive myself!"

"You must indeed, my friend; for I forgive and thank you."

Andrew retired back, but Margery came forward; she looked earnestly on Edmund, she then threw her arms about his neck, and wept aloud.

"My precious child! my lovely babe! thank God, I have lived to see this day! I will rejoice in your good fortune, and your bounty to us, but I must ask one more favour yet; that I may sometimes come hither and behold that gracious countenance, and thank God that I was honoured so far as to give thee food from my own breast, and to bring thee up to be a blessing to me, and to all that know thee!"

Edmund was affected, he returned her embrace; he bade her come to the Castle as often as she pleased, and she should always be received as his mother; the bride saluted her, and told her the oftener she came, the more welcome she should be.

Margery and her husband retired, full of blessings and prayers for their happiness; she gave vent to her joy, by relating to the servants and neighbours every circumstance of Edmund's birth, infancy, and childhood. Many a tear was dropped by the auditors, and many a prayer wafted to Heaven for his happiness. Joseph took up the story where she left it: he told the rising dawn of youth and virtue, darting its ray through the clouds of obscurity, and how every stroke of envy and malignity brushed away some part of the darkness that veiled its lustre. He told the story of the haunted apartment, and all the consequences of it; how he and Oswald conveyed the youth away from the Castle, no more to return till he came as master of it. He closed the tale with praise to Heaven for the happy discovery, that gave such an heir to the house of Lovel; to his dependants such a Lord and Master; to mankind a friend and benefactor. There was truly a house of joy; not that false kind, in the midst of which there is heaviness, but that of rational creatures, grateful to the Supreme Benefactor, raising their minds by a due enjoyment of earthly blessings to a preparation for a more perfect state hereafter.

A few days after the wedding, the Lord Fitz-Owen began to prepare for his journey to the north. He gave to Edmund the plate, linen, and furniture of the Castle, the farming stock and utensils; he would have added a sum of money, but Sir Philip stopped his hand.

"We do not forget," said he, "that you have other children, we will not suffer you to injure them; give us your blessing and paternal affection, and we have nothing more to ask. I told you, my Lord, that you and I should one day be sincere friends."

"We must be so," answered the Baron. "It is impossible to be long your enemy. We are brothers, and shall be to our lives' end."

They regulated the young man's household; the Baron gave leave to the servants to choose their master; the elder ones followed him (except Joseph, who desired to live with Edmund, as the chief happiness of his life); most of the younger ones chose the service of the youthful pair. There was a tender and affectionate parting on all sides. Edmund besought his beloved William not to leave him. The Baron said, he must insist on his being at his brother's wedding, as a due attention to him, but after that he should return to the Castle for some time.

The Baron and Sir Philip Harclay, with their train, set forward. Sir Philip went to London and obtained all he desired for his Edmund; from thence he went into Yorkshire, and settled his affairs there, removing his pensioners to his other house, and putting Lord Fitz-Owen in possession of his own. They had a generous contention about the terms; but Sir Philip insisted on the Baron's accepting the use of everything there.

"You hold it in trust for a future grandchild," said he, "whom I hope to live to endow with it."

During Sir Philip's absence, the young Lord Lovel caused the haunted apartment to be repaired and furnished for the reception of his father by adoption. He placed his friend Joseph over all his men-servants, and ordered him to forbear his attendance; but the old man would always stand at the side-board, and feast his eyes with the countenance of his own master's son, surrounded with honour and happiness. John Wyatt waited upon the person of his lord, and enjoyed his favour without abatement. Mr. William Fitz-Owen accompanied Sir Philip Harclay from the north country, when he returned to take up his residence at the Castle of Lovel.

Edmund, in the arms of love and friendship, enjoyed with true relish the blessings that surrounded him, with an heart overflowing with benevolence to his fellow creatures, and raptures of gratitude to his Creator. His lady and himself were examples of conjugal affection and happiness. Within a year from his marriage she brought him a son and heir, whose birth renewed the joy and congratulations of all his friends. The Baron Fitz-Owen came to the baptism, and partook of his children's blessings. The child was called Arthur, after the name of his grandfather.

The year following was born a second son, who was called Philip Harclay; upon him the noble knight of that name settled his estate in Yorkshire; and by the king's permission, he took the name and arms of that family.

The third son was called William; he inherited the fortune of his uncle of that name, who adopted him, and he made the Castle of Lovel his residence, and died a bachelor.

The fourth son was called Edmund; the fifth Owen; and there was also a daughter, called Emma.

When time had worn out the prejudices of Sir Robert Fitz-Owen, the good old Baron of that name proposed a marriage between his eldest son and heir, and the daughter of Edmund Lord Lovel, which was happily concluded. The nuptials were honoured with the presence of both families; and the old Baron was so elevated with this happy union of his descendants, that he cried out, "Now I am ready to die—I have lived long enough—this is the band of love that unites all my children to me, and to each other!" He did not long survive this happy event; he died full of years and honours, and his name was never mentioned but with the deepest marks of gratitude, love and veneration. Sweet is the remembrance of the virtuous, and happy are the descendants of such a father! they will think on him and emulate his virtues—they will remember him, and be ashamed to degenerate from their ancestor.

Many years after Sir Philip Harclay settled at the Castle, he

received tidings from his friend Zadisky, by one of the two servants who attended him to the Holy Land. From him he learned
that his friend had discovered, by private advices, that he had a
son living in Palestine, which was the chief motive of his leaving
England; that he had met with various adventures in pursuit of
him; that at length he found him, converted him to the Christian
religion, and then persuaded him to retire from the world into
a monastery by the side of Mount Libanus,* where he intended
to end his days.

That Walter, commonly called Lord Lovel, had entered into
the service of the Greek emperor, John Paleologus,† not bearing
to undergo a life of solitude and retirement; that he made up a
story of his being compelled to leave his native country by his
relations, for having accidentally killed one of them, and that he
was treated with great cruelty and injustice; that he had accepted
a post in the emperor's army, and was soon after married to the
daughter of one of the chief officers of it.

Zadisky foresaw, and lamented the downfall of that Empire,
and withdrew from the storm he saw approaching. Finally, he bade
the messenger tell Sir Philip Harclay and his adopted son, that
he should not cease to pray for them, and desired their prayers
in return.

Sir Philip desired Lord Lovel to entertain this messenger in
his service. That good knight lived to extreme old age in honour
and happiness, and died in the arms of his beloved Edmund, who
also performed the last duties to his faithful Joseph.

Father Oswald lived many years in the family as chaplain; he
retired from thence at length, and died in his own monastery.

Edmund Lord Lovel lived to old age, in peace, honour and
happiness; and died in the arms of his children.

Sir Philip Harclay caused the papers relating to his son's history

---

* Mount Lebanon, a range of mountains in Syria (now Lebanon).

† This is John VIII, the Byzantine emperor who succeeded Manuel II (whom Sir Philip served)
and reigned from 1425 to 1448; the dynasty ended in 1453, when the Turks completed their
demolition of the Holy Roman Empire.

to be collected together; the first part of it was written under his own eye in Yorkshire, the subsequent parts by Father Oswald at the Castle of Lovel. All these, when together, furnish a striking lesson to posterity, of the over-ruling hand of Providence, and the certainty of RETRIBUTION.

FINIS.

ABOUT THE AUTHOR, HORACE WALPOLE

HORACE WALPOLE (September 1717–March 1797) was born in London, England, son of the first British Prime Minister, Sir Robert Walpole, who was the 1st Earl of Orford. Horace (born Horatio), through descendancy, became the 4th (and last) Earl of Orford.

Horace was the youngest of six children, born sickly, frail, and expected to die young, as had two siblings before him. Yet he survived and, indeed, flourished. Thereafter, he seems to have lived a not-unexpected life of English privilege and leisure to someone of his family's high esteem. He studied at Eton and at King's College, Cambridge, and after schooling travelled Europe with the soon-to-be famous poet Thomas Gray. Upon return home, Horace's father secured for him various administrative positions, and Horace became involved in Parliamentary politics.

Horace was an avid reader and antiquarian, and a devout admirer of author William Shakespeare. In 1764 he wrote *The Castle of Otranto*, his most famous work and widely considered to be the first Gothic novel. He wrote little else of fiction (primarily the novel *The Mysterious Mother* and speculative history *Historic Doubts on the Life and Reign of King Richard the Third*). Besides fiction, however, Horace earned claim as one of the most diligent letter writers of his generation, with a private correspondence that is still in existence today, catalogued through forty-eight volumes that collect much of his nearly four thousand letters, a timepiece to the history, etiquette, and culture of his era.

In addition to writing, Horace also made fame through the design and construction of his home, Strawberry Hill, a facsimile Gothic castle (built into a small, fashionable suburb), which included towers, battlements, and elaborate "gloomy" decorations, and came to prefigure the nineteenth-century Gothic Revival architectural trend. It was within this eccentric setting that *The Castle of Otranto* was written (the result of a strange, Gothic-infused dream, he later revealed). Strawberry Hill has been restored several times in the past quarter-millennium, and is still a tourist landmark today.

Horace Walpole passed away in 1797 at the age of 79, after suffering gout and other lingering illnesses. He never married nor had heirs. The title of Earl of Orford died with him.

ABOUT THE AUTHOR, CLARA REEVE

CLARA REEVE (January 1729–December 1807) was born in Ipswich, England—one of eight children—and lived all her life in that general area, where her family had long been resident. Her father was descended through a lineage of ecclesiastical reverends, of which occupation he also engaged. Clara's mother was daughter to the goldsmith and jeweler for King George I.

Clara was educated firmly by her father, whom she later credited with "teaching her everything she knew"—an impressive amount, as she translated books of Latin, debated politics, and wrote on a wide range of authoritative subjects.

She published at least twenty-four books of fiction, essays, and translations over thirty-three years, most notably the epistolary novel *The School for Widows* (1791) and the novel *The Old English Baron* (1777), the latter which encouraged Gothic fiction to relate more toward "the realm of probability" and away from the supernatural, and was influential upon author Mary Shelley's *Frankenstein*. Many of Clara's other works have been noted for tones of morality, prudence, philosophy, and romance.

Clara Reeve passed away in 1807 at the age of 78, leaving little other biographical material. She never married nor had heirs. She was granted the wish to be buried in her hometown cemetery next to a reverend with whom she'd been close friends.

SUGGESTED DISCUSSION QUESTIONS FOR CLASSROOM USE

1. *The Castle of Otranto* blends elements of realistic "literary" fiction along with the supernatural, creating thrills, intrigue, revulsion, and fright, all set in the rich backdrop of a crumbling castle and fading nobility, which is regarded as establishing the first novel of the Gothic tradition. Where do your own reading preferences lie? Do you favor realistic tones to stories or supernatural, or else a fusion of the two such as reflected in this book? Why do you think your tastes have developed this way?

2. *The Castle of Otranto* is not only considered the first Gothic novel, but it is also said to have founded the horror story as a "legitimate literary form." If art and creativity are subjective, why do you think this is important to grant the art form of horror literature as legitimate—in the sense of normative acceptance? If a certain reading style was abnormal or unconventional (i.e. not "legitimate"), would that affect your decision to read it?

3. The first edition's preface to *The Castle of Otranto* gives a fascinating and entirely falsified backstory to its origin

as being a translated and "found" document. The second edition's preface backtracks, and author Horace Walpole admits it was all written by his hand, confessing that originally he was not sure how the public was to react to it, and if it proved a failure then no one would know he was behind it. Do you think this strategy to be wise by the author or to be sneaky? If you created something new, would you mask your identity until learning how it is received, or would you proudly display it regardless?

4. Manfred is lord of the Castle of Otranto and soon revealed to be a terribly villainous antagonist. The day of his son's tragic death, he romantically pursues Isabella, the young woman who was to have been his daughter-in-law, planning to marry her and divorce his wife. Most of the characters in this book are aware of his intention, yet overlook or even accept it. What do you think of the attitude in this book as it relates to women in the eighteenth century? Essentially, Manfred's wife, Hippolita, has little say as to Manfred's womanizing and his plans to leave her; she and daughter Matilda are both painted as submissive and obtuse. Do you think that is how women actually behaved and/or were treated in that era? Would such a literary attitude be accepted in modern day?

5. As terrible as Manfred's character proves to be, his actions are prefaced upon the tragic and sudden death of his only son, stated to be his "darling." Do you think Manfred's ensuing choices can be explained or apologized for due to the emotional trauma he surely must have faced with his son's death (especially occurring on his wedding day)? Or is Manfred's wretched behavior found to be strictly without justification? Do you find anything redemptive in his character?

6. What is the significance of the ghost of Alfonso unexpectedly rising from the grave to proclaim Theodore the true heir of Alfonso? There's no rational explanation in the story, but it is accepted by all characters present that a ghost appears before them, cries out a singular line, and then ascends upward. If in the same circumstance, would you believe or act on a claim made by a ghost? Have you ever seen a ghost or known someone who has seen a ghost? How was the experience?

7. After Conrad's death, Isabella's father, Frederic—who initially despises Manfred—arrives at Otranto Castle to bring Isabella home but then makes a deal instead with Manfred, essentially for each of them to marry the other's young daughter. In an era when arranged marriages were practiced, especially among royalty in order to gain alliances or wealth, what do you think of Frederic's decision? Have you ever known someone to completely change their stance on an issue you felt strongly about? How did that make you feel?

8. *The Castle of Otranto* is filled with plot twists, unexpected appearances, and melodramatic revelations. Do you enjoy suspense and surprise developments in the plot, or is it too disconcerting or unreliable? Is there anything in the plot that you would have written differently?

9. *The Old English Baron* was written as a critical reaction to *The Castle of Otranto* and set off a literary feud between the two books' authors. Although each book shares thematic similarities, there are many differences, notably that *The Castle of Otranto* relies upon supernatural elements, while *The Old English Baron* remains in the realm of science and reality. Why do you think these two books of

contrasting approach are so often held together as "book-ends" to Gothic literature?

10. Which did you prefer more: *The Castle of Otranto* or *The Old English Baron?* What about that work appealed to you most?

11. *The Old English Baron* makes use of an uncommon literary element called a lacuna, in which there purposefully appears a gap in the story under the guise of it having been caused by decay from the original manuscript. Does this add atmosphere to the story, as if it is truly a work discovered from bygone times? Does it spur your imagination to fill in the gaps of a missing story? Or does it bother you for lack of continuity or other reason?

12. In her preface, author Clara Reeve states that supernatural elements "destroy the work of imagination," and that "instead of attention, <they> excite laughter." What does this statement mean to you? Do you agree or disagree with it? How far would you allow a supernatural event to push along a storyline before "suspending your disbelief" is no longer viable?

13. In *The Old English Baron*, Edmund states, "You have raised my curiosity...and I beg of you to gratify it." What are you most curious about? Even in this age of modern-technology, are there things you wish to understand, but find the answers to be elusive?

14. A work of literature is said to fall into the Gothic tradition if it includes certain elements such as: inducing feelings of suspense and fear, utilizing gloomy setting particularly of a castle or graveyard, usage of overwrought or

melodramatic emotion, inclusion of supernatural activity, and inclusion of certain role stereotypes, such as a damsel in distress and a villainous male in a position of power. Examples of other Gothic novels include *Frankenstein, The Fall of the House of Usher,* and *Wuthering Heights.* What other works of Gothic fiction are you familiar with? Which ones have you enjoyed reading? What do you look forward to reading next?

SUGGESTED FURTHER
READING OF FICTION

For readers who have enjoyed *The Castle of Otranto* and/or *The Old English Baron* and wish to further read works of similar voice, theme, or literary style, consider the following, which represent just a small selection of available great and commensurable books.

The Ancestor by Danielle Trussoni (2020): A young New York woman discovers unexpectedly that she is the sole heir of a wealthy noble family and their inheritance, including an isolated castle in the Italian Alps, which she then visits only to learn her ancestors harbored ghastly secrets.

Beloved by Toni Morrison (1987): This Pulitzer Prize–winning novel is about an escaped slave, haunted by guilt and the revenant of her infant child, whom she had killed years before, rather than have the child live enslaved.

The Betrothed (Italian: *I promessi sposi*) by Alessandro Manzoni (1827): This epic tale of religion, 17th-century politics, and passion, follows two young lovers who are forbidden to marry by a powerful tyrant who wants the bride for himself, and will stop at nothing to despoil her, even by chasing them across a landscape filled with strange characters and fearful dangers.

The Bloody Chamber: and Other Stories by Angela Carter (1979): This collection of ten short stories revisits classic fairy tales and legends with Gothic twists.

Dreadful Hollow by Irina Karlova (1942): In this Gothic horror-romance, danger pursues a woman when she enters the strange mansion of the mysterious Countess Ana Czerner; she turns to a young local doctor for help…but is he friend or enemy?

"The Fall of the House of Usher" by Edgar Allan Poe (1839): In this short piece of Gothic fiction, the narrator arrives at the home of an aged brother and sister who believe the house is sentient, and its life as well as their own are enjoined, and soon all are beginning to show cracks and decay.

Frankenstein; or, The Modern Prometheus by Mary Shelley (1818): In one of the world's most iconic science fiction and horror novels, a young scientist, Victor Frankenstein, creates a hideous sapient creature in an unorthodox scientific experiment, and then abandons him…much to his later regret.

The Hound of the Baskervilles by Arthur Conan Doyle (1901–1902): Acclaimed detective Sherlock Holmes investigates an attempted murder at a gloomy estate, shrouded by the legend of a marauding and diabolical hound of Hell.

Jane Eyre by Charlotte Brontë (1847): A lonely young woman is hired as governess in a mysterious mansion by a brooding, proud master, where she falls in love and uncovers a terrifying secret.

Justine, or The Misfortunes of Virtue (French: *Justine, ou Les*

Malheurs de la Vertu) by Marquis De Sade (1791): Before the French Revolution, a young woman awaiting execution recounts the tragic events that befell her throughout life, leading to her unintended crimes.

Melmoth by Sarah Perry (2018): A depressed woman, working as translator in Prague, comes to learn the myth of Melmoth, a legendary character who is doomed to wander the earth and witness all of humanity's cruelty.

Mistress of Mellyn by Victoria Holt (1960): In this Gothic romance, a young woman is hired by a mysterious widower to be governess for his spoiled daughter; they reside in a haunted mansion, filled with the memories of his first wife who suffered a tragic death.

The Monk: A Romance by Matthew Gregory Lewis (1796): A Spanish monk forgoes his monastic vows when giving into temptation of increasingly depraved acts of sorcery, murder, incest, and torture.

The Mysteries of Udolpho by Ann Radcliffe (1794): In this novel, cited as a quintessential Gothic romance, a young woman suffers the death of her parents, supernatural terrors in a gloomy castle, and the intrigues of a contemptuous Italian nobleman.

The Mysterious Warning, a German Tale by Eliza Parsons (1796): This classic of Gothic tropes includes dark family secrets, incest, seduction, and ghostly apparitions, in which a dead count's youngest son flees his older brother after a ghostly voice warns him his life is in peril over stake in an inheritance.

The Name of the Rose (Italian: *Il nome della rosa*) by Umberto Eco (1980): This historic Gothic murder mystery set in a 1300s monastery includes literary puzzles and "intellectual studies" amidst mounting deaths of monks.

Nine Coaches Waiting by Mary Stewart (1958): An orphaned governess in a French chateau encounters an apparent plot against her young charge's life, also an orphan, in this Gothic mystery-romance.

Northanger Abbey by Jane Austen (1817): An innocent young English woman learns harrowing, and oft satirical, life lessons while travelling across the county and immersing herself in tales from "trashy" Gothic novels.

The Phantom of the Opera by Gaston Leroux (1910): A deformed and bitter man known only as the Phantom lives underneath the Paris Opera House where he falls in love with an obscure chorus singer and privately tutors her while terrorizing everyone else.

Rebecca by Daphne du Maurier (1938): A young bride, hastily married to a man she barely knows, goes to live in his mansion, and in the shadow of his deceased first wife, whose memory is kept resolutely alive by a sinister housekeeper.

The Séance by John Harwood (2008): In this novel of horror and mystery, a young Victorian woman who suffers from grim visions of the future inherits a house in which her relatives have mysteriously perished.

The Silent Companions by Laura Purcell (2017): A Victorian-era young and recently widowed mother, having married into wealth, is left with an unfamiliar estate run by hostile servants and a strange wooden figure, locked away in a spare room, that begins to "watch" her.

The Thirteenth Tale by Diane Setterfield (2007): An elderly and reclusive author, once famous for a collection of fantasy stories, reveals that she has been penning a series of alternate lives, which act as therapy for herself and her biographer.

The Turn of the Screw by Henry James (1898): This classic novella tells of a deceased English governess's found manuscript detailing her claims of haunting ghosts while she tries to care for two young children.

Uncle Silas by J. Sheridan Le Fanu (1864): In this Victorian Gothic mystery-thriller, a young, naïve heiress is plagued by her cruel governess and goes to live with a reprobate uncle who has a sinister past.

Usher's Passing by Robert R. McCammon (1984): Descendants of the Usher line (from Edgar Allen Poe's seminal "The Fall of the House of Usher") live on in North Carolina, where family fears and madness must be confronted within a massive and evil estate.

We Have Always Lived in the Castle by Shirley Jackson (1962): The last three surviving members from a deadly tragedy live a reclusive and ostracized life in their Vermont estate, when an estranged cousin arrives, determined to extract what wealth remains of the family.

The Woman in White by Wilkie Collins (1859): A recently married woman is confined to a mental asylum by her deceptive husband who wishes to control her wealth, until she escapes and seeks help from a former lover and his sleuthing partner.

Wuthering Heights by Emily Brontë (1847): A passionate and forbidden love in youth leads a young man to run away, and then return many years later for revenge against the slights—both real and imagined—he endured by his ex-lover's family.

Zofloya, or The Moor by Charlotte Dacre (1806): A purposefully melodramatic Gothic tale of scandal, sexual deviancy, and violent revenge, in which a wicked heroine shuns the mores of aristocratic views to reach her own ends.

ABOUT THE SERIES EDITORS

Eric J. Guignard has twice won the Bram Stoker Award®, been a finalist for the International Thriller Writers Award, and been a multi-nominee of the Pushcart Prize for his works of dark and speculative fiction. He has more than one hundred stories and nonfiction credits appearing in publications around the world, has edited multiple anthologies, and has created an ongoing series of primers exploring modern masters of literary short fiction titled: *Exploring Dark Short Fiction*. His latest books are his novel, *Doorways to the Deadeye*; novella, *Last Case at a Baggage Auction*; and short story collection, *That Which Grows Wild: 16 Tales of Dark Fiction* (Cemetery Dance).

————

Leslie S. Klinger is the *New York Times* bestselling editor of the Edgar®-winning *New Annotated Sherlock Holmes* and the Edgar®-winning *Classic American Crime Fiction of the 1920s* as well as numerous other annotated books, anthologies, and articles on Holmes, Dracula, Lovecraft, Frankenstein, mysteries, horror, and the Victorian age. Twice nominated for the Bram Stoker Award® for Best Nonfiction, his work includes the acclaimed

New Annotated Dracula and *New Annotated H. P. Lovecraft,* as well as the World Fantasy Award–nominated *New Annotated Frankenstein* and five anthologies of classic vampire and horror fiction, three of them with Lisa Morton. His latest books are *New Annotated H. P. Lovecraft: Beyond Arkham,* also nominated for a World Fantasy Award, and *Annotated American Gods* with Neil Gaiman.